KA-CHI-FO

Good Bye

Tressa Olden

Library of Congress Control Number: 2011908486
ISBN: 979-8-89465-032-6 (sc)
ISBN: 979-8-89465-059-3 (e)

Printed in the United States of America.

Integrity Publishing
39343 Harbor Hills Blvd Lady Lake,
FL 32159

www.integrity-publishing.com

CONTENTS

CHAPTER 1

Honor Deserved

Beulah Mae Reeves" her name rang out among two others in the very large auditorium. She was being honored for her work with under age and under privileged young ladies. Surely over the years there had been hundreds of young ladies, who had found themselves pregnant, with no one to care for them, or their unborn children. By the grace of God and not by mishap as some would say they found Beulah. She helped them to secure a place to live, and taught them how to care for themselves, and their children and unborn children as well. She would assist some with their medical bills through a fund she had set up when she graduated college. It was always a passion for her to help those less fortunate than herself. Beulah was an only child. Both of her parents had a good income so she did not have to deal with a lot of the issues and pressures that fell on her peers she grew up with.

As a young teenager in her church, she worked with a group called Youth for Christ. Beulah was able to help people in her neighborhoods. After returning home from graduating college, she began her work. Beulah met and later married a young intern at the local hospital while she was there helping a young mother get care for her child. Her passion for helping others became his also. She along with her husband and grandmother started a group called W.A.S.H. (Women Asking Someone to Help) Most of the young women were getting some kind of assistance but without proper training on what to do with it, they were losing out on the benefits that were available to them. Beulah was there to intercede on their behave if one wanted or needed her assistance. She assisted by talking with the powers that be and helping them to get and understand what was available in helping them succeed. And if that was not enough, she had brought many of their children into the world. Beulah was a registered nurse and a midwife. Many of the young women came to her when it was time for them to deliver and she and her grandmother assisted them with the birthing of bringing their little ones into the world. Now her husband Dr. Reeves an (obgyn) was escorting her to the beautifully decorated stage to thank those who had selected her for this honor and the prestigious award that accompanied it.

"Thank you, thank you all very much," she said as she walked slowly to the stage on the arm of her husband of fifty-five years. The applause seemed to go on forever, from those who were standing around the room, sharing in this great celebration of love, dedication, and devotion, to a great woman. "My, my" she said as she took her position behind the podium looking at the mass of smiling faces on the people. "I never thought when I started doing this work fifty some years ago, it would lead to this." "I most certainly wasn't looking for anything in return in this lifetime, though you have certainly warmed my heart to the point of unspeakable." Pausing for a minute to compose herself and wipe tears from her eyes she continued speaking. "Looking back over the seventy -two years that I've lived this makes all the disappointments, frustrations, and misunderstandings, I've faced in my life, all worth it." Beulah went on to impress and warm the hearts of all listening. She took her time allotted and informed the cause and thanked those who had supported her and stood by her over the years. She made it a point to speak to the success stories of those who had turned their lives around and had become productive citizens of which she was very proud saying, "Those of you who took what was available to you and made the most out of it, I personally applaud you. By the time she concluded her speech there were more tears being shed from the smiling faces all over the room. Then with her final thank you, the applause started all over again when she departed the stage to return to her seat after having received her coveted award.

Doris had just returned from her doctor, putting her key into the lock to open the door. "Hello my lady, Finley said seeing her come in and head straight to her room. "Well, madam what did he say? Finley was questioning her because he knew today was the day, she would get the news results regarding the test she had taken over the months. She stopped and looked back at him. "Finley please get me a cup of hot tea with lemon, and draw me a hot bath." "Yes, my lady" he said hurrying to get what she requested. Finley had worked with her long enough to know that something was bothering her and if she wanted to share it, she would, but in her own time. She put her things down by the chair in the sitting room and hung her head thinking. Only minutes had pass when Finley came back with her tea. "Madam" he said quietly standing over her. "Here's your tea you requested. "Why, why Finley did this happen to me? She cried out! Finley had no clue of what his lady was talking about. He quickly sat the sterling silver tray on a table in the room and kneeled by Doris Wright his lady whom he worked for as her butler. "Madam, please tell me what's wrong? He asked again seeing she was very upset. "Well it looks like I'm going to need a kidney transplant after all", she voiced. Oh no my lady, I'm so sorry" Finley was now holding her hand. "Thank you so much for being here, she acknowledged, "I don't know what I would do without you! She said now hugging him around his neck crying. "Don't worry my lady", I will be with you through all of this". "You will be fine". Doris said nothing she just continued laying on Finley's shoulder crying.

Beulah sat at her table after dinner was over looking around at those who had come to share in her honor. Jon this is so wonderful, she said holding his hand and still surveying the room with her eyes. "Well Beulah, I know you're deserving of this honor. You worked very hard and sacrificed a lot of things in life for others. And I love you." He confessed. "You would say that but you know I wouldn't have got this far without you" she replied smiling, "Dear we did it together" gently reaching over to kiss her softly on her lips. They sat talking with other honoree couples sitting at their table when up walked two young ladies. "Hello they said walking up to the table. "Hello" Beulah smiled returning the greeting. Looking at Beulah you would never guess her age. For that matter her husband either. Her beautiful white hair enhanced her gorgeous wrinkle free skin and bright smile. "You may not remember me but I'm Rowena, and this is my daughter Lilly, you delivered her," she said leaning over to hug Beulah. "Oh my, she's so beautiful Beulah replied. The young lady stood smiling. Her very short hair was corn rolled styled and her tall thin frame looked very stylish in the outfit she was wearing. "Hello young lady Beulah said turning to the daughter. "So, you're little Lilly, how old are you dear?" "I'm almost twenty ma'am," she said confidently. "Oh! You were the one who gave me such a scare," she said smiling and pausing to remember. "I couldn't get you to cry when you were delivered and I was so worried," Beulah explained. "Your mom had a hard time with the birthing process. I feared the worst. She was crying so hard I had to leave the room with you. I remember wrapping you in a blanket and taking you into the other room, laying you on a table, massaging you until you started to cry." Then Beulah laughed, once I got you started crying you wouldn't stop! That was a good thing!" "I was so glad to hear you crying, I really was afraid to stop you. You frightened me". She said letting out a sigh, "had never gone through that with anyone of my babies, Beulah confessed. But looking at you now it sure didn't stunt your growth at all" looking up at the young lady. "Thinking of being a model some day? Mr. Reeves asked. No sir, that's not in my immediate future. But winning a championship sounds great! She said sounding very excited. "Oh! Beulah said looking for an explanation to her statement. Well are there plans in your near future now that you have graduated high school? "Yes ma'am" she said very confidently. "I will be heading back to Gonzaga in the fall. It will be my second year. Our basketball team was pretty good last year and we hope to go to the big game this year, she sound very excited "I'll be starting point guard for my team," she expressed proudly "Well that's impressive Mr. Reeves said, Beulah and I will most certainly keep up with you on television and newspaper. Heck! We may even take in a game or two he added smiling. He took a business card from his inner jacket pocket and handed it to Rowena. That has our email address and phone numbers dear," Beulah explained. 'Thanks, she said handing it to her daughter Lilly. "I will write you and let you know how I'm doing" and thanks to you both, giving Beulah a hug and shaking her husband's hand before walking away. Rowena stood smiling and hugged Beulah and Mr. Reeves too and started to walk away. "Thank you for sharing your success with me dear, Beulah added. "I love you" Rowena said to them and waved goodbye. Rowena was truly a success story. She had failed school and was on a fast decline to failure before meeting Beulah in the grocery store buying formula for her little ones, as she calls them. She was a pregnant teenager without a clue of what to do next. Rowena was from a single-family home with younger sisters and brothers and a mother who worked tirelessly to care for them, though came up short. Rowena was left to care for them most of the time. When she wasn't, she ran the streets with her older friends. Beulah helped her get attached to a non-profit agency that helped her and her mother to have a better life. 'She returned to school and though she had missed a year with Beulah's constant encouragement she graduated high school. Beulah sat sharing with her husband at the table how she had spoken with her in the grocery store and asked her to stop by and she would help her. And Beulah and her grandmother were so happy one night when Rowena showed up. Beulah sat smiling. Rowena had shared with her she now also had a younger son who was home with his father. Soon others seeing that the couples didn't mind being interrupted walked up to their table. "HELLO! Mrs. Reeves. "Hello dear"

Dana Williams was one of the ladies who attended Beulah Reeves celebration award banquet honoring her. Dana had come with her son David Michael and her sister Doris Wright. Beulah had delivered both of their children and they came with others to show their respects and give Beulah her flowers of love by being there. Dana had stepped up on the platform in front of the large banquet hall. She remembers it was beautifully decorated with Beulah's favorite colors and lots of flowers all around the room. The tables sparkled brightly from all the crystal dinnerware and stemware for each setting. The coordinator who had planned this day for Beulah through W.A.S.H INC. told Dana that the chosen colors were Beulah's favorites. "Good evening" Dana starts out. Her lovely "Versace" gown shimmering with its' beaded rhinestone bodice throwing streaks of light across her face. "My name is Dana Williams I too was helped by Mrs. Reeves, as you have heard so many other's say who have stood here tonight before me. She is a remarkable lady. Caring, kind, and I've found her to be very understanding. My sister and I were wayward teenager's who turned to Beulah Reeves for help." Dana had everyone crying including herself when she was near the end. On behave of myself and my sister Doris we would like to donate to W.A.S.H. in the name of Beulah Reeves one hundred thousand dollars!" so that what she started some forty-five years ago will continue." Then she turned to Beulah and began clapping. Everyone stood and joined in along with her. And the now new president of the struggling organization W.A.S.H. and coordinator of the event fainted when she heard the amount of the donation. Beulah only smiled.

CHAPTER 2

Should all acquaintance be forgotten?

A donation of that magnitude was nothing for Dana Williams. She was loaded. Her adoptive parents had left her wealthy. Her father was a businessman and C.E.O. of a major chain of retail stores. He was found dead with his wife in their home the night of her high school prom. "What a memory" The couple they say, were surprised by someone as they sat having lunch together in their dining room. What a horrible day! Shot to death in their home. Dana sat writing in her journal and remembering. Not ever wanting to return to the home she had sold it and all of the furnishing and had now decided to donate a large portion of her proceeds to the W.A.S.H foundation, founded by Beulah Reeves. The ranch her grandparents had left her in Oregon defaulted to her after the settlement with other siblings in the Demato family. Dana sat thinking about what she wanted to do with it in her room at the Sheraton Inn. Doris and David Michael her son who had come to the event with her had gone out exploring the sights.

Aunt Doris did you grow up here? He asked as they drove along headed to the mall. "Yes, but not this area." I lived much further away across the tracks." "Can we take a ride through it and see what it looks like now? David asked at the curios age of nineteen. "It probably looks a lot different now, he added. David I'm sure it does, just looking around where we are right now, she continued, this lot was once covered with trees." "Trees, aunt Doris? He questioned now sitting in the parking lot of the huge mall and all the retail stores. "Yes, she said, a lot as changed." "Let's go in the mall first and then if time allows, we will ride by the old neighborhood, o.k. "Cool!" he said getting out of the car heading into the mega mall to shop.

Dana had just got off the phone with David her son's grandfather who lived up the road in Washington. She had promised to stop by for a few days while she was here in Oregon since Spokane was only a few hours away by car. "Doris her sister was heading back to Los Angeles where she lived. Her flight was scheduled for early tomorrow morning. Dana looked at her watch. "Now where are those two? She questioned in her mind. Our dinner reservations are for six, she thought to herself as she walked around her room. "Ring! Ring! The hotel's phone was ringing. "Dana put a questioning frown on her face. She could not imagine anyone calling her here at this number. No one other than the foundation she had just donated her parent's things to have this number in case of questions, she thought as she answered. "Hello! Dana Williams, "Mrs. Williams, a voice came back. I do apologize for disturbing you." The voice continued. "Who am I speaking with? Dana asked very pointedly. "I'm sorry I'm Hester Birch, I am one of the committee members at W.A.S.H. "Yes, Dana replied. "First of all, thank you for your generosity to the organization." "Yes dear, Dana replied not wanting to get more calls thanking her, so she said very little hoping Ms. Birch would get the hint and get to the point of this call. "Well, she paused; we received a box here with your name on it. We did not know if it was something you wanted us to have" she went on to say. "Yes, go on, a box? "What kind of a box? Dana asked curiously. "A cardboard box filled with papers" Hester replied. "Papers" Just toss it out! And thanks for calling" Dana said bringing the conversation to and end. "No! Hester said quickly. "You may want to look at these. They look like important documents you might want to save," she suggested. Not wanting to continue the conversation with Mrs. Birch regarding some probably useless old papers Dana gave her the address to her office at the hospital in Maine where she worked. "Please send them there, and again thanks for the call" hanging up before Hester could say another word.

David and Doris were just about to the old neighborhood when her cell phone rang. "Hello she answered. It was Dana. "Are you two headed this way? She asked. "Our dinner reservations are at six o clock you know." She stated. "I'm aware of that, we are riding through what use to be the old neighborhood" Doris said very surprised at its transformation. "Oh, what does it look like? Why didn't you ask me before you took David there? How is he doing?" Dana questioned over and over again. Dana, calm down! David Michael's fine. "He asked to come here, he's nineteen you know and in college."

"I know that Doris, don't be funny! Doris and her nephew had become close. He was planning to attend U.C.L.A. in Los Angeles where she lived and baseball was his passion. All of his family had attended colleges on the east coast he wanted to come out west for a change he explains. "Dana we're sitting in front of the W.A.S.H Center." It's nice. Though the money you donated will really help" It sits where the corner market use to." "Is it that small Doris?" "Oh no! It's huge, maybe three or four floors covering a city block including the parking lot," she laughed. "David's over looking at the names of the founders and those who have contributed to this foundation." "It's a magnificent building "Would I recognize the place Doris?" "No Dana, this does not look at all like the place we left." The Henny place is gone and so is the little house Beulah started in" she shared. The Henny place, wow! That could only be a blessing" Dana acknowledged. They continued talking. David Michael walked up to the door; it was locked with closed hours posted on the glass door. "Another time I guess" he mumbled walking back to the bench where Doris had sat looking around at all the new office building's that saturated the old neighborhood. "We better head back, your mom called," she said as he walked toward her. "Is this where I was born Aunt Doris? He asked still looking at the building. "Yes, she smiled but I'll let your mom tell you that story.

Dana and David Michael waved goodbye to Doris as she entered the terminal to board her flight home. "Dana how long are you staying in Spokane at grandma's this time? He asked as they drove along the highway enjoying the scenery. Just a few days, I promised your grandparents I'd stop by before heading back to Maine. Your dad is flying in also, I spoke with him this morning." Dana added. "He wants to see you too!" "What has it been? Six months are eight since you last visited Washington," Dana asked. "Dana it's been about eight" David Michael replied. "Remember I asked if you and dad would mind if I go and visit Tommy in Texas". He has a large ranch there with lots of horses and cattle." It was fun. "That's great, it just seems funny little Tommy is a bronco rider". "Yes Dana, and he loves it" says he's riding in a big rodeo in June". "That's wonderful but so dangerous, I'm glad you chose baseball over bronco riding" Dana added. "Well after seeing those bulls throw more than one rider from their backs, I'm glad too! David Michael acknowledged laughing. "Well how is the season looking this first year of college?" "Any new recruits" Dana asked? "There are some hopefuls" David replied. "There's a new guy rooming down the hall from me. He is a senior. Coach wants us together". Says nothing gets pass us in the outfield, "His name is Ray" real nice guy." David confessed. They rode along the highway only stopping to rest and fill up the tank to finish the drive to the state of Washington. Near the gas station was an airfield with all kinds of planes for public viewing. David Michael and Dana casual strolled over and walked around from plane to plane looking inside. "Look at the wings on that one Dana! He said jumping up on it to take a picture. Dana snapped the shot looking through her digital camera's lens and gave the camera to David Michael. Then she went and posed by a beautiful red airplane and smiled. They spent about an hour just looking and laughing and getting inside of most of the planes. "One last pose" she said asking a passerby to take the camera shot as she and her son stood in front of a 1936 fighter jet plane. "We'd better get back on the highway Dana suggested walking toward the car. "There is still about an hour to go before we get to Spokane to your grandparents' home". Securing herself into the seatbelt of the car," Ready?" David Michael was positioning his seat to the reclining position to relax and Dana knew eventually go to sleep.

Finley! Finley! I'm home," Doris said entering her front door. "Oh, madam why didn't you tell me you were due in today? He said hurriedly coming from the back of the house to get her luggage the cab had left by the front door. "Why didn't you let me pick you up at the airport my lady? Weren't you inconvenienced being there all by yourself? Finley questioned still bringing the huge pile of luggage into the living room before heading to get a luggage rack that was stored in the large pantry closet. "Actually Finley, it was at times an inconvenience to get my own drink or call for a bell hop but I did it! And it feels great!

Finley had just come back to get the last pile of suitcases in the luggage set and carry them to her room. "My lady, are you, all right? He asked coming over putting his hand on her forehead. "Finley, I'm fine. "I have just had a real dose of reality!" Oh, madam what do you mean?" he asked standing with a puzzled look on his face. "Finley I will tell you all about it after I get out of these clothes and get comfortable" Doris replied heading to her room. "Madam may I draw your bath?" No! No! Finley I can turn water off and on! she said leaving Finley standing outside of her bedroom door scratching his head.

CHAPTER 3

No place like home

"Mom I'm here! Billy yelled coming through his parent's front door. Tetra moving a lot slower since earlier years came in from her great room. "Son, it's good to see you, are you by yourself? She asked looking around for someone else. "Yes mom, I'm supposed to be meeting Dana and David apparently they haven't arrived" He said hugging his mother. "No, I have been here most of the day," accept the two or three hours earlier I put in at the Center each week." The Center, how are things there? He asked being the one who initiated the building of it in honor of a dear friend. "It's still going strong! James just recruited a new energetic coordinator on staff and a much-needed activity planner for our seniors." "Well that's good, but how are you adjusting to all the changes? You know someone coming in and doing things you've been doing so well." "Well, you're right, two or three years ago I fought James tooth and nail on every change he tried to make to ease things for me. I thought he was trying to move me out of the picture all together. Then he asked if he and I could sit down and talk. We talked all the time for years but he asked if we could really talk! I finally conceded knowing he was right anyway, and said yes. He convinced me to share my knowledge with those who would carry the baton on" she smiled. "I know that was his nice way of saying I was getting older. But he was right and I knew it! Things have started to easily nerve me and I am not as patient with something's as I use to be. So, I'm very happy helping out and leaving all of what I use to do to the younger at heart" Tetra shared with her son. "Come in sit you can get your luggage out in a bit." "Tell me about life? She said pulling him over to the sofa in her great room. "Mom I know when you ask me about life, what you really want to know is who is she? And when do I get a chance to meet her? Billy replied obliging her by sitting next to her on the sofa. "Now son, that's not entirely what I mean" she smiled. "Well mom, I date often. You met Annie; she's one of the secretaries at the firm. Dana and I have become close again. We've shared a few dinners together. But honestly I have not found anyone since Jillian that I would even consider marrying" William said in a stated tone. "Annie seems like a nice young lady; William". "Mom she is. And Annie would marry me today if I asked her to. We have discussed it a lot. But I don't love her mom like I think she deserves to be loved." He must have sat there for half and hour talking about his future with his mother when the front door opened. "Tet! I'm home" came a voice it was his dad. Hurriedly getting up to meet him Billy went toward the door. Hello dad" walking over to share a hug. "Son, my it's good to see you" "Are you alone? I mean did Davie come in with you? "No dad it's just me right now but David Michael and his mother are meeting me here." If that's all right," he said walking his dad into his study to put down his briefcase. "Sure, that's fine with me. "Is your mother in? Yes dad, you just rescued me from another one of her talks about marriage. "Well son, that's your mother". They walked into the great room where Tetra was putting photographs in an album. Hi honey! David acknowledged walking over and kissing and hugging his wife. "How was your day? She asked, "Can't complain just another day at the office, usually happenings". "Son let's get your things from the car; David suggested. We can discuss a matter I had on my mind. "Great there's this case I'd like to run by you too" Billy replied getting up heading out. Tetra went into the kitchen to discuss the dinner menu for tonight with her new head chef.

Finley had set a gorgeous table for his lady. He had her favorite seafood meal prepared for her by the kitchen staff. He paced along the wide hall waiting for her to come from her room for dinner. 'Madam! He said gently knocking on her door. "Yes, Finley, do come in" she replied. Finley slowly opened the door. She was sitting over in her comfy chair in the corner reading. "Madam your dinner is ready" he said standing waiting for her to acknowledge his presence. She kept her head down in the book. "Madam! What has your interest so? He asked seeing that she never looked up at him. "Finley I'm reading, she said again softly. "Can't it wait my lady your dinner is being served? "I've waited long enough and I don't want to stop reading now." She stated. Madam what are you reading that can't wait until tomorrow" Finley asked looking back at the maid waiting for instructions on dinner. "My bible, she acknowledged". "I have been talking with Tetra Parker and Masony the detective" since they visited me years ago. Do you remember Masony? She asked Finley. He said nothing just stood and cringed recalling that horrible day. "I have been feeling very depressed and down since I received the news of the transplant from my doctor. And just recently when I visited Oregon, I found out how much God loves me". Finley was still in the dark about what his lady was talking about so he stood and listened. She explained about how she was living on the street there and things she had done to people to survive. She continued sharing with him as he waited for her to come for dinner that had been set out for her in the dinning room of her home. She explained if she were still there, statistics suggest she would be dead by now she confessed. "First hand Finley I saw some of those people I hung out with still doing the same things! Seems life had stood still for them", she said sadly. Doris stood up shaking her head and gently laid her bible on her night table. "Will you sit and have dinner with me Finley? She asked securing his arm and heading to the dinning room.

Tetra walked into her kitchen to ask the newly hire chef if he knew how to make blackberry dumplings. It is a dessert her husband David loved. He had shared with her he was treated to this delightful dessert at Mrs. Wheatley's home in Arkansas when he went for a visit. She wanted once again to surprise him since they were having their son and grandson joining them tonight for dinner. "Alfredo, she replied walking into her kitchen seeing him pulling a pan from the oven. "Oh, hello madam Parker" he said turning around after sitting the hot dish on the counter. "Sorry I didn't mean to startle you". "Did I pronounce your name correctly? She asked "Al-fredo? "Well madam it's French. Alfred or Alfredo, long o sound is the correct pronunciation". But I've had it pronounced both ways" he confessed standing smiling at her with his dark skin in his all white uniform. Mrs. Laine her previous housekeeper/cook had retired now and David insisted Tetra replace her with a full-time chef. Especially now with the family gatherings and large dinner parties they have from time to time. David knowing that he and his wife were getting older wanted to make sure things at home stayed consistent with their life style. Alfredo had come to them by way of Hurricane Katrina. He was once owner of an exclusive restaurant in the devastated area of New Orleans that had been washed away with the floods. Not only had he lost his thriving business but his home had also been destroyed. Discouraged and heartbroken he and his daughter packed up what was left and salvageable and headed out to find a place to call home. Alfredo Francois thought after losing his wife to cancer two years prior to the disaster that rocked the nation, he had rebounded fairly well. When is daughter a professor working at Xaiver college called to tell him the university was being evacuated and they are asking everyone to leave he fell on his knees praying? When she arrived at their restaurant to check on him, he was standing holding a beautiful lead crystal vase that once sat in the corridor of the restaurant's entrance. His wife had purchased it on their last trip together. It and he was all that remained of the family's restaurant. After getting her dad into the car and heading toward his home they were stopped short of going into the area he once lived in. It was months before they were able to see all that had been taken from them. He had shared his story with David and Tetra meeting them at a gathering held at the Mt. Nebo church. Alfredo can you make dumplings? Tetra asked. "Dumplings? He chuckled. "Madame I don't think there is a southern dish I cannot make" he confidently responded. "Good! She replied, wow me with blackberry dumplings for dessert tonight. I want to surprise my husband" she said walking out heading up the stairs. Alfredo shook his head looking around still not quite familiar with the kitchen's layout and where all things were placed. "Dumplings! He repeated she is a southern girl he thought getting all his ingredients ready to prepare Tetra's requested dessert for tonight's dinner.

Hello! Hello! Grandmother" David Michael yelled standing outside the front door ringing the doorbell. Billy came hurriedly to answer opening the door. "Dad! What a surprise he said hugging him with a father son embrace. "Dana did not tell me you would be here" he continued saying walking in with Dana right behind. "That's because you were not listening young man! I'M SURE I DID BUT YOU JUST WEREN'T LISTENING" She replied embracing Billy too. "Mom and dad are in the great room, put your things down right there and join us. We'll take them up in a bit". David Michael ran in quickly to meet his grandparents who embraced him with hugs and kisses. "Granddad, you're suppose to shake my hand, he said wiping his cheek from the kiss he had planted there. Dana and Billy had made their way into all the embracing to. "Well I guess he's growing up" David said to Billy his son. He wiped off my kiss" he shared lovingly. "Well he'd better not wipe of any of my kisses, Tetra replied. "I'll just plant two more! she laughed. Everyone sat down and joined in conversation. "Gram can I have the room next to dad's old room? He asked getting his things from the foyer and heading upstairs. 'Sure, as a matter of fact I had a decorator in to make it look like your school's mascot colors" she told him. I had some new shelving put in for books and lots of bright colors to fit your personality" she added. 'Thanks grandma" running up the stairs. That child as so much energy! Well Dana how have you been? Life seems to be treating you well". Tetra asked sitting back on her chair. "Yes, I'm doing very well," she responded thanks for asking. 'I'm enjoying my career at the hospital and life with my son keeps me busy enough not to get bored." "That's wonderful dear." "How is Doris these days, she shared with me about the transplant?" I have been praying for her." "She seems fine, Dana responded. We were together at Mrs. Reeve's celebration this week." "Oh, that's right! Beulah I'm sure she enjoyed herself, seeing all of you again. "It was very nice. Her foundation has grown so much since we were there, Dana shared. Mrs. Reeves deserved the honor she was bestowed," she added. "That's great they gave her flowers while she could still smell them, Tetra explained. I agree Dana concluded. The ladies continued to talk and Billy and his dad David went into his study. After everyone had got settle in the doorbell rang. It was a group of young college students from the church. "Hello Mrs. Parker they all said coming in to get David Michael. They were heading out to go skating for a while since finding out he was down visiting his grandparents again. Tetra hugged all the children as they chattered loudly with everyone trying to speak at the same time. Tetra introduced Dana to the young adults making all the noise in the house right now and they ran upstairs to meet David Michael. After a few minutes they all came hurriedly down the stairs saying their goodbyes. "Hi David", Frannie Ardion replied she had come in while the others were upstairs. Seeing David Michael come down to leave, she came running over to hug him. "Hi Frannie, I didn't know you were here too" David said responding back to her warm hello. "You're down visiting too, "Great! Let's go, hugging the other two girls and slapping the guys a high five heading out the door. "Dad I'll be back before dinner!" he yelled passing the study where Billy and his granddad David were having a continual conversation. Dana had gone up to her room to relax and make some phone calls before dinner and Tetra was in fussing with getting Mrs. Laine's things, she had left there sent to her from her room she once occupied.

Taking out her treo style cell phone she dialed "Hello, this is Dana Williams, may I speak with Dr. Baisden please?" "One moment please came a voice on the other in, I will see if he's in. "Pam, this is Dana, if he's busy please give him a message for me" she stated hurriedly. "Oh, Dana I do apologize I have been so busy today I didn't recognize your voice." 'Dr. Baisden is in a board meeting right now, but I would be glad to take a message for him". "Thanks Pam, it's regarding the ethics meeting we had last week" Dana shared the information she wanted his secretary to pass on to him, thanked her for her time, and hung up the phone. She sat in the big chair in the room and made other calls that needed her attention. After she finished her last conversation she sat looking around in the bedroom and writing in her journal. "Wow she thought! I can't believe I'm back in this room! Of course, the decor had changed but its layout was the same. She remembers the desk over under the window. She smiled as she looked at the fresh flowers Tetra always kept in her home. Dana had not been in the home or room since that tragic night in high school when her parents were murdered. She got up from the chair walking around to clear her head from those thoughts. Looking around she saw how Tetra had chosen such soft and warm colors to make this guest room feel inviting. A beautiful day bed was tucked in the alcove covered in white, beige and crème pillows trimmed in white lace. That theme flowed throughout the entire room. It was very bright and airy Dana thought as she sat down at the desk looking over papers. "Hello" Dana looked around to see Billy's head peeking into the door. "Oh, come in, I'm just looking over my client list. "I came to let you know dinner will be served soon". "Oh, thank you, I'd better get cleaned up. I want to change after that drive down from Oregon". "Well I'll see you then, he said turning around to walk out. "Billy? It feels very strange being in this house again." I mean, the last time I was here it was not a pleasant time for me" Dana confessed standing near the open window looking out. "Dana" he said coming over putting his arms around her to comfort the thoughts she was having now. I know those are thoughts that will probably never go away". Though I'm hoping you'll turn it over to Jesus, just talk out loud in your alone time. He really hears and understands". And Dana you know I'm always here." "Thanks Billy," she replied wiping her tears on his shoulder.

Alfredo had set a gorgeous dinning table. The Parker family including Dana all gathered in the huge elegantly decorated dinning room for dinner. David Michael had invited Frannie Ardion for dinner also. She had come down to visit her mother who lived in Washington. She met David Michael on one of his many visits to his grandparent's home over the summers. She was a student at Oregon State University. Her mother attended Mt. Nebo also. "Well Frannie it's good to have you with us tonight" Tetra said sitting down putting her napkin over her lap. "How's your mother doing?" "She's fine Mrs. Parker," Frannie replied very gracefully remembering her taught manners of the table. Tetra nodded to her husband David sitting at the head of the table to begin saying grace. Everyone bowed. Alfredo had made all of the southern dishes Tetra requested taste magnificent. The fried catfish was golden brown, potato salad, macaroni and cheese; green beans smelled and tasted delicious. "My, my David replied. You have out done yourself he shared with Alfredo" He stood silently after he had placed the last entrée on the table. The crisp salads and fried prawns, scallops, and something David Michael found out were hush puppies. Very little conversation regarding any topic was voiced except "Umm, that's good, try that! "This is wonderful" the baked salmon and asparagus spears were Tetra's favorite of the evening though she sampled some others.

After everyone seemed to have had their last bite Alfredo appeared again with the dessert blackberry dumplings" David looked and smiled at his wife. Then he turned to his son "Oh Billy who have got to try this! He said getting a large serving spoon.

Nada was busy helping her dad put the last of his things into the small bungalow that set at the back of the Parker home. "Dad, she yelled to him coming into the door. "Everything is out of the car." Nada flopped on the couch. 'Thanks, dear, I'll get things organized tomorrow." "Now I want you to go home and get some rest," he said pulling her up from the couch and pointing her to the door. "Dad, I can help you! You have worked so hard today already". Nada, the work I do now is nothing in comparison to running a restaurant." "I'm fine" he told her. "Are you sure daddy? She questioned standing now by the door where Alfredo had guided her. "Yes! Yes, call me when you get home." "Alright daddy" Nada said reaching to kiss him on the forehead and leaving closing the door behind her.

Nada got into her car and drove silently down the highway home. She and her dad had purchased a small two-bedroom house not far from Mt. Nebo where they attended when they arrived in Washington to live. "Dad, I'm home" she said calling him on the phone as soon as she got into the house so he wouldn't worry. Nada was very concern about her dad especially after her mother died. She left everything she had worked for behind to relocate with him. It was her choice; she didn't want him to be alone. Besides there were some personal things she wanted to leave behind also. Alfredo says he just didn't have the strength to start all over again in New Orleans. Everything besides her that meant anything to him IN THIS WORLD WAS GONE! "There was a call from Renetta Jackson on the answering machine," she told him. "Oh, what did she want? He asked?" "I don't know she just asked me to call her tomorrow, says it wasn't important". "Well knowing Renetta it's probably gossip, but call her anyway you never know" he replied. "You're right she did state if I choose to. But I'll let you know if it's something worth repeating" "Alright dear, sweet dreams to you". Alfredo replied. "Goodnight daddy".

CHAPTER 4

Feeling a Need

Doris was so focused on everything she wanted to do this week. She stayed in touch with her boutique staff daily by phone and any business matters that needed her attention. Finley was concerned that his lady had not gone out at all and knocked on her door to speak with her. "My lady, he said walking up standing at her bedroom door. "Oh, Finley do come in" she replied smiling her greeting. "My lady I just stopped by; you haven't been out all week is everything alright?" "Yes Finley, everything is fine, I just needed some time alone". Thank you for leaving the tray at the door and not asking a lot of questions" she said again smiling motioning for him to sit down. "Finley gave her a questioning look. "Oh, sit Finley! Relax, I have something I 'd like to do today," she voiced. Feeling very uncomfortable he threw the tails of his uniform in front of him and sat up very straight in the chair in Doris' room. With his fingers intertwined across his lap he asked. "My lady what is it you want to do today? "Are you having health problems? He questioned knowing of her condition of needing a transplant. "No Finley, I feel pretty good right now". But I do have an appointment for next Tuesday with my physician" Doris openly shared with her butler and long-time friend. "What I'd like to do is to walk downtown in South Central". "SOUTH CENTRAL!" my lady I thought you said you were all right! "That's crazy! "What do you expect to find in South Central besides trouble?" "I have a passion to help some people Finley, and I read there's a mission there that does just that! She shared very excited. "No! No! My lady South Central is not where you want to be! There are lots of charities My lady you can donate to." Finley said jumping up from the chair and heading to get the brochures. "Stop Finley, Doris replied grabbing his tails holding him. "You know I give to those all the time". What I need to do is to get up close with the people. Maybe really help some of them to change their way of thinking and see things differently" she said passionately to her butler. Finley shook his head, he knew he was not going to stop her and he could see her mind was made up. "My lady, have you thought this through? he asked again. "Yes, Finley, I have" she said walking over to a closet getting out a pair of jeans and a plaid shirt giving them to Finley. "What is this? He asked now holding the hideous clothing in his hand. Go! Finley, we want to get an early start!" Doris stated pushing him gently out the door.

Billy and Dana and his parents had just come back from taking David Michael to the airport. He was headed back to U.C.L.A. to begin another college semester. And Billy and Dana were heading back to Maine later that tonight. 'I see Alfredo has moved in" David said walking into their home. 'Yes, I finally got all of Ms Laine things sent to her." Tetra replied. "I went by the retirement home to see her last week, she seems much better. Her nurse says her appetite is improving and her children and grandchildren come all the time to see her". "Oh, that's wonderful, I really enjoyed having her here all those years" David said. "She like you Tetra, kept us eating" he smiled hugging his wife.

Dana had made her way to the kitchen to get something to take up to her room to snack on. Did you find what you where looking for dear? Tetra asked seeing her standing in front of the open refrigerator door. "Yes, a piece of fruit", thanks she said holding up the large red apple taking a bite. She needed to get her things prepared back into the suitcases for the flight home tonight. Billy had walked back outside to get something from the car and ran into Alfredo's daughter startling her going down the pathway at the side of the house to visit her dad. "Oh, hi each said standing looking at one another. Billy quickly extended his hand. "Hello, I'm William Parker, this is my parent's home" How are you doing? He asked looking at this stranger, but very beautiful women standing along the elegant path leading to the bungalow. Hello, she returned the greeting extending her hand to connect with a shake. I'm Nada François; Alfredo is my father she said very proudly. "Oh, I see the connection Billy said now laughing with the met stranger as they talked. "Just call me William. "Do you live here also, he asked. "Oh no, I'm bringing some of my dad's things he left at my home" she replied. Billy had got very comfortable standing chatting with Nada. He wasn't even thinking about the time. He had shared about how he grew up in this house and she was sharing about the Katrina devastation. "I'm sorry to hold you up, I'm just talking and you're standing here with all this in your hands, can I help? He asked reaching for the lamp and some books she was holding securely. I'm not in a hurry but thanks I do have some other things in my car that I can get". She replied relinquishing the things she was holding over to him. He put them on the bench near a sitting area along the path and ran out to meet her at her car to get the other things. With everything secured in their arms they walked along the very long path to the bungalow's door. Knock, knock, Daddy! She said entering the unlocked door. "Oh, he's up at the house. We just got back and he's preparing brunch," Billy said remembering. Would you like to join us? He asked. "Oh no! Nada replied, that's unheard of I'm from the South! She acknowledged very seriously. I'll just stay and arrange some things for him since he's out" she said, he wouldn't let me do it yesterday", she added. 'Are you serious about what you said? Nada looked at him wondering about his question. You really think that because your dad cooks for us that you can't eat at the same table? He questioned. "William it's a long story, but thanks for the invite, she stood smiling at him and "Thanks for all your help." Nada said now standing at the door. "It's been a pleasure maybe I'll see you around from time to time when I come for a visit." Nada said nothing she just smiled at this handsome man thinking all the good ones are taken.

Dana had packed her luggage and sat looking out of the window at Billy standing in the distant doorway of the bungalow with a woman. "I have no rights to him, she stood thinking as she watched them sharing laughs. He isn't committed to me, or anyone for that matter! We share a son and that's all. But why was she feeling jealous. They had been together with their son and his parents all week but between them there was very little to no intimacy at all. Dana stood for a moment surprised at herself at what she felt for Billy at this moment. She saw him smiling and laughing like they use to. She and Billy dated occasionally over the years. But getting together again! "Love, real love." It just couldn't happen. "I was different AND most certainly Billy was different. We are older now and more mature she reasoned in her mind. Besides he also dates Annie, which honestly doesn't bother me. He had shared with Dana on many occasions, Annie wouldn't replace Jillian. And honestly with him no one could. She sat and watched as long as she could before heading down the stairs. "Dana could you let Billy know brunch is served" Tetra shared seeing her go hurriedly toward the front door. Dana hurried down the path toward the bungalow. Billy saw her coming and gazed down at his Rolex on his arm, checking the time. "Dana, I'm sorry have you been looking for me?" He asked quickly seeing her coming toward him. Dana was so angry she couldn't speak and didn't. "I'm sorry Nada, this is Dana Williams" Billy turned to say standing watching both women that stood on either side of him. "Please to meet you," Nada said extending her hand. Dana managed a very cold heartless handshake. Then turned to Billy, "I'm all packed for our flight and Tetra says brunch is on the table" turning her back walking away without another word. "Ooooo, I didn't mean to cause problems with you and your wife?" Nada said seeing how Dana was reacting. "Oh, who Dana? No, she and I are just friends". We do share a son". Billy said "as a matter of fact we just saw him off to college, that's one reason we're here together this weekend". "Ummmm, college" Nada responded, "I'm a professor at Washington State." "Well I most certainly never had a professor that looked like you" Billy smiled thinking "But I'd better go mom will be out here next! He replied shaking her hand again and walking away "Nice meeting you, Nada said going in the bungalow closing the door.

Doris hurried along the wide boulevard in South Central. Finley was walking along side of her but he wasn't happy at all. "My lady what has gotten into you?" 'You had better talk with your physician about the medication you're taking! You are not thinking clearly! "Oh, Finley I'm fine". "We are out for a wonderful day in the city" she said bouncing along down the street in sneakers as the fast-moving traffic swiftly passed by. "Swish! Madam? Where are we going? Finley asked after about three long blocks. He couldn't remember the last time he dawned a pair of jeans and tennis shoes. "Just two more blocks to go she said heading into a group of men standing on the side walk. Finley slowed down. "Oh, come on Finley" Doris replied grabbing his arm to keep him moving. Then one of the guys stood in front of them. They stopped. "You got some change? He asked not letting them move on. "NO! Finley yelled trying to get past him now holding Doris's arm. "Hey, he asked if you had some change? Another one said pushing lightly on Finley's shoulder. "Stop that! Doris admonished, where are your manners? She asked moving with her back to the wall with Finley on her other side now and moving to the opposite side of the sidewalk where the men were gathered. "I know you won't hurt me for some change?' Doris replied sounding like them. Finley looked at her in astonishment at her word usage. "Now I'll tell you what, I'm on my way to the mission right up the street. Come by there and I'll have some change for you!" she told them moving past the gathering and trying to catch Finley who had made is way hurriedly down the street. "Finley? Finley, she yelled to him. Slow down Finley, they're just trying to frighten you! "Trying my lady, well they have succeeded and I want to go home! He said moving hastily down the block. Doris ran to catch up with Finley who was headed to the next bus stop and was getting on a bus going anywhere! he shared with her. After a few more blocks Doris stopped and looked around. She had past the turn on Pleh Street. "Wait Finley she yelled holding his arm to stop him, let's turn around." She shouted. "No! No! Finley yelled trying to push her away gently and keep her from holding on to him. "Excuse me miss, is this gentleman bothering you? They had now caused a scene with their disagreeing and someone was questioning it. Finley stopped and stood straight up looking into the gentleman's face. "Oh no he's not bothering me. I'm trying to get him to go to the mission on Pleh street and he refuses" she replied to the stranger passing by. Miss why are you going to the mission? Are you hungry, or do you need somewhere to sleep? He questioned with concern. Finley said nothing, he just looked at Doris, he was angry. Doris started to say something off color or out of line to the man but then she noticed his collar. "You're asking a lot of questions," She said looking him up from head to toe. "Well dear, I'm on my way there now. I'm a pastor and I come down often to speak with the men and women who somehow end up there" he shared. Finley took a deep sigh to relieve himself, "Hello my name is Tyrone", he said extending his hand to the stranger who had now confided he was a preacher. "Tyrone? Doris looked at Finley and wrinkled her brow in question regarding the name he had made-up obviously. He shrugged his shoulder. "I'm Octavia, Doris said extending her hand to the pastor. Finley laughed silently to himself about that one. "Well it's a pleasure to meet both of you. "Octavia is it? You passed the mission a block up and around the corner if you still have a need to get there." "I'm headed that way; you both may walk with me if you like" he replied. Doris nodded and affirmation to Finley with her head in the direction the pastor had given them. He looked at his watch, "I can't be late" he said starting to continue his walk down the street. Doris got in right beside him and beckoned for Finley who still wasn't convinced that's where he needed to be. "Come on Tyrone!

David, Tetra and their son along with Dana enjoyed a wonderful brunch. They enjoyed conversation regarding careers, children, friends and family. Billy shared with his dad about some work he had completed for his aunt Sarah, his dad's sister. And she seems to be back to her old self again, he said putting a strawberry in his mouth from his plate. She really took their parents death hard. After the brunch Billy and Dana prepared to leave. "Great time again mom as always" Billy said going to the door. "And David Michael touched ground also I spoke with him last night". "That's wonderful son. David and I plan to go up and visit him in a few weeks" Tetra explained getting her purse walking out the door to the car. After a short time, they were in the car and headed to the airport. William and Dana were headed back home to Maine. "Tetra and David said their goodbye's and watched their son board the plane. "I will call when I arrive, he told his mom, so don't worry". They waved to Dana who had already rolled her carryon through the boarding door. After securing their seats in first class William asked, Dana, what was that attitude I got at the brunch table earlier? She knew exactly what he was speaking of but hesitated to answer. "Excuse me!" she said looking surprised. "No, no let's back it up further" he replied. "Your attitude showed up when I was talking to Alfredo's daughter the night before". "Oh, is that who she is? She exclaimed.

"I thought she was someone you had met while you were there", you know another one of your dates!" she scolded. "Ooo that hurts, he replied putting his hand on top of hers' on the arm rest. She smiled from the attention. She really had not thought about getting back with Billy. She had steered clear of men after the disastrous ones that failed terribly. She dated rarely and until today had not even given Billy the chance at love again with her. She knew him as a great father to their son and a good friend when she needed him. He hinted several times for more but her heart wasn't in it. She was always thinking about the horrible way he treated her after Jillian his fiancée died in that plane crash on September 11. She had befriended her to get to him. 'She hated her and wanted her so far from him, though she didn't want her hurt. But it happened! She smirked a devilish grin. She had taken him from me and I was a woman scorn, Dana sat remembering. "It took years before I could even be in the same room with him. And now I'm sitting here with him holding my hand! Dana smiled as her thoughts went through her mind. "I guess there is a God!" "What? What did you say about God? He asked hearing her thoughts aloud. "Oh, I was just thinking about our son" she told him. "Oh, he squeezed her hand and reclined the seat to relax for the plane trip home. Dana just smiled.

Doris and Finley walked into a crowded room of wanting people. Most were homeless and in need of a bath and a good meal. Finley looked down at his plaid shirt and smiled, it didn't look so bad after all. Most had layers and layers of clothing on of all colors. Finley surmised it was to keep them warm at night. During the day they pushed around a loaded shopping cart filled with anything. One man had an old recliner in his. He was standing in this long line waiting to get in for a hot meal. The pastor looked at Octavia and Tyrone, he still had not figured out the reason they were here but he knew they didn't belong in this crowd. He beckoned for them to follow him in through another door. Finley sighed relieved moving quickly in the direction with Doris and the preacher. Inside they saw rows and rows of long benches in a very large open space of a room. There were others busily getting food set up in a buffet style Finley surmised. "Well you're here! The pastor turned to say to them. "Now Tyrone and Octavia what can I do for you?" He said somehow knowing they were not from around here. "Doris looked at Finley. "Sir we just want to help! I was reading my bible this week and I felt a need to" she said twisting her hands in a wringing nervous motion. Soon a very loud buzzer sound filled the room. "Buzzzz, buzzzzz, take your positions it's time! Someone yelled. "I haven't seen Rose this morning who's going to take her place?' another yelled. "I will! Doris yelled out before she knew it. "Over here then I'll show you what she does". And you! Someone yelling in Finley's direction, "you look strong we need those boxes brought in from the pantry!" Finley looked around for Doris, who at this point was nowhere in sight. "Well come on we don't have time to waste, that line ain't getting shorter! Finley hurriedly followed another gentleman to the pantry area filled with boxes. On his way through he spotted Doris with a plastic cap on her head and a big spoon in her hand. She was probably going to serve up something he thought. Finley reached down for a box then he noticed the other gentleman was having trouble with his. He stood up looking for a cart of some kind to carry the heavy boxes of potatoes to the kitchen. After a struggled or two they came up with a system that worked. They both would help picking the box up on this rickety small table and it was easier from that level to secure the boxes and carry them into the kitchen. Box after box of potatoes were carried in for preparation of today's meal. Sweat was coming from their brows. Finley couldn't remember the last time he needed to sweat. He was a butler out of Beverly Hills for God sake! The other gentleman was really having a hard time. Finley reasoned looking at him he needed to eat something. He had shared with him this is how he gets his meals each day by coming here and helping out. Finley took a candy bar from his pocket and handed it to him. It was his favorite a Snicker bar. "THANKS! He said quickly opening the wrapper and swallowing it down. "Okay guys that's plenty" "now I need them peeled!' he shouted out. This big guy in statue who had been barking out orders to everyone most of the morning came over with a red apron on. He pointed at two chairs sitting next to a sink and gave them two knives that Finley reasoned couldn't cut butter they were so dull. But it would be a change from running back and forth with those 40 lb boxes of potatoes. Finley and Russell sat down and started to peel the potatoes. They were going to be boiled and mashed for the large crowds coming in all day. The snicker bar had helped a little but Finley could see that

Russell was growing weary. Finley had a great breakfast earlier and all that he had done here was wearing on him too. He looked over where Doris was standing and made a gesture motion of eating and then pointed to Russell the gentleman with him. Doris had been watching all the activity Finley had been doing all morning and knew he must be pretty tired. The heaviest thing Finley lifted during a day was probably a teapot she reasoned. Again, he made the motion for her to sneak some food for the gentleman. They had said they would let them eat a little later but Finley sensed the man needed to eat now. Doris was spooning mashed potatoes on each plate as the endless line of needing people came through. She smiled. Hopefully being unnoticed she spooned a large scoop of mashed potatoes on a plate that sat unused under the counter. She looked around to see who was looking. The line was still moving the place was busy and loud from all the conversations. She looked at Madry the lady who was in charge of the chicken they were serving today. She was keeping account of every piece it seems. Madry turned to give attention to another worker serving at one of the other tables and Doris quickly grabbed some chicken with her hands from the large tray. Madry came back. She looked at her tray, "umm" she said looking at the space now showing. Then she looked at Doris who flashed her an innocent smile. Really Madry couldn't remember if she left it or not it had been to busy. Besides she had this very hungry gentleman standing in front of her and he wanted food now! Madry quickly dismissed her thought and kept the line moving. Doris motioned for Finley to come and get the food for the gentleman she was hiding near her standing spot. "Can you serve for a moment while I take a bathroom break" she asked Madry who wasn't happy about it but "if you have to go you have to go! Doris handed her the big spoon and quickly turned grabbing the meat and potatoes from its hiding place. She walked in the direction of the lady's room and met Finley who intercepted the plate and went back to his spot where he continued peeling more potatoes after giving the mash potatoes and chicken to Russell who really needed it.

CHAPTER 5

Boom-a-rang

Hello Renetta, Nada greeted her returning her call the next day. "Oh, hi girl, I didn't think you would call me back, I have not talked with you or your dad since you all left Naw leans" she replied eating something as she spoke. "I know, we were trying to get settled, it hasn't been easy you know" Nada responded. "I got your number from Mother Phillips" she said your dad left it in case she needed something." Nada stood shaking her head. 'That's just like dad. Mother Philips and her mom were very close she remembered. She didn't mind Mother Phillips having the number but she most certainly did not want Renetta having it with her loose mouth. Renetta was a busy body and told what she knew and what she didn't know. She worked at a little fish and chips franchise in the city near the University. "Colvin came by the other day" Nada flopped down in her chair. She was praying Renetta had not given him her number. "Yes, what did he want? She asked holding her head in her hand. "He asked had I saw what direction you went in after the floods. He had not heard from you." "What did you tell him? She said still hoping for a good out come. "Well! She said smacking her lips as she spoke, "He said he heard you had drown trying to save your dad." As horrible as that sounded Nada wished in this case it were true. She did not want Colvin Murphy to ever find her. He owned a shipping business in New Orleans. He was one of her dad's fish suppliers for his restaurant. They began dating after continuous business meetings she attended for her dad after her mom's death. After a few months he became very controlling and abusive to her. She kept it a secret for the most part from her dad and her close friend Anna Lisa. Although it was a disaster that rocked the nation, to Nada it was a blessing to be able to leave that situation. Well! You know I couldn't let him believe that! She said laughing loudly. "Well what did you tell him? Did you give him my number?" "Girl! Please! First thing I have no idea what city you're in there in Washington. I got this much info from the operator". She said there are three cities with your area code in that state!" Whew! Nada sighed. It sounds as though she was looking for information to give him. "Where are you anyway? She questioned. Mother Phillips said you all are close to California and all those earthquakes. "Renetta, we're hoping to come home soon! Have they started rebuilding in our neighborhoods? She asked to throw her thoughts off. She watched the news everyday. She knew exactly what was happening there. "Oh, you guys are coming back here? "We hoped to that is our home" she said convincingly. "Well, she sighed, "they haven't done nothing, and it may be a while" "Look Renetta, I have to go I'll call again soon" hanging up feeling she had not given him her number anyway. But just in case Nada called the phone company and had it changed immediately. She would work something else out with Mother Phillips later through the church in New Orleans.

Billy and Dana had secured their luggage and were in their cars headed home. She had thanked him for a wonderful visit they had shared at his parent's home. He reached over to hug her before saying goodnight and getting into his car. She wanted more than the peck on the cheek and a buddy hug they had been sharing before. Dana felt they bonded during the plane ride home. Reaching over to confirm the friendship she kissed his lips "Good night she smiled holding his hand as they stood by their cars making small talk. Her car was dusty from being parked in the lot for two weeks. 'Billy looked at his watch as they stood in the dusk of the evening, "I'll call you tomorrow" if it's all right he said seizing the moment. "Promise?" She flirted getting into her Porsche and driving away.

Dr. Reeves paced the floor next to his wife's bedside, stopping only to stare out the window. She had been a little under the weather these past few months though now her health had worsened. "Jon you know I have been thinking about Sonjee a lot lately" she said sitting up in bed to sip on a bowl of soup. Not much was staying down in Beulah's stomach and eating had become a challenge. "Thinking about what dear? He asked coming over sitting on the chair near her bed. "Well, I spoke with her the other day. She was telling me about some of the difficulties their mission team is having with placing some of the children whose parents have died of Aid's". Sonjee was over in Africa and she had been there about two years now working with Save the Children Foundation. She always said she was following in her mother's footsteps. She had a passion for helping and she didn't mind the hard work that came with the task. It was rare that she got the chance to speak with her family in the states. They were stationed out in a remote area with very little modern immunities. Only in the past few years some of the cellular services had been improved to provide much needed communication in the bush areas. "Oh, you spoke with her too?" he asked. "I had put a call in to her and left a message. They were out in one of the villages checking to see if any of the children had been left stranded," he was told. "She had shared it had become a weekly activity going from village to village often finding abandon children lying by their deceased mothers." Jon said removing the half empty bowl from the bed tray placing it on a cart. "She said you had left a message saying I was ill". "I did honey, you and I are both aware of your health of late. I would hate for her to be surprised with a phone call," he said now holding his ill wife's hand. "Jonathan, I know you're right," she paused. I think we should tell her the story of her birth". I thought for years there would be no need to. No one ever questioned it", Beulah said letting out a frightening cough. Dr. Reeves jumped from his sitting position and leaned over the bed. After a few minutes things with Beulah had calmed again. "When I saw the girls at that banquet earlier this year, I knew I would have to tell her the truth someday." She said looking at her husband's concerned faced. "Jonathan, she has a right to know! "I know Beulah" we gave her a good life, didn't we? He questioned with a tear regarding the truth. They sat talking over the years when their phone rang. "Hello Reeves residence". "Hello, may I speak with Beulah Reeves" the voice replied. "Mrs. Reeves is resting right now; this is her husband may I be of assistance to you. "Oh hello Mr. Reeves this is Doris Wright, she paused. I was one of the young ladies your wife helped out a long time ago. My sister and I were so glad to see her again at her award dinner this year" she went on to say. "Yes, yes I remember he replied. "Is everything all right? "Things couldn't be better! She said in and excited delightful tone. "I wanted to share with Mrs. Reeves that I had picked up her passion for helping the poor." "Oh, Dr. Reeves acknowledged waiting to hear what Doris Wright was saying. "I have been helping down at a local shelter for about seven months now" she said thinking over the time when she and Finley first made their way to South Central. "But Dr. Reeves they just keep coming" she said sadden by reality. "I am getting ready to launch a venue to try and help as many of our homeless people as possible". "That's sounds wonderful, what has God laid on your heart?" "Thank you for confirming that" she said with a smile in her voice. "I am opening a chain of thrift stores all over the Los Angeles area and someday the world". It will be running and employed by the people who frequent the missions and the homeless." It will allow them to make a better life and take care of themselves as well as their families, Doris added. I'm even looking into providing low-income housing, she said continuing to paint and even bigger picture to Dr. Reeves. "Well that most certainly sounds wonderful! I will give Beulah the news when she awakes" he said. He had looked at her lying in bed and she had nodded out again as she did often of late. "I was hoping she would come and speak at the opening of our first store in February' Doris suggested. "Dear, the vision that God as given you is wonderful. I will speak with my wife as soon as possible and get back to you." "You be blessed and I will continue praying for you and your effort". Dr. Reeves hung up the phone and stood over by the window in their bedroom starring into the heavens praying. Again, the phone rang. After turning the ringer off as not to wake Beulah he answered. "Hello Reeves residence". "Hello dad, I'm headed home" the voice said. Tears that had filled his eyes now flowed down his cheeks. Neither he nor Beulah had seen their little girl in three years. She had chosen to do mission work before graduating high school. Most of her studies were home schooled through the mission program she was with. She had left in her sophomore year after having major struggles in her classes of studies. In spite of all the tutoring the Reeves had paid for nothing seemed to help. Beulah admitted they had spoiled her. The Reeves were blessed to have Sonjee late in life.

They had raised their two children and now in the prime of their life God had given them another child to care for. They finally conceded after she pleaded to go, explaining to them it would help change her life. She said she really felt that's what she was placed on this earth for. They researched the organization thoroughly before agreeing to let her go to Africa, a foreign land. She loved the work she was doing over in Africa, and was able to complete her graduation requirements. Now this call said she had graduated high school and her plans were to come home attend college and graduate of course. Get a job in a field helping people, just like her mom she shared with her dad. Her desire was to attend college near where her parents lived. "See you soon dear!

Dana and Billy dated more often after the last visit to his parent's home. Her hidden feelings had once again surfaced for him after that long weekend with his family. Not to mention that plane ride home. "Billy, I will see you at 7 0 clock." "Sounds great, I'll be there" he said hanging up the phone. Mrs. Williams? Dana looked up to see one of the maintenance men from the hospital coming in with a box. "You asked me to store this in the storage a few months ago when it came, do you still want it? He asked holding it in his hands. "I was going through our storage to clean out some things and ran across it" "Oh I forgot about that, ummm just toss it out back. "Are you sure?" "Yes, it's just some old papers from years ago. Something I want to forget" She said dismissing any questions. "He paused for a minute. "You sure, remember this package required a signature". "I'm sure! I'm sure! She yelled now take it out of here! I don't want to be asked about it again! 'Hey! Hey what's going on Dr. Justin Parker acknowledged walking in. "Oh, he keeps questioning about and old box of papers! Dana replied "A box of papers? What kind of papers could cause that much commotion from you? "I don't know they were papers found after I sold my parents home, I guess? "You guess? Have you looked at the papers to see if they are worth keeping? He questioned. "Now there you go! Then she turned to the custodian "put the box over there, pointing to a corner of her office and "I'll look at them and throw them away myself." Okay hurrying out while Justin was still in her office. "Dana, why don't you want to know what's in that box? Whatever it is isn't going away! Let's look and see what's inside. 'Go ahead then maybe I will be rid of this darn box! He picked the box up from the corner of the room and placed it on Dana's desk. The shipping tape was wrapped around and around it several times to prevent damaging or having it open during shipping. Justin was just about to get where he could lift the flap of the box when "BUZZ HONK BUZZ! A very loud alarm went off. Soon it was followed by a code blue announcement "CODE BLUE! CODE BLUE! Justin quickly stopped what he was doing and headed out of the room leaving the box partially opened on the desk. Dana stood at the door as she saw other employee's, doctors, and nurses scurrying about. After a bit she looked over at the box again. I will just look at this quickly and toss the box in the dumpster on my way out she stood thinking. Dana finished opening the box and looked inside taking out some cards. She looked at the signatures they were from Richard Demato, her dad. She sat for a moment thinking about them. No! I know what's in here will not make me happy" she thought. She put the cards back and looked moving some of the papers around. Oh, this looks interesting she said pulling out a pile of letters secured with a large rubber band. All the letters were to her father. She turned them over and read the name of the person who had sent them "Faye Wright". Ummm I've heard that name before. She looked at the pile of letters and then she looked at her watch. Oh, that's right I'm meeting Billy at 7 0 clock. I'll have to take this box of papers home I can't be late meeting Billy.

CHAPTER 6

Getting together

Nada enjoyed her new position at the University. She had meet many of her colleagues and was finding her way around campus life pretty well. "Hi Nada, Hello you all, she replied walking into the lounge for a much needed break. "Girl you look like you need a cup of coffee! What's been happening? One of her associates asked. "Coffee yes, just a long question and answer period before an exam, though I haven't rested well lately," she confessed. "Oh, what's going on? Is it something I can help with? The two gentlemen who were standing with them excused themselves to let them talk. "Later" one man said and walked away. "Nothing really, I'm probably making more out of it than I need to! Nada voiced, "Well if it's causing you to lose sleep, it must be important! Her friend Carin said. "I heard and old friend was looking for me". Carin Wilson starred into her face. What do you mean friend? Carin said holding up both hands making a parenthesis motion regarding friend. Good or bad? "Well put it this way if I never saw this person again it would be fine!" "Ooo that hurts! So, you think they will try and find you? "I hope not, but honestly I'm not sure what he might do! "You said he Nada! Is this and old boyfriend?" "Yes! But one I want to forget! "Well, I just hope he doesn't come around here" Carin said very serious faced as Nada drank down her coffee. "Thanks for the concern. I'm probably worrying for nothing" "Whew, for a minute I thought I would have to take off my shoes and earrings" she said bringing much laughter to the conversation. "I'd better head back to my administrative desk, this semester classes are quite large when they all show up", Carin acknowledged getting up leaving the table. Madison Green another colleague had now walked in the break room. Hi Nada mind if I sit with you? She asked going over to get a cup of coffee. "No, I don't mind, but I've been here for a while so I will be leaving soon, Nada replied. Madison gathered her condiments and came back to the table. Nada are you planning to attend the staff party next month? "Yes I do." "Do you have a date lined up already? No Madison! And no, I'm not going to have you ask your friend! Madison was always pawning him off on somebody! She wants him married to a good woman she confesses. "Oh, that's good. He gets mad when I set him up with dates anyway". Good! Then you should stop! Nada explained "He's a nice guy for an accountant but certainly not my type Madison". He's to shy and you must admit a bit of a recluse".

"I want you to meet my husband," Madison replied. I shared with him you were from the New Orleans area. He grew up there and left after he joined the armed services," Madison confessed. We all wanted to meet him that's all she talked about in our girly circles! Would love too! Hey, don't worry about a date. I'm coming if I have to come by myself, I'm very independent," she added. And I do look forward to meeting and talking south with your husband" Nada explained. I'd better get out of here I have a lecture to get ready for, she said standing up to leave the table. Nada walked out pass Emily the librarian giving a friendly wave, leaving Madison sitting looking around sipping her coffee.

Dinner was great Dana! Billy said getting up from the table. "Oh, thank you, twas nothing, she explained taking credit for all entrées. 'Billy please take the wine into the den; I'll get the stemware and ice." She suggested. Billy took the left-over bottle of costly wine and walked into the family room. Dana came in clicking a switch on the wall igniting a fire in the fireplace. "Nice! "Very nice" Billy said taking a glass from Dana and pouring the expensive wine into it. "Dana changed the music to set a mood for the evening's conversation. She and Billy sat watching the fire and catching up on their past lives. "After about an hour he put his arm around her and drew her close and kissed her. She didn't refuse his approach and returned his affection. Dana what are we doing? He said after sitting back realizing what seems to be happening. "What do you mean? Dana asked still cuddling near him vying for his attention. "Do you think we can find what we once had?" "I do Billy, I really want to" she said honestly. "You do, you mean after all these years you're willing to start all over? "Well Billy, we're much older and a lot has happened to the both of us. But my feelings for you never faded" Dana said lying on his shoulder clutching his hand. Billy poured another glass of wine and gulped it down. He had been trying for months to recapture feelings for his old girlfriend. He knew she wanted more. They shared a child together. And although he cared for her and knew he always would he didn't see them married and living happily forever. "Billy, Billy, she said noticing he was starring into the distant. "Are you still dating Annie? "I do see Annie from time to time" he answered. Dana pulled away. "Well do you love her? Her mood and questions were sounding defensive. "Dana, I know these are questions you don't really want to hear the answers to let's just drop it" Billy said reaching to hold her hand. She stood up and moved across the room. "Look Dana this was a beautiful evening" let's remember it that way." Dana crossed her arms and said nothing. Billy stood up to leave when his cell phone rang. 'Excuse me Dana". "Hello, he said moving in another room to answer his call. "Oh, hi Annie" is what Dana heard. She slammed the emptied wine bottle on the cocktail table and stomped into the kitchen with the stemware they had been using. Billy was still talking when she made her way back to retrieve the bottle from the table to dispose of it. She was not happy. But what she needed was to win her man's affection again. She was not going to hide this time. She was going to do whatever it takes to get Billy to love her again. "Soon Billy walked back into the den. There were no signs of Dana. "Dana? He called out not knowing what she was doing, are where she was. "I'm in here Billy she finally said. Her voice was coming from here bedroom. "Ok! I'm just letting you know I'm leaving," he said again. "What? She said pretending not to hear what Billy said. Dana was not coming from her room, she wanted Billy to come to her. She knew it was Annie on his phone and she was not about to spend the evening with him and turn him over to her. Billy there's another bottled of wine in the frig in an ice bucket please bring it to me" she requested shouting her sultry voice from her bedroom. Thinking manly thoughts Billy raised his brow and walked in her bedroom with ice bucket and bottle of expensive champagne in hand. Dana was sitting on her bed in a beautiful gown draping to the floor. She had let her wavy hair down. "So, did I hear you were about to leave? She asked enticing him with each word. "Wow! you look awesome Dana". 'I have to admit getting use to the new you was not easy. But seeing you sitting there now is a turn on. He confessed flirting with hand gestures. "Pop the cork Billy please? She requested knowing it was probably the wine talking for him right now. But if it was keeping him from running to Annie, she didn't mind it. He poured the wine into the beautiful gold trimmed flutes and handed one to Dana. She stood and walked around allowing Billy's imagine to run wild as he sat in her big chaise style chair sipping down his second glass of wine from this bottle. The soft silky fabric fell just right across her hips. The dim lights and the mood music were setting a stage filled with romance. Not really being much of a drinker he was feeling a little light headed. He knew the wine was getting to him. "Come here" he said beckoning for her to come over from her place on the bed.

"Me! She teased pointing to herself looking around as if someone else was in the room. "Yes you! opening up his arm allowing her to walk right into them. Whether or not they finished the expensive bottle of wine or not we will probably never know. But don't worry! No one did any driving home that night anyway.

Sonjee was back in the states with her family. Her experiences she shared in Africa would never be forgotten. She wanted to attend the university in Oregon because it was closer to home but she was accepted at Gonzaga so she made her way there with her parents blessing. They had just arrived back from two weeks visit with her sister Candace and their brother Bailey who lived in Arizona. They were Jon and Beulah's older children who had moved to Arizona for better job opportunities and Beulah loved their yearly visits together. This one was especially delightful because Sonjee was back home with them. "Candace purchased me a gorgeous sweater when we went shopping" she said to her mother finishing up her packing to leave for college. Oh, that's wonderful! Did you enjoy yourself? "I sure did Bailey and Aunt Katherine invited me with them when they go to Disneyland "she said. "Good the twins will love that I'm sure" Beulah replied preparing herself for bed after the plane ride home. "Marlon their neighbor who Sonjee and her parents had known for years had come by to invite her out for a burger with some of the others in the neighborhood who were also going away to college. "Bye mom, bye dad, she said kissing each one before leaving.

Dana had prepared the coffee and brought it in to the dining table in a sterling silver serving pot. Billy was moving around in the other room getting his things together to leave. "Coffee's ready she yelled softly but loud enough to be heard. "Oh, I'm coming! He replied back, my mornings don't get started until I get a hot cup of coffee" he shared coming out of the room with coat over his arm and palm mobile in hand. "Are you in a hurry? I want to make breakfast for us" Dana suggested not ready for him to leave. 'Dana hold that thought! I'd love that but I'll need a rain check". He moved to a chair to sit and tie his shoes and stumbled slightly kicking a box sitting near the chair. "Sorry about that! He acknowledged looking at Dana. "No worries it's just a box of papers, no harm done". Billy quickly drank down the hot cup of coffee Dana had handed him. 'See you soon" Billy said kissing her and opening the door with his cell phone ringing. "Oh, hi Annie, I know I'm on my way! Dana heard him say as he left with her standing in her front door listening.

CHAPTER 7

Can this be happening?

Doris was helping all she knew how with the mission. She had met with some of her executives and business partners. Some others were potential partners in her newest venture with low-income housing. She had met again with them to close up all matters. Finley I'm going in for my dialysis this morning, are you coming with me," she asked getting her coat heading out the door. "Sure, my lady, I'm just making sure the order made it to the mission." He replied standing with the phone receiver to his ear. Doris was having regular donations of food sent to the mission on Pleh Street. Finley was overseeing that matter keeping it running smoothly. "Let's go my lady" following her out the door. Doris had been going for the treatments now for about a year. She was going once a month but her body was shutting down so her doctor insisted, she now come twice a month. She had been put on a list awaiting a kidney transplant but still no matches were found and her need for it grew worst. Finley if I feel up to it, I'd like to stop by the boutique on my way home." "Sure, my lady we will do that." "Finley are you aware I have hired Russell to work for me in the office. "Yes, he told me," Finley laughed. "Who would ever know that he was a fortune 500 executive" Doris replied. "Oh, did he tell you his story?" Finley asked. "I guess some of it" she replied. When I saw his resume, I began to ask him questions" Doris confessed. "I wanted him to work repairing furniture in one of the thrift stores. So, I asked him to bring me a list of some things he likes to do and I received a well-prepared resume. I was very impressed and surprised when he said he had prepared it himself."

He shared with me" Doris continued "that he ran out of money and the interviews they were sending him on, he was over qualified, some said under qualified, and a lot just closed the door in his face when they heard Tri-ron. He confesses he worked a lot of odd jobs. Door after door was shut in his face. He tried selling everything from vacuum cleaners to automobiles. Divorced, Depressed, discouraged, disappointed, and tired he grew weary and was about to give up all together until he met you". "Well you mean I helped someone? Finley asked driving along down the highway. He said you did" Doris repeated. "We talked quite a bit peeling those potatoes for three weeks, I guess you get to know one pretty well" Finley reasoned. "Did he tell you he worked for Tri-ron that company the went belly up". Yes, that was on his application". His wife blamed him for losing his job. She hired a good lawyer took him for everything, sold their home from under him and left him virtually with the shirt on his back" he says. When we came to the mission that day and showed compassion for the people, he confesses it gave him hope. He had been there about two months doing odd jobs for his daily meals, he told me "I admit I sat in my office and cried when he left" Doris said it wasn't until later I had my human resource department to call him back at the mission and offer him the job". "And yes, he was grateful and very surprised" Doris said getting out of the car heading into the hospital for her weekly treatment.

Dana sat back on her chair sipping her coffee and thinking about the night before. She looked over at the box. Okay it's not going to go away! She picked up the box and poured out the contents on the floor, sat down and began reading the pile of letters she had removed from a rubber band. The letters she found out were from her real mother Faye that she had written to Richard Demato her adopted father. She had heard Edith talk about a Faye with Mrs. Demato often. She was my mother? She fell against the sofa throwing her head back. She felt like crying but nothing would come out. She regrouped her thoughts and shuffled around some papers finding a picture of a lady. "Wow! She's beautiful turning it over it read love Faye. Tears instantly filled her eyes. This was the first encounter she had with her real mother. She starred and starred at the photograph she couldn't take her eyes off of it. Dana put it in her hand and held it to her heart. Could this really be happening to her! She thought. "Come on Dana get it together! She said in her mind. Soon she began reading again. She carefully arranged the papers on the floor. So far from the letters she had read Faye was having an affair with Mr. Demato for years. He had paid for her home and took care of all her needs. She had letters thanking him for the new car he had just purchased for her to get around in life. Seems this was something he had done two years prior. This was just a later model she was referring to. Dana sat reading and putting together Faye's past life. There were pink slips and mortgage statements and other important papers Richard Demato had kept for records of his purchases for her. Best Dana could figure from looking at all the documents and papers she had read Faye and Richard had been dating for over ten years. She even mentioned time and time again that she loved him. There were letters that talked about her daughter. Then Dana burst out crying when she read about Faye being pregnant. She was telling him about the troubles she was having carrying this one. She explained that this pregnancy was so different than when she was pregnant with Doris she mentioned in the letter. Clutching on to the letter in one hand and the photograph in the other Dana sat and cried for a very long time.

"Hi Billy, Annie said seeing him come through the door. He had gone home and changed his attire from his evening out before coming into the office. 'Hello, he said to her with a smile. She stood talking with him holding some important files in her hand. "Are those the files my dad asked us to look into? He asked. "Yes! She replied excitedly moving again toward the filing cabinet. That was also the reason she had shared with him for her early morning call. "I had just begun to pull the files for you and place them in your office" she replied. "Oh good! He said going into his office hanging his coat on its hanger behind his door. Annie followed him in vying for attention. "Oh, I guess a girl can't get a hug anymore?" she teased standing in front of his large oak desk. He and Annie dated for years off and on even when Jillian Mcfinney his fiancé was still alive. Jillian and Billy were separated during that time then reconciled before she was killed in the fatal plane crash of 911. Annie could never get him to commit to the relationship she confessed but since the two worked together they remained friends and even dated occasionally. "Annie you know I always have lots of hugs for you" he said coming from behind his desk to hug her. "Melvin stood in the door and cleared his throat" Annie was a bit startled as they both turn to see him standing there smiling. "Good morning! "Good morning to you sir, Billy replied extending a good morning friendly handshake. "Yeah! Melvin said, "Want to chat a bit about that Bitterman case. "Can you spare a moment or two?" Sure, my day is fairly light today. "Came in to get some folders to go over at home", Billy shared. "Let's head down to your office". Annie had quickly moved out of the conversation range after the handshake. Melvin headed down the hall stopping to get a cup of coffee from the break room and went into his office to wait to talk with his boss, director and owner of Parker & Associates law firm.

"Dad" Billy said calling him at his office. "I had a chance to go over the files you sent me. "That's a big undertaking you're stepping into. Are you sure you want to commit to something of this size at your age, he joked, "It's going to require a lot of time". "You're right son! But it's not my undertaking I'm only involved financially. "Well I'm going to help get this venture off the ground. "But for me it won't be putting in man hours" he explained to him. "This proposal you have drawn up is right on target." The outlined agenda seems to be on point for the time frame you have indicated" Billy went on to say. David and his son discussed the venture in great detail before saying goodbye. He and Billy had scheduled several meetings to meet with the other persons who David was partnering with in this endeavor.

Billy had tried earlier to call Dana to explain the need for his swift departure but got no answer. After sitting at home watching a favorite show Dana came to mind again. "Ring, ring, ring he let it rang until her machine answered. Leaving a message, he went to bed to get some needed rest. He had booked a flight to Washington for a Monday morning meeting planning to return home hopefully by noon of the same day.

After what can be viewed as a good night's rest Billy woke to the sun shining in his window. A good hot shower and warm robe he pulled the serving tray from the hall into his room for breakfast. "Thanks, he said closing his door as the staff walked away. His big house had started to get lonely without the laughter of David Michael and all of his friends running from one end to the other. He sat thinking about his last evening with Dana. Could there be a chance for us? "He really didn't feel what he thought love should be, but they have a child together maybe his feelings would change and he was getting older. He was rapidly approaching his fortieth birthday. He knew he wanted to have someone to spend the rest of his life with. After all the glamorous parties and dating for him now just wasn't what he wanted. He had done it all. He and his buddy Glen had visited the Hawaiian Islands, Greece, Brazil more than once and any other place on the map. He most certainly has sown his oats. His mother had reminded him of that during every conversation lately. Annie cared a lot for him but had for the most part conceded on marriage for now anyway. But like all the rest she hoped for a Parker ring! He walked over to the telephone and dialed Dana again. Letting it rang he got only her machine to answer. "Oh well, I'll get her later at the office" he reasoned before sitting down to breakfast again by himself.

Dana was still sitting after hours looking through the papers. She had composed herself enough to call her office and arrange for a week's vacation she said to clear her head. She looked at the message light on her phone. She didn't want to speak to anyone! Not right now she was grieving the lost of her mother and father she discovered from reading the legal papers he had left stored away. "She loved me! She really loved me! She said moving around fighting the tears from her eyes. She took me to my daddy! She knew he would take care of me! She kept saying. Ring, ring, Dana stood in place until it stopped ringing. Then she heard Billy's voice. "Dana! Please call me; I have been calling you since yesterday. "I've tried your cell" and the hospital clerk said you were on vacation after much prompting for an answer for me." If you're trying to avoid me, call and let me know! Then I won't call as much," he teased. Call me, bye! Dana knew she would call but right now she wanted to be alone. Several other messages came in. "One message caused her to fall back on her chair. It was a voice from her past. "Dana it is Rusty".

CHAPTER 8

Can this be real?

Nada most certainly was enjoying her new life and feeling quite comfortable in Washington State. Her friends and colleagues embraced her openly and welcomed her to the staff of the University. "Nada a few of us are going out for pizza and bowling tonight, want to come? Carin asked walking briskly to catch up with her at her car. "Sure, sounds fun whose going, all singles? She asked. "For the most part, though Remelda and Simon are going". "Okay, that's fine count me in". "Where are you going now in such a hurry? She asked noticing Nada didn't want to stand around talking. "I have to pick up a prescription for my dad and get this kitchen off the back of my head" she said rubbing the back of her neck and hairline and laughing. "What salon does your hair? Carin continued to question. It always looks great! Carin confessed. "It's a salon call "Felicia la Clinique, on Pershing. "Umm I'm scared of you! YOU GO GIRL! She acknowledged "that's swank! "Let me go! She laughed, getting into her car. "My hair will be gorgeous but my pocketbook will be a lot lighter" she teased pulling slowly out of the faculty parking lot.

Doris was in her room getting dressed when her phone rang. It was "Beulah Reeves" Finley announced knocking on the closed door. "Thanks Finley, walking over to her phone." Hello this is Doris Wright" she said greeting her caller on the other end. "Hello Doris this is Beulah, how are you? she asked sounding a bit weak in body, Doris thought. "I'm fine, I'm just on my way out for my weekly treatment" she explained. "Oh, I understand! Well I'll talk with you another time," Beulah replied. "Oh no it's alright. "I am not in that big of a hurry that I can't talk to you, I have plenty of time," she said looking at her watch on her wrist. "There is a personal matter I want to speak with you about" "Oh! Doris said now curious about Beulah's call. "I would like you to meet with me. I have something that's very delicate in nature and much too important to discuss over the phone". "Are you alright? Doris asked trying to figure out this important quandary. "I'm as well as a woman my age could be right now" she said assuring Doris this matter had very little to do with her health. Doris sat talking on the phone and Finley had knocked a couple of times regarding them leaving for her appointment. "Okay! She said very loudly to Finley on the other side of the door but made an excuse to Beulah when she asked about it. "Oh, I see, thank you Beulah. I know it took a lot for you to tell me that". "You're right I love her very much! Doris hung up her receiver and walked slowly to her front door. Finley was standing out front anxiously waiting to drive Doris to her appointment. She got into her car and sat quietly. Doris did not say one word to Finley on the long drive to her dialysis appointment.

David and Tetra walked into Mt. Nebo and found their familiar seats down front. The large congregation was all gathered into the sanctuary for praise and worship after prayers had been rendered. The worship team took the platform down front and the joyous music rang out. Those who chose to do so was asked to stand in the present of the Lord as the worship leader ushered them into praise song after praise song. The Parkers stood lifting holding hands unto the lord. Many had tears of joy streaming from their faces. "Hallelujah! rang out across the auditorium as God's presence entered into the sanctuary. "You are welcome in this place" came from the saints of God. Their voices blended together in harmony. What a time to be present in God's house. When Dr. Hathaway took the podium to deliver the message the saints of God rejoiced mightily.

Billy had decided not to call Dana for a few days. He had left lots of messages. And some were sounding pretty desperate. He wasn't trying to rush into anything with her but things had started to grow between them since their last visit to Washington. "Ring, ring hello William Parker, he said answering is mobile phone. "Hi dad". "David Michael! hello what are you up to these days? He asked greeting his son. "Oh, the usual, he paused. "Studying, practicing and cramming" he replied. "Yes, those are great answers and what you should be doing but what have you really been doing with your time?" Billy asked again sharing a laugh with his son. "Ah! You know how it goes! But I'm keeping it together". "Good I believe that" Billy added. "So, have you spoken with Dana lately?" David Michael asked. "Not since Thursday we had dinner together, Billy shared. "Well I've been calling her and leaving messages she hasn't returned my calls". "Son you know Dana, but I'll go by and see what's up. I know she's on vacation from work and maybe traveling somewhere, though I'll find out and let you know". "Thanks dad." "Well how's that backfield going." "We're looking good, Ray and I are a force in the outfield David explained. "Great! Dana and I will be there opening day" that's the plans anyway" he said reassuring him he would be there". As they were talking Billy could hear loud talking on the other end of the line. "Okay dad it's good talking to you" I look forward to seeing you and Dana soon". "Plans tonight son?" "Not really just headed to a frat party" and they're calling me? "Billy shook his head remembering his years in college. "All right son I love you. "I'll have Dana call when I speak with her" disconnecting the line and calling Dana.

"Hello, her voice answered. "Well hello, I thought you were out of town? He questioned surprised she had answered her home phone. "No, just needed some time alone" Dana replied. "Is it something I can help with?" and with that question Dana broke down and started crying all over again. "Dana, Dana, what's wrong? He asked over and over again. Dana I'm on my way! He said rushing out of his office with Annie looking and wondering as he passed her desk in a hurry.

When Billy arrived at Dana's home, she to him was fine. She opened the door speaking on her mobile phone. She beckoned Billy in. He stood looking around as if looking for what had caused her out burst over the phone. "All right dear, I love you" she voiced disconnecting the line to her caller. "That was David Michael" she confessed he had been calling since yesterday he told me". "I can't believe I got so emotional after all these years! I'm angry with myself for letting you and David Michael worry about something so foolish", Dana replied walking around her home. Billy walked over to her and stood directly in front of her and caught her by both arms. "Dana what in heavens name are you talking about?" He stood looking puzzled waiting for an answer. 'I'm sorry I made you all worry about my whereabouts" I needed time to reflect and I didn't think about anyone else" Dana confessed. He let go of her arms. "You frightened me! What was that all about on the phone? I thought someone was here hurting you or something, he admitted now going over to sit on the sofa. "Oh Billy, it was that box." "Box, what box? "Dana please sit down" he said. "Let's start from the beginning because nothing you're saying right now makes any sense". Are you on a prescription of some kind Dana? "No Billy! she replied sitting beside him on the sofa. "I received a box of papers from my parent's estate that I sold." After finally reading through some of the papers I found out that Richard Demato was my real father! "What! Are you kidding! "No, he and Faye my real mom were having a ten-year affair from what I've read thus far. He kept all the letters she had sent him over the years. "He took care of her" Billy. "He took very good care of her! She said leaning into Billy's embrace as she continued speaking. They sat embraced and Dana shared with him about things she had read in the letters. That's incredible Dana! You have both parents now Billy said, seeing how pleased Dana was about the realization. "I know what that means to you" Now you have closure. "I'm just sorry they're not still around that you can get to know them. "Me to Billy", Dana replied "me too."

When Dana arrived at her office Monday morning there was a delivery of a bouquet with a dozen beautiful yellow roses. She smiled and thanked the gentleman who had carefully sat them on the credenza in her waiting room. She gave him a tip, went over and took out the small envelope removing the card and sat down at her desk writing in her journal.

CHAPTER 9

Thank you

Sonjee had settled into her dorm. She had called her parents to let them know she had arrived safely. "Now what will I do with the rest of this day she thought" folding and putting away the last few pieces from her luggage. Her roommate still had not shown up so she got first choice of everything there. She thought for a moment and chose the bed over near the window for starters. Out of her window you could see the tall beautiful trees that covered the campus. Sonjee sat looking out of her dorm window watching the busy crowds of students' scurry from place to place. She had come earlier with her parents and took a mini tour around campus. Jon and Beulah being older they didn't see all that was available for their daughter around the huge campus. Walking or riding a golf cart for them was only minimum. With her mother's health issues and their ages a lot of things were limited. They knew enough regarding the University and its curriculum to know it was a great chose for the younger daughter and very close to home. Sonjee put on her coat and walked out of her room to explore the outdoors. She was very independent. After all she had spent the last three years in Africa learning about its' culture and its' people. She walked across the huge campus looking at all the diversities of people. She remembered the long walks she and her core group took from village to village. Sonjee was looking at the styles the girls were wearing. She had gone shopping before she left home getting some of the latest styles. Her attire in Africa was minimal though in Johannesburg the people are Americanized and fashion too many of them really didn't matter much.

She walked along the designated paths very quickly. She looked up to see a Willow Goldfinch sitting on a branch. She stood for a moment watching the tiny yellow and black bird move from branch to branch then flew away. She smiled and continued her journey walking up to a small eatery on the corner near the university. She ordered a hamburger and pulled the money from her blue jeans pocket to pay for it. Wow, she thought sitting down biting into the juicy burger. This is great! She had almost forgotten the taste of the delicious sandwich. She most certainly had made up for it since coming home from Africa these last three months. And having this place a few steps away from her dorm was going to be very tempting. "Hi! A voice over her shoulder said. "Hi, she returned the greeting without even turning around. "You're saying hello do you even know me?" the voice replied. "You spoke first do you know me? The sassy Sonjee voiced. She took another bite finishing her burger. The voiced moved around the table. "I was admiring your dreads! I think they're beautiful like you". How long have you been growing them? The voice asked. Sonjee looked up to see a very blonde-haired young man standing in front of her. "Are you serious? She asked looking puzzled he complimented her hair. "Well yes, I'm serious, are you from here? "Who's asking and why? Continuing her answers with her sassy attitude, "Okay rewind! "I do apologize, he said extending his hand out to her. "My name is Fonsworth Erickson and I will be attending the University" he replied still waiting for her to reach out her hand, "And Fonsworth that's your pickup line?" She asked. He raised his brows and they both laughed. Well it broke the ice anyway. "I'm Sonjee Reeves" she said reaching to connect with a handshake. "I would ask you to join me but as you can see, I'm finished and getting ready to leave. But to answer your question for about three years". "May I say, I have seen lots of dreads but yours are fabulous! He replied flirting with his gorgeous hazel colored eyes. His accent Sonjee could not distinguish. "Oh! Sonjee paused waiting for the next line. "Maybe this guy had saw her leave campus and followed her she thought feeling a bit uneasy getting up from the small bistro style table. "I am new here in the states and your hair reminded me of home! My hair! Now don't you think that's taking a line a bit far? Sonjee asked now standing up in her sassy way "Where are you from? "I only arrived last week from my homeland in South Africa". Sonjee stood with her mouth opened. "Oh, what you think that's a line too because of my skin color?" he asked motioning an uncertainty gesture. "No, she smiled walking away. "I believe you, and thanks for the compliment".

Billy had called his dad to let him know when his flight would arrive. He was sure Dana had her footing back and things with her were fine. They had enjoyed a wonderful opening day game with their son David Michael who by the way was turning out to be a great baseball player. Their U.C.L.A. team had won their game opener and his roommate and another team player had hit a homerun to put them back in the game. "Hello! Miesur Billy may I help you? Alfredo asked answering the Parkers phone. "Hi Alfredo is mom or dad in?" Mrs. Parker is in the den reading, please hold I'll let her know it's you" he replied taking the phone receiver to where she was sitting in her family room. "Hello son! She said greeting him warmly. "Hello mom, how are you?" He asked in his playful way. "Just wonderful Billy" "I left a message on dad's cell phone regarding my flight time. His secretary says he was in a corporate meeting and could not be interrupted. I wanted to make sure he knows I will be meeting him at the Hyatt at 6pm for our scheduled meeting with his investors." "Oh yes he did mention something about that". "I'll surely let him know. "Are you going right back home this time out son? "I don't know we'll see how this meeting goes. We may need to talk over some vital details and it could take a bit longer." "That's' fine I look forward to seeing you son". Me to mom! Billy replied hanging up. I think she had given up on me marrying anyone. I admit I was spoiled and had everything I needed but someone I really loved. Mom had stopped asking me whenever I spoke with her. I guess she was content having David Michael my son and her only grandchild. But I wanted someone for me. I was growing lonely in that big house all by myself.

Nada had just spoken with Carin her young friend about the staff party tonight. She had made up her mind to go alone. Knowing there were lots of single professors on the University's faculty staff she felt totally comfortable. "Nada girl may I borrow your diamonds if you're not going to wear them? Carin asked her close friend. "I'm wearing my hair up and they will look fabulous with this outfit". "Carin, you're asking a lot. My dad bought my diamond earrings and as a rule I don't lend them out. Besides I'm wearing them myself." After a pause in conversation Nada spoke again. "I'll bring you another pair I have, they are gorgeous too." "But will they compliment my outfit and better yet are they diamonds, Carin asked in a close friends' way again. "I will get there a little early and you can decide if they work for you" she said hanging up the receiver. Nada looked stunting in her black strapless dress she had purchased at the high-end outlet store. It was a Klein original. Her make up was flawless and her beautiful small but hand cut diamond earrings sparkled against the reflection in her mirror. She was just about to walk out of her door after one last look and "you go girl!" when the phone rang. "Hello, she answered just knowing it was Carin again. "Hello dear! The voice replied. "Daddy, I was just leaving is something wrong?" "I just walked back to the bungalow and realized you still have my prescription." "Oh, you're right daddy," she replied walking to get her larger purse she usually carries. "Yes dad, I have it right here". "Are you completely out? She asked trying not to make a trip across town right now. The University was in another direction and she had promised Carin she'd get there early. "I should be fine I took my last one about four hours ago". "If you get them to me early tomorrow it will be fine dear". Alfredo said knowing of his daughter's plans and the reason she was hesitating. "Are you sure dad?" she asked just to hear him say it again thinking that would make her stop thinking about it. "Go forget about this call, have fun sweetie good night" he said the phone buzzed in her ear. Nada looked at the bottle of medicine putting it in the small purse she was carrying tonight. It was full with just lipstick and makeup. She rushed out the door. She thought she heard something and looked around before getting in her car and driving off quickly. She drove along to the freeway. But instead of merging to enter the freeway to the University she veered to the right and circled around going in the other direction to take her dad his prescription. It would be about thirty minutes no matter what! She drove as fast as she could, watching for patrol cars. After a while she made the exit to the Parkers home. When she arrived, a cab was out front letting someone out. She parked and hurriedly got out and was heading to the bungalow using the side path entrance of the yard as the cab pulled away. "Hello, where's the fire?" the voice yelled. She looked back it was dark and she couldn't make out who it was. Taking a chance, she asked

"Mr. Parker" "Yes." She thought it strange that he was getting out of a cab but who knows? "I'm taking my dad his prescription" she yelled still moving. "Is he alright" the male voice asked running to catch up with her. "He's fine, I just forgot to bring it today and I'm in a hurry! She admitted. "Slow down you can't be that late" he held her arm, she stopped! Oh my, it's you! She smiled I thought you were Mr. Parker? "I am Mr. Parker". Oh, William you know what I mean" what are you doing here? Weren't you here last week" I mean daddy said you were here", 'He's right, my dad and I are working on a project together so you will be seeing a lot of me for a while". Okay, if you say so! Where is she? looking up to the main house. "Oh, I'm by myself this time. Dana's in Maine." We're only friends not an item! She walked a little further and knocked on her dad's door. Billy waited by the bench along the path. She gave her dad the prescription, kissed him and closed the door and headed quickly back toward her car. "Well it was good seeing you but I really must go. I'm headed to a faculty party and I don't want to be late. "A party, mind if I come along?" he asked. "Are you kidding? No! I'd love to come with you". "It's very formal attire" she informed not wanting him to feel out of place. "Give me a few minutes in the house and I will do you proud" he told her running into his parent's home with his luggage in tow. Nada sat impatiently in her car in front of the Parkers home. She thought she saw a shadow watching her but dismissed it when a cat walked across the yard. She quickly locked her car doors. After about thirty minutes of waiting and two phone calls from Carin, Billy came out to find her coming from the bungalow. "I didn't want my dress to get wrinkled so I waited with daddy until I saw you coming out of the house" she confessed. "Sorry about the wait. I apologize I'll make it up to you." "Park your car I'll drive dad's jag if you trust my driving." "OOOKAY! A man who knows what he wants" Nada said going over parking her car in the wide driveway of the home and getting into this fabulous silver jaguar heading to her faculty party.

Billy drove speedily along the highway with Nada on the passenger side. She was sharing with him about some of her colleagues and fellow faculty members he would be meeting tonight. They shared with each other light conversation about their lives and of course they talked about careers. Neither could believe how comfortable they felt with each other. Nada with her leadership qualities was impressing William Parker. Billy, Nada thought for a lawyer is quite hip and easy to relate too. She surely mentioned her friend Carin right in the beginning knowing that would be drama! Billy felt so comfortable with her. He repeated it to her several times during the ride to the University. It was as if he had known her for a long time. Nada directed him to turn at the next corner. He had forgotten the exact route. It had been a few years since he had even driven by the University's campus. They pulled slowly into the lot. "Sorry Billy I don't think there is valet service here. You will have to park it yourself" she teased taking another look in the lighted mirror in front of her. Are you sure? He said laughing as he pulled the car into the parking space. There were other couples and faculty persons she knew getting there at the same time. She stood over on her side of the car and adjusted everything in place from the long ride in. Billy looked very handsome wearing a casual Valentino tuxedo. "May I say you make me look very good!" Nada voiced to Billy walking around to join him as they walked to the entrance together. "You took the words right from my mouth, he replied. But I would have said fabulous! locking his arm with hers before entering the magnificent transformed room of the University.

The décor for the evening was very warm and inviting. The enormous space was lit with hundreds of candles strategically place all around the room. The tables were draped in white linens and covered with crystal stem wear sparkling across the nights' atmosphere. The band had set up on the stage and was playing softly as the now crowded room was buzzing with the faculty and their guest. Immediately seeing them come through the door Carin presented herself. "Hello Carin, Dana said greeting her as she strolled to meet them. "Um so that's why you're late? She said in her humorous teasing way. "Oh, am I late? Dana teased back. "Well you're not exactly early". Billy cleared his throat. "Excuse me! Nada interjected looking directly at Carin to stop her from speaking. "Carin Wilson this is William Parker. "Please to meet you Carin" he said extending his hand for a shake. "Hi she giggled then pulling herself together. "Carin was one of our youngest staff members. She works in the administrative office and hangs out with the ever-increasing black faculty members on staff at U.W. We all know she still has a lot to learn though we agree she is open to bettering herself about a lot of things as well. "Please to meet you", Carin greeted with her extended hand joining the shake. "You look very nice Nada said motioning about her earrings she was wearing. She stood looking at Billy like a deer in headlights. Carin! Nada voiced to get her attention. "Oh, did you bring them? Nada closed both eyes and shook her head. She opened her small purse and handed Carin the small box containing the earrings she had brought for her to borrow. The earrings Carin had on looked fine. She took the very small box and hurried off heading to the lady's room to put them on. "Nice meeting you" she yelled waving. Nada and Billy looked at each other "drama!" and continued walking across the room. They stopped along the way to their table meeting others who had come out for the welcome festivities. Some of her close associates were surprise to see this handsome man on Nada's arm. Heads were turning all around the room and few even whispered. They soon found their reserved table with their named seating arrangements. "I imagine you're the guest" Nada said turning to tease Billy making light of the fact that his name wasn't on the name display on the tables. 'She had called ahead while she waited in the car for Billy and had a place reserved at her table for him as her guest for the evening. Billy pulled out her chair and they sat with two other couples greeting and exchanging names all around the elegantly set table. "Hi Nada! She heard Madison's voice. She stood up looking as she and her husband were coming toward the table. Billy got up from his seat and stood next to Nada. He was having a wonderful time. They sat with a science professor with her husband the realtor. And English professor and her husband a chiropractor, Billy a lawyer and Nada a science professor also. Conversation had wide range. It had been a long time since he let his hair down. He socialized a lot. But he was having fun! Relaxing fun and yes, he talked politics with the small group listening, but even that in this setting was fun. "Hi! Madison Nada said greeting her with a friendly hug. Madison always made it a point to sit at the faculty tables with the minorities. No one ever questioned it but we did talk about it for a while. She was ever the lady, gorgeous very prim and proper with shoulder length blonde hair and blue eyes. Everything about her said money! Her father had an important job in Washington D.C. So yes, we all knew she had the silver spoon treatment growing up. I guess the trip was until you get to know her everything about her said snooty and stuck up though she wasn't at all. And until now Nada couldn't figure her out. Nada looked up from hugging Madison into the face of the very tall black gentleman in full dress uniform. And her thoughts were handsome looking and quite the officer. There was brass all over his chest. His name badge read Lieutenant Green. But his face said "Junebug" a familiar friend from her childhood. He looked at Nada he knew exactly who she was though his look was wishing she didn't remember. The silence was broken with introductions. "Nada Francois this is my husband Charlie Green, Madison said very proud of her husband and his accomplishments. "Honey this is my dear friend and fellow professor Nada Francois". Madison was smiling as the two shook hands. I'd like you all to meet William Parker" my date for the evening. Nada said looking directly at the couple.

"Please to me you" Billy replied and again handshakes were exchanged. "Honey Nada is from New Orleans where you were born." His answer though true set the tone for the rest of the conversation. "Sweetheart, New Orleans is a large place with lots of people" he replied in his very proper all business sounding voice. "Am I right? He said looking at Nada. "You're absolutely right! Nada realized that "Junebug" that's what the bayou crowd affectionately called him wanted to put his past behind him. He was from a large family with lots of children Nada recalled. He was one of the younger ones very close to her in age if memory served her correctly. They attended school together. His dad worked very hard to earn a living but with all the mouths that had to be feed and the upkeep of daily living he fell on hard times most months. He would come by the restaurant and her mother would always have their restaurant staff leave what she called leftovers from her day's preparations. Often times she would even cook more than was needed which always included whatever dessert that was on the today's menu. Mr. Green would leave with several grocery bags of food to feed his family daily. He was a very proud man.

Charlie looked at Nada it had been years since he graduated high school and joined the Armed forces to make a better life for himself. He was handsome she thought as he stood so tall and straight in his

Army uniform and spit shined shoes. "My parents past quite a while ago" he confessed. So, if it had not been for Hurricane Katrina I don't know if I would have returned. "Now that made a lot of us stop and take a look at life" Billy replied now thinking of the world tragedies that has happened. "Yes, daddy and I had nothing. He lost everything when the floods came" Nada added in. "It's funny how things work out" Charlie intervened "I was assigned a troop to go over and rescue some of the families that were caught in the flood waters. "I hadn't been in the trenches since being stationed in Iraq five years ago. It was certainly an eye opener! he added. My wife and I are still very involved in helping some of the families that are still struggling from that disaster" Lieutenant Green continued. Nada extended her hand to Charlie, "Lieutenant Green it is and honor and great privilege to have met you" she said shaking his hand and then her friend Madison's hand. The Greens walked away to find their table. Nada felt Junebug knew his past was safe with her and he could walk away secured with his future.

Billy and Nada had a blast at her faculty outing. From the ones who braved the karaoke on stage, to the laughing and the patterned movement of the electric slide ending the evening with a slow methodical style of an embraced slow dance to close out. It was a fun filled time for everyone. They stood for a short while in front of the Parker's home expressing what fun was had and bidding goodnight. Friday night had come to an end. Nada got into her car and drove home smiling.

CHAPTER 10

A Second Chance

"Come on Finley! Didn't you say Russell is meeting us at the church?" Doris expressed standing in the door in her large stylish hat covered in flowers. "I'm coming my lady, I'm coming" Finley returned tugging on his collar to adjust his jacket. "My! Aren't you dapper this morning! Doris voiced noticing Finley's new suit. "Oh, it's nothing! He replied walking lively using a sporty bounce movement out the door. Doris was pleased she had found a church home that she attended regularly. The past few Sunday's Finley had come along also. He had invited Russell to join them for this morning's service and Doris most assuredly did not want to be late on any account. Her treatments at the hospital thus far had kept her life normal as one could expect under those circumstances. With all of her projects coming together her life was starting to have purpose for her. Doris was pretty happy. Involving herself in many of the offered classes the church had and her business involvement she kept busy. "Finley you did remember to tell the staff we're having guest today?" she asked as they entered into the doors of the massive sanctuary on another glorious Sunday morning. "Yes, my lady no worries! He replied greeting ones coming in with them. As the crowds made there way through the doors to their seats Finley stood looking across the foyer in the now thinned out-group still waiting to enter. "Good morning! Russell Woods greeted him. He had gotten there early and was awaiting their arrival. Doris had already entered and secured her seat to begin praising the Lord.

"Hello mom" Sonjee called greeting her mother Beulah who answered the phone. "Sonjee it's good to hear from you are you all settled in?" "I am and so far, I like it". There are lots to do around campus" she shared with her bubbling sounding personally. "I'm coming home next weekend, did you remember?' "Yes dear, how could I forget that" your dad and I are both looking forward to spending some time with you" Beulah expressed knowing her health issues and age was a big factor. "Mom did you remember I have a birthday also next month?" Sonjee continue with questions. Beulah smiled she had sat remembering it all. She and Jon were headed to visit an old friend. She painfully with love and tears went through all of her younger daughters' photographs and made albums to carry along. "Yes, Sonjee I remember every birthday and every party you ever had" Beulah replied laughing thinking over the years. "Mother, remember when dad pretended to be a clown at my party?" she said laughing from her thoughts of childhood. "Oh yes! Beulah had almost forgotten about that one. It was Sonjee's fifth birthday and she wanted to go to the circus. They planned for the invent sending out invitations to all of her young friends. They were later told the performances were cancelled. Weather conditions in another state where the circus was previously had caused delays in the travel schedule. Sonjee couldn't understand. So, Dr. Reeves pulled out his red nose and oversized shoes that he used many years prior for his performances on the children's ward of the hospital. "He was a great clown! Sonjee recalled laughing at her thoughts. "He was", that he was! Beulah added.

Dana couldn't understand why she was getting theses flowers from Rusty. She read the card and tossed it in the trash under her desk. The flowers she'd give to one of the candy stripers passing by she thought as she directed her next patient into her office for her session. "Please sit down and share with me the concern that's on the top of your list" sitting in her comfy chair with legs crossed holding a pad and pencil in her hand awaiting her client's response. "Where should I start? The client thought out loud. Dana sat silent and allowed her patient to gather her thoughts. "He made me feel special" he was open and honest. And I felt we connected on every level". Dana looked at her client as she spoke her story. It sounded so much like hers regarding Rusty the man you had left the state with his wife after she had fell for him. "I guess what I really want to know is why he chose her over me! I knew he loved me! She continued standing up to gaze out of the large window in Dana's office. "See that couple sitting on that bench" she said pointing and looking back at Dana for her to come over to the window. Dana got up and went and stood next to her looking at a couple that was having a picnic lunch she guessed. "That was us. We spent that kind of time together for two years". His job had relocated him here and we met. I never asked if he was married so he never lied" Just when I knew he was going to ask me to marry him she showed up and spoiled everything! 'I had planned a life with him! We were an exclusive with all my friends." Dana realized all those same questions her client wanted to know were her questions too regarding her past relationships. It seemed this year was a closure year for her and maybe that's why she had received the flowers and the phone messages from Rusty. Finding out about her mother and father was the start of her healing. She felt she could surely take talking to Rusty. Her client returned to her seat and finished her hourly session in tears remembering being jilted by her lover.

Dana looked at her daily appointment schedule. Her next appointment wasn't until one thirty and it was ten o'clock in the morning. Her first thought was to get caught up on paperwork. She had spoken with her sister Doris in Los Angeles keeping an open connection since their reconciliation. Dana decided since they had reconciled after her change of appearance she wanted to bond again with her older sister. Who by the way saw more of Dana's son these days than Dana had? He attended college at U.C.L.A. She looked over at the flowers, grabbed her purse from the desk drawer and headed out of the office for a couple of hours. Sharing her plans with the clerk at the front desk she was out the door. Within minutes she was in her car and headed out to Rusty's ranch. It had been close to five years since she drove to the ranch. David Michael was now in college. "What am I doing? She thought driving down the once familiar stretch of highway. He had left a message, but it still hurt, Dana remembered. "Why was he back? Was he back? She drove on questioning every mile of road. After a while she came upon the turn. The "for sale" sign had been removed from the roadside. Dana turned off the highway onto the small dusty road and drove slowly toward the ranch. She continued driving down the narrow road coming up on a wooden gate she could see in the distance. SHE PULLED UP CLOSER to the large wooden gate. The last time she saw the gate it was locked with a huge padlock bolt. Now it was swung wide open. Dana sat for a moment in her car wondering whether to go through the gate. She could see that life had returned again. There were small groups of cattle grazing in the distance. The drive out had used up thirty minutes and now she sat procrastinating on her next move. "No!" she thought out loud "this could be Pandora's box. "I should just leave this alone and close this chapter of my life" she continued thinking. "And that's exactly what I'm going to do! She turned on her ignition starting her engine, put her car in drive and proceeded to make a u turn when up galloped a lone cowboy. "Howdy miss! He replied looking down from the saddle he sat upon. Startled Dana stopped abruptly not finishing a complete turn around. "Hello", was Dana's returned greeting after a sigh from being startled. She didn't recognize the cowboy at all. Though she knew it wasn't Rusty he was much younger. "May I help you Dana? He asked which sent shock waves through her as she sat in her car with the engine still running. "Excuse me! Do I know you? Dana miffed immediately questioning the strange cowboy. "You most certainly do," he said with his strong twang and southern accent. Dana turned off her engine and got out of her car and stood beside the door. The cowboy got down from his tall saddle still wearing a big wide smile. Dana looked and looked soon she formed a smile. Through his handsome physic and a cute little curl in the middle of his forehead when he removed his hat, she saw Corky! Oh, my forgive me! she said coming over to give him a big hug. I didn't recognize you. You're all grown up! Corky was only three years younger than Dana but to her he was Rusty's little boy. "Yes, ma'am I have" he replied rubbing his horse's mane to keep him settled down. "Well are you coming up to the house? He asked. Dana hesitated with her answer. It was certainly good seeing Corky but she didn't know about Rusty. "So, did Donna come with you all? She asked continuing conversation before making up her mind to go further. "No, I convinced the old man to come back here". He loved it here and that placed was depressing him" he confessed. "Oh, did something happen to Donna?" Dana knew his love for his wife could conquer anything. "Donna, Donna he repeated with a smile. Oh no, she's fine" he said being sarcastic. "Oh, what do you mean? Dana was now curious wanting to know why Donna had not come back with him to the ranch. "Well honestly, she traded him in for her physical therapist" he said almost smiling himself. Oh no! how did he take that after all those years of devotion to her?" "Well needless to say he's been depressed" I got him to come back here after she called and told him that her physical therapist understood what she was going through better than he did. So, she released him of his commitment" he put his hand over his mouth to hide a laugh that was forming. "Personally, I think there was more to it butttt! Corky admitted. "He's probably up there gazing out the window if you have a mind to come up" Corky suggested. "Not this time but I'll be back" Dana said heading back getting into her car. "Well it was good seeing you' reaching over with his powerful hands and embracing her in his arms as he spoke. "You take care" he told her. Dana relaxed in the embrace of her younger friend. "Rusty sent me flowers! She shared as she stood in Corky's armed embrace. "No ma'am I did".

Doris was back home and awaiting her guest to arrive. "Finley did the guest room get fresh linens and towels" she asked making sure everything was in place for her overnight guest. "Yes, madam everything is in place for your guest and they are here! Finley replied walking toward the front door. He saw the limo pulling up which Doris had sent to the airport to pick them up. She smiled and hurried to the door to greet them. Moving very slow Beulah and Jon Reeves made their way through the front door. 'Hello! Doris greeted with a warm smile and embraced both of them. "Hello, they returned the greeting. "Well hello Finley" the Reeves voiced seeing him come in from the wide hall of the enormous home. "My Doris you have a lovely home" Beulah said standing admiring a huge wall mural on the wall. "Thank you for coming, please come this way" I have your room ready if you need to rest or just relax after that plane trip" Doris explained showing the Reeves to the guest room of her home. They walked down the spacious long hall turning a corner to reach the guest room Doris had prepared for them. "Dinner will be ready for you in an hour" she said walking out closing the door allowing the Reeves to unwind and Beulah to rest if she needed to. Finley had already brought in the luggage and placed it on the luggage rack in the room. Beulah Reeves had come to be one of the speakers at Doris Thrift store opening to help the poor and homeless. This adventure had come full circle for Doris and she believed God had given her this work to do.

Jon helped Beulah into a large comfy chair in their room putting her feet up on the ottoman. He knew she needed to rest before the big evening got started. He opened their suitcase putting some things in the dresser drawers and hanging the clothes from their garment bag into the closet. "Knock, knock". "Come in" Dr. Reeves said going over to open the door. It was Finley with a rolling cart tray. "Why thank you sir" he said to Finley standing outside of the door pushing the cart into the room. "Madam insisted" he said with a nod and smile walking away down the hall. Jon rolled the cart into the room and placed it near the armed chair where Beulah was sitting. Lifting the sterling lid, he saw two bowls of fruit, fruit juice, some small sandwiches, two china coffee cups and a silver coffee pot. "Well that was nice wasn't it dear"? Beulah stated 'I'd like to rest a bit before tonight." "So, I will eat this and take a nap if you don't mind". Beulah got up and refreshed herself in the beautifully decorated adjoining bathroom suite of Doris's guest room. Jon followed changing into something a bit more relaxing. Beulah prepared what she wanted from the tray and sat down to eat and then retire for and hour or so before they would head out tonight for the opening. Jon and she sat eating and talking about the plane ride from Oregon. Often, they mentioned the beauty of Doris' home and warm welcome and the hospitality they had been shown and given since they had been there. Doris was one of Beulah's success stories but the real reason she had made her way to be here with Doris against her doctor's orders was her younger daughter Sonjee.

Billy had met all weekend with his dad and the investors who were partnering on this housing project. "Dad I think negotiations went well; wouldn't you say" Billy asked walking out of a two-hour meeting with David. "Son, I'm somewhat concerned about Fratus, he seems to be dragging his feet on the final bidding of the project." "Yes, dad I sensed that to but he really is small potatoes. We can do this without his input." "I'd really like him in on it, he is a vital asset to the community we have targeted" David replied. We'll give him a week to think about it and I'm sure he will come around" if not we will proceed with Macoon in order to keep the project moving." "Wonderful son", what time does your flight leave? David asked knowing his son was heading back after the meeting. "Oh, in two hours but I'm heading to the airport now." David and his son drove along the highway to the airport discussing the meeting and his wanting to have someone to spend his life with. "I had breakfast with mom this morning so I'll get something to eat at the airport before my flight". Alright son then I'll see you next month" standing now in front of the airport's pickup area hugging his son goodbye. "Yes, dad that's the plan" Billy replied. "Oh, is Dana coming to the gala that's planned for next month also," David asked now assisting his son with his luggage out of the trunk of the car. "Dad I asked her several weeks ago". She said yes, so we'll see you then and give my love to mom" he stated shutting the car door and beckoning a bellhop for his luggage.

Billy got his luggage all checked in and went looking for a place to sit, eat, and relax before his flight leaves. He had almost walked from one end to the other before he found the elegant restaurant sitting near the escalator. He had an hour and a half before his flight so sitting up near the gate would surely not be relaxing. He found a table looking out on the runway and took out his laptop, looked at the menu and ordered quickly and waited opening up his laptop to a document. We don't know what he was looking at but it did remind him of a friend "Nada". He pulled out his cell phone and dialed her. "Hello, she answered. "Hello Nada, just thought I'd called to thank you for a wonderful outing this weekend. "Oh, it's you" she said smiling, you're very welcome". "But all thanks go to you, Carin is still asking questions about my handsome man" she teased continuing the built relationship they shared. "Well I was sitting here ordering something to eat waiting for my flight to leave," Billy said still waiting for his order to come to the table. "Funny, I'm just leaving the airport I had to see a staff member off to a conference" she confided. Billy could hear lots of noise and laughter in the background as they talked. "Are you still here? In the airport I mean? He expressed a little excited but hoping to have her to talk with while he waited for his flight. "Yes, I'm upstairs she just boarded her flight and I'm headed home when I leave here' Nada added. "I'm here" just downstairs near the escalators in that Italian restaurant "Pellini's". "Would you join me for a bit? My flight doesn't leave for an hour" he informed her. She had waited enough in airports to know how boring it gets by one's self. So, Nada agreed to meet with Billy in the airport restaurant. He watched anxiously for her looking as each one traveled down the large stairs of the escalators. He sat remembering how beautiful she was all dressed up Friday night and the fun they shared when he honed his way in to her faculty party. After a few minutes Nada was standing by his table. She was wearing blue jeans and her hair was in a ponytail. "Hi again old friend" she greeted with a big smile. Billy stood, he still only saw her beauty and embraced her with a welcome "hello" in return.

Everyone was gathered out front of the first thrift store to open in the Los Angeles owned by Doris Wright. They had the mayor of city and other city dignitaries at the ribbon cutting ceremonies held in the stores parking lot. The crowds watched as each spoke of helping the community to become a better place. Russell Woods spoke of how he was helped through the efforts of the mission and was now challenged to help by giving back. Beulah Reeves was unfortunately rolled up to the speaking area in a wheelchair. She had become ill since waiting for today's event. Mrs. Reeves wasn't feeling well but wanted to keep her promise to her friend Doris Wright. She shared that each one should use this opportunity to better themselves and improve on their lives. She spoke about the compassion that it takes to give of oneself as Doris Wright has done to help so many. She admonished all the employees who would be working in this store to realize the chance they have been given and move forward. Everyone applauded as she was wheeled back to the limousine. The ribbon was cut and balloons were released in the air. Doris, Russell and Finley stood at the door as each new employee entered the thrift store and rehabilitation center filled with bargains for the homeless and needy in the community.

Doris left instructions at the store with her new field director. Thanked all who had come for the opening as she hurried off to see how her guest were doing. When she arrived at her home Jon had started packing their suitcases and they awaited the limousine to take them to the airport. Doris knocked at the door. "Come in dear" Beulah said still sounding weak in body. Doris walked into the bedroom and sat next to the bed where Beulah was resting until the limousine came to transport them to the airport later in the evening. "Beulah how are you doing?" She asked very concern about her friend. "Oh, for my age I'm fine" Beulah answered trying to bring a smile to Doris's face. Jon had gone out for a walk on the grounds with Finley and Beulah, he left resting. "Dear please give me that book over there" she said pointing to a stack of albums she had Jon place on the floor. Doris picked up one from the top, Beulah nodded to affirm, and she brought it to her. "My doctor didn't want me to make this trip, but I wanted to give you these myself," she began. "May I have a drink of water please? She asked. Doris put ice in a crystal glass on the side table and poured some cool water from the pitcher sitting near it and handed the glass of water to Beulah. "Thank you! "Jon and I are not getting any younger. God saw fit to bless us with Sonjee in our latter years. We have two other children and grandchildren also. We most certainly have been blessed" finishing her cold drink of water. Beulah still held on to the book she had asked Doris to bring to her. Doris thought Beulah wanted her to carry on the work she was doing at the foundation W.A.S.H. so she continued to listen. Beulah caught Doris's hand. "I'm very proud of what you have become dear". "You have a heart for giving and compassion of love for helping that is so big". Beulah looked right into the face of Doris as she continued to speak. "You are deserving of this delayed blessing that was yours from the beginning. I was chosen by God to watch over it until which time you came back to claim it," she said with a smile. Things were making sense to Doris and then they were not making sense. She thought Beulah was talking through the medicine she had taken. "I understand Beulah" she said sympathizing with her patting the top of her hand. Beulah handed her the first book. She opened it to a picture of an infant child. "That's a pretty baby Beulah" Doris said looking at the picture. "Yes, she is" Beulah replied. Doris kept turning the pages in the book. The child in the photographs was getting older. "Are all these the same child? Doris asked. A beautiful little girl I see! Is she your daughter Beulah?' Doris paused for a moment "Beulah I often think of my child." Dana raised a beautiful son". "One of my biggest regrets in life is that I didn't keep my child" she said wiping a shed tear. "You know Doris, God always allows us another chance" Beulah stated. "I know that now. I often pray that I would see her and get a chance to know her. "Could God do that Beulah? She asked with a hopeless look on her face. Beulah sat up on the side of the bed with Doris's help. "Thank you dear" Then she pointed at the picture on the opened page. "She was my little girl? She said now starting to cry. But I've grown old now and I can barely care for myself" she said. "Don't cry Mrs.Reeves" I'm sure your little girl loves you even at your age" Oh I know she does! She gave Beulah a tissue to wipe her tears, embraced her, and went back looking at the photographs. She was asking questions and Beulah was explaining an event or time that pertained to it. When she got to the third album, she began to see this little girl for the first time. She dropped the album and ran out of the room. "My God! Beulah said what have I done? Then she began to pray. After what seemed like an eternity Doris was back with a very old black and white photo of a woman and her as small child maybe three standing holding her dress tail. She looked at Beulah with tears streaming from her face. "You kept her for me didn't you Beulah? You kept my little girl!

CHAPTER 11

True commitment

Sonjee bounced along to her chemistry class early in the morning. She was remembering a happy African tune from her three years stay there. She moved along swiftly as not to be late with her backpack over her shoulders. "Hey! Someone stepped out in front of her and startled her. She threw up her arms causing her backpack to fall on the ground. "Sorry, I didn't mean to frighten you home girl" he said in a playful tone. "Well you did! She said reaching down to pick up her backpack, a little embarrassed knowing he was Fonsworth. "Why did you do that? She miffed hitting him lightly on the shoulder. "I apologize." Can I walk you to your class? he asked now heading in the same direction. "Can't stop you" She said still moving fast but enjoying taunting with a friend, she guessed. She had only seen him around campus a few times since their first encounter at the Burger Shack. "What are you doing up at this hour? she asked, I thought I was the only one silly enough to register for classes this early. "Well now you know we have something in common" he said tugging on her dreads and causing a smile. They walked along bantering with one another and enjoying each other's conversation regarding their college curriculum. "Well this is it", Sonjee replied I have to go this way! She went bouncing off in the other direction. "Will I see you later? Fonsworth yelled a short distant from her. "Maybe, Sonjee responded loudly, maybe!

Nada left the airport after seeing Billy's flight leave. She walked out to her car and looked back over her shoulder feeling a little uneasy as she walked across the parking lot in the dusk of the evening getting into her car. After giving the parking lot attendant the ticket securing her car she drove out of the lot to the highway. She drove along thinking about her week ahead. Her plans were to send an email to Billy when she arrived home since they had exchanged email addresses vowing to keep in touch as friends. Nada looked in her rear-view mirror. She noticed the same car had been following her when she left the airport. She slowed down trying to get a look at the person behind the wheel but the car slowed down also. She looked at the sign on the freeway. Her direction was to merge to the right in the other direction. When she merged the black car followed. Oh, it's just a coincident" she thought taking out her cell phone to call her dad. "Hi dad, she said still keeping her eye on the car still following her down the highway. Hello sweetheart, he returned the greeting, "How was your day? She asked making small talk to ease her concern. She drove along talking with her dad and the car was still following her every move. When she turned the corner to her home the car turned right behind her. She pulled into her neighbor's driveway and the car kept going. Nada sat for a moment and gave a big sigh before backing up and pulling to her own driveway. She looked around again before going into her home for the evening.

"Alright son, Billy said hanging up from a weekly conversation with his son David Michael. "Annie did those briefs come in from Hamilton? He asked now focused on a file that had come to him on his computer. He sat down and began reading it when a visitor interrupted him. It was Dana, she didn't always come by but when she did, she always made her presence known. Looking up from behind his desk Billy said, "Dana I didn't expect you," getting up and giving her a friendly hug. "I was in the neighborhood and came by to say hello," Dana replied putting her tote on his office credenza and sitting with her legs crossed smiling. "It's good to see you're in a much better mood than a week or so ago? Billy stated. "I know, thanks for checking on me". Not a problem, hey are you still going to that big gala with me next month? He asked sitting back behind his desk. Before she could answer Annie returned with the briefs. "Here they are Billy" she said in a flirtatious way walking slowly into his office stopping short after seeing Dana sitting over by the credenza. "Hello! She said looking at the face of a woman you clearly despised her. She put the briefs on Billy's desk and walked out without hearing a returned greeting from Dana. "Dinner?" Dana asked. "Yes, there are some things I must share with you" Billy replied "Oh what kind of things William? "The kinds of things that involves a commitment," "Sounds serious" Dana teased getting her Truex tote from the credenza and standing in the door waiting for Billy to shut of the computer and put things away for the day. He had been thinking seriously about what he wanted in life. He wasn't getting any younger and he wanted someone to spend the rest of his life with him. He had feelings for Dana that could possibly change into real love. She was always butting into his relationships anyway, she wasn't going anywhere, and he was tired of playing games. Dana let's go! He said leaving out with goodnights to all as they entered the elevator. Annie sat at her desk pretending to read some documents until Keith Poulton another attorney in the firm came over to the desk. "Hello Annie," "hi Keith what can I help you with? She asked awaiting his instructions. "I'd like to take you out to dinner tonight" he stated. Keith wasn't a bad looking man by any means but as square as a box. And dressed, well let's just say he covered himself. Sharp mind, very intelligent, polite and cared about Annie and everyone in the office knew it but her. She was hoping for William Parker but so was every other woman that laid eyes on him. He was one of the town's most eligible bachelors. "Okay, she responded without hesitation. Annie stood and talked with Keith for a while until everyone else watching settle down from the shock of her answer and went back to whatever a firm does when its not preparing for court proceedings.

Doris had asked Beulah and Jon to stay until the following Sunday. She wanted to invite Sonjee for a visit and ask if they would be there also. Doris wanted to have a chance to meet her. After remembering Sonjee had a birthday this month and she knew her nephew David Michael's birthday was later this month also Doris wanted to do something for them hopefully together. But she wasn't ready to take on motherhood without Beulah being there. Getting things cleared with her doctor the Reeves agreed knowing even though it would be tough giving up their child, they hoped telling her that Doris was her mother would be the best thing for everyone. They didn't want her to be alone. Beulah with poor health and she and Jon were both in their late seventies. Their older children would certainly make sure she wasn't alone but now that Doris had entered the picture Beulah wanted, she and Sonjee to bond in a relationship. Doris thanked the Reeves for their sacrifice in keeping her child. She was grateful that they wanted Sonjee to know her and not exclude her from their lives. Doris did not want Sonjee's life interrupted to the point of confusion either. Sonjee had been told she was adopted by the Reeves when asked by her why did they wait so late to have her? But she was never told about her mother or father mainly because until recently the Reeves really didn't know where Doris was. Doris even shared with them about her sister Dana and some of what she went through in her home. She most certainly did not want to bring confusion to the Reeves or Sonjee she kept repeating. After a good night's sleep and praying she had a suggestion that would keep parenthood in tact and allow a bond between her and Sonjee. With the Reeves in agreement Sonjee arrived at Doris Wright's home in Los Angeles. Her parents the Reeves and Doris greeted her warmly also. And early Sunday morning stood before God, her home church, and with the Reeves blessing, became Sonjee's Godmother.

Billy drove along the highway to the restaurant with Dana following close in her Porsche. She had made reservations at the Fire Pit Restaurant in midtown. It was one of their favorite places to have dinner. He pulled in up front and a valet was waiting to park his Jag. Dana was close behind in her Porsche handing the valet her keys and walking into the doors with Billy. "Hello", came the greeting, "Welcome to the Fire Pit" Mr. Parker and Ms. Williams right this way" the mater de stated walking slowly in front of them. "Billy noticed as he walked to their table there was a live jazz band playing. 'Oh, that's why you asked me out, my favorite band is playing" "something like that she replied smiling waiting for Billy to push her chair under her as she sat down at the table. 'Thanks, gently kissing his lips. He took his seat and the waiter brought over the requested bottle of expensive wine. Billy had been thinking about commitment all day. He was getting close to his fortieth birthday and he was ready to settle down from the single scene and get married. It would surely make his mother happy. She has been waiting for him to begin building a life for himself with someone he loved. Tetra knew firsthand how lonely it can be being alone. As soon as the waiter came back with the wine Billy brought up the topic on his mind. "Dana I've been seriously thinking about marriage" he said while the waiter poured a sample of the wine for him to taste. He nodded for him to fill the glasses. The waiter poured two glasses of wine and moved away from the table. "Oh, so you're really wanting to make an honest woman out of me" she teased. "Dana I'm really serious about this. For the last three months on Sunday's I've been attending church again. I want to settle down Dana, and raise our son and who knows maybe another" he smiled holding her hand across the table. The waiter had brought the appetizer and they now sat enjoying the Portabella mushrooms sautéed to perfection and mouthwatering good! What do you mean church? Dana asked. "I would like to be a family and do things families do, like attend church" he stated. "But Billy you know I don't go to church; well I think once with Mrs. Bea to a holiday function with David Michael," she replied taking another bite of the delicious treat. "But there are so many other things in life I want to do with you, why are you talking about attending church" she miffed. "Dana I don't think there is anything else in life that we can't do or places we can't go" But I do want us to bond as a family" "Are you saying that we can't be a family without attending church," she asked now moving the saucer to the edge of the table allowing space for their main entrée's. Billy put his hand over the top of his wine glass. "I'm driving" he replied looking up at the waiter. Dana had him pour another. When the waiter moved away again Billy stated. Dana, I believe we need a solid foundation on which to build a marriage". Wouldn't you agree? Dana gave a pondering look. "Billy, I love you but we will have to make an adjustment when it comes to that," she voiced. "Dana you and I have known each other practically all of our lives" you know what I value." You're always around and you're not going to let me be with anyone else I've noticed," he said taking a bite of baked potato from his plate and trying to lighten a very tense moment. "For now, I'm asking you to consider it," it is very important to me! He said standing up and going over to kiss her. "Okay I'll think about it but no promises," Dana replied. "What's the big deal of attending church on a regular basis anyway? Dana continued. What does that have to do with marriage? Dana questioned still trying to make her point of not attending church. "Well for one thing there is a self-sacrifice required to make a marriage work," You know a give and take." Dana, I realize this may be hard for you to grasp right now but a true marriage commitment defies earthly logic!" Billy pointed out finishing up his meal. Dana sat back in her chair. So, are you telling me that marriage is about choices?" she asked still letting what Billy is saying sink in. "Yes, the choices you make in a marriage can increase the quality, durability and the longevity of your marriage" he added smiling feeling certain about his facts. "You sound so sure this will work for us." Dana it can't hurt," I happened to visit Mt. Nebo the church where mom and dad goes in Washington and they had this minister there doing a marriage seminar, he called himself "The Relationship Doctor" I was helped so much in my thinking process of relationships. I was fascinated by the style of teaching and his facts and his presentation keeps you on the edge of your seat." What he said made sense to me". I went up after it was over and had him autograph his book I had purchased, and I also asked how we could get him to Maine. "I gave the information to the church clerk here and he will be here in two months Dana!" he exclaimed very excited remembering how good it really was. "I really would like you to think about it" Billy suggested still driving the importance regarding attending church and having a good marriage and home. Dana gave a nod and I understand your point" and smiled to him sitting across the table waiting for a yes. "I said I would think about it! Now please may I have another glass of wine" and a dance if you don't mind".

CHAPTER 12

Again

Doris had just come out of the hospital after her weekly treatment. Finley sat reading a magazine in the waiting area as she walked toward him. "Well my lady, how are you feeling? He asked getting up from the seat. "Honestly Finley, I am quite tired today, and I have a meeting to conduct at four o' clock regarding the stores inventory." My lady can't Marple go in your place? Well I thought about that but I have him doing so many things right now I'd hate to spring this on him with such a short notice" she replied getting into her Bentley with Finley driving away. "Oh, my lady what about Russell, he knows that store in and out" He will probably be glad to go down town for you" Finley explained driving along awaiting Doris' answer. "Finley are you sure, I don't want to overwhelm him to soon. But I will admit he is doing a great job with the staff and the store". He has sat a great example for the other two stores we opened last month in the Los Angeles area, Doris replied wiping sweat from her brow. "I must do something" she explained taking out her cell phone to call him. Doris had purchased cell phones for her store managers so Russell had a cell phone also. "Ring! Ring! Hello came his voice across the line. "Hello Russell this is Doris". "Hello Mrs. Wright is everything all right? He asked knowing her schedule for this morning. "Yes, as well as they can be, though I'm very tired right now and I need you to do me a favor?" "Me, Mrs. Wright, are you sure? "Yes, Finley suggested you to me". He says hello, and he knows you can do this" Doris stated. She proceeded to tell Russell what she needed from him giving him the meeting time and location. "All the slides are on my desk and the blue folder has the information you will need to present." Again, Russell I do apologize for such short notice just do your best" and thanks" she said hanging up the cell phone heading home to get some rest.

Sonjee started most of her days with a phone call to her parents and swallowing down a breakfast drink and heading out the door. She hurried along meeting Fonsworth near the same place each time. "Want to get a burger today for lunch? He asked pulling on her dreads as they walked. Okay, but I'll meet you there. I'm in the middle of a big rehearsal in my performing arts class and I'd hate to have you waiting for me if I can't make it" she explained heading away but stopping to squeeze Fonsworth's hand before going to class. "Fonsworth man!" Someone yelled crossing the lawn to meet him. I know you didn't get up again to see that girl" he laughed. "What do you see in her? He laughed hitting him on the shoulder. Fonsworth was of the Dutch Descent and has a very strong Swahili dialect. His dad is a safari operator with money it stands to reason he usually gets what he wants. "She's my home girl" and I kinda like her" he said to his buddy. "You know what I think? his friend Chipper said now walking with him back to the dorm. You were not able to be with the dark-skinned African's there so that's why you chose her." He said laughing hard knowing Fonsworth's motives. "First of all, she's been to Africa she's not African she has dreads like an African woman and I think their neat! He said with his strong African accent from being born there. "But even that's not entirely true, my parents wouldn't let me go into the village with the young teen girls wearing hardly anything and I use to see the women in the village too. Most wore very little clothing." He explained knowing the culture. "I always heard they were different and their skin was tough like shoe leather" Fonsworth said causing his friend to laugh uncontrollable as they headed up the stairs to their dorms to wait for their class to start before heading back to the campus.

Russell hadn't presented before this level of a group in years. His career at Tri-ron had experienced him in much of corporate America. He struggled to prepare the documents he needed to present before Doris Wright's board of directors. Nervously he paced lining up his words before the mirror in her office. He looked at his suit clean but very much out dated from today's style. "Oh well I'll have to live with that! He thought adjusting his collar over his shirt. The meeting place and time for him to be there was in two hours. He had about five hours to prepare since Doris's call at nine o clock this morning. "Whew! he sighed hope she feels better soon, releasing some of the butterflies from his stomach. He paced around the office going over his notes he had prepared. "One more time through working this slide overhead projector" okay I think I got it! He put his cell phone clip on his side and reached for his briefcase Doris had given him his first day on the job. "Knock, knock, come in Russell voiced hearing the sound as he paced around Doris's spacious office. The employee walked in with a garment bag. "A gentleman named Finley left this for you" he explained handing the bag to Russell. "Is he still here? He asked rushing to the door to see. "Oh no! he left about an hour ago. I did share with him you were here though" he said going out the door. Russell smiled knowing his newfound brother in Christ "Finley". He zipped opened the black leather garment bag to find everything including shoes and cuff links to look just like a Wall Street executive.

"Thank God! He found came from his lips. "He had never even realized what that meant until now. He had started attending church with Finley who had shown so much compassion for the homeless at the mission. He was only going with Doris Wright his lady to whom he was a butler, who had spoken with Detective Masony who had helped her find her sister, who was shared the word by David Parker as he helped him to close a case concerning his son. David heard the word from an evangelist who shared about another chance that was so loved and forgiven by his wife Tetra Parker. "It works! Russell Woods said loudly leaving for the meeting "it really works!

> Sonjee hurried back to her dorm after having a hamburger with Fonsworth. She was feeling her way around his friendship though wasn't committing to it. Her roommate was rarely there so Sonjee spent a lot of time alone in her dorm room. Her roommate confessed she spent most of her time with her boyfriend who was older and had an apartment off campus. So,

she and Sonjee were saying hi and bye most of the time. Sonjee sat waiting for time to past until her next class when her cell phone rang. She didn't have a clue it was her father at this hour of the day. "Sonjee dear the voice came across the line. "Daddy, hi daddy?" I usually wouldn't answer my phone now" I was sitting home studying for an exam this week for my chemistry class but I'm glad I did" she said explaining her point. "How are you doing since our conversation this morning?" "I'm fine dear, it's your mother! He said very somberly to his daughter over the phone. "How is she daddy, do I need to drive home? She asked knowing of her mother's illness. "I think it's best dear that you do" he replied. "Daddy can I speak with her to let her know I'm on my way" Sonjee asked with sadness from thoughts. "She's resting now but I'll let her know you are on your way" he replied in a fatherly tone. "Sonjee please drive carefully I'll see you soon". Mr. Reeves hung up his phone after asking his daughter to come home from college. He wanted her close to him when he shares that her mother had passed away after their conversation this morning.

Russell rushed out of the office heading to the meeting downtown. He left instructions with his assistant at the store and jumped into his clunker of a car and drove hurriedly down the highway. He wanted to get there early. He surely couldn't drive up anywhere near that Sheraton conference room in his jalopy that wasn't guaranteed to get him from point A to point B. But it was what he had so he made provisions by parking about three blocks away securing the club on the steering wheel and walking to the meeting. He sat out in the lobby still going over the materials he was going to present. As the group gathered in the reserved meeting place Russell shook off the final jitters. He walked in and found his place at the table. After two other executives had presented their overheads Russell was called to present. He started off slowly but accurately getting his footing before the group. He found himself getting comfortable and right back into what he had be doing in prior years before the debunk of the company he worked for. After his presentation that went very well according to all the calls Doris had received regarding her new executive she had hired. He was just relieved it was over.

What a sad day when the line of limousines and automobiles to the grave sight were endless. Beulah Mae Reeves left a legacy of helping that would go forward from generation to generation. Sonjee sat in the back of the Hearse styled limousine resting her head on Doris Wright's shoulder. It had become too much for her standing by the grave site viewing the close casket. She was waiting for her dad and her older siblings who were greeting many of their guests who had come to share in their sorrow.

CHAPTER 13

Oh no!

Dana sat in her office behind close doors with her client. When the session was over, she walked into her waiting room to find a beautiful bouquet of flowers. Reading the card, it read Rusty. She smiled knowing they were probably from his son Corky again but this time she decided to call. "Howdy" came the voice. Dana hesitated with her response knowing the voice was Rusty's. "Howdy" the voice rang out again before silence came. The voice who she was sure was Rusty had hung up the line. She stood reasoning a minute before dialing again. "How-dy," the voice stated. "Hello this is Dana" she responded awaiting the next line from the voice. "This is Rusty, how are you dear? he asked in a mellow sounding country twang. "I'm fine and it's good to hear you voice. "How are things? She asked after hearing about Donna. "Well truth be told I should have never left Maine." But you live and hopefully learn" he responded sounding a bit livelier since the conversation started. "Did you get the flowers I sent you?" I did they are lovely; my favorite thank you very much". "Dana, you know I can't change what happened and I hope you don't hate me" really I was just trying to be true to my marriage," he admitted explaining his reason for leaving her. "Hey, I wasn't blindsided I knew going in you were committed" things happen" she confessed. "Those flowers were just to apologize and hope I didn't cause damage to you ever trusting men again," Rusty added. "The flowers are lovely and you take care I must go now". Goodbye Dana, Rusty stated and hung up the phone. "Sweet guy, really sweet guy" she said feeling sorrow for his misfortune but allowing her client to walk into her office and close the door.

Billy sat down at his computer reading his emails. There was and email from Nada stating how she enjoyed the airport visit again and her conference she had attended recently. Months had passed quickly and Billy and Dana's relationship seemed to be growing. He was totally committed to Dana and his friendship with Nada was intact and growing as well. "This is dated today from her work address so I can assume everything was fine" he read quickly emailing Nada back and kept reading. Oh, that's right! This Thursday the Relationship Doctor will be at our church. It's in two days so I'd better inform Dana to put it on her calendar. He didn't want to push to hard she had come with him last Sunday and had to admit it wasn't bad. He also made a note to remind her at dinner tonight and emailed Dana just in case something comes up. He was just about through his emails for today when in a bright flashing email came BOWLING TOURNEMENT FINALS. "Hey guys he said getting up heading from his office to the main lobby. Our firm is in the finals against Mcnairs attorney at Law on Wiltshire. The office was a buzz! hey! Way to go slapping high fives, laughing and sharing stories leading up to this moment. "Annie, are we going to partner again this session? He asked with assurance. Every year for the past five years it's been him and Annie. No! she yelled from her desk as they all stood around talking "What are you kidding me? What color shirts are we wearing guys so that Annie can get them ordered?" We've got to win this" Billy said going back into his office. Annie walked in behind him. "Good morning Annie, you're telling jokes early in the morning" not be my partner! he said coming over laughing to hug her and greet her warmly. "No Billy I can't be your partner" I want more from you and it's obvious to me you've moved on with Dana". I wish you well! Keith and I are going to partner together this year," she stated walking out of the office going back to her desk. Billy stood up to go after her but he knew she was right. He could not with a clear conscious keep stringing her alone. He'd partner with Corbin in the mailroom he concluded sitting down at his desk.

Sonjee had arrived back to college after bereavement for her mother and two months on Campus had past quickly. Her dad told her it would be best for her if she got back to doing things again. She sat around the house for weeks sad and crying most of the time. "Hi dad she said making her morning call. "Hello dear, how are things? Okay still trying to catch up in my courses though I'm making progress" she said assuring him she was starting to recovery through the pain. "How are you doing daddy? Sonjee asked concerned. "I'm going on, I know Beulah would want it that way for both of us," he said lovingly. "I'll be home again this weekend," she said reminding him. She had been home every weekend since her mother past to be with her dad. "Sonjee, Wilbur and I are going fishing this weekend". "All weekend daddy?" "We're going up to Big Bear Lake with his son". "I just got off the phone with him and was getting ready to call you." "Daddy are you sure you won't be alone?" Sonjee I'm fine. "I have my friends at the hospital who I visit from time to time. My Nazareth men's group at the church, Wilbur everyday you know that". Alone, sometimes I wish I was" he chuckled. "So, you find something to do with the younger folks" he said wanting her to start being around people her own age. Sonjee had cut everybody off and spent weekends moping around and feeling sad. She was so full of life and since her mother's passing, she felt like she had to take care for her dad. He missed his wife dearly. But she was not suffering anymore and that brought him peace. "Love you sweetheart, I'll call you from the lake. He said hanging up the line. Sonjee took out a book to study when her cell phone rang. "Hello daddy did you change your mind? She asked quickly answering the phone. "Hello" the voice said whom she recognized to be Fonsworth. "How did you get my number? She asked sassily. "Tina gave it to me I shared with her I had not seen you in a while and wondered why? "I'm sorry about your mother," he said surprising Sonjee that he even cared. "You can always change the number if you don't want me to call it anymore". "That's true! she replied but thanks for calling", Before Sonjee could disconnect the line he asked "There's a band playing in the quad tonight want to go over with me? He asked. "With just you?" she asked. Where are the guys you hang with? She questioned. "Oh, I'm sure they will be there or somewhere else but I'm asking you?" Sure, why not I'll get Tina and the others' to join me and we'll meet you there" she said not feeling where he was trying to go. "Sounds good see you then" Fonsworth added disconnecting the line.

Finley had just checked in on Doris. She had come home early from the office again at 10: 0' clock in the morning because she wasn't feeling well and went straight to bed. He slowly opened the door as not to wake her. Oh! my lady! he said loudly running over to her lying on the floor. "Finley please call an ambulance" she said under her weak voice. Finley picked her up and laid her on the bed and then dialed 911. He paced nervously from the front door to her room until it arrived. The paramedics quickly put Doris into the ambulance and drove away with Finley close behind in the family's Bentley. Moving quickly through the cities traffic with the sirens blasting the ambulance soon came upon the huge Medical facility downtown. Finley quickly parked the Bentley in a secured space and ran inside to wait. He sat about and hour before her doctor came out with news. "We got her stable now". Finley got up smiling and shook her doctors' hand. "She really needs to have her kidney replaced. We are actively looking for a donor right now" he shared with her friend Finley. "Another episode like that could prove fatal" he explained standing outside of her door. "Does she have family her in the states? Her doctor asked Finley. "Yes, she has a sister and a daughter too" he said hesitantly. That was information he was to keep to himself regarding her daughter. But Finley knew Doris's life was at stake here so he didn't think twice. "We will need to speak with them, if we are not able to locate a match donor in our database" he informed Finley who was anxiously waiting to see his lady. "Russell had now arrived after making sure things at the store were secure. "How's she doing? he asked walking up to see Finley and her doctor discussing her illness.

The doctor looked at Finley making sure he could speak freely in front of Russell. "Well the disease Doris has is called Pyelonehritis though common long term it could destroy the kidneys and prove deadly" he informed letting them know the seriousness of this disease. Both were anxious to schedule an appointment to be tested for a donor. They assuredly want to help Doris. "Thank you doctor they both said shaking his hand and going in to see Doris who until recently didn't realize how long she had been there. It was now around 8:30 in the evening.

Sonjee and Fonsworth met with the others in the quad. The band was very entertaining and there were many couples dancing around the floor in the night's air. "Would you like to dance? Fonsworth asked Sonjee who at this point was standing alone near the music's speaker. Her friend Tina had secured a dance partner and was on the floor moving to a line dance. "Sure" she said she loved dancing. She hadn't danced since she returned from her mother's funeral and jumped at the chance to enjoy it again. Fonswroth she thought was lovingly adventurous to ask her since he was just learning the electric slide himself. And she thought herself to be vivacious, enthusiastic and full of live and needed to have some fun now. She couldn't mope forever. "Mother wouldn't want that" she reasoned walking out into the crowd already on the dance floor. Fonsworth caught her hand, as they began to dance he saw the twinkle in her eyes and of course he liked the dreads in her hairstyle swinging on her shoulders as she turned in another direction mimicking everyone's movements. "What drew you to me? she asked stepping backward to the beat. "I told you that you remind me of home, Africa" he said getting into the dance with a rhythmic motion. She moved around swirling her hips in front of him to the music with others in line doing the same. She laughed, he laughed, as they conversed on the floor and danced over and over again. This dance was very popular with the college crowd. "Tina are you having fun, she yelled across the quad a few feet away". Yes, Tim's a great dancer! she said swirling around on the floor. The crowds danced and danced for hours to none stop music far into the night. After a very slow tune to close out the night Sonjee looked at her watch. Chipper and Fonsworth had moved over and were dancing with some other girls whom they knew from some of their courses she guessed. "Tina had left with Tim about thirty minutes early and Angie was still moving gleefully to the beat. Sonjee made her way through the now thinned crowd still left. "Ang! She said speaking above the music. "It is 1:30 I'm headed in. "It's been fun but if you're riding with me, you'd better come now! She stated moving toward the exit area of the partying place on campus. She looked back to see Angie kissing her friend and she soon joined her at the car. They got into her car and off they went to the dorm. Where is Tina? She left with Tim, Sonjee replied. "Girl that was a blast! I needed that" she said letting Angie off as near as possible to her dorm door. "I'll sit and watch until you get in. Just flick the lights so I'll know you're in safe" Sonjee said watching her run quickly through the night to the main dorm of Carver Hall. "See ya, tomorrow Sonjee! Angie yelled from an open window while waving her hand goodnight. GOODNIGHT! Sonjee yelled back and drove off not far to Beamer Hall. She parked her car and looked around the area before opening her door. Getting out she was startled by and owl in a nearby tree. She quickly locked her car doors and ran up to the main door of the hall. OH! She screamed as she bumped someone in the dark stairway. "Shhh he said it's me Fonsworth. "Fonsworth! You scared me don't you ever do that again she said hitting him on his chest. Shhh! He repeated the lights in the dorm's hall came on and then went off again. They stood for a moment in silence. "What are you doing here? She asked after getting over being frightened to death. "I came to see you". "Me! "You left before I could say goodnight and tell you I had a wonderful time tonight' he whispered now holding her hand. "You're right it was fun' she said softening her tone. "I'll see you tomorrow it's late," she whispered not wanting to wake up anyone sleeping. "I'd like to talk with you is there some where we can talk? He asked running his hand down her bare arm". Her first instinct was to say no and walk away. "Don't look so sad there's always tomorrow" she said touching his forehead affectionately with her index finger giving it a slight push. "Can we talk in your dorm room?" "I have a roommate you know? She said trying to discourage that thought. "She's still at the quad with Robert. "I won't keep you up long I promise" he said putting his hands together in front of his lips in a praying motion. Sonjee didn't mind talking she was wound up from the evening and she hadn't planned anything for tomorrow it was Saturday. "Wait here she said going a short distant from the main door." She went into her dorm room making sure her roommate was still out. She wasn't there most of time anyway. Sonjee went back to the door and beckoned Fonsworth in closing the door behind him. "Nice place you have" he said looking around the room. "Our dorms are crowded and girls smell so much nicer" he joked. "Would you like something to drink? We have soda and tea if you like" she said leaning over to get to the small refrigerator filled with goodies. "I have something" he said pulling a beer from his pocket. "No, don't you dare drink that in here! She exclaimed. "Fonsworth please leave! she insisted pointing to the door. "Okay I'm sorry I won't open it I promise! he said again with a grin on his face. "You'd better not or you will leave and that I promise you! turning to take a soda from the frig for herself. "Not a lot of choices! She admitted. Mind if I sit on your bed?" he said making her smile with his antics. "Sure, over there" Sonjee replied pointing to the other side of the room. He sat on the bed and motion for her to sit next to him. "Besides dance what's your favorite course this semester? He asked starting a conversation that interested the both of them. They talked and talked for a while about everything including Africa. She hadn't smiled or laughed in months, she thought as she looked at the clock on her wall and yawned. "Fonsworth this has been fun but I really must go to sleep it's four o'clock. "You're right but I really enjoy you and you make yourself scarce around campus" he paused. "And besides I have missed you! he explained rubbing her dreads of hair. "Is that what this is about? she teased making reference to her hair. "Not really" he replied and kissed her gently on the lips. Sonjee cleared her throat. "Now where did that come from". He had never approached her in a manner other than an acquaintance. But she did tease him on the dance floor and honestly, she was starting to like him. Okay so you're saying you didn't like it? He asked. Sonjee got up from the bed "I didn't say that did I" she replied in a sassy tone. "I did! he said bringing a surprise look to her face. What? Her expression read. "I kissed you but you didn't kiss me back? What kind of goodnight kiss was that? He returned waiting for her next move. Sonjee most certainly did not want this to go to far. The fact that he was in her dorm room was too far and she most surely had heard the warning more than once about having males in the dorm rooms. Fonsworth stood up in front of her looking into her face. He puckered his lips and they both laughed at his gesture. Then he held her in his arms and closed his eyes. She laughed at him again. "You're silly" she said. He stood with his arms around her and gazed into her eyes their emotions meet and soon their lips followed. When Sonjee woke up the next morning she had become a woman.

CHAPTER 14

The Relationship Doctor

With Doris out of the hospital and safe back in her own home Finley sat out to find a donor on his own. He decided to start a blood drive. He had several persons including Russell and many of their now church members who wanted to help. He scheduled blood donor trucks for all the missions in the areas throughout the city. They served several purposes. Volunteer doctors and nurses assisted those who needed medical attention when showing up to give blood. And other medical staff members were there to help find a blood match and a possible donor for Doris. Finley single handedly had set up the Doris Wright donor Transplant Campaign. "Mrs. Wright? Russell voiced slowly walking into her home. She was sitting in her family room at the desk going over her books. "Do come in Doris beckoned. "Thank you Mrs. Wright another store manager from her boutique said leaving." "I'll get those samples over to the designer and give you a call "she said making her way to the front door going out. "Come in have a seat, I'm sure Finley is off doing who knows what! she teased making her guest feel welcome. 'Did you find those papers I was asking about? She inquired. "Pull up a chair and let's go over the employee's schedules and payroll for this pay period and then we will look at the project you have purposed. Doris's doctor had her on bed rest until after her much-needed kidney transplant. So, she was having her manager's meet with her at her home. She couldn't stand being idol but she had to be careful and not over due it. She most certainly did not want an episode like a few weeks ago.

Sonjee sat remembering how she felt the next day after her visit from Fonsworth. She couldn't believe she had let that happen. She realized it was nothing like she read in those romance novels or even what her roommate had shared with her. It hurt and all she could think about was "I'll be glad when it's over!" is what she remembered thinking lying there that night. She was so ashamed. Her dad had called over the weekend, and she didn't want to talk, so she ignored the call and hoped he was having fun on his fishing trip. Finley had called to share about Doris's emergency and to let her know Doris was now at home but she wasn't answering that call either. The person she thought would call or even show up never did. She lay in bed all weekend and cried her eyes out. Now it was Monday and Angie and Tina had called her wanting to meet at the burger shack at noon. She slowly got up and headed again to the shower where she had spent a lot of time trying to wash away all that happened this weekend. She kicked over the opened beer can that had been left beside her bed. After walking over to the basin pouring the remainder of its contents out Sonjee tossed the can in the large trash bin outside. She looked at the clock and knew she'd better hurry or she would be late for her first course. She moved slowly around the dorm room wiping tears that continued to flow from her eyes. After what seem like an eternity she was dressed and ready to walk out of her dorm when her cell phone rang. He was her dad. "Hello she said greeting her caller. 'Why hello sweetheart it's good to hear your voice." "Oh, hi daddy how was your fishing trip? It was wonderful dear" he said with excitement in his voice "I caught a whopper of a fish for bragging rights over the guys" he stated laughing with pleasure. "That's great daddy" she said locking her door and heading out as not to be any later. "Baby doll what's wrong you sound sad this morning? He questioned not hearing her usual bubbly self over the phone. "I'm fine I was just thinking about mom. "I sure wish I had her to talk to" she said that wasn't quite true. But she could have used her mom who would probably understand better than her dad who she was not going to breathe a word to about what happened. "Sweetheart I understand I miss her too. Two months just isn't enough time to stop hurting for a loved one" he replied feeling hurt for his daughter. "Dad can I call you later? Sure dear, and call your Godmother too, goodbye" bye daddy. Sonjee couldn't bear to keep lying to her dad besides a few more steps and a turn around that corner was Fonsworth's usually place to meet her. She had been anticipating what she would say to him or even what he would say to her. She took a deep breath and turned the corner. She looked around. Fonsworth was nowhere in sight. It was the first time in three semesters he wasn't standing there greeting her to a new morning. She didn't know what that meant or how to feel. She walked quietly to her class meeting other students as she walked into the door. 'Morning, Sonj!

Billy finished some briefs he had been working on and was meeting Dana at the church where the seminar was being held. He was excited he had read the book and was now looking forward to sitting through the session with Dana. He had called her earlier that day to remind her about tonight and she said she would be there. He waved goodnight as everyone left the building's law office headed in all directions. "Good evening Annie" he said seeing she and Keith walking out together to her car. She waved and smiled but kept going not stopping to converse. In his car he got on the highway and headed toward the church. Dialing from his car phone he rang Dana's cell phone, ring, ring, ring, ring! No answer soon her voicemail came on. He left a message and hung up. Soon his phone rang. "Hello sweetheart! He said glad she had called back. "Hello! The voice surprised him on the other end. "Oh, dad sorry I was expecting Dana but, how are you?" he replied with the proper greeting. "Great son, headed to the golf course. Just called to say we closed that deal! Anderson and I are going out for a relaxing game of golf. Though you know Anderson we will probably end up talking logistics" he laughed. "Hey that's wonderful, I know how long you worked on that one! CONGRATULATIONS! "Hey son, so let me get off the phone so you can get Dana, I'll see you all soon," "Sure dad give my love to mom! I will son, bye". Billy drove all the way to church and Dana still had not called. He turned into the parking lot of the church and parked in front as to see her coming in. He looked at his watch as he waited for her to come and meet him there at seven o clock. Time to start was getting close and still Dana had not shown up or called. He had left several messages on her voicemail and answering machine. He was feeling very disappointed, and a bit worried that she had not joined him as he sat and watched lots of couples going in. There were some single guys and ladies he could see going in also. Tried of waiting in his car he decided to go inside and wait in the corridor that housed a coffee shop for its members. "She's probably running late I'll go inside he reasoned and wait besides its 7.00pm and it is about to start. He sat for a cup of coffee and Dana he felt at this point was not coming. He walked into the now crowded sanctuary and sat near the back still hoping and watching for Dana. He checked his cell phone which he had put on vibrate as not to disrupt the crowd, no messages. A director from the marriage ministry was now up front introducing the facilitator known as the Relationship Doctor. Everyone stood and applauded. Billy sat down and got up again after the applause and was about to leave when he heard him say. "If you are married and want to know the person you have chosen, you're in the right place. If your special someone is on the way, you're in the right place. If you have jumped the broom once and at some point, you have jumped back over again, you're in the right place." The crowd was at the end of their seat with just his opening dialog. They were whispering softly as he delivered a fresh insight to their relationships. Married, single, divorced, widowed or just looking WELCOME YOU'RE IN THE RIGHT PLACE! Now intrigued by just the opening monologue Billy sat back down alone and listened to everything the Relationship doctor had to say again.

CHAPTER 15

This can't be happening

It had been weeks and Sonjee still had not seen Fonsworth. She had spotted Chipper is friend in some of the familiar places but he would only laugh and squeeze his nose as a tease she guessed. Then one evening when she was leaving for Los Angeles to see Doris her Godmother, she dialed his cell phone number. Getting his voicemail, she hung up without leaving a message. Finley had met her at the airport and she sat looking out of the window as he drove to their home. "How is she really doing? Sonjee turned and asked Finley who was very quiet thus far on their ride in. "Oh, she's in good spirits after that scare weeks ago" he replied. She keeps herself busy around the house" doctor's orders you know! I heard they found a donor for her" Sonjee asked knowing of Finley's campaigning. "Yes, we did! he exclaimed. But the doctors aren't saying yet though they have scheduled my lady's surgery in a few weeks". That's great! Sonjee replied I would hate to lose her" she confessed sadly as Finley pulled the Bentley up the long driveway allowing the huge gate to close behind them. "Hello Sonjee, Doris greeted her with a hug coming in her home with Finley following behind with her luggage. "Hi, you look well" Sonjee replied heading into the formal living room to sit down with her to talk. Finley had headed up to the guest room with Sonjee's luggage after his lady's instructions of where it should go. "Sit dear; is there something I can get for you?" "I'm having Finley bring us something after you get settled in." Doris said. "No, I'm fine, Sonjee replied. "Sonjee you seemed bother by something is your dad all right? "Dad?" she laughed is wonderful. He keeps busy with his fishing buddies and he as gotten involved with the retired doctor's organization." He and I talk everyday. He's thinking about selling the house and moving to a retirement village he shared the last time we spoke." "That's great isn't it? Doris asked still trying to put a finger on Sonjee's mood. Yeah, I guess, that's good, I'm glad for him. I was worried that after mom's passing he would just wither you know, they were together so long". "That's right over 50 years! "Doris surmised. "I do understand dear," she said hugging her as she sat next to her on the beautiful sofa of her home. "How's school going for you? the year is half way over you know." "Yes, you're right though it's fine, it's okay" she said getting up walking around the spacious room looking at some photographs. "Who is this Godmother? she asked picking up a picture of David Michael. "That is David Michael" your cousin, my sister's son." Then Doris paused after she realized what she had said. "Your sister? Sonjee questioned looking at David Michael's photograph. Doris slowly got up from the sofa chair and walked over to a picture of Dana handing it to Sonjee. "She is gorgeous, she looks like a movie star" she concluded holding the beautiful photograph of Dana in her hand. "That she does! Doris said going back to sit down. She was still having difficulties with her kidneys and daily now she had to have the dialysis to keep her going. Where do they live was her next question? Well David Michael lives here" Doris replied. Here? Sonjee came back surprised she had never met him in all the visits since becoming Doris's God daughter. She continued looking around the huge place. "No, he goes to college at U.C.L.A. so he lives here as in Los Angeles. He comes by often to say hello. We have gotten very close since he moved here" she confessed. "Dana lives in Maine and we talk, I see her occasionally when she comes to visit her son." "I'm sure we will all meet soon maybe after my surgery in a few weeks" Doris added. "'Wow, here I am feeling lonely and I have all this new family" she admitted not knowing all of what Doris was thinking. "I would love to have her tiny little nose," she said sitting the photograph back in its proper place on the mantle. "That's what she hated about herself. Sonjee felt her nose was big and flat. She often shared her feelings with her friends. So perhaps that was what Chipper was making fun of she thought. Sonjee was a beautiful girl in so many other ways. Over in Africa she was often taken for one of the natives looking at her God given features until she spoke.

She kissed Doris and headed up to freshen up from her plane trip there. She had come down not only for another bonding visit with her Godmother but to speak with the doctor regarding her blood test. Doris sat thinking about the conversation she just had with Sonjee "Anything is possible in Hollywood" Doris whispered quietly under her voice. Anything!

Dana had left a message by the end of the seminar. Billy looked at the message driving home very pleased that he stayed there but disappointed Dana had not come. His first instinct was to return her call. He dialed the number and hung up before it rang. He drove home thinking about everything. She knew how much this meant to him yet she still had not made it. For weeks he had tried convincing her of the importance of a great marriage and a good relationship. He was tired of dating and going home alone. He wanted to get married and settled down with a wife. Perhaps she was telling him she wasn't ready for a commitment? As he parked the Jag in the first space of the five spaced garage area of his estate, he saw a light on. Getting out with his briefcase in hand he walked through the door leading into the house. Not long after he had gotten through the door Dana greeted him. "I'm sorry Billy I got tied up with a new client" will you ever forgive me?" she said putting her arms around him as they walked into his wide hall way. "How did you get here? Where's your car? It wasn't in the driveway or garage? He said moving away from her heading into the kitchen. The staff had left his meal in the oven as always but he wasn't feeling very hungry he had eaten appetizers and hors oeuvres at the church. "I had a cab bring me here" you mind? She asked cooing her questioned to him" He looked at her removing his jacket throwing it over his shoulder. "I going to change my clothes and get ready for bed it's late and I have to get to the office early in the morning" he stated to her. The two-day seminar had lasted about two hours on it's first night and due to conclude Friday after it began and right now it was close to ten o clock on a Thursday night. "Can I prepare your food from the oven?" she asked still trying to get into his graces. "No Dana they served food there also!" He said heading out of the kitchen. Dana knew he was upset right now. But by morning things will be different she concluded as she slowly walked into his bedroom suite wearing her soft silky Fredericks' lingerie touching the floor and a bottle of her favorite expensive wine from the family's cellar she had chilled.

"Hi Aunt Doris" David Michel said coming into her room. Frannie is down from Washington and I just came by to see how you are doing?" "That's nice sweetheart" Doris replied allowing him to lean over toward her chair giving her a big hug. Frannie hugged her too and they sat and talked with Doris in the bedroom suite for close to an hour. Sonjee had left to go and get the results of the test she had taken to help Doris her Godmother. She was nervous as she walked into Dr. Brewer's office. "Come in" he said standing up to shake her hand before sitting back down behind his big desk. She walked in and sat in one of the chairs placed strategically in front of it. "Well it's nice seeing you again" he smiled to make her feel at ease somewhat. "How have you been feeling lately? he asked which surprised her. "Just fine, she said looking a little puzzled. Something earlier had caused her upset stomach but how would he know that she thought to herself. "Good! He replied giving her some relief from his earlier question. I'm sure you have heard that we found a donor for your Godmother and that she is scheduled for surgery in three weeks". "Yes, Finley her butler shared that with me. She confirmed the surgery date so I'm very happy" she confessed. Then Dr. Brewer stood up "I was considering you for a donor Sonjee because you are a perfect match for Doris's needs." "Me! You mean I'm the one who will help my Godmother with a kidney! She was ecstatic trying to keep still in the chair without screaming. "Yes, dear you were our first choice however we had to keep looking. "Your Godmother needs this surgery right away". "I can be here! The college semester is ending in two weeks we can do the surgery over the summer and I won't miss any time and I still have lots of time to recover before it starts again" she pointed out to the doctor now back at his desk chair. "Yes, Sonjee that's what we thought until a slight problem came up with you and surgery." Me! She said again pointing to herself. I am as healthy as a horse! I'm a dancer! I'm very active and I take good care of myself with regular checkups" she said smiling at the doctor as she spoke. "When was your last checkup? he asked. "Every six months I go for my checkups" I learned to do that from being over in Africa" she added. I was scheduled to go in but I cancelled it to come here for my

Godmother." So, when I return, I will see my regular physician near the University, Sonjee stated. "But I would like the opportunity to help my Godmother" she said looking into Dr. Brewer's face. "Sonjee she can't wait that long" he told her. "But you said her surgery is scheduled for three weeks from today! That's right" Dr. Brewer repeated "three weeks! Dr. Brewer was still being oblique with his answers to Sonjee. She took out her calendar from her purse. When do you need me here? She asked "Sonjee we can't use you as a donor right now" Why? She questioned standing over his desk. "Because Miss Reeves your test results came back positive. So! She replied. You're pregnant dear, you're pregnant". Sonjee flopped back down in the chair. She couldn't believe what she had heard. NO! NO! This can't be happening to me! She screamed. "Please doctor do not tell anyone about this!" she asked with him leaving his office. "You take care of yourself" he said closing his office door allowing her time inside to sit a while.

Dana knew she had ground to make up. Her beautiful lingerie and expensive wine were not enough to win Billy over and he had turned his back on her and went to sleep. He had gotten up earlier and took her home vowing to see her later were their plans. Dana miffed around most of the morning still thinking about how he had ignored her. "That was childish! She thought as she put on her business suit and shoes. Dressed for work and now headed to her office at the hospital she got a call. "Good morning Dana came the voice on the other end. "Good morning, she returned the greeting. "I was wondering if you had time in your schedule to meet with me for about an hour?" The voiced asked. "Honestly my day is quite light because I have a meeting tonight at 6pm that I can not miss" she said speaking of part two of the marriage seminar. "Before Billy wouldn't even think twice about their wavering relationship, A bottle of wine and beautiful lingerie was all it took to make up. Now he's listening to some Relationship doctor and he wants commitment and longevity." She thought as she spoke to her caller on the phone. "I'm not sure if I want marriage but I don't want to lose him! She reasoned so I'd better show up tonight. "What did you have in mind? Was there a specific question I could answer? No charge" she teased the caller. "No Dana I just need to explain why I chose Donna over you." I knew I had strong feelings for you but I loved Donna and was determined to make our marriage work." Rusty shared. "Oh, Rusty thank you for that, I really needed to know you cared" she replied. When we were talking last night, I wasn't sure from the answers you were giving me." I know you have moved on and I understand that but if sometime we could just talk, I would really appreciate it" Rusty said. Dana looked at her watch. She was headed to her office to get some paperwork completed. Nothing was going to keep her from meeting Billy tonight. She merged over in another lane allowing her after a few miles up the highway to head toward Rusty's ranch. "I'll meet with him in his home for about an hour. Go back to the office do my paperwork and meet Billy at his office and ride to the church with him. "He will be happy! She thought driving along turning on the dusty rode to the ranch.

Sonjee wasn't up to doing any fun stuff this trip. She did meet her cousin David Michael and his friend Frannie as they were leaving when she arrived from her appointment. "Next time we'll do something fun you can take me sight seeing" she suggested and gave he and Frannie a hug as they left. Sonjee sat around the house the rest of the weekend playing board games and watching television with Doris and Finley. Sunday, they attended church service and she caught a flight back home immediately. As soon as she landed, she called again and left a message on Fonsworth's voicemail since he had not responded to the first one, she left after finding out about her condition. She unpacked her luggage changed clothes and called Tina and Angie her running buddies. She wasn't going to tell them yet she wanted to speak with Fonsworth first! "Hi! How was your trip? They asked walking up to meet her for practice. Sandra Motobia the dance instructor was calling a practice for a special production they were putting on before the semester break. "Glad you're back, bring your tights" we're headed to the gym to practice some moves for the play" Angie said. "I have my gym bag right here! Sonjee stated. "Can we go by the way of the burger hut? Sonjee asked now walking with her two friends toward the gym. As they got closer, she could see a crowd of students sitting at the tables. Not unusual most students hung out there between classes and at the lunch hour. As Sonjee got closer she could see Fonsworth sitting with his arms around a female. "Hello, she said, I haven't seen you in a while? She questioned standing near him and his friend. "Babe who is this?" The girl asked him. He got up from the bench and whispered something into his friend girl's ear. Angie and Tina were over at the window ordering food to take with them. "I thought you would get it when I didn't return your calls! He said standing directly in front of her. "Oh, so you're saying you got what you wanted and now you're done with me! Sonjee chided back. Chipper was now looking and laughing. "Fons you want a milkshake? His friend yelled from the window. Sure! he responded back to her. "Hey, what happened is what happened, no love lost! Why are you sweating me? You're not the first and you won't be the last" he replied and ignored her by making a joke with Chipper who sat across at the other table falling over in laughter. "Fonsworth I really hate what happened between us". I wish I would have continued to ignore your advances and I would be better off!" she voiced to him. Soon his friend was back in his arms. With Sonjee standing there he threw his hood on his head and walked off hugging and kissing on his blonde blue-eyed babe. Chipper looked at Sonjee and smiled as he and his group followed Fonsworth. "Leather man, real leather Chipper snickered. Sonjee, Angie and Tina headed toward the gym. Tina and Angie asked Sonjee nothing about Fonsworth. But they knew whatever was going on she was upset about it! Practice for Sonjee was futile her mind was on telling this guy who really didn't care about her she was pregnant with his baby.

Howdy Dana" Corky said seeing her driving up to park her car. He walked over and hugged her and walked with her to the door. Rusty was surprised Dana had shown up all ready or at all since she hadn't said she would come. Howdy! He said looking quite rested and happy despite of how he spoke yesterday in her office. "I'm glad you decided to come out" have a sit" showing her to his large sitting room. "Can I get you something to drink? I have your favorite", he stated looking for an answer before sitting. It was near noon and Dana liked wine with her lunch meal so she opted for a drink of her favorite expensive wine and lunch. She and Rusty sat down immediately at his dinning table and began eating talking for about and hour when Corky came in. "Rusty, they just brought the horse back. I've tied him in the stable." He reported. "Thanks, he replied. "Dana you remember Cork don't cha? He asked looking at the handsome cowboy he had become. "I do but he sure looks different! she teased reaching to shake his hand across the table. Corky was handsome and very stylish in his alligator boots and large cowboy hat and his big smile. Rusty stood up and put his napkin across his emptied plate. "Well I'd better see what I've got" he said. "Sugar is one of my favorites". "That's great timing Dana said, I have to go anyway but I enjoyed our conversation" she confessed giving him a warm hug as Corky looked on. He took his hat from the back of the chair where he had hung it. He tipped it slightly and walked out the door. Dana reached for her purse and headed for the door. "Good seeing you again" Corky said opening the screen door as she walked out. "Dana have you ever thought about line dancing? Corkey asked walking her to her car. "Line dancing? Not really. Is that what you do for entertainment? She asked inquisitively. Yes, Rusty and I use to spend hours at the OK Corral in old town." When you have some time let me know, I'd love to show ya how it's done," he said closing her door gently and allowing her to pull away with Rusty waving far in the distant from the stables.

Tetra had left the church heading to the grocery store three blocks down the street. She had a special surprise she was making for someone in her woman's group and needed a special spice of which Alfredo had shared with her she had run out of at home. She parked her car and got out entering through the automatic door of the small grocery store. She looked at the shopping carts secured one and headed down the isle. After finding and putting into her basket things she had not come to buy, but sense I'm here I'll just get. She headed to the counter to pay for her wares. Not long was she standing in line when she felt a tug on her dress tail. She turned to see a young child holding a loaf of bread. "Miss could you buy this for me? The child asked very politely. Tetra looked around for an adult that should be accompanying him she reasoned but there was no one insight. She didn't mind paying for the bread but she was concern for this child who was maybe five or six being out by himself. "Please miss please" he repeated standing at the end of the counter. The clerk shrugged his shoulders indicating he didn't know or had never seen this child in the store before. Not wanting to hold up the growing line behind her she quickly paid for her groceries and headed out to the car. The child walked quietly beside her cart. "Where do you live sweetheart? she asked leaning over gently in front of him. "Over there! Pointing to an apartment complex whose driveway joined the stores large lot on the side. "Okay, well you run along home now. Handing him the loaf of bread and a candy bar she had pick up near the counter. He took the bread and stood looking at Tetra for a minute. "Thanks ma'am! He said and ran hurrying toward his pointed direction. Tetra quickly put her groceries into her car and started out the lot when she saw a lady looking franticly all-around yelling for Joey! Tetra's heart stopped she knew without a doubt that was probably her child. She stopped her car and got out. The woman kept yelling franticly for her child. As she got closer to where Tetra was standing, she could see that she was crying. "Miss, have you seen a little boy? She asked. 'He's only five years old! He ran out of the house! She exclaimed very concerned. I was trying to prepare him something to eat in the kitchen but all he wanted was a peanut butter sandwich, and he left out the front door. Then she broke down and began crying again. Tetra was feeling bad. She should have taken the child home she thought. She was afraid to tell this mother what she had done, buying bread and sending him on his way. "I'll help you look for him he can't be to far" she said holding the crying woman's hand and leading her back to the complex. As she got closer, she let go of Tetra's hand and ran swiftly back to her apartment now seeing the door wide opened. Much to her surprise he was seating on the worn couch eating a peanut butter and jelly sandwich. The jelly he had spilled on the floor and coffee table. "Oh, thank you" she said "for calming me down. I would still be out searching had I not saw you." You're welcome dear" Tetra said turning to leave. "Thanks miss" the young child said smiling finishing his sandwich. The young mother looked at Tetra. "Have you met my son before? She asked surprised the child seemed to recognize her. "Dear I saw him at the store and he asked me to purchase the bread for him" Tetra replied. The mother looked concerned. "I can't pay you right now but I will" she explained. "Oh no, I'm just glad your child is alright! Tetra expressed heading out of the sparsely furnished though clean apartment. Then she stopped before leaving out of the door. "Dear do you have time to go to the store with me? she asked. "Ma'am, can I be honest, I really don't have much money right now" as soon as I can get someone to care for my child I'm going to work and make something of myself." I believe you dear" but I have an idea, lets talk about it at the store, maybe I can help". The young lady was hesitant but Tetra was persistent and she and Joey accompanied her back to the grocery store. He would not have to worry about bread or anything for a very long time. She was able to fill all the cabinets and refrigerator after getting all the bags from Tetra's SUV. While still there Tetra called James Captain the director from her cell phone. He ran the Parsons Center and she asked if he would find a job for her there and Joey would be cared for in childcare facilities ran but the church. "Mrs. Parker, I don't know how to thank you but Joey and I will see you Sunday" she shared with Tetra as she stood in the door leaving. "Oh, know dear the job starts Monday morning". "I know! She said looking at the paper Tetra had given her with the address, phone number, time and also the person to report to. "Joey and I will be at church when the doors open Sunday morning. That last dollar I had left hidden away to buy food stretched."

David and Tetra had just finished dinner and sat watching twenty, twenty in their great room after she had shared about the young lady she had met today at the store. Mrs. Parker the phone is for you one of the staff said bringing her the receiver. "Hello mom Billy said calling to share his plans for tonight. "Why hello dear, it's good to hear from you" she replied to her son. "Mom my flight leaves out later I'm here at the seminar now with Dana and we're looking for a great time" explaining that the Relationship doctor was ending the seminar tonight and he really learned a lot. "You know I'm glad to hear that" she laughed. 'I'll see you all in the morning" knowing she would be in bed when they arrive. "I love you and give our love to Dana" Tetra said hanging up the line.

Billy was standing in line waiting to walk into the sanctuary again for the end of the marriage seminar and Dana was by his side. She had come to his office and they rode in together. With the room full to capacity the Relationship doctor opened again with those familiar words "No matter how far you have come or what it took to be here you're in the right place! The applauses consumed the room for what seemed ten minutes before it stopped to allow him to begin speaking again. Dana and Billy sat through the first half hour, Billy was very intrigued by what the facilitator had to say. "Dana isn't he right on about me? He asked turning to Dana who was reading her email from her palm handset cell phone. "Dana what are you doing aren't you interested? He asked. She put the phone back into her purse and seemed to be paying attention to what was being conveyed. Billy was very focused on everything that was being said. Everyone in the large room seemed mesmerized at times by his definitions of manhood and womanhood pertaining to marriage. About how men are wired and how women are wired was very informational to Billy. There were laughter and familiar recognitions to situations many couples had encountered. "Remember when" Billy leaned over to Dana whispering quietly in her ear. She nodded and smiled at what the doctor was saying. It made sense to her but she still didn't think anyone could tell her about relationships. She spoke with people everyday. What could he say that was different she thought sitting beside Billy in the row of comfy chairs? "I'm here for the sake of argument tonight" she thought patting the top of his hand that rested on her crossed legs. The facilitator posed questions around the room.

EVERYONE got involved. Most shared information about their marriage or relationship that enhanced the seminar greatly. Dana's phone rang just before the break, "BILLY WAS SO EMBARARASSED quickly helping Dana to turn it off. "Alright we will take a quick break and stretch for a minute" the facilitator said hurrying out of the room toward the back. "Dana had gone out to the corridor and was returning the call she had abruptly disconnected. "Dana, do you have to bring work home with you tonight?" Billy asked teed and a bit upset. Another young couple their age came over to introduce themselves. "Nice to meet you" Billy said looking for Dana to acknowledge the couple. She ignored them and Billy and walked away still holding her conversation. "She's always so busy that's one reason we're here" he joked with the couple. "Tanner and my wife Lauren we've been married six months and I only wished we could have got this advice before marriage" he confessed. "We have complied so much information here tonight we just might get our vows right" they confided." The couple was still speaking with Billy when they made the announcement for everyone to reconvene. "Dana! he voiced very sharp seeing she was not getting the hint to get off the phone. "Look Billy! She stated very loudly "I have important matters to take care of! She then realized there were on lookers waiting to go in staring at them. "How much longer is this going to last? I'll meet you at home! Dana replied looking at her Rolex trimmed in diamonds on her wrist. Billy did not want to make a scene. He pulled Dana over to the now empty coffee shop that was in- housed in the large corridor. "Dana this is very important to me why can't you understand that" he reasoned. "You're acting childish! He voiced. Everyone had gone back into the sanctuary and the seminar was well underway. "Billy somehow this means more to you than me, but to say I'm childish when you are forcing me to be here! "Forcing you! I'm not forcing you to do anything! He replied sternly "I know you would ignore me if I didn't come tonight" she said wiping her alligator tears. "Is everything alright? Someone stuck their head out the door and asked. "We are fine" Billy voiced back allowing the usher to close the door free from concern. Dana, it's obvious that this does not mean to you what it means to me". "I love you Billy, and I don't think it takes a Relationship doctor to validate that! She said hugging him around the waist. "But let's go back in" she said knowing he wanted to. Billy went in and sat close to the back listening but his heart wasn't in it not with Dana anyway.

Sonjee knew she had made a terrible mistake with Fonsworth in not protecting herself. It happened so fast she thought as she reasoned her next move. Her dancing practices were taking a toll on her as she tried to keep up with her peers. Those early classes and most practices were very drooling and long. Sonjee was very determined to keep her pregnancy a secret for now. Feeling uncomfortable a lot lately she knew something had to be done. Dr. Brewer in Los Angeles had explained to her some options in which she told him she'd think about. A couple of times during practice she had to rush out to the ladies' room she said for general relief but often it was for an upset stomach in which she needed to throw up. Her thin frame to others was not noticeable but Sonjee could certainly feel some changes that were taking place with her body. "Bye! She yelled heading to her dorm after a long rigorous practice day waving at Angie and Tina as they continued on to their dorms. Tired she hurried and showered got dressed and headed to Planned Parenthood in midtown a few miles from campus. "Boy this car sure comes in handy she thought" She had gotten her car for her birthday and so far, it was worth it's weight in gold. Especially right now she wouldn't know her way by bus. She had got all her directions out and was headed to speak with a counselor or nurse there with whom she had made the appointment. Fonsworth had ignored her and failed to return any calls. He avoided her on campus she surmised for the last time. She was glad she hadn't told him the truth on the one encounter he had showed himself civil. "He could have owned up to it she thought a least acknowledged what happened, she thought driving along checking each mile of her odometer. What would I do with a baby? I saw to many young girls in Africa she thought" as she pulled the door opened going in. Sonjee sat waiting for a moment looking at a Parent's magazine. She wiped a tear that had somehow found its way down her cheek. She looked at a young girl probably her age sitting with a young guy across the room consoling her or so it seemed. "Sonjee Reeves" a person came out calling. Sonjee got up and made her way pass others sitting in the waiting room too. She was shown into a small office. After an hour of decision-making thinking things through again and one more time with "are you sure this is what you want to do? "Yes! She answered and left.

Billy drove home along the wide dark highway. He was quiet and Dana's advances were getting on his nerves. "Babe, want to stop by Raffe's the old crowd will probably be there? She suggested running her hand through the curls of his hair. "No Dana! He replied very stoic and continued down the highway. "Is this what I am to expect all weekend from you? she asked now upset because her charm wasn't working. "You shouldn't expect anything from me this weekend Dana! he returned. "She was furious now with his response. "You expect me to sit through a boring seminar on marriage with some man who puts his pants on just like you and then get on a plane and end up at a very boring business party of your father and his prehistoric friends! AND YOU'RE TELLING ME NOT TO EXPECT! She screamed sitting on the passenger seat of his car. Very calmly Billy spoke "I have had enough of you Dana" you want everything your way and if you think I'm going to continue to play games with you, you're wrong!" She was crying and screaming loudly when he turned off the highway on the road that leads to her house. Pulling up in her driveway he got out and walked to the trunk of his car and took out her luggage. The plans were to head directly to the airport after the seminar for Washington State to an Investors Ball his father was giving for the now closed real estate development deal. He went to his passenger side of his car and opened her door. She had sworn at him all the way driving along the highway. He sat quietly which caused her to be even madder because it showed her, he didn't care, she had confessed to him. When she finally realized he had brought her home and not to his house she became enraged and pound on his chest. He caught her arms and hugged her to calm her down. He walked her to the door. "Aren't you going to kiss me? She asked standing inside her doorway. He looked at her eyes still wet from crying. Her makeup and mascara had smeared across her face. Dana was still very beautiful even in her present state. But only on the outside he thought to himself looking back at her at this moment. He turned and held her in his arms for a long-time saying goodbye.

CHAPTER 16

Grant me the serenity to accept

The university was buzzing with students going in all directions. Sonjee's time was very limited. She only had a few days before her appointment with the clinic and Fonsworth had belittled her one time to many. "He's not going to win! She acknowledged to herself as she and Carolyn entered into their English lecture prepared for the big exam. Leaving heading for the administrative office Fonsworth confronted her. "Hey home girl, where are you going in such a hurry? He asked surprising her. "Excuse me? Are you speaking to me? She asked in a matter of fact tone. "Hey, I'm sorry I didn't return your calls. "What did you want from me anyway? "Nothing she replied "absolutely nothing! Sonjee stated walking away knowing she had a scheduled appointment with her class advisor of the university regarding her next years class curriculum. "Well I'm dating someone now and you're causing questions when you keep showing up in familiar places" he shared with her now civil in nature anyway. "Look it so happens we frequent a lot of the same places and our class courses are in the same direction or building and you're tripping about me following you! She said determined to not let him know he had broken her heart. "I thought you were mature enough to take it, I just knew you had done that many times before" he said looking at her. "But when I realized you were a virgin I got scared and wanted nothing to do with you." You are just a big tease! He added. "Oh, so what happened is my fault! She exclaimed pushing him in the chest. "You came to my dorm, you kissed me and things went too far and now you're blaming me! She started to cry from the sheer accusation that he was making it her fault. And she felt hurt because she knew better, honestly, she had never done that before and if that's what love was about, she'd pass she had reasoned within herself. Sonjee had a lot she could have said to him in that moment but what was done was done and she just wanted to forget him and move on. There was still one thing left to do. "Hey, don't cry I'm sorry" he said coming over to console her. She held her hand out to stop his advance. She never wanted him to touch her again. She wiped her eyes and walked away. Leaving Fonsworth wondering why all the fight had left her. And honestly, he missed it.

Doris lay in the hospital recovering from her recent surgery. "It went well! Every thing is healing fine" her doctor shared with her after his morning checkup visit to her room. Finley was coming by at noon and had call to asked if she would mind if Russell came also. "Dr. Brewer thank you so much I'm feeling much better this morning. Do you have an estimated time that I can go home? Doris asked smiling at him as he stood by her bedside. "Well Doris if your health keeps improving and your new kidney continues to accept its new home, you should be out of here next week," he teased to keep her smiling. "Dr. Brewer that's great news" "I'm ready to start moving again," she stated sitting up in bed picking up some folders she had been looking at earlier before his visit. "Now Doris when I release you from the hospital you must take it easy for a while". "I will doctor besides you've got Finley watching me! They both laughed. "You're right no worries there" he added still laughing "I will check on you later" heading out the door. "Oh yes, how's your daughter?" He asked. "My goddaughter is fine, if fact she called and said she will be here at the end of the semester," she acknowledged. "Why are you asking was everything all right with her testing? Doris inquired now concerned. "No, I was just wondering because she was such a close match to you, that's all". "Oh, Doris paused relieved. "She's fine my little girl is just fine". "Good! Dr. Brewer replied and walked out.

Sonjee was more determined than ever to get things right again. She left the administrative office heading to practice. Angie and Tina were waiting outside the door. "Sonjee, where have you been?" "Sandra is on a tear today, and we are all feeling it! They said speaking very fast as she dressed into her tights. "Sonjee! What is this? Tina asked coming over putting her hand on her stomach. "Girl I just had the best shrimp pasta and too much of it! "I hope I can dance," she said quickly putting her leotards on and running to meet the others. Truly in five weeks she had got a little pudgy stomach and tried hiding it wearing a different style of clothing but with leotards and tights it was getting hard to hide it. "Quickly! Quickly! Sandra announced clapping her hands to get everyone's attention "I need everyone to get in place we must get this right! We have less than a week before we perform for the student body and faculty. Then another before going to the convention center before thousands each night" she said with her native African tongue. They were performing one of the great Alvin Ailey's pieces and perfection is what she was striving for. With everyone about to drop on their feet the instructor ended the practice session. "KO-CHI-FO" she said leaving the room. They all knew that meant good-bye in her native tongue. Each dragged themselves to the showers.

Billy parked his car in the long-term parking at the airport and walked in to check his luggage. The lines were extremely long and security was very tight. "He walked to the counter and being a frequent flyer, he was rushed right through the long line of people still waiting before he walked up. Luggage checked; he made his way up the escalator walking toward the assigned gate of his flight. He sat down and opened his briefcase; he had used as carryon luggage. He removed a beautiful jewelry box he had purchased earlier as a gift for Dana. "I wonder if she would have appreciated it! He thought. She's just not getting this commitment thing, I guess? He closed the box back and put it securely in the velvet case and sat reading a Fortune magazine when his cell phone rang. "Hello" he answered. "Hello Billy". "Mom, I'm sitting at the airport right now waiting to board my flight is everything all right? He asked surprised she was calling. "Well that could be my question to you". I just spoke with Dana, she was apologizing for not being able to make the trip, work or something" she explained. Billy didn't reply he couldn't. What lie could he make up to cover Dana's lie! and besides his mother knew Dana very well. Dana had sat in her home writing in her journal as always. She knew she was right is what she told herself and he would be the one making the change if he wanted a yes from her concerning marriage.

I was broken so very long ago
By a door I feared would open creaking
Trying to find my inner child
And peace I was continually seeking
Anger and bitterness, I could not rid
Though I sought with intelligence to find
I reached for those I thought should help
Though some I found very unkind
As I grew older, I found someone to love
But the connection to him I couldn't reach
He gave up on me and sought someone else
And shared he'd found solace and peace
I fought him with this flesh I had perfected
I'm right I'm right I continue to tell myself
I won't let myself be taken in with his reasoning
Leave that bible and those help books on the shelf
Where will I go, I have often wondered?
Not ever giving in to what he says is right
As long as I live and intelligent as I am
This battle I will continue to fight!

Dana Demato-Williams

After her call to the Parker's home she left for a get away to teach William Parker a lesson on LOVE!

"Mom they're calling for boarders now, I'll see you soon" he shared disconnecting the line. Billy boarded and got comfortable for his flight to Washington. After the flight attendant had cleared them to remove seatbelts and walk around, he took out his cell phone. "Hello the voice came from the other end. "Hi old friend" he replied. "William, funny hearing from you I was thinking about you" Nada replied "Good thoughts I hope" he said with a smile in his voice. "Umm the girls and I were out shopping and your name came up a coupled of times" she said falling on her sofa enjoying the fact he had called again, "just a couple?" He teased to make her smile "Umm maybe a few more" she added. "So, are you in town or is this a call to check up on me? She asked with her fingers crossed hoping he was in town. She and Billy were emailing each other often and had built a relationship even though no kiss had been shared or intimacy had not been attempted. Their relationship was built strictly on friendship. She liked their accidental encounters thus far. "Actually, I am headed your way and need a favor," he asked hoping she would say yes. "You need a favor from me? She was spinning around her living room feeling anxious. She, Carin, and Madison were sitting in the faculty lounge talking about dating and she was hoping to see him since it had been two months since his last visit. Nada had relieved herself of the threat of her old boyfriend ever finding her again and was starting to enjoy her life at the university. "I do" he replied with just a few words. "If I say yes and I haven't yet because I don't know what your favor is" when? She asked now curious though glad knowing he wouldn't ask her to do something out of the ordinary. "Tomorrow night, say around 7 o clock" he replied to her. "Are you asking me out? "You could say that but actually I'd like you to accompany me to an Investors Ball at the Regency". "What! Are you kidding William? I know you're teasing right! She questioned over and over again. "No Nada I'm not kidding. I do apologize for calling you this late but if you say yes, I promise I will explain it to you later" he confessed. "Tomorrow" she smiled. Okay, but this explanation better be good, she teased hanging up and jumping around the room being silly. Billy had come to grips that after two years of seriously dating Dana she was not going to change from the girl he knew in high school. All of her successes she had achieved. College and her Practice, a world traveler and she was still the little girl he met oh so many years ago his kindergarten friend. She didn't want to commit and it seems she certainly did not want to be a part of anything Christian and that was causing a real strain on the relationship. He had tried to reconcile with her, having David Michael their son who had now gone off to college. He cared very much for her, wanted to marry her and built a home together but all he did to help the relationship was futile Dana wanted it her way!

Sonjee was up bright and early the next morning. She had made her call to her dad and found out he was going to a golf tournament on Friday and would not return home until Sunday afternoon. "Perfect! She thought no need to explain my visit continuing to place her clothes into her luggage for the trip home later in the day. Quickly out of her shower dressed in sweats with her dreads tied back in a bow, no makeup she headed out of the dorm with luggage in hand. The morning air was still brisk as she used paper towels to wipe her windshield covered in frost. She started her car and drove pass the university where on a normal day she would be attending. This wasn't a normal day! Nothing could have prepared her for this moment. This came after marriage! Somewhat irritated with herself having to go through this alone Sonjee wept. She most certainly was not going to tell her friends or Fonsworth. Sonjee had estimated it to be around ten miles from her dorm to the Planned Parenthood clinic where she was headed. She drove slowly giving herself time to go over everything that was about to happen to her. Is this what she wanted? She had to be sure! So many emotions were going through her head, nervousness, anger, remorseful and confusion. It's going to be fine," she kept repeating over and over again as she pulled into the parking lot and walked inside for what seemed like an eternity. As she entered, she looked at a bulletin board covered with announcements on the wall. Someone had pinned up a flyer that read: Grant me the serenity to accept the things I cannot change! Change the things I can and the wisdom to know the difference! Before continuing inside Sonjee stopped and smiled limited in her knowledge of prayer she recited the twenty-third Psalms which her mom had taught her years ago.

CHAPTER 17

Will I ever forget?

"Russell did you get those employer issues addressed and resolved? Doris asked calling him from her hospital bed where she was still recuperating from kidney surgery. "Yes, Mrs. Wright I hope so" Marvin is still constantly having to be called out for drinking on his lunch hour." He's a good worker and a fine craftsman when he's not drinking alcohol" he stated making his point why he had given him so many chances. His wife came by the other day and thanked me for letting him continue to work". She says believe it or not he's gotten better. "Well, for now I'll let you make that call." How is everything else? Are there any other issues that I need to address?" "None I'm aware of "he replied. Russell went on to share with her about the productivity of the store, donations that were coming in and other administrative issues Doris had entrusted to him.

Billy had arrived that evening late to Washington. He was still hurting from the way Dana had acted earlier that evening. He needed some alone time by himself to think. As not to disturb his parents he got a room at the Hilton near the airport for the evening. "Good morning' he said calling from his hotel room the next day. "Good morning David replied. "I thought you were coming in last night what happened? He asked concerned something had. "I'm here in Washington, my flight came in very late and I didn't want to disturb you all coming in so I just decided to get a room near the airport." Billy replied. "I was just about to check out and head your way will you be there this morning?" "Hey, that's wonderful! I'll have Alfredo start breakfast and later you can join me and Anderson on the course". "Sure, dad that sounds great" Are you going to the Ball tonight? David asked. 'Your mom said Dana's not coming with you! "That's right dad, Dana isn't coming tonight" he paused "I don't think she is the one" he added. "Son I'm sorry to hear that, I know you tried to make it work". "Dad want to know what's so funny, I really love Dana" but I know now she's not the one! He confessed. David didn't know how to reply. "Son I'll see you in about an hour" feeling his son's hurt and sharing what he was possibly going through at this moment.

Sonjee had arrived at seven thirty in the morning and it was now five o' clock in the evening and the staff at the clinic was preparing to leave. Having to drive herself she stayed at the clinic as long as possible to get her bearings to get behind the wheel. She was wiping tears from her eyes as she headed to her car in the lot. What had just happened was very vivid in her mind. She held a small plastic bag filled with birth controls pills and her signed consent form of this life-changing event. Her original plans were altered from heading home right after the surgery for the weekend and return Monday. She didn't have any complications. The doctor had told her since she was in such good health things should be back to normal for her in a few days. Sonjee thought about the drive to her parent's home and thought it best to go back to her dorm and rest a bit before hitting the highway. When she arrived at her dorm, she noticed a familiar car parked out front. She walked hurriedly pass Fonsworth's car without stopping, and entered her dorm locking the door, and ignoring the knocks at the door from her dorm sisters, who answered the shared phone in the hall, or the calls of her cell phone. She did call Tina and Angie letting them know of her weekend plans. She said her dad was moving into a retirement community and she was helping with some of the packing. That wasn't totally a lie that was his plans he just wasn't doing it this weekend and Sonjee was going home to rest peacefully. When Fonsworth came looking for Sonjee the next day she was gone.

Nada had gotten Madison to go shopping with her for a ball gown. "Thanks Madison, but I love your taste in clothes and I could surely use your help in this matter" she confessed to her as they strolled through the boutique stores at the Pavilion. Designer fashions galore were staring her in the face. Nada wanted to live up to the fact that Billy had asked her to this gala affair. She felt he could have any woman he wanted and he asked her. Even the single women on the faculty at the university stilled remembered him from the gathering months ago at the beginning of the year. Her colleague having attended many of the social events in Washington D.C with her husband, Nada wanted Madison's expert opinion on her gown purchase today. "Okay how are you going to wear your hair Nada? Madison asked as they entered the posh boutique. "I'm hoping up if I can fine the perfect gown to compliment it" she replied. "A ball! Madison said now thinking about colors. Nada's smooth dark skin would look gorgeous in a fire engine red or bright canary yellow, she reasoned looking a Klein's, and Purcell and Wang designs along the side of the wall. After about an hour they found what they agreed was the perfect gown for the evening. They had so much fun shopping and trying on gowns before deciding on a white Versace gown with a split on the side to show off the sparkling ankle strap heels she had purchased also. "Thanks Madison, for all the tips and advice and for accompanying me, Nada said leaving out of the final shoe boutique for the day. "Have fun and I'll see you Monday if you get your feet back on the ground" Madison teased her, hugging her, as they left going their separate ways. That evening when Billy picked Nada up in a limousine and presented her with a gift of a handset pair of diamond earrings and a necklace fit for the queen of Sheba from Tiffany's they shared their very first kiss! When they walked into the magnificent Regency Ball room arm and arm Tetra and David were both very surprised. The elegantly decorated room was filled with businessmen and investors from all over the world. William Parker was with his newfound friend and enjoying getting to know her in his world. His parents were pleased too. They said nothing to him to influence him though together they agreed with his choice hands down!

The familiar stretch of highway seemed to have shortened Sonjee felt on her drive to Oregon. She pulled up in the driveway letting up the garage and pulled in next to her mother's car still parked in its place where she probably parked it. Her dad had thought about putting it up for sale or giving it to Sonjee but parting with Beulah's things he said were a bit uncomfortable right now. He'd wait awhile. She unlocked the door from the inside of the garage and went inside. Her small luggage she had packed for the drive down was in her hand. "Wow! It's so quiet here she thought walking around the large empty house. She stood remembering how she a small girl ran all around the house hiding from her mom or dad at some point when playing hide and seek. She walked out back to see her mother's favorite place on the porch where she'd be when she returned from grade school. It was their time with a book that she would bring home from the school's library for her mom to read to her. She stood there fighting tears when she looked a Beulah's portrait hanging over the fireplace. It had been there as long as she could remember. "Oh mommy! Oh, mommy I need you!" She cried out falling to the floor with her hands covering a face of tears.

Dana was not going to sit at home tonight because Billy was being selfish! "I think I'll go and see what that O.K. Coral" is like she thought. Our friends are probably at Raffe's having a great time but they'll be expecting Billy. I really don't feel like explaining his childish behavior tonight! She reasoned going into her bedroom to dress in her country wear. Dana had never been to the "Coral," as it was affectionately called by the patrons who frequented it. Heading to go inside, she walked up, "Howdy partner!" A gentleman stood in his big black hat and plaid scarf around his neck greeting everyone coming in. Dana was very surprised when she stepped in the door's foyer filled with security. "Howdy ma'am, may I have your ticket? Another gentleman asked as she stood there in line waiting to enter. She then noticed others were moving around her handing him their ticket to keep the long line that was forming moving. Sir I'm sorry I didn't know I needed a ticket" she replied waiting for his response. Well ma'am, normally we don't" but there is always a cover charge" tonight we have Ms. Rhimes performing and we sold tickets" he said reaching around her allowing the line to keep moving. "Ma'am, you can't stand here! If you go on the other side of the rope you can purchase a ticket if they have any left." He shared pointing back out the door and through the other side. Dana was miffed but she pushed her way back out of the door and looked at the long line waiting for tickets. "This is ridiculous! I'm not going to wait in this line to find out they have sold out of tickets for tonight's performance" she voiced walking to the front of the line. Dana removed a large bill from her wallet and showed it to the person in the front of the line. "Sure! "Thanks, she said walking up purchasing a ticket and entering the spacious nightclub. First thing she noticed was the hay on the floor along the wall. There were bales of hay on the stage and large wagon wheels hanging from the very high ceilings being used for chandeliers. It was surprisingly elegant she thought finding a stool at the bar. She looked at ladies in wide skirts and men in plaid shirts arm in arm swinging each other around the floor. "Howdy miss" what can I get for ya? The lone bartender asked running from end to end of the long bar trying to fill every request being yelled at him at one time. 'Thanks Dana replied after he finally got back with her ordered drink. She turned on her stool as she heard them announce "let's Welcome LeAnn to the Corral" the place buzzed, Hee-haw! Yee haw! Yippee! could be heard throughout the establishment. Hands clapping loudly as she took the microphone in hand and began to sing one of her favorite songs. Heads were swaying, knees were being slapped, and everyone was getting into the music as they moved to her country beat. Most stood watching and clapping along to familiar words. Many of the patrons were singing along, some echoed every word that came from her lips. After several songs ranging from happy and lively to a sad ballad that everyone enjoyed her set was ended. The crowds were pleased. Many now in the spirit of things hit the dance floor with a favorite line dance. Dana watched the festivities from her stool. She had ordered another drink and turned to get it from the bar when. "Howdy pretty lady! This cowboy walked up in full dress including chaps and a white hat. "Hello, Dana replied with a friendly greeting. "Is this here stool taken? He asked pointing to an empty stool that had been vacated when he approached. "Doesn't seem to be" Dana said looking around for the gentleman who was sitting there. "Well do ya mind if I join ya? He again asked with his country drawl. "Free country", Dana responded moving around on her stool toward the floor. He sat there patting his feet and the lively patrons made time to the country beats of the live band. After a while two young ladies walked up vying for his attention pulling him on to the floor. Pretty soon all attention was on the two ladies and the dancing cowboy. He spun then over his head and under his legs. Around and around they went taking turns dancing with this cowboy who made cowboy boots look like ballet shoes. He was showing off his skills and the crowd was watching and clapping their hands to his beat. Do-si-do arm and arm each bowed and curtseyed before him and then to the patrons standing around watching. When the music stopped, he walked back proudly to his stool next to Dana. "Pretty fancy foot work for a cowboy" Dana voiced making reference to the speed at which he moved back and forth. "Oh, taint nothing! Anyone can do it if they put a mind to it" he responded chugging down another cold one. The band struck up another upbeat tune and the dancing patrons hit the floor. "Come on he said pulling Dana by the arm? "No, I'm not ready yet" she said pulling back with little force. "You can do it just follow me" he said still trying to convenience her to take the floor. Dana turned and swallowed down her drink and made her way to the floor with the dancing cowboy still tugging her arm. "Now be gentle she said timidly moving to the fast-rhythmic beat." "Just follow me! He replied catching her hand and with his other around her waist and away they went. Dana felt awkward the first few times around the floor after awhile it became smooth sailing. "Oh, I'm getting it. I'm getting it" she kept repeating as they danced. By the next song she was twirling and clapping enjoying the evening of country music and the new learned dance steps. She still would not attempt the line dance as she watched it being preformed over and over again. But she'd certainly be ready when she returned again, she promised Frisco the dancing cowboy.

Sonjee lay in her bed at her parent's home all day. The phone had rung a few times. One call was her older sister Candace her message said she would try her dads cell number. Sonjee knew she'd reach him there she wasn't answering any calls. She had come home to recoup. She went into her mom's large kitchen. She remembered all the good smells that use to come from there when she was growing up. She looked on the shelves at her mother's worn cookbook thumbing through the pages. She smiled as she came upon some of her favorite recipes. She put the book back on the shelf and took a can of chicken soup from the cabinet. "Not the same but it will have to do" getting out a small pot and the can opener. She poured the soup into the pot and put it on the stove to heat. Sonjee was feeling rested though she knew she still had a ways to go. While waiting for the soup to warm, she quickly went to the living room closet where her mom kept her homemade quilts. She remembered the stories her mom told her about her great grandmother when she was growing up. And how all the ladies would gather in one another's home putting the magnificent quilts together. The patterns were simply amazing she thought. She took one of the very heavy quilts from the closet and took it to the family room throwing it over the arm of her dad's big comfy chair. She ran back to the kitchen, got a tray table from the side of the refrigerator, a bowl from the dish cabinet, and poured the soup into the bowl. Umm she said thinking before going back to the family room. "Crackers, that's it! Sonjee expressed getting some from the opened cracker box and putting them back. She went back into the family room carrying the tray carefully as not to drop it. Sonjee then sat it in front of the chair and got the remote sitting it on the tray as well. She hurried down the hall to relieve herself from discomfort in the bathroom and quickly came back and sat down in the chair wrapping up in the big quilt. She carefully pulled the tray to her lap got the remote in hand and pushed the button allowing the television to come on. Hurriedly moving through the channels, she saw a movie title she liked. "Okay I'll try this one, it's one of my favorites she said getting the channel in sight and pushing the button again. Big spoon in hand to now eating the soup that was to hot moments ago. She put a big bite into her mouth as she heard a character from the show sing; "The sun will come out tomorrow" Sonjee spent the rest of her weekend watching old movies and reminiscing over her life. She cried when she remembered what had happened just two days ago. "Would that thought ever go away? Will it?

CHAPTER 18

Get Away

Billy sat in his office thinking about the wonderful time he had with Nada at the Ball. He remembered the embarrassment Dana had caused at the seminar. How was he going to tell her it's not going to work? Sure, she knew he was not going to back down on his beliefs. She knew full well going into the relationship. I want to remain civil in this matter for our son's sake. I'd like to remain friends, but it's up to her. "I will have to tell her soon that I'd like to see someone else. Billy smiled opening his email addressed from Nada. She was thanking him for the wonderful present he had given her. She explained how she had read it once and was going over it in detail. "She read it she gets it! he said getting up walking around his office. Nada said she most certainly would cherish this gift. "Wow he was impressed. He had given her diamonds and she was writing to thank him for the Relationship doctor's book he had given her. "Wow he exclaimed sitting back behind his big desk to start what he knew at this moment to be a great day!

Nada hurried around gathering her things going out the front door to her car parked in her driveway. She lived in an older neighborhood not far from Mt. Nebo church where she and her dad attended services since coming from New Orleans. After losing everything in the flood she and her father had purchased this small home very reasonable when they first arrived in Washington State. A few coats of paint and a gentle cleaning it served them well. Now that her father was working for the Parkers and living in the 1700 sq. ft. bungalow she lived there alone.

Nada liked the neighborhood, and the older folks she lived around were to her priceless. If something took place on Filbert Street Ms. Manuel knew all about it, if you cared to listen. She met Nada out by her gate most mornings. Nada would always invite her to the women's social every week trying to channel her meticulous gift of chatter. Some Sunday's Ms. Manuel would attend with her, every now and again" is what she would say. Nada walked quickly down her walkway meeting Mrs. Manuel standing by the gate holding her cane. "Morning Nada Jean" she said loudly. "Good morning Mrs. Manuel, how are you today? She asked stopping to acknowledge her. Ms. Manuel insisted on calling Nada, Nada Jean, she said she reminded her of someone back home named Nannie Jean. So as to not keep correcting her Nada just answered to the name. "Now that's what I should be asking! She exclaimed with a smile in her voice. "Ma'am? Nada asked waiting for an explanation. "I saw that long car in front of your house the other night" she said smiling. "Oh yes, Ms. Manuel I had a date" Nada replied. "Um I see." "It was dark I tried but couldn't see his face is he handsome? She again asked wanting all the details for sharing, Nada knew. "Ms. Manuel, I think he is a nice-looking gentleman." Nada responded looking at her watch hinting to leave. "Gentleman, um, I see." 'Well do you plan to marry him? She stood waiting for each answer to her questions. Nada was trying hard not to laugh at the expressions Ms. Manuel was making after every remark she made. "I know you got to get to school" she shared with Nada stepping back inside her gate and closing the latch down. "Nada Jean! She called out as Nada was opening her car door "is he rich?" holding her hand over her mouth giggling. Nada just smiled. 'Ms. Manuel you have a good day okay! "You to sweetheart" she said walking slowly back to her porch and wooden rocker.

Dana had fun the entire weekend. She had returned the next night to the O.K. Corral on the outskirts of town for what she saw as relaxing fun. She walked into and all out square dance they called it was just about to begin. "She wore all white covered in rhinestones and was the prettiest Philly in the place someone shared when she arrived. Dana looked around for a table. The place was not as crowded as the previous night when Ms. Rhimes was there, they just had the usual great country band "The Good old Boys "playing. "Ring ring as she sat down at the table after ordering her drink. The caller I.D said it was Billy. "I'll call him later" she said looking around the room for the dancing cowboy. The place had now started to fill up. "Grab your partners! was yelled loudly across the microphone. The band struck up the music as the music master called out the steps. "Well now you all join hands and you circle the ring. Stop where you are and give your honey a swing. Swing that little gal behind you, now swing your own cause you're a lucky fellow. Now you allemande a left with the corner gal and do-si-do your own, and now we all promenade with a sweet corner maid singing oh Johnny oh Johnny o! Dana had missed the first circle of dancers but others were coming out as he called the second and third verse of the swinging square dance song. Wanting to join in she pulled a cowboy gently by his arm to the floor. They made the circle around laughing and having fun. After the swing set ended, he introduced himself as Peter Wyatt. "Please to meet you she said shaking his hand and thanks for the partnership it was fun," she added. "Have a seat Dana voiced catching her breath from the fast movement. "Naw, I better not my girl wouldn't take kindly to that" he said pointing to her sitting across at another table staring him down. "Oh, I'm sorry hope I didn't cause any problems" nice meeting you" and she waved at the girlfriend as he walked over to meet her. Dana sat watching line dance after line dance before she had drunk enough to brave the floor. Precisely everyone on the crowded floor mimicked the two-step form of movement of each person. They shadowed each other so to be off on a turn or back step showed. "Oh, excuse me! Excuse me! Dana said again and again bumping into others in the line dance. After a while she conceded and sat down to watch each movement again. Some she mimicked well others needed more concentration. "I'll keep trying she said obliging a patron who had asked her to dance with him. And off they went hand in hand bouncing around to the yee haw movement.

Now the day had come to face Billy. She knew he was back and even though she had ignored his calls, she would one day have to face up. But nothing prevented her from stalling for another week until she got her thoughts together. So, she signed up for a Physiatrist convention in

Europe for a week to give her a legitimate excuse not to talk right now. He is still calling maybe he is seeing it my way, Dana reasoned.

Dana was calling to let him know from the plane that had just taken off from the Maine airport headed to Europe.

Doris was following her doctor's orders and not rushing into things to fast. Her managers over the staff had kept her a breast on all of the business affairs for her thrift companies. And her boutique as always was doing very well. Doris felt very competent in taking as much time as needed to allow her body to heal. "Finley! She called standing by her intercom system in her bedroom. "I will be attending church services this bright Sunday morning" humming a tune as she dressed. "Wonderful my lady!" they have missed you" he replied. She felt their love. Her hospital room had been covered in flowers from her church congregation and well-wisher's, over and over again her entire two weeks stay after surgery. "Oh, I missed everyone too. I will be down in a bit" she added and went back to buttoning her blouse she was wearing. On the drive in Finley did share that Dana her sister would be paying her a visit in a week. She was in Europe but was stopping in for a few days to see her. "Now that's great news maybe we will make a family gathering out of it." I will call and invite Sonjee, it will be a wonderful time," she thought riding along to the Los Angeles Praise Center. "I agree my lady, I agree!

Knowing Dana was leaving the country for a few weeks Billy decided to use this time to go and visit his son at U.C.L.A. He had spoken with him earlier in the week and shared he had some concerns regarding a few of his courses. "Nada, where are you going in such a hurry? Madison yelled seeing her pass by the university bookstore. "Oh, hi Madison, I'm headed to my class across campus. I'm trying to get there before the class does so that I can pass out these copies of facts for the next exam" she responded. "Someone will still say they didn't get the information but this at least helps those who study! She added. "Well look, call me later, we need to talk I'm planning a party for Charlie" I'd like you to attend if you can? "Sounds fun I'll call, bye. Still rushing across the campus when her cell phone rang! "Hello she answered walking to her class putting the papers on the desk. "Why hello there! Billy said very calmly. "William, I was just thinking about you, the book you gave me is wonderful," she said now totally focused on her call and not on the students coming in. "So, you like it! "Umm very good! He replied. "You don't know how happy that makes me! He voiced. What? Nada asked, not understanding the significance of the book to Billy. "I'm really committed to finding my mate using those techniques," he teased knowing of their built relationship. "Oh, I see, well I do agree with that, I've been through it twice." She teased back smiling. "I have too. As a matter of fact, when I met the author and sat through his seminar it was unbelievable." "You met the author of that book? And actually, sat in two of his seminars! Wow I could only imagine" Nada confessed, "that must have been awesome! She finally looked up to see her class just about filled with students and her handouts were on the desk in front of her. "Hey, I got his itinerary from his website so I'd love to do it again deal? He suggested glad she was interested. "That would be fantastic! she thought to meet this wonderful sounding facilitator. "I'll call you later but will you think about going with me on a ski trip in Kansas next week? "Next week are you serious William? "Yes, I'd love for you to come. I'm visiting a friend who lives there and would like you to accompany me if you have the time are even want to?" "Class is about to start. Please call me later." "Oh I will have a good one," he said disconnecting the line. He was going to visit and old friend, and another week away from Dana right now to think things through, is really what he needed. Nada smiled as she passed her handouts to each one there to aid in their study for the big exam. She had never even thought of skiing. But she had envisioned a life with William after attending that fabulous Ball with him. "Skiing ah!" she smiled starting her class lecture excited.

"David Michael please" Billy said calling the dorm room phone looking for his son. David! David! Yeah is there a David in here? He yelled while Billy listened. "No sir no one is answering right now". "Thanks, would you leave a message on the board for a David Parker" "Yeah I can do that". It was quiet so he must have been writing out the message to put up on the board. "Oh, hold on here he comes. "David it's for you! He yelled. Billy waited for a minute or two before he heard, "Hey what's up? David Michael asked. "David Michael, Billy asked after he answered the phone. "Oh, hi dad how's things going? That's what I should be asking you. "Where's your cell phone? I've been calling it all day" "Oh yeah ah I left it in my room, I think". I'm headed back there now to find out" he replied. "David is things getting better since our last conversation?" "Our last conversation dad?" asking as if what his dad was talking about was foreign to him. Look son, I'll be there probably around noon". I will see you then" okay thanks dad! see you then!"

When Sonjee got back to the campus on Monday morning she was feeling better, but still had a lot of healing ahead. Heading across campus early in the morning, she saw Fonsworth. He looked bad. "Hey home girl can I walk you to class? he asked. "You look terrible. How was your weekend?" She asked being cordial as she walked to class and a bit frighten of his demeanor. "Slow down why are you walking so fast" reaching to put his arm around her. She could smell the alcohol still on his breath. "Fonsworth, you'd better stop drinking it is addictive you know! pushing him away from her and advising him of his problem. 'Look stop for a minute! He said grabbing her arm tightly. Her first instinct was to pull away and keep walking. "Okay but please don't touch me! She stated looking directly at him. Sonjee, I told you I was sorry and you still avoid me like a plague". He stood looking for her to say something to ease his pain of neglect from her. "Fonsworth, I heard you apologize, but what has happened has made me empty and I can't help you. I do forgive you because I was taught if someone asks for it I should". 'I'm trying to do that but you hurt me badly!" please leave me alone! Sonjee stated walking quickly away heading to class. Fonsworth found a quiet hidden place on campus and drank a beer he had packed in his backpack then headed to class, I guess. He was probably sorry for what had happened but for Sonjee it was to late now. And she wanted nothing to do with him ever again.

The remainder of the week in Billy's law office was uneventful the Mcnair's law firm won the bowling tournament so things were pretty gloom around the Parker & Associates law offices. Billy had just finished reading and email from Nada when his phone rang. "William

Parker, he answered after his announced call. "Billy it's Dana how are you? "I'm wonderful, how's the convention?" "Oh, the usual, lots of talking and reasoning" she replied. "Oh, that's exciting ah?" Billy said positioning himself to talk. "Pretty much" "Well Dana I wasn't aware of your sudden departure to the convention, was it planned? We really must talk you know". "About what now Billy, I've explained I will think about what we talked about earlier" what else can I say? She said sounding put out he wanted to bring this subject up now. "I saw some beautiful sights since I've been here," she said changing the topic. "I got a chance to see a Greek drama in Athens, Greece, which featured the ancient temple called the Parthenon in the background" she said very excited. Billy didn't want to discuss sights and knew she was avoiding the issue. "A few of us went out to an opera last evening it was wonderful." "That's nice Dana" but we have to stop pretending that everything is fine when it's not". "What do you mean? She asked as if she didn't have a clue for his statement. "Dana, we want two different things. I want commitment and longevity in a marriage relationship. And you, I'm really not sure what you want". "I know what I want and that is not to discuss this topic with you right now! She said slamming down the receiver leaving a loud buzzing in his ear. Billy sat for a moment in disbelief from Dana's childish behavior. How was he going to reason with her? First thing, he would have to get her in the same room with him, and that was proving to be a challenge? He needed to speak with her face to face. Though right now he was headed to court, and then to the airport, for his flight to be with his son in Los Angeles for a few days.

CHAPTER 19

Let's get together

Hello Sonjee, how are you doing? Doris asked after getting a call from her. "Great! She replied enthusiastically. "The performance got a standing ovation from the student body and staff! She said laughing. "Wow Sonjee, that's wonderful, see all that work you where telling me about paid off", Doris replied. "It sure did! But I see now what Ms. Motobia our dance instructor was after in our practices" when she kept having us do it over and over again".

We want to really wow the crowds expected at the convention center next weekend! Sonjee added. "Dad was down for the first performance and he really liked it." "Dr. Reeves how's he doing? Doris asked with concern. "Dad's fine he says, he's keeping busy and just about moved into the retirement community which I think is good for him". "Retirement community" Doris questioned. "Yes, some of his friends who are retired physician's live there and persuaded him it was the way to go. He really didn't want to leave the house he and mother had together. But honestly there was so much house for him to try and maintain by himself, it was virtually impossible. He wasn't going to let anyone move in to help him, so it was best, we agreed" Sonjee confided. "Well if it's what he wanted that's alright," Doris added. "He loves it there, and they have lots of activities, including golf for him to participate in, and he comes and goes as he pleases, you know! He still drives everywhere he wants to go" Sonjee shared very pleased that her dad still has that ability. "So, you have been there to visit him? "Yes, it's gorgeous! Candace, Bailey, and I were there two weeks ago getting him settled in. He had us laughing at the large kitchen he had by choosing this model. He informed us he wanted us to be able to come especially around the holidays and sit and eat together". He was also able to keep the beautiful dinette set he and mother had purchased a few years ago" which we were all delighted to hear" Sonjee shared. "That's good he didn't have to store or give away all of his memories" Doris affirmed. "He's fine, I know he thinks of mother all the time but he's going on with living as she had express to us is what she wanted many times during her illness." So, it sounds like your dad is fine so what plans do you have after your year ends", which by the way is in a month! Doris asked inquisitively. "Well honestly, I was thinking about relocating and transferring schools" she said. "Oh? Doris replied waiting to hear her plans. Sonjee was silent. She had already spoken with her advisor about it and was having her credits transferred to another University away from Gonzaga. "Sonjee where are you planning to transfer"? Doris waited with her heart pounding. She and Sonjee had started building a relationship and she most certainly did not want anything to come between it. She knew wherever Sonjee went she would stay in touch. She didn't want to lose her again. "Well if you must know I was planning to come your way," she said hesitantly. "My way"! You mean to Los Angeles! YOU ARE! THAT'S WONDERFUL! "I would love to have you closer and we could spend time together and shop together and get to know each other better, would you like that? Doris asked overjoyed Sonjee wanted to come nearer to her. That answer was precisely what Sonjee had prayed for while spending that long weekend recovering at her parent's home alone. "I would love you in my life mother" she said with tears streaming down her face. "She knows" Doris said to herself. My little girl knows!

Nada and Madison went shopping for new winter outfits. They had become shopping buddies mostly due to Nada. She wanted to mimic Madison's style in everything. "You have very good taste in clothes Madison, I hope you don't mind that I purchase some of the same things you do". No, it's actually a compliment, it's fun to see the different accessories and colors that make an outfit look so different" she replied. "I agree thanks anyway," giving her a hug as they looked around the department stores. 'How do you like this? Madison asked trying on a beautiful white knitted hat as she pranced around in a mirror. That's gorgeous! Look at this cashmere one! Nada said putting it on and pulling it to the side. They laughed a lot as they stood trying on winter hat styles. I'm getting this one" Nada voiced "Billy has asked me to go skiing with him and I think this will be perfect don't you think? She said putting the beret style hat on her head looking at Madison smiling. 'Skiing? This sounds pretty serious! Are you to getting there yet? She asked as they move around looking at the coats. Umm we talk a lot, and email each other a lot" she smiled. We enjoy being together on our dates though most have been unplanned." I'm thinking that this ski trip would be a chance for me to get to know him better. Just relax and have some fun" she shared looking into the future.' Oh, I see, Madison replied but is there any chemistry between you two? You know have you kissed him? "Madison! Nada shoved her gently on her shoulder. "There is lots of chemistry and yes we've kissed twice to be exact. And no, we haven't to your next thought or question. I want this to be special! He's looking for Mrs. Right, he has confessed that! Nada said walking out of the store loaded with shopping bags. 'So, you're saying this could lead to wedding bells? "If what I know about him so far rings true yes! Nada voiced helping Madison put her bags in her trunk. She had twice as many as Nada on this trip. Madison assisted Nada as they stood by their cars still talking. Well he seems very nice. You think he will accompany you to Charlie's party next month? Madison asked getting into her car. "I will let you know when we get back from Kansas" Are you sure you want to go to Kansas with this man? 'I'm sure, I know his family very well otherwise I wouldn't be going I don't think? She said getting into her car and starting the engine. Thanks Madison it was fun, see you tomorrow" "It was fun for me to she said pulling away leaving the parking lot. Ring! Ring! Hello, Nada voiced answering her cell phone as she drove along. "Hi there, Billy's voice returned a warm greeting" how are you this evening? He asked. "I'm wonderful! She said in a very upbeat tone'. That's good to hear, so what has put you in such a happy mood." "You called! She said. Easy Nada you don't want to sound anxious she thought silently to herself. 'Well I'm glad my calls bring you a smile" he said "I will have to do it more often. "Okay I agree. "Soooo any particular reason for this call". Umm maybe" Billy said in a teasing voice. "I'm visiting my son for a few days on the west coast and I thought I would stop by and see you on the way back home" "Oh are you going to your parent's home? Nada asked. "No, I really don't have a lot of time I have to be in court Thursday and Friday but I wanted to stop by and see you! he said waiting for her to respond. As she pulled into her driveway Ms Manuel was sitting in her rocker, Nada waved? "Billy you know I always want to see you" she said in a very charming way. "Great I'll call when I get in town, take care," he added hanging up the line. Nada had her arms filled with packages as she got out of her car walking into her house. She stopped near the door to see Ms Manuel getting up slowly heading to her gate where Ms Hazel her neighbor on the other side of Ms. Manuel's fence was standing looking up at her kitten who had ran up a tree. Ms. Manuel walked over closer to her fence yelling at Mr. Garvey two fences over. He was trimming his edges. He had one of the nicest yards on the block. "GARVEY! GARVEY! She yelled. "That's alright Virginia I'll walk down there and ask him to help" Hazel said. GARVEY! G-A-R-V-E-Y! Ms Manuel yelled trying to be heard over his electric hedge saw. "I declare that man is a deaf as a fence post! Ms Manuel stated frustrated he was not hearing her. Nada hurried in to put her packages away coming back to be of help. She wasn't in her house very long it seemed before she came out to find Mr. Garvey coming down a ladder with the small kitten in his arm. "Thanks Garvey, Hazel Ross said rubbing her kitten's head. "Umh! He could've had him down yesterday if he wasn't so deaf! Ms Manuel exclaimed going back to her rocker. Nada went back into her house laughing at her elderly neighbor's antics.

Doris had got back in the swing of things with her businesses but remembering her doctor's orders to take it easy. She had got his permission to travel to Washington to Gonzaga University to see Sonjee perform at the convention Center. The show had sold out crowds and plenty of standing ovations nightly. Doris, Finley and Russell were enjoying watching the African dance being performed. They oooo'd watching as the dancers form from a single file into two parallel lines. Often, they would make a circle moving precisely to the music. Sonjee had a solo part where she was able to showcase some very expressive moves Finley thought. They also noticed the beautiful and colorful body paint each used to draw attention to all the movements being made. Each part of the dancer's body, the head the trunk and the arms and legs were moving to a different instrument at the same time. Doris watched smiling proudly as the group made precise controlled flowing continuous, natural movement.

'I can hear several rhythms going at one time" Finley voiced to Russell making movement with his feet tapping the floor. "Look at the instruments, one, two, three, four, five different ones Russell concluded after carefully counting again. The story was one that emphasizes the unity among the members of a village Doris shared reading from the program layout given when they arrived. It was a wonderful production and though Doris had to get back to Los Angeles that same night Sonjee was glad they shared what she thought to be the being of a great career. Doris, Finley, Russell and a few chosen friends of Sonjee's went out to eat before she saw the three of them off from the airport.

C H A P T E R   2 0

University Life

Billy had arrived in Los Angeles and went directly to the university. He looked around as he entered the campus filled with students going in all directions. Wow! He said standing back and remembering those days. He continued on headed to Fenton Hall where David Michael's dorm was located. As he walked up some guys were headed out of the door. Billy quickly walked in before the huge door close behind them. He then looked at the arrows pointing with the numbers getting higher or lower depending on which direction you went. He had been here a few times in the past so he headed in the direction of David's dorm room. As he walked down the narrow hall, he passed several more guys leaving the building. "Good morning! He greeted each one as they passed. Good morning could be heard over and over in a short span of time. Soon he was knocking on David's door. "Come in! A voiced yelled from the other side. Billy slowly turned the knob. The small room looked like a tornado had hit it! There were clothes everywhere and underneath it all somewhere was his son. "Oh dad, come on in I'm on the phone with Dana! He yelled looking over a pile of clothes he was laying under on the bed. Billy beckoned for him to not mention he was there, just finish your conversation, he whispered. "Dana that sounds great! Is there anything you didn't see? He asked still hearing about her travels around Europe. Okay Dana I look forward to seeing all of the pictures." "No! Dad, ah I should be talking with him soon why? "I won't bad mouth you to dad" I'm sure he knows you needed to get away". "Dana, I have a class to get to call me later on my cell. Yes, it was

129

in my athletic bag" Love you too, bye! "WHEW! Sorry about the room dad, we had friends over last night, well every night" he said moving the clothes to the floor finding a chair. Billy just looked. "How do you find anything in here? He asked moving some books and papers lying on a table or desk out of his way. 'We argue about this all the time. "Kyle is a slob! A smart slob by a slob nonetheless" David said defending the way the small dorm room looked. Dad that's kinda what I wanted to talk with you about? Billy sat looking around he couldn't believe this place. "I'd like to get my own place next year, I know, I know before you go off on me hear me out." "I'm listening" Billy said crossing his arms. There are some really great townhouses near campus and I could get more studying done in a quieter environment" he shared making his point. Kyle doesn't have to study as hard as I do it seems" good grades just fall out the air for him or something" he added. "I'm sure that's not true but I hear what you're saying" his dad confided. "We attend lots of frat party's and a lot of guys come in here, dad it's rough to try and study around here", he said putting on his shirt buttoning it as he talked. "David Michael after looking at this place I'm seriously considering your idea. "I'm a bit surprised the university hasn't said anything about it. "Oh they have, and we pick it up for a while and boom! It's right back after a few days" he confessed. "Where is the slob, I mean where is Kyle now? "He stayed down stairs last night playing cards, I guess, he hasn't been through this morning yet" "Umm, are you ready, lets get out of here and get some breakfast and discuss this problem. "Cool, he said heading out of the door behind his dad. Walking out down the hall they ran into Kyle, Remy and two girls headed up to their dorm. Hey David how's it going? Kyle said coming toward them. Headed out? He asked. "Yeah man, hey want to get together later and clean up our dorm? David asked as the four stood in the hallway. The girls were giggling as they beat on the dorm's door, both stood together after sneaking into the building. Remy asked for the key so they could go in the room while David Michael stood still talking with Kyle. "Kyle you remember my dad? He stated introducing them again. "Oh, didn't know man! Nice meeting you sir, Kyle replied extending a shake to Mr. Parker. "That sounds great, cleaning the room I mean but there's a party near the girl's dorm tonight! He yelled heading down to their room. David Michel and his dad headed out the dorm's building and walked across the campus to his car. "We've been warned several times about having girls in our room so I may get kicked out anyway! David Michael added riding to the restaurant with his dad.

Doris walked in to her thrift store ran by Russell unexpectedly one afternoon. "Hello" everyone said seeing her entering and passing the registered in front of the store. She acknowledged each one and kept looking around at the new displays and clothing arrangements that had been put in place. "Oh, good afternoon Mrs. Wright"! Russell voiced coming from the back of the store with a hat assortment in his hand. "I was just putting up this hat display on those shelves over there," he said pointing to the shelves to the left of the store. "Do you have enough hats? She asked looking at the long shelves he was making reference to. "Doris, we have hats and caps of every kind, season and color" Chloe has a great knack for displays. She put the one up in front" he shared with Doris. "Chloe Burcher! Please be sure and share with her I think she's done a great job" Doris shared with her store manager and continues looking around at how well planned out the store was. "Ms. Wright if you have time,

I'd like to go over some paperwork with you" Russell asked. I'd love to Russ" walking into his office in the back of the huge thrift store.

Billy and David Michael sat at a chain restaurant very near campus. They had finished eating and were still talking about his dorm situation. "David if you're sure you can maintain living on your own, I'm going to seriously consider it. There's only a month left in this semester year so we will see what happens" "You can always get a new roommate too' Billy suggested. "Yeah, possibly, we'll see." David Michael replied finishing up his breakfast orange juice. "Son something else I want to talk with you about" David looked at his dad waiting to hear "It's about your mother Dana". I don't think we're going to make marriage," he confesses sitting across the table. "You and Dana"? Gee that sounds funny! He said chuckling under his breath. 'Well son, we've been together for a while and I want to get married and settle down. Maybe give you a little sister or brother." Is that what Dana wants? David Michael asked now relaxing back on his seat. "I seriously doubt it son.

She's been evading me again regarding commitment". So, I'm seriously looking somewhere else." "I can't be upset about that," David Michael admitted. Dana is not an easy person to live with". "Well son don't bad mouth your mother, even though I agree with you, she is". "I haven't shared this with her yet, but I want to see someone else who I have been building a friendship with". "Oh, dad she already knows about Annie and you know how she feels about her! He said looking over at Billy with a smile. "I know! But it's not Annie son". She's dating someone else now" "Annie! Wow I liked her dad". I know, I liked Annie to, but I was trying to make a go of it with your mother. Annie got fed up with me always putting her second to Dana and I understand her point," he said thanking the waitress for the meal ticket she had placed on the table. David Michael shook his head regarding his newfound information regarding his dad's former girlfriend. "Son I'm seeing Nada now" Nada? Nada Francois, Alfredo's daughter. "Oh Nada! She's hot, I mean gorgeous, very pretty" Don't get me wrong Dana is pretty to but she's my mother. "Are you serious about her?" "We shared a kiss or two but I want to be free to pursue a lasting relationship with her" he shared openly with his son. "Well dad I wish you the best" but Dana won't like it". "I know you're right about that son though I'm hoping Dana can be very mature about this and we can still remain friends, he replied walking out of the restaurant rubbing David's hair on his head. Hair cut time son? He asked as they got back into the car heading back to the campus.

Sonjie had just finished talking with her dad for the morning. She had shared with him her plans for transferring college for next year. They had shared a night out earlier in the week with Mr. Reeves keeping a promise from his late wife, came down to see one of the young ladies, Beulah had delivered, play in a championship game for their team. "Hi Mr. Reeves, she said coming up to him after the game" great game, hard fought though" he said acknowledging her work on the court. "Yes, the team plays pretty dirty most time but we got this one! She said smiling from ear to ear. "Oh Mr. Reeves I so sorry to hear about your wife" my mom and I came to the service but trying to get to you to shake your hand afterward was impossible". "Thank you dear I understand". "This is my daughter Sonjee Reeves" she attends here also. "Lillian Graham, please to meet a fellow student" extending a hefty grip on Sonjee's very small hand. "I enjoyed your game Lillian" she replied looking at how tall Lilly was. "Thank you but most people call me Lilly, besides I like that better" she confessed. "So, is this your first year? Yes, Sonjee replied. "It's a great University Lilly smiled, "I'll be starting my third-year next year and I'm enjoying it. Maybe we can keep in touch.' "Well, I would love too but I'm transferring moving to Los Angeles for my continued education. "Wow that's a bummer; we have a great curriculum here. "What's your major? "Performing arts, I love to dance". Mr. Reeves was now down speaking with the winning coach as the two girls continued conversation. "So, you got a chance to see the show the arts department put on? "I did, I was one of the lead dancers" Sonjee acknowledged. "Now that was an awesome show! "Are you the one who had the solo in the beginning of the show?" Lilly asked. "Yes, I was! Sonjee exclaimed proud of her accomplishment. "Ms. Motobia comes in to some of our practices showing us different body movements to help us on the court" Lilly confessed. "LILLY! LILLLY! A group of teammates were yelling at here from across the court ready to go and celebrate after the big victory. "Sonjee, its good meeting you maybe I'll see you around campus before the years out. I'd like that" she said sharing a hug with the tall basketball player. "Tell your dad thanks for the game visit" she yelled being pulled by her arms toward the door. Sonjee and her dad went out to dinner before she saw him off to the airport after another very wonderful visit.

Doris left Russell and headed to Rodeo Drive to her boutique. Everyone was very busy putting in the new fashions that had just arrived earlier in the week. Doris browsed around for a while looking at her inventory. Then she went to her beautiful office space on the second floor going over some paperwork for about and hour before heading home to rest for the evening.

CHAPTER 21

We met

Billy left satisfied that his son wasn't going to be tossed from the dorm anytime some. He and David did speak with Kyle about the amount of company coming into the room. Kyle promised he'd keep it down during the week anyway. So far now Billy was satisfied with Kyle's answer but would certainly think hard about getting David his own place for next year off campus. After spending an entire day with his son Billy boarded a plane to Washington State. He was headed to see Nada. He hoped to spend some time with her getting to know her better. He had not formally shared with Dana his feeling but he had given up on her uncommitted relationship. Dana had called again letting him know she would be home soon and for some reason looked forward to seeing him. He sat on the plane thinking the scenario through. He would soon be landing in Washington and his heart was beating fast just thinking about Nada. Somehow, he felt good about the fact that his son had for the most part given him his blessing with Nada and he was feeling jitters. After landing getting his luggage, and a car he headed to see Nada. "Hello she said answering her phone. "I'm headed your way, I'll be there in about forty-five minutes, he said after reaching her by phone. "Okay, I'll see you then" she said shyly. "Whoa what was happening she thought? I'm so nervous, but anxious to see him, I'm nervous, but at the same time I'm looking forward to being in the same room with him! Nada got up looking around. She, Carin and Madison had added some newly decorative pieces to her small but very elegant home. She was pleased. SHE KNEW BILLY'S WORLD!

SO MUCH BIGGER THAN HERS! HOW COULD SHE FIT IN? Okay settle down," she said using self-talk as she paced the floor waiting his arrival. He called you remember? She thought out loud while she waited. After a while she heard the car pull up out front. She stayed in her kitchen busily waiting to hear the knock or bell ring on her door. Maybe that wasn't him," she thought cutting fresh tomatoes on the salad she had prepared with dinner. After about fifteen minutes of waiting she walked to her living room looking out the window. "Oh no, she said seeing Ms. Manuel out by her gate speaking with Billy. "HELLO YOUNG MAN! She yelled standing behind her gate "YOU COMING TO SEE NANA JEAN? She asked, being, let's say inquisitive. "YES MA'AM! he yelled back surprising the nosy neighbor. "COME OVER HERE SO I WON'T HAVE TO YELL she yelled across to him. Billy got out of the car with his arm full of flowers and headed toward Ms Manuel's fence a few yards out of the way. "Umm pretty flowers! She acknowledged checking Billy out from head to toe. "Thank you, ma'am, I'm William Parker, he said extending his hand making her blush. She shook his hand smiling. "Oh, I see you have a different car today? She noticed looking around him to see it. "Yes ma'am, I don't live here. I'm just visiting from Maine". "Maine? She asked surprised. "But it was you I saw that night in that long car wadn't it? She again asked for clarification (nosy). "Yes ma' am that was my family's limousine, we were going out! He said smiling moving away, getting away, from her many questions he sensed was not going to stop. "YO FAMILY, THEY LIVE HEAR? Yes ma'am, Billy replied. "Do you know if Nada's home?" "Umm I don't know you might want to ring her doorbell," she said laughing quietly and going back to her rocker.

The last semester was going by so fast for Sonja. She loved the performances at the convention center and the fact her body had gotten back in shape and all seemed well. Except for a reoccurring nightmare involving her life decision life was pretty normal. She sat up in bed with beads of sweat pouring from her. She wiped her face. She had been crying, she reasoned. WOULD THIS FEELING EVER GO AWAY! WOULD SHE EVER FORGET WHAT SHE DID? She got up and walked to the door and then walked back to her bed. Boy was she glad her roommate wasn't in tonight again. Sonja got on her knees and laid her head on the bed thinking quietly to herself about prayer. After a few minutes she recited the Lord's Prayer, which she was taught long ago as a child. Soon she began just talking like her mom and dad had taught her since she came back home from Africa. She wasn't sure what she was doing but it had worked nights before when she was awakened like this during the night. After repeating the same words, she had heard over and over again she got back in bed and went to sleep until morning.

"Come in" Nada said after hearing her doorbell ring. "Well how are you Nada Jean? He teased coming in handing her the beautiful flowers. She laughed, "oh I see you met Ms. Manuel" she replied. "That would be a yes! He smiled breaking the ice and starting a great evening that would be one to remember for the two of them.

David Michael went out to the practice field to meet with his baseball team. "HEY GUYS! He yelled coming toward them from across the field. "David! Hey man good to see you! His friend Ray acknowledged seeing him get closer. The coach called all the guys together to discuss the strategy for the big game this Sunday.

"Alright guys we've come a long way to get to this game. We've sacrificed a lot to be here today! I know most of you did not participate in a lot of the activities that has taken place during this spirit week. I promise you will have plenty of TIME TO CELEBRATE AFTER WE WIN THIS ONE! He expressed getting louder with each word. YEAH! YEAH! They exclaimed slapping high fives and waving their caps in the air. "Let's make this practice a great one!" he suggested watching each player take his position on the field.

CHAPTER 22

To close for comfort

Billy sat in his office preparing some paperwork for his court appearance later that day. He had spoken with Nada reminding her of her flight time since she had agreed to accompany him to Kansas. She was leaving from Washington State and he from Maine. Billy had coordinated the flights so neither would be waiting around for the other. "William, Mr.Winegardener left these papers at the front desk for you" Annie explain coming into his office. "Thanks Annie, please put them in my in basket" he replied. "I haven't spoken with you lately how are things? He asked standing up coming around his desk. "Things are fine" she replied getting ready to walk out the door. "Annie you seem happy? he said now close enough to hold her hand, though hesitant. "Billy I am, I really am," she said walking out of his office going back to her desk. "Ring! Ring! Ring! "Hello William Parker, he answered after the announced call. "Hi Billy", Dana's voice came across the line. "I'll be landing in and hour could you please pick me up at the airport, I would appreciate it" she asked with a smile in her voice. "Oh Dana, I can't I have to be in court in an hour. But I will send a car to get you" he added. "I'm glad you're back! He said to her sounding excited, she was soon to arrive in Maine. How was your trip? "OH WONDERFUL, I HAVE SO MUCH TO SHARE WITH YOU! Dana said excitedly. "That's good "I can't wait to see you tonight either, we have so much to talk about! Billy explained, waiting for Dana's response. "I know Billy, I missed you too! She cooed over the line. Billy paused for a minute, he realized this was going the wrong way, she was thinking everything was alright, and nothing had change in the two weeks she had been gone sight seeing around Europe. Dana had decided to stay another week after the convention to see more of the beautiful sights. And who could blame her. He just didn't want to mislead her, though he knew she had not changed her mind regarding anything, since the last conversation. "Dana a car will be there for you" he said again hurrying to get off the phone. "Billy make it a limo"! She huffed, hanging up the line.

"Daddy here is your prescription" I got it early so that you won't run out while I'm on vacation. She explained removing it from her tote before going over sitting next to him. "Oh, that's right" her father exclaimed, you're going on a ski trip, right? "Yes, dad I shared everything with you about it and whom I was going with" she said sitting next to him on his bright orange leather sofa. "I know dear, I admit I was a bit concerned about it at first, but the Parker's think it's a wonderful idea". "They do? "Yes, I just came right out and asked Mrs. Parker the other day." "What did she say daddy? What did she say? Nada asked anxious to hear what Tetra had to say. "Well, she thought it to be a wonderful idea. She was taken by the way you presented yourself at the "Investor's Ball," and was very please her son had asked you". "She said that? "Yes, and why not, I'm very proud of you. And I would choose you over anyone" Alfredo said hugging his daughter. "She loves to ski by the way so if you need some pointers, just ask" he smiled taking one of his pills from his prescription bottle. "Daddy, thank you, I'm getting ready to go home, busy day tomorrow with finals close". Oh, Nada that's right, I got a call from New Orleans today" Oh? "Yes, dear we lost Mother Phillips" Oh daddy, I'm so sorry to hear that Nada replied. So, while you're on vacation I'll be there" Alfredo said. "No daddy I can't," he stopped her in mid-sentence "you continue with your plans" no! Goodnight. Nada kissed her dad on his forehead and picked up her tote and purse and left going home.

Sonjee was headed back to her dorm after a very long day on campus. Tina and Angie had turned to go in the other direction to their dorm when up from behind her came FONSWORTH! "Ohhhh! She screamed. After seeing it was Fonsworth, she pushed him away. "I've asked you not to do that" And walked hurriedly toward her dorm.

"Yeah home girl, I'm sorry I didn't mean to frighten you," he explained walking fast trying to keep up. "Fonsworth please leave me alone! If you don't, I'm going to scream" "Please don't I'm sorry" he repeated again. There were not many students moving around in the area by the dorms but if she screamed loud enough someone would hear, she reasoned. "Stop, for a minute? He asked vying for her attention. She was only about a block away from her dorm's door. He reached for her arm. "Don't touch me! "All right, all right! But tell me why you're so mad at me". "You don't return my calls what's a brother to do? He said motioning with his hands. She stopped for a minute she could smell he had been drinking. "I haven't returned your calls because frankly I have nothing to say to you! "Why, I said I was sorry! He admitted sitting down on the ground to keep from falling over. "You're right you are sorry! I thought you were more mature. I thought you would own up to what you did! Now you're coming to me with this "I'm sorry! Well, I sorry too! She stated walking quickly toward the dorm leaving him sitting on the ground with his head down. "Sonjee! Sonjee! He looked up yelling. "Don't you dare follow me"! She yelled back going into her dorm.

Billy had arrived at Dana's around six o clock. He certainly didn't know how she would take the news he had to share with her about their ending relationship. "Come in, come in sweetie," she said hugging him and kissing him passionately as he entered. Billy kissed her in return and moved further into her home. "Look honey, I purchased so many gifts in Europe I'm surprise they all got here in one piece, she confessed showing him an expensive mat print waiting to be hung on the wall. "Dana it looks like you had a good time" he admitted looking around at the merchandise she had lying around the den. "I did, but come over here and sit down I've missed you," she said pulling him by his arms to the big comfy chaise sofa in her family room. She sat on the chaise and beckoned for Billy to come and sit beside her. He sat down. She put her hand on his shoulders and began a massaging motion. "You seem to be tense, long day in court? She asked still massaging his shoulders. "Ah you know," he shared getting up pacing the carpeted floor. 'Billy, I missed you, come and sit here and we can talk" she cooed at him across the room. "Ring! Ring! It was his cell phone. Excuse me Dana I need to get this," he said walking away to another room to talk. "I'll make something for us" she said walking pass him as he was speaking, patting him on his behind, to tease him as she flirted about. "I'm busy right now, I'll call when I get home, I promise" he said disconnecting the caller after a few minutes of talking. Dana had come out of the kitchen with a pitcher of Margarita's and sat back down on her beautiful chaise beckoning for him to join her. He had her in a room alone, but now could he go through with his plans? "Dana you know what I'd like to talk about, are you sure you're ready to talk," he asked looking at her sultry motions she was making. "I just want to be near you right now, I miss you," why are you being so evasive? She asked taking a sip of her salty drink. Billy sat down and moved himself next to her on the long chaise sofa. A click of the remote and the room was filled with romantic music. "I missed you Billy Parker, she said kissing him on his face over and over again". He didn't say anything but this is not what he envisioned to happen. He had planned a ski trip with Nada! "Stop, stop, he said pushing her away gently. Let's talk! Okay she said now stopping her behavior of the way she was acting. "I'm listening. Billy sat for a moment and swallowed hard, Dana had riled him up. (no, no in a good way) It had been a while since he was with anyone. He had ignored Dana. Then she was gone for two weeks. He certainly had not gotten that far with Nada yet! "Now he was being tempted again! "No, he said getting up again from the chaise. Dana offered him his Margarita filled glass. "Relax, it's obvious you had a long day," she said so innocently to him. "Whew, you're probably right, he said taking it and quickly drinking it down. After a fleeing thought he moved up beside her again. "She kissed him gently but very passionately and he didn't try to fight it. "It had been to long without a woman's touch. And though Dana didn't know all of what was going on she knew her man. She snuggled up closer allowing him to smell the expensive perfume she was wearing. "Umm" he exhaled having his senses aroused from the fragrance. Dana breathed in his ear. He moved slightly to fill their glasses again, but admittedly she had him. "What was that we were going too talked about? she asked rubbing her body up next to his. Billy wasn't quite sure of what was happening, he only knew he didn't have the power to stop it at this point. Dana had the upper hand and she was playing it for everything it was worth. "Cooing and moaning and being playful next to him on the chaise getting her point across. He's not quite sure either when it happened but about 2am in the morning he crept quietly out of Dana's home headed to his.

Nada was up early and headed to the campus for another day. She was hoping Billy would call soon so she could share the sad news with him. "He promised he would call, she thought driving along in the morning breeze. She pulled into the parking lot hearing her cell phone rang. It was Billy. "Good morning! She expressed cheerfully glad to hear his voice. "Good morning! He returned. "I'm sorry I didn't get home until very late," Billy confessed to her feeling guilty. "Oh, I understand, but I really need to speak with you about the trip" Nada shared getting her materials from her car headed into the faculty lounge. "The trip" Billy wanted to cancel the trip himself. He wasn't sure if he wanted to begin another relationship when the one with Dana was so uncertain. He had begun to care for Nada but after last night with Dana he wasn't sure if he wanted their relationship to end. He knew he wanted more from Dana like marriage and home life. He owed it to himself and her to try. It wasn't right, he reasoned to have arranged to go on a trip with someone else simply because he was upset with her. I missed her, and yes I must admit I think I love her," he reasoned as he spoke with Nada regarding their planned ski trip. "You will probably hate me, though I would hope you will understand," he started out. "Are we speaking about the same thing? She asked curiously. "The trip right" "Yes, she teased but I called first! Nada said being playful in her conversation. Billy felt bad he had to tell her about Dana. "How did I get myself in this mess? He said pacing around his bedroom. "I feel bad" Nada began, I really wanted to spend some time with you, old friend" she admitted with a smile in her voice as she spoke. "Oh? He asked waiting for what she had to say. "I called to say I need to cancel, but please don't be mad I have a very good reason". Billy said nothing but breaths a quiet sigh of relief. "I'm going to accompany my dad to New Orleans for a funeral." "Oh, I'm sorry to hear that are you, all right? Billy asked after hearing the news. "I'm fine, Mother Phillips was a very good friend of my family and we're going back for her home going" she shared waving as Carin and Madison walked into the teachers lounge. "Well I understand" Billy replied. "So, you're not angry with me?

She asked him honestly. "No Nada I'm not mad or angry with you." "Okay, so what were you going to say to me? She questioned. "Me? Yes you! "It's not important now." You have a wonderful trip and give my condolences to your dad". "Thanks, I will, Billy we'll talk again soon" disconnecting her line. "Hey girl, are you ready for that big ski trip? Carin asked seeing she was off the phone and coming toward their table where she and Madison sat having morning coffee. "I was but I'm headed to New Orleans with my dad". What? You chose your dad over all that man! Carin asked surprised at what Nada was telling them. 'Hey anything worth having is worth waiting on" she said gathering her materials and briefcase heading to her classroom. She was really looking forward to being with Billy, though she really didn't want to rush things. She wanted a lasting relationship and so far, they were building that she thought happily.

Tetra and David sat talking in their great room when Alfredo came in to let them know he was leaving for the evening, and would be heading out early morning for his unplanned trip to New Orleans, to a friend's home going. "I'm heading out now," he said coming in from the kitchen. "Oh, David said getting up from his chair coming toward him. "I wish you a wonderful trip though I know the occasion is a sad one". Thank you, sir," It will be wonderful to see old friends and even though I heard not much has been done there, it is something I look forward to seeing" Alfredo admitted. Tetra stood and gave him a friendly hug and David shook his hand. "God Bless you" both said standing in their door waving as he left going to his bungalow. His flight was leaving very early in the morning. His daughter Nada accompanying him was coming to drive him to the airport for two weeks stay in New Orleans their hometown.

CHAPTER 23

Revisiting a disaster

Billy had committed to a ski trip with his old friend in Kansas, so he decided to go asking Dana along. He thought to himself how tacky to bring Dana, but I'm trying get married and if it is to be Dana then so be it! He reasoned putting his carryon luggage in the overhead compartment. Dana was really trying to be everything Billy wanted. They had dinner every night since she came back from Europe. The whole week she worked hard at keeping him happy, she admitted it to one of her close friends at the hospital. Skiing was really not her thing but if Billy wanted to go then she would come along. "I hope I brought enough warm clothing for the week," she voiced sitting next to Billy on the plane trip to Kansas. He had plans of seeing Desmond his old buddy from Harvard while he was there. But since Mostaliga his wife, Billy understood was visiting family in Yugoslavia, he'd wait to see. Dana laid her head on Billy's shoulder, as they flew the friendly skies, to a wonderful week of skiing on the Snowcap Mountains, at the beautiful resort.

Meanwhile Nada and her dad were landing in the state of New Orleans, amiss all the ruins of devastation they had left behind. Nada hurried over to the Avis rental counter right out side of the terminal, and quickly secured a reserved automobile, getting their entire load of luggage in the trunk and off they went. "Nada are you planning on staying here? Her dad asked seriously as they drove along. "No dad, what would cause you to ask that? She responded driving speedily down the highway. "Just looking at all that luggage we put in the car," he said laughing hard at what he was saying. "Well dad, for your information, a lady never knows what she's going to wear". "Well you won't have that problem, now will you? he continued laughing. Leaving the airport, they soon were in downtown in the main business district. "Turn at the corner their Nada," her dad suggested as she drove slowly through what was now the French Quarters. Continuing on slowly down to Bourbon Street they could see where many business owners were trying to put their lives back together. "Stop for a minute dear" Alfredo said looking at the hallowed-out building, that was once his restaurant. Nada pulled the car to the side of the street and parked. Alfredo sat for a moment before getting out walking around to the entrance. Looking around, you could see some businesses were up and running again. While some like the restaurant he once owned, was left abandon, after the terrible floods. Alfredo looked around for a minute through the opened windows. Nada watched as he wiped a tear from his cheek more than once. "Dad are you alright?" she asked as she stood looking through an opened window of one of the near by buildings. "I'm fine dear, lets go" he replied walking around to the passenger side to get in. "FRANCOIS! FRANCOIS! He turned to see a gentleman running toward him from across the street. FRANCOIS it is you! now standing directly in front of him. "Pierre! Oh, my you're all right! He exclaimed hugging this small gentleman wearing a chef's hat. "You too sir, I thought I never see you again! They were both very excited that each were okay. "Oh, dear Nada it's good to see you too" he said turning to embrace her as she stood beside her dad. Nada returned the affection causing a tear to fall from her cheek. Pierre saw her grow up into a woman. He was the head chef at her father's restaurant for many years. "Mario said he thought he saw you over here". I thought he was joking me again" but it's really you!" The small gentleman exclaimed as he jumped around in the street. Alfredo looked to see smiling faces staring at them from across the way. "Yes, and you made it out safely too. How's the family? Alfredo asked. Pierre put his head down. Alfredo lifted it up. "The children are all fine" he nodded with a smile but we lost momma" he confessed sadly. "Oh Pierre, I'm so sorry to hear that" choked up embracing his dear friend again. After Pierre stood for a moment and composed himself, he suggested, "Come, come have lunch we can talk," he said looking up to speak with Alfredo to his face. "Nada? Her dad asked, getting her opinion on the matter. "Sounds good," she said making her way across the street after securing the car and getting her purse. "Come we eat! leading them across the street for lunch of Creole cuisine, and conversation with old friends, who cheered and greeted them warmly as they walked through the doors of the neighboring restaurant.

Doris was singing happily around her home awaiting her decorator. She was having Sonjee a room redecorated especially for her. Doris was ecstatic that her daughter was moving to Los Angeles to attend college and to be with her. She knew she would be getting a place near campus, because Sonjee had shared that with her. But she wanted her to have a home to come to also. "My lady the phone is for you it's Miss Sonjee" Finley voiced. "Oh, and my lady I'll be out for an hour, or so, at the men's meeting" he shared heading to the door. "That's right, is Russell planning to be there too? "Yes! My lady, he is conducting this one" Finley replied proudly heading out of the door. "Have a great time! She yelled putting the receiver to her ear. 'Hello dear! 'Hi! How are you doing? Sonjee asked gleefully. "I'm just wonderful and you?' "I'm fine, I'm here with daddy right now visiting him for a while, he's teaching me how to score a golf game! She said laughing at the thought. "In turn I get to teach him some of my dance moves" she added still laughing. So, are you ready for my move to the big city?" "Oh, Sonjee I can't wait! My decorator will be here in an hour, I'm decorating your room! "My room" But I shared I had found a place near campus, through our campus directory". "I know, that's wonderful, if that's what you want, but you still can have a room at home" she said hesitantly hoping Sonjee would approve. "Wow, thank you! Thank you, very much" I'm overwhelmed! Sonjee replied pausing, relieved Doris is openly accepting her move and she was content. "Godmother, daddy would like to speak with you." "Sure, I'd love to speak with him also." "Hello Doris," "Dr. Reeves, it's good to hear your voice". "Please take good care of my little girl" is how he started his conversation.

David Michael had gotten back to his dorm room after a very intense practice with his baseball team. "Hey Kyle, a few of us guys are going downtown to that club! Wanna come? his roommate asked walking out of the dorm with yet another girl. "No man I'm exhausted all I want is to sleep peacefully through the night". "Well okay but you're going to miss out". "True, probably true, but we have got to win this championship for the uni man" and I have got to sacrifice for this one" David Michael replied. "Call me later if you need me to send one your way". "Yeah got it, have fun" closing himself in the dorm room flopping on his bed before getting up taking a very long shower.

Billy and Dana had settled in the very posh resort ski lodge in Kansas, and he stood looking out at the gorgeous snowcapped mountain-view from their window. "Wow this is magnificent" "Look darling". She came over and stood in front of him and he put his arms around her waist. "It is beautiful" she conferred. "Dana we're alone now, I'm truly hoping we can resolve some issues and get on with our relationship," he said squeezing her tightly as she stood happily in his arm. "Umm now the truth comes out about this trip," she teased. "No, that's not the only reason I asked you here" he said moving away across the room. "I'm listening," she said turning to face him in an inquisitive manner. "Dana will you marry me? "Ha! Ha! Ha! Who are you kidding?' I know you're making fun of me because I totally disagree on the church thing". She said getting her ski jacket from the closet heading to the door. "No Dana, this is real, I HAVE FEELINGS FOR YOU, AND I want to marry you," he pleaded almost with her. "Billy I'll be right back, I need to get some air, and something from the gift store at the lodge," and walk out still laughing at what she knew to be a joke. Unfortunately, Billy was serious about his proposal and thought she would change after marriage, even after all he had read and heard about relationships. He wanted a commitment from Dana. He cared for Nada, but he was willing to give her up and make a good marriage with Dana. Sadly, he put the very expensive diamond ring back in his pocket, disappointed in Dana's love and commitment, but felt free now to pursue Nada. Knowing for certain Dana had not changed.

Nada and her dad left Bourbon Street headed to the downtown area where most blacks lived, including Mother Phillips's once small home. They understood from Pastor Ridgeway that it had washed away in the floods, and she had been put in a senior residential care facility, since that fatal disaster that struck the nation. A year since the disaster things still looked pretty much the same. Abandon structures, dilapidated buildings, debris scattered all around showing signs of things that once belonged to families now in ruins. If they found anyone still there it was a miracle! Sad to say though almost everyone living there, had been scattered all over the United States. The home going of Maudie Phillips was still two days away, so they decided to visit Canal Street, the business district. Things there, they could see were coming back together more rapidly. The residences that had survived the storm were getting their lives back on track. Some were going about their day-to-day lives shopping with armloads of packages from the department stores. Slowly driving along looking at their once thriving city Alfredo was feeling a bit tired from the long plane trip. "Dad lets ride by my old apartment then head to our room alright? Nada asked seeing he was tiring and somewhat heartbroken in all he had seen. Sure dear! He acknowledged seeing she really wanted to go by there. "Ah! It was a breath of fresh air Alfredo thought. Nada's apartment was west of downtown in and area known as Uptown. It was also near the family home where she had grown up with her mom and dad. Nada lived in the Garden District one of the oldest and most famous neighbors in New Orleans. "The gardens are still as beautiful as I remember! Nada said stopping the car aside of the road to reflect. Nada always had a love for the neighborhood going by it everyday heading to Tulane University her alma mater. "Look daddy! She said pointing up to her old window. "My flowerbox mom and I planted, is still blooming" she said smiling. Alfredo acknowledged by wiping tears that had formed in his eyes. The lower part of the buildings still had boards over the windows. Looking around there were construction crews working busily throughout restoring the once beautiful city back to life. Both stood for a moment in an embrace looking around the area. A few hellos's at passersbys and waves from other smiling faces before getting back in their car and heading to the hotel room. Alfredo decided to rest for a while in his room at the Sheraton Inn and Nada headed to the Xavier University where she once worked as a professor for three years. Upon her arrival Nada went into the main office. "Hello! She said to the lady who had her back turned to the counter going through some paperwork. She turned to respond coming toward the counter adjusting her eyeglasses. "Flo! It's Nada!" she said excitedly seeing her friend coming to the counter. "Nada, oh Nada! She responded coming from behind the counter and running over to embrace her. "My! My! It's good to see you again, how are you doing? She asked not taking a break between sentences. "I'm wonderful and you look great! Nada acknowledged after hugging her and looking at her smiling face. "So, what brings you back? Are you here to stay? She asked. "Oh no, we're here for Mother Phillips funeral. "Oh, I see, I did hear about that". "It's good to see you, most of our professors are still here they would love to see you" are you staying around for a while? "Sure, I'll head over to the lounge, it's close to break time isn't it. "It sure is but I'll announce it so everyone who wants will get a chance to see you? Is that all right? She asked again hugging Nada and smiling going back behind her counter. See ya there! She acknowledged waving as Nada walked out the door to meet more old friends in the faculty lounge of the prestigious university.

Billy and Dana enjoyed the day on the slopes neither were avid skiers but could handle the run pretty well. "Dana be careful on this one it tends to run very fast" he said coming up beside her on the slope. "All right" is all that came out before she fell head on into a roll landing on the bottom before stopping. "Dana! Dana! Are you okay? Billy asked hurriedly skiing down to aid her. "WHEW! That was some fall," she laughed. "So, you're alright? I wasn't going to laugh until I knew you were alright," he said starting a laugh both shared. Billy was still laughing as he helped her up and brushed the snow from her shoulders and her mink fur hat she sported on the slopes. "You're laughing now just wait I noticed your skiing skills buddy! She teased. Back on the ski's the two started back up to the top of the lift to do it all again. "Let's go! And off they went. They were enjoying the fun of the day but as night fell tension set in for Billy. He had made a fool of himself earlier proposing to Dana who thought it only to be a joke. She flirted with him throughout the day just knowing at night he would be hers for the asking. After a long hot shower for the both of them Dana curled up on the sofa waiting for his affection. "Dana I'm heading out to the lodge for a while shouldn't be to long" he shared turning the knob to leave. "I'm tired I thought we were staying in tonight near this cozy fire I made for us". A bottle of our favorite champagne and soft music won't entice you? She asked getting up walking toward him provocatively to the door. "I'll be back" closing the door and heading to sit at the bar in the main lodge having ginger ale. When he decided she was fast asleep he returned to the cabin. The rest of the week was pretty much the same with him evading Dana's advances all together. "Okay, so tell me why are you treating me like a red head step child? She asked going into the living room where he sat early in the morning drinking coffee. "Dana what are you talking about? He questioned back as if he didn't know. "You stay out until I'm fast asleep and most mornings are gone before I get up! And in case you hadn't noticed you've made this sofa your bed in the living room! She scowled. "Dana I just can't keep letting you do this to us! "Do what? What are you making references to now? She asked going over to pour a cup of coffee and sitting in the big cozy chair. "It's simple, I want commitment! He replied now pacing the floor. "Oh, is this about that foolish seminar again! She stammered getting up leaving the room. Billy sat quietly for a moment. "Dana I will not compromise my values to be with you" "You think sex is the answer for everything and it's not! "Will you ever understand that? He yelled to her from the living room. SHUT UP BILLY PARKER! Was heard before a very loud slamming of the bedroom door TO EXPRESS HER DISAGREEMENT ON THE MATTER!

CHAPTER 24

It made a difference

Sonjee had most of her luggage bag packed and what she hadn't given to her closest friends she had packed in boxes for shipment to L.A. "Sonjee let's go over for one last burger before the year ends! Angie yelled up to her dorm window. "Sure, hold on a minute I'm putting my tennis shoes on I'll be right down" she yelled back. Sonjee grabbed her jacket and headed out to the Burger shack with her friends. When they arrived, they noticed a large crowd was gathered around. "Hey! What's going on? Angie asked someone she knew standing in the crowd. Tina and Sonjee had made their way to the window to order burgers. As they walked back to meet Angie they heard, really! Are you kidding me! Last night! WHAT ANGIE? Tina questioned. That was all that commotion we heard last night" remember when I woke you and you hit me saying it goes on all the time" Fonsworth and Chipper were in a bad accident and hit that tree over there! She said excitedly. Sonjee ran over with Tina, Angie and her informant close behind. "Look right here" the guy said pointing to the paint the car had left on the tree. "I heard the car was smashed up pretty badly," he added. "Tina they're calling your number! Someone yelled from across the street. Tina turned to go back across the street. Sonjee! Sonjee! She asked before tapping her back to reality. "You want me to get your burger?" Sure, here's my money" she said still standing staring off into space. She had been in Oregon visiting her dad and drove back early this morning and clearly had missed all of this excitement. Had she been in her dorm she would have heard it all she thought as she hurriedly left Tina and Angie still standing in the crowd heading to her car. SONJEE! SONJEE! They yelled.

Billy knew things with Dana were not going to go well but he still invited her to join Desmond and he on the slopes. Of course, as expected she angrily turned him down. Desmond had drove up for the day from his home in Langley Estate. He lives in Kansas so the hour drive to meet and old friend was a no brainier for him. "Des how was the ride up? Billy asked as Desmond stepped out of his black shiny Hummer. "Great, I've come to love it up here" the air is so fresh and clean" he said taking in a deep breath. "Man, how long as it been? They shared a manly hug. "How's the family? Billy asked. Then added how many are there now? with a smile in his voice. "All four of them are fine," he laughed back in a fatherly manner. "And you? How's David Michael" "He's great a sophomore in college, loving that game of baseball still". "No! When you two were here before he was what in junior high?" Desmond smiled "My how time flies" "Let's head up to the main lodge for a cup of coffee to warm up before hitting the slopes. "Wow sounds good! I can't believe we're actually going to spend time together that's not court related" Desmond confided as the two former Harvard grads went to the ski lodge for coffee and conversation.

Sonjee slowly made her way into the crowded elevator going up to the third floor arriving at the intensive care unit. She noticed it was very quiet and there was little to no movement of anyone that was visible. She looked around and slowly peeked through the door. Besides all of the machinery and tubes that was visible she saw nurses moving around setting gages and checking patience's Sonjee reasoned. She got up on her tipped toes trying to see if she saw Fonsworth. "Why was she here? She wondered. He had caused her so many restless nights and bad dreams but for some unknown reason she still cared. She had to know he was all right. "Drinking! I told him it was not good," she stammered again around the entry door. Giving up after very little success in seeing through the small window Sonjee sat in one of the chairs with her head down. "Hey! Someone lightly tapped her on her head. She slowly looked up into the face of a delicate blonde hair blue eyed woman. "Oh, I'm sorry" Sonjee replied jumping up from her seat. "Oh, it doesn't madder," she said with her strong African dialect. Sonjee knew then she must be African. I know who you are," she said looking with a smile on her face. "You know who I am? Sonjee asked looking at her. "Yes, my son wrote many ledders bout you". Sonjee was surprised but said nothing. "He wanted me to tell his fodder bout you" He knew his fodder would never except his black African queen is what he say to me." His fodder is very proud and I hate to admit stuck in his ways". "He would never give Fonsworth his blessings for you" she confessed now sitting beside Sonjee. "But how do you know? Sonjee searched for words to say to this woman whom she had just laid eyes on. "Oh, besides your dreads" she smiled "a mutter knows". "How is he? She finally asked the reason she had driven all that way across town to the hospital. "His fodder is in with him now" they say if he lives much rehabilitation is needed." "Oh, I'm sorry to hear that". Sonjee replied looking for a comforting word to share. "Yes, yes that's what they say" but I serve a higher God who has the finally answer" she said going back toward the intensive care door. "I tell him you were here," she voiced closing the door. "Kachifo" Sonjee replied quietly. She then pushed the button on the elevator. After getting in she cried all the way back to her dorm room.

Nada and her dad arrived early at the small Baptist church that had withstood the mighty floodwaters. They drove in slowly parking off a way as not to be blocked in while trying to leave in time for their planned flight home. Where Nada had parked the car, they had a view of the cemetery only a mile away. After a short discussion and of course being quite early they decided to visit it for a while. "Okay daddy, are you sure you're ready? Nada asked as they walked up the narrow path of road leading to it. He couldn't bear to visit his wife's grave in the past saying he did not want to remember her that way. Nada held his hand tightly. She could feel the sweat starting to bead up in it. "Daddy are you sure? She asked again meeting Cyrus Greedly coming from the other way. "Hello, Mr. Frances" he said greeting the two of them. "Cyrus sir it's good to see you sir, Alfredo said giving the elderly gentleman a hug. And this yo lil girl? He asked lovingly. "Yes, sir this is my daughter Nada. "Please to meet you ma'am," he replied reaching to tilt his worn hat from his head. Nada smiled and gave him a hug also.

Daddy knows lots of people she smiled to herself. "Going up? he asked throwing his head to point the direction of the cemetery. "Yes, for a little while", Alfredo replied. "Yeah, I was just up talking with Bertha." Ya gotta look pass all the mess up there" he said "them waters sho messed thangs up around these parts" "I agree sir, are you still living here? Did your home survive? "Oh no, everything I ever worked fo is gone". We's down in West Texas now with Bessie Mae". "Oh, I see, well I relocated to Washington". Washington? Uh uh" he laughed, "so you up there, wit the president? "Oh no sir" Alfredo replied Washington State is where I live", correcting the geographical area. "Well alright, let me let you, git on up there" not much to see now alls dim pretty flowers done gone. Some of the headstones been broke by something I reckon." He shook their hands and started on down slowly. "Hey Mr. Frances? "Yes sir," Alfredo turned to the old gentleman to give him is undivided attention. "Remember she's in a better place now! He yelled. "Thanks sir, I'll remember that," Alfredo responded as he and Nada made their way to his wife gravestone. After looking for a while they discovered it covered under mud.

Billy and Desmond had a wonderful time on the ski slopes and enjoyed warm lasting conversations about careers, family, and reminiscing the past years of their lives. Desmond had met Dana when he arrived. Billy introduced them when he asked if she wanted to accompany them out for the day. Desmond felt since he had interfered in the ski outing, he would at least thank her and apologize for taking her ski buddy. "Not really necessary man" Billy shared but if you feel you have to, be my guest". He thought he had honestly explained the whole situation to Desmond on the slopes. "Man, it just wouldn't be right to just leave" he acknowledged coming in the door behind Billy. DANA! DANA! She must be at the lodge man, really it's not that big of a deal". Alright if you say so, but I know women". "Yeah! Give my love to Mossy and the children" I'll do it! With a manly embrace and let's talk soon, Desmond was gone. Billy sat in the cabin for a while using this time alone to listen to all of Nada's sweet voicemails, she left on his cell phone. After a while he reasoned he should find out where Dana was. The night air was starting to set in so he went to the closet to get a jacket to put on and there it was. She had written in bright red lipstick on the bedroom's closet mirrored doors. "ENJOY THE REST OF YOUR VACATION. GOT A FLIGHT HOME! DANA, she was gone. The lodge confirmed she had indeed left in an airport taxi at 2 0' clock pm. Desmond and he were probably still inside the lodge at the time having coffee.

Nada and her dad stayed by her mom's graveside clearing it off with water from a nearby water fountain. After a time, they both headed back down the path to the church. "Dad it's amazing these houses are still standing after all that water" she stated walking pass a small house sitting off the road by itself. "How do! Someone waved from the porch as they walked by. "Hello! responding to the greeting with a smile and a wave. A few more steps they were in the car and headed back to the church. Pulling up they could see others had started coming. The small church looked to hold maybe fifty to seventy-five people comfortably Nada thought as they made their way in to sit on the long wooden benches. "Why did they pick this place? Nada asked whispering to her dad. Alfredo was ready to give her an answer when up walked Reverend Thaddeus Augustus Ridgeway the pastor. "Good morning sir" he greeted Alfredo." "Good morning Pastor Ridgeway" he said getting up to embrace his former pastor. "It's good to see you! And my look at little Nada" "Hi pastor Ridgeway" she voiced reaching to shake his hand. "Now it's so unfortunate that we are coming together for this but it's certainly good you came back home," the pastor confessed. "Yes, pastor we wouldn't have missed it for the world." Maudie Phillips was a God sent to my family" he added. "Well, I know that to be true. But what I don't know is how we're going to put all these people in here" he laughed. "But it was what Maudie wanted her children said" As the two stood talking and reminiscing the times some more huge flower arrangements were being brought in. The ladies in very large hats and Sunday outfits were making their way down front to the first pew. "Excuse me Alfredo I'm going to look over the sermon" shaking his hand. "Hope to talk with you later" he stated walking across the church and through a closed door on the side of the pulpit. "Excuse me! Sorry, could be heard as other's began crowding into this over crowded space. The benches along the back wall were filled. The faithful ushers had sat out extra folding chairs in all the space available and yet they kept coming. When the music started for the processional of the coffin into the church it was standing room only in the small corridor. Pastor Ridgeway dawned a long white robe and led the six pallbearers in black suits and ties carrying the beautiful white coffin Maudie had pick out, and paid for, all by herself. After the coffin was positioned in front of the pulpit her three children and the family were escorted in. The choir stand was behind the pulpit and was filled with the faithful choir members whom she had heard sing praises every Sunday she attended. Nada looked at her daughters and thought about when she had sat in that position only a few years ago. Though her mother died of cancer at age fifty-nine Maudie lived to be ninety-four before God called her home. After the choir sang her favorite songs Pastor Ridgeway stood to read her favorite passage of scripture. He was a grandson of the church's founder. His grandfather was the pastor after his great-grandfather Thaddeus's father, was skipped over. He said it was because of behavioral issues he missed out on the family jewel. "I would apologize for being in this small place but it's where Maudie wanted to go home". "Most of you knew Maudie was a schoolteacher to most of our children, grandchildren, and even great grandchildren". There was a quiet laughter that spread throughout. "Well! What some of you may not know is that Maudie taught her first students right here in this church". Build in the late 1800's the church served as a one-room school. It had one teacher who taught all grades. Of course, it has been renovated somewhat but still it only holds about hundred people comfortably. So please bear with us". Nada looked over at her dear friend Katherine one of Maudie's youngest daughters. Maudie had made a career for herself before deciding to marry and have children. Maudie had her first child in her late thirties. That for most was late in life. Sitting behind her Nada put her hand on her shoulder to comfort her as she wiped her eyes of tears. Reverend Ridgeway then asked for words from the Superintendent who has since retired but was on the school board and knew Maudie Phillips personally. "I wouldn't have missed this day for anything". She stated after being helped up to the front of the small church. "I know, this is exactly what she wanted" she giggled "everyone in a school of learning". She then caused laughter in the room that was healing for the soul. "Maudie wouldn't want us crying" "She said by being a teacher she'd live on through others. "I see

Maudie what you were saying, I see!" she said looking around the many that had come to be a part of Maudie Phillips's home going. When she had completed her say that became very emotional for her near the end speaking of her love for Maudie, how tenacious she was for equal rights, and her challenging the school board more than once! There wasn't a dry eye to be found. As she was being escorted back to her seat those who could stood and applauded her. Pastor Ridgeway asked for 2 min comments that lasted for about fifteen minutes before he again went behind the pulpit. The choir then sang "I going up yonder to be with my Lord". Pastor read a scripture and talked about a lady who lived her funeral. "Just look around," he said reaching his arms out to the over crowded congregation. "What and impact she had on so many lives." When he concluded and the crowds began to view Maudie Phillips remains for the last time. The single line seemed to go on forever, as each wanted one more look on a lady who made a difference!

CHAPTER 25

A bold stand

Billy arrived home earlier than planned and was up sitting in his office when his office staff arrived to start the day. "Good morning! each said as they passed his office door near the conference room. "Good morning! You're back early one finally said. "Yes, but no complaints about the skiing, it was wonderful! 'The lifts were not overcrowded and the packed powder on the slopes couldn't have been more perfect." he said sharing a cup of coffee with one of his staff attorneys. "Sounds fun, look I will be in court most of the day" and Annie should be here shortly." She said she was coming in late but Keith may know definitely,' he stated heading to his office down the hall. "That's fine I have lots of paperwork and briefs to go over I'll stay busy," Billy turned heading into his spacious office to work. "He liked his lifestyle he had built for himself. Of course, his parents and grandparents had left him worry free in the finance department. Along with other assets he owned the law firm that had four of the best lawyers in Maine he 'd brag. He sat down at his desk going through his email when his personal line rang. Annie still had not come in. "Hello, Dad glad I caught you, I left several voicemails on your cell!" his son said very excitedly. "Whoa son, what's going on? he asked the overly excited voice. "WE MADE THE PLAYOFFS DAD! WE MADE IT! "Hey congratulations, I watched that last game you guys were down three to zero." "YEAH you're right but you gave up and stop watching but we didn't. "Mays hit a grounder ball that loaded the bases for us and Ray hit a homer to put us up by one! "Okay but there was still another ending. Our pitcher struck out their next two batters but the third hit a long fly to the fence AND I CAUGHT IT DAD! Wow! Sorry I missed that" feeling equally as proud for his son. "Well we're still celebrating here." "Think you might make some games?" "Son from now on I won't miss any part," he stated, whether on television or in person." "I'm very proud of you! He added. "Thanks dad". "Did you talk with Dana? "Yeah, she said she'd come but something always comes up", you know dad" he confessed. "Well don't worry I'll be there and probably the loudest cheering section in the stands" laughing and causing his son to laugh at his antics over the phone. Oh dad! Aunt Doris and Mr. Finley were at the game, she's doing much better now". "Son that's great, Okay dad gotta go, my fans await! He shared. "Have fun love ya! hanging up the phone. Then Billy sat for a moment smiling before calling his dad who had witnessed the game play and was certainly going to be in the stands when the playoffs opened.

The gathering after Maudie Phillips home going was held at a huge new state of the arts Living Life Center near the dome. Room and food were not an issue. Several local restaurants had volunteered to cater the re-pass and thought it to be an honor to be asked. It was decorated beautifully. Many of the flower arrangements were sent there since this church was much larger. Many were there already when Nada and her dad arrived from the grave sight with the family to share their loss. My goodness! Nada expressed walking into the room with her dear friend who was a principal at one of the local high schools. Nada! Nada! She turned to see Renetta yelling her name from across the large dining hall. "Hi Renetta, she said embracing her old friend. "I saw you at the church, but I was outside I came late". "Yo daddy came with you? "How long you been here? Not long" Nada replied keeping her answers very specific. "Colvin traveling right now he told me last time he was through". Hey, so when you leaving? "Not sure yet, I'll be here, look let me see what Rita needs and I'll see you hopefully before I leave,

"Nada stated walking back to the family now sitting at the table. "Mother was a go getter" she heard Rita say as she approached the table. Rita stood proudly shaking hands and hugging well- wishers. The southern food was not in short order. There were reds beans and rice, catfish, collard greens and mustard greens, dirty rice and jambalaya and fried chicken, barbeque ribs, sweet potato pies, banana pudding and many more Cajun dishes for anyone's pallet. Family and friends again gathered to celebrate a legacy that had influenced many lives. After prayer from Pastor Ridegeway everyone sat down to their choices of entrées with the room buzzing with laughter and sharing. Nada wanted to share her experience in knowing Mother Phillips. "Well she smiled looking at her friend. "Rita and I got lots of whippings from her mother and my mother" she laughed. "Mama would call her when we were anywhere downtown" I don't know how they did it" I know they didn't have cell phones! She caused much laughter. "Mother Phillips would call mama when I even thought to do wrong at school" she continued. I didn't see it then but I most certainly appreciated it now". "She will live on! Looking up Nada added holding Rita's hand. "Rest in peace"

Dana had seen her first client for the day and sat reading through a medical journal awaiting a conference in the large boardroom downstairs. She calendared her son's event for his baseball game since she had spoken with him last evening about it. Reasoning that Billy his dad needs to stop whimpering over commitment and attending church she will steer clear of him until he sees things her way. When in walked a gentleman. "Howdy miss," he said standing outside looking into the opened door. "Dana looked up and smile. "Hey! She teased, "What brings you this way? "Well just stopping in to say hello" was over across the way seeing my doctor". "Oh, Dana expressed concern "is everything alright?" "According to my doctor everything is peachy king! Just my annual" you know! "Well that's good to hear," she confessed. "Been to the Corral lately? He asked. "I haven't, I've been distracted with a lot of things but I do need to relax more or I'll need a doctor" she shared smiling. "Well don't know if you heard but Brooks is supposed to be there Friday night". "Really! You're telling me Garth is going to be on my doorstep and I hadn't heard. "Okay I admit it I've been working to hard" she said standing coming from behind her desk. "What's the chances at this point of getting tickets?" Dana asked. "SOLD OUT I'm told! He said looking at the disappointment on her face. "But I got a couple extra ones if you need it! He smiled pulling then from his jeans pocket. "Oh thanks! Snatching the priceless tickets, he held up in his hand and hugging him placing a kiss on his cheek. "Not a problem see yaw there! He noted with a wave and was gone. "Um that was very nice," she said of her new friend the dancing cowboy.

Nada and her dad pulled away heading to the airport after spending a glorious week in New Orleans ending with old friends who were still there near the French Quarters. Pierre had brought the family by to see them off also. "We keep in touch no! He asked saying again goodbye. Nada pulled slowly down the street and stopped to watch a small gathering of girls playing along the sidewalk. As she listened, she heard some familiar words. "Jimmy crack corn and I don't care, Jimmy cracked corn and I don't care, Jimmy cracked corn and I don't care, the master's gone away! Shoe fly don't bother me, shoe fly don't bother me, shoe fly don't bother me, for I belong to somebody! "Daddy, do you know it was Mother Phillips who taught us what that song was about". "I believe it dear, she taught us all," he responded smiling as they drove out the city to the airport for a return flight home.

Nada waved as her dad's flight left heading for Washington State. She had another hour before her flight left heading to Maine to visit Billy. "No daddy I'll be fine, he knows I'm coming, and I will call as soon as I arrive, and you do the same okay," she said to her concerned dad about leaving her in the airport alone. She hadn't spoken with Billy; he wasn't answering any calls. Surely, he was probably upset because she changed plans on him at the last minute! Calling again at his office she got his secretary Annie.

"Yes, Mr. Parker is in but asked not to be disturbed". Not being pushy Nada thanked her and proceeded with her plans now putting her carry on above her head and reclining her first-class seat. "This is bold Nada! She thought to herself as she flew high in the heavens. "What if you" What are you thinking you'd better call! She dialed, her thoughts in her head were screaming loud. "Hello! the voice happily answered on the other end. "Hi, Mrs. Parker, this is Nada". 'Oh, hello dear is everything alright?" "Oh yes everything is fine" she said hesitantly. "Um okay" Tetra paused. "Daddy should be there shortly. His flight left about two hours ago". "Dear aren't you coming back too? She asked concerned. "Well I thought I would spend my last week visiting Maine." Tetra now had a clear picture of where this was going but said nothing. "I felt so bad canceling our ski trip, so I'm headed there, think it's alright?" she squeamishly asked. "Well have you spoken with Billy? Tetra asked. "No, his secretary said he was very busy and asked not to be disturbed". "Oh, I see, well dear you go on with your plans, I mean it would be silly now that you're on your way already". "I'll call and if there's a problem I'll call back." "Thanks Mrs. Parker" she smiled. "Sure, enjoy your visit" hanging up and immediately calling her son's office. Tetra called his private line no answer and cell phone's voicemail was full. "Parker attorneys at law the voice answered. "Hello Annie, how are you? "Mrs. Parker? She questioned. "Yes, dear is Billy in? "Not at the moment but he will be back in about and hour or so. He had an unexpected trip to make down at the courthouse". "Well, two things dear" have him clear his messages mailbox from his cell phone, they both laughed it wasn't the first time. And have him please call his mother." "I will Mrs. Parker, Annie affirmed. Tetra put the receiver back on the phone. "With Dana being in Maine, one can only pray! She said dialing Nada back but only reaching a voice that informed her to try her call later.

CHAPTER 26

A New start

Doris looked again with her decorator over the beautifully decorated space. "MY LADY! Finley yelled excitedly Ms. Sonjee's things are here," he said coming in to meet her in the room. "My it looks like a palace" he shared touching all the elegant wood pieces of furnishings and silk drapes the decorator had used to embody the feel of this magnificent space. It mirrors Doris' exquisite taste shown throughout her fabulous Beverly Hills home, Finley could clearly see. "Think she will like it? She said holding Finley's hand showing him the huge walk-in closet and tile she had chosen for the adjoining bathroom. "Oh yes, knowing Ms. Sonja, she'll love every inch! He stated causing a smile on Doris's face and the flamboyantly dressed Mr. Designer. "Wonderful! he stated heading out the room behind Doris. "Finley have them bring all her things in here". "Yes, My lady!" Finley was so happy for Doris; her once lonely miserable existence of a workaholic was going to be filled with much laughter from Ms. Sonjee. Doris had become very involved in her church and Finley thought she needed someone close to her besides him. She and Russell had a few dinners out together but being a very private person, she kept everyone at bay. Ms. Sonjee! Perfect, he said as he handed out instructions on getting her belongings she had shipped to her home.

Tetra was still waiting for her son to return her call when Nada's flight landed in Maine. After landing she turned her cell phone back on after following flight instructions of turning it off at certain times before landing. "Good! She sighed no message from Mrs. Parker. Getting her luggage, and reserved car, she pulled into a gas station to set her gps system. After getting the address from Billy's business card "whew she sighed, thank God for directions!" she confessed pulling out of the station headed to Billy's office. With the modern technology of the GPS system Nada was pulling into the law firm's parking lot within forty-five minutes. "Not bad for never having been here! She said nervously getting out and walking into the huge building that held the law office. After getting instructions from the clerk at the front desk, she pushed the button on the elevator. The ride up seemed to go faster than her thoughts wanted it to. "Okay one last sigh before walking in. "Good afternoon," Annie greeted her standing confidently in front of her desk. "Yes, William Parker please," she stated in an "I have business" tone. "Mr. Parker is in a meeting, is he expecting you? Annie asked to clarify matters. "No, he isn't, but I need to speak with him, is it possible you could let him know I'm here," handing Annie one of her business cards. "Just a moment, you may have a seat in there, I will be right back". Annie voiced going to her phone at the desk. Annie called Billy's line. "Billy there's someone here to see you and did you remember to call your mother". "I didn't thanks, for the reminder, can you bring in the folders for the cases that are on the court docket tomorrow" he asked and hung up. Annie looked over at Nada sitting down reading a magazine as she patiently waited for William who was probably not going to see her anyway, she reasoned. She gathered all the file folders Billy had requested and headed quickly into the meeting. Tapping lightly on the office door she walked in. "Thanks Annie" he said before she began falling backward onto a chair. Billy and Keith both jumped to aid her. "Annie are you alright? They asked in unison. "I'm fine, just a little lightheaded sweetheart" she shared with Keith. "I'd better get some lunch" she voiced. Billy came over with a cup of cold water handing it to her. As she reached for the cup of water, he noticed her diamond wedding ring. She looked and then covered her face as she drank. The very concerned Keith was giving attention to her every need. "When were you two going to tell me? He asked smiling at them. "Keith wanted to immediately, but I asked him not to". You've been going through so much with Dana I didn't want to bother you" she said now feeling better but still sitting getting attention from Keith her husband. "So, you two are married? "Yes, in a small ceremony of family and a few friends". O I see! No Billy it's not like that" It actually came sooner than we expected. "They looked at each other. We're having a baby! WHAT! Congratulations! Really I am happy for the both of you" he admitted hugging Annie and shaking Keith's hand. "Now you two get out of here and go to lunch, we can finish this briefing later or I'll do it myself" he acknowledged opening his door for the smiling couple to leave. "Thanks William" Annie said standing in the hall outside of his door waiting for Keith to come back with their coats from his office. "Hey don't mention it, you take care of yourself." Thank you, I will". Billy stood watching Keith assist her with her coat and turned to go back in his office. "William! She yelled softly, I almost forgot, you have someone waiting to see you". Me! Is it a client"? "I didn't get that impression from her but she's sitting in the lounge up front." The card Annie must have left on her desk when she pulled the files. "Okay you two have a good time I'll take care of the person out front". Billy walked past Annie's desk and down the long hall. When he got close to the waiting area, he hesitated a moment before going in. He was not expecting anyone today. "Nada! How long have you been sitting here? Oh, it doesn't matter come down to my office". "It's so good to see you! William was surprised Nada thought. "Good surprise, but nevertheless surprised. Whew! She exhaled as she walked into his beautiful decorated office space. "So, when did you arrive in Maine? Sit down, here give me your things" reaching for her briefcase and overcoat she was holding. "I've been here about and hour and a half". "You've been sitting out there for and hour and a half! "No, I've been in Maine that long most was spent getting my luggage and the car." Why didn't you call? 'I tried, first your secretary informed me you asked not to be disturbed and your voicemail is full!" "Oh, sorry about that bad habit of mine". "I have been so busy, my mother even called and I haven't gotten back to her either if that tells you where I'm at" he confided. "She was calling to let you know that I was coming". "Wow I sure messed that up, didn't I?" He asked needing a comforting word right now. "Don't feel bad, everything worked out. The GPS system is a God sent to women! She admitted with a smile. "So why didn't you return any of my calls earlier in the week? She asked now in his embrace. Nada it's a long story lets get out of here and get something to eat and I will tell you all about it.

Sonjee moped around campus the next two weeks feeling sorry for herself and Fonsworth's condition. "Fonsworth Erickson's room please? Hoping to speak with whom ever was there. "I'm sorry he's no longer with us" the voice replied. "WHAT? Sonjee asked shocked. 'Who am I speaking with? The voice asked, "We've been having his friends call all morning. "Yes, I'm a friend from the university." "Is his mother still there? "No, she's gone also". "They all left this morning". "Oh, is that what you meant, about gone". Yes, I'm sorry if I confused you", he was up to traveling and his parents took him back home to Africa". "He has a lot of work ahead of him but there is certainly hope. "His mother gave us permission to share this news with who ever calls." "Gee thanks that's good news! Thanks so much" Sonjee said disconnecting the cell line.

"Just a minute, I will let the guys know I'm leaving and Annie and Keith should be back soon," Billy said leaving Nada alone in his office as he went down the hall. She looked a Billy's degrees he had framed and displayed on the wall. William John Parker Master's degree in business administration and his law degree from Harvard. "Not bad" she thought looking at the classic style décor used to display them on the wall. "Okay ready? He asked putting his overcoat on and heading out of the door. "Let's take my car. Its park underneath, lets' go this way," he suggested leading Nada down the back staircase to the parking garage that housed the attorney's cars.

Billy had called and spoken with his mom as he and Nada headed out for lunch. "Mom says hello and she's glad things turn out so well" "I am too! she replied now sitting in the passenger seat of Billy's Jag. "I'm hungry what place do you have in mind? Nada asked. How about some seafood? "One of my favorite meals sounds great". Billy headed out to Barnum Tavern. The seafood was great but it was another place he owned as an investment. "So, you're going to explain to me why you didn't return my calls? Nada again brought up the topic. "Honestly, Nada I have been struggling trying to decide what to do." You know

I have been trying to make a go of it with my son's mother". "I'm listening. "Dana and I can not see eye to eye on family and church". "Okay so you're going to explain right? Nada asked. "I have shared with you that I am looking to get married but I'm not sure who are what God has for me". "Have you tried asking him? Nada questioned. "Since God had given me a son with Dana, I assumed she was my soul mate so I wanted to make it work". "I have to apologize to you for putting you in the middle but I got so angry with her." Umm, Nada said looking directly at him as they drove out to the restaurant by the sea. "She was supposed to accompany me to the Investors Ball but like always she chose not to come, we had a big fight before I left and I called myself deciding it was over! Billy reached over to hold Nada's hand as he drove along sharing. "She left for two weeks to Europe to get back at me I reasoned, and I found myself missing her. When she returned, we spent the night together, and I swore I was not going to jump back and forth between you and she," "You were never committed to me, we are just friends, you could have told me that" she stated. Billy could feel her hand tremble in his, though she never pulled it away. "So, if I hadn't called and cancel the ski trip you would have?" "Yes, he said pulling into the parking lot of his family's restaurant. Billy walked around and opened Nada's door and both walked in and found seats. "Mr. Parker! Good to see you sir" the restaurant manger expressed coming over to the table. 'What can I get for you? "Let's start with two cups of coffee, and give us a moment with the menu". "Thank you, sir," Hurrying off and coming back with two hot cups filled with coffee and a huge smile. Billy and Nada made small talk until their entrée's were served with an expensive bottle of red wine. "The ski trip was a disaster! Billy shared opening the conversation they had started in the car. "So, you did go? "Yes, and unfortunately I asked Dana along". "I was going to call you and shared all this with you in person but you beat me to the punch" taking another bite from his delicious meal. "How's the lobster? "It's very good! Go ahead what were you going to share with me," Nada replied looking across the table. "Dana and I decided together that we are not right for each other." I shared with her I was not going to compromise my values to be with her. She got angry and flew out three days into the ski trip." 'I did get to visit my bud Desmond who lives there, I told you about him". "Umm yes I guess I recall a Desmond" she responded a bit lifeless at this point. "So where does this relationship with you two stand now? Am I in the middle of a spat" she asked a bit teed he could tell? "No! I know now she's not the one for me". She got angry and left because I chose to sleep on the sofa". She's good at getting her way in the bedroom so I chose to take it out of the equation". He explained. "We have to remain friends or cordial anyway for our son. But I 'm not in love with Dana. I was willing to make it work but she chose not to". Nada wiped her eyes. The cool winter breeze from the seashore was blowing through the opened windows giving her an excuse. "Is everything alright? Billy asked seeing she was a bit confused as too why she was here. "I'm fine the breeze is a bit strong coming from this side" she replied making a gesture with her hand. "We can go if you'd liked". "No right now I'd like to know where I stand" I'm sorry Billy but I really thought you cared for me not that I was just a fill in for Dana". Billy sat holding his head down trying to process so he would give and intelligent answer. "Nada, I shared all that with you because I needed accountability for my actions". Nada listened. "I care for you very much" but Dana was always a question in any relationship I had. Simply because I wanted to do the right thing." "I want a good marriage that last." "So when I saw you sitting there in the office I knew what I had did at the ski lodge was right! I hope you will forgive my actions, and give me a chance to prove to you, that I mean what I'm saying." He looked up with tears in his eyes. Nada handed him a napkin from the ones she had been using to keep her tears from showing. He reached across the table to hold her hand. "A new start" she asked holding him with an uncertain trembling hand. "Please! William replied.

CHAPTER 27

Happy Times

"Mollie, I have two tickets to see Garth at the Corral. "Who? Garth you know the country singer" Okay so you want me to go with you? Girl's night out." "Yes, I think I went with you the last time downtown to Havana Night's, that trendy nightclub that caters to the career single I'm told". Okay you're right "The Corral is huge I've heard lots of country singer's come through there". "It's nice, I like it and I've learned the line dance! "All right so you're going to show me what that is? "Sure, when you have time come by my office". Will do! disconnecting the phone. Mollie and Dana both worked at the hospital. Mollie worked in the administrative office and she and Dana were good friends. Dana helped Mollie through some tough times and relationships due to her weight she says. Deciding to get her stomach stapled and losing hundreds of pounds she looked stunting in a size eight dress. Considering she use to be a size twenty-two. So, hello world here I come! was her philosophy and she and Dana ran together?

Tetra was up early moving in the kitchen. "Alfredo hello, how was your trip? "Sad occasion but wonderful to see old friends." "Good, so you and Nada had a good time? "We did". He responded handing Tetra the serving tray he had already prepared for her and David. "Have you heard from Nada? Yes, Mrs. Parker, she's fine, she went to see Billy in Maine" I hope you approve?" "Oh, Billy and Nada are intelligent adults, I think they know what they're doing," "if it helps, I've given them my blessings," she said going upstairs with the tray. "Thanks Mrs. Parker".

Billy and Nada went back to the office so Nada could get her luggage and relax. Letting Annie know he could be reached at home he left the office with Nada following close behind in her rented car. They decided they would take the rental car back to the airport tomorrow as they drove down the highway to Billy's estate. Billy rode along wondering what he and Nada would do to fill the week, and Nada was still in shock about even being there, and now she was following him home. After driving several miles, around several winding turns, and what seemed to be a long distant for Nada from his office, he drove up a hill to his luxurious estate. Billy waited while the huge gate opened to allow entrance into the beautiful manicured lawns and grounds. He drove slowly down a gravel path leading to the spacious driveway. Pushing his remote the garage went up as they drove toward the entrance. Billy pointed for Nada to park the car to the left of the long five-car garage. Soon he was helping her get her small luggage from the car and she walked through the garage behind him. "So, this is where you live? She asked walking into the house following him putting her hand on his shoulder. "The grounds coming in are gorgeous will I get a chance to see more? She asked smiling walking further into the beautiful home. "Umm that's up to you, I'd love to show you later, other parts but it's quite large, and it will take more than a day! He replied going into the guest room he had his staff prepare for her. She walked in with her small carry case. "I've asked Spence to get the large pieces of luggage from the car" he should be here in a minute". "Oh, thanks William" I certainly didn't expect this treatment. Nada voiced looking at the magnificence room. "Well I don't know how to take that?" he responded. "In a good way, a very good way, you're giving me my own space and a girl really appreciates that," she said coming over to kiss his cheek. "Nada? "Yes William? He embraced her and gently kissed her cheek. "I'm not trying to rush you into anything, but I do care". He confessed looking into her eyes.' "Thanks for making me comfortable in this awkward situation," embracing him as they stood in the middle of the room. "Do you mind if I just relax for a minute, I need to make a few calls and take a long hot shower?" she asked holding his hands. "Sure, I understand, I need to call the office as well, so if you need something let me know I'll be in my study" on the second floor". "What if I get lost trying to find you" she smiled and teased him looking at the enormous house. "Believe me there are people here to help you" he smiled "just push this button in any room", pointing to show Nada the small button to the intercom. "Thanks again William, she said as Billy walked out of the room leaving her by herself. Nada looked around the beautiful room. Spencer had brought her luggage in from the car and placed them on the luggage rack in the huge walk-in closet. Nada walked in and sat on the soft chenille bench to unwind. "I CAN'T BELIEIVE I CAME HERE! She thought out loud. "What was I thinking? This could have gone really bad!" Nada reasoned, doing self talk. "She got her cell phone from her purse and dialed her neighbor back in Washington. "Hello! Ms. Manuel answered. "Ms. Manuel? Yes, this is Virginia Manuel" she stated in a matter of fact tone! "Ms Manuel, this is Nada your neighbor". "Nada, Nada Jean, where you at?" Ms. Manuel I'm still on vacation, remember I asked you to watch the house for me?" Child! I remember. "You having fun?" "Yes ma'am, it's very nice here". "They ever clean up from all that water? "Oh, New Orleans", well not much has changed except the floodwaters have gone down, Nada explain patiently to her elderly friend. "Are things alright there, in the neighborhood I mean?" "Nada Jean, things are fine, I read your newspaper everyday, shame what folks do! "Thank you Mrs. Manuel I was hoping you would, I wouldn't want them piling up on the porch". "Well don't worry bout that, King and I go over every morning and walk around the house" brave dog you know? Yes, ma'am, German Shepard's make great pets and he's a great watchdog! "Well, when you do back home? "I should be returning from Maine at the end of the week". MAINE! Now I know enough to know Maine ain't in Loosanna". "You're correct Ms. Manuel. I flew to Maine this morning to visit a friend before coming home". "Oh, I see, yall chi-dren git on them planes and fly all over the place." "One day ya here the next day ya somewhere else" she giggled. "Ain't seen that man around here" you with him? She inquisitively asked. "Ms. Manuel thank you, and King for keeping an eye on my home until I return. I'll see you soon okay". "AH um, Yes, it'll be nice to talk with you, Hazel sits here all day and talks up a blue streak before I have to make her leave". "Now be nice"

Ms. Manuel, are you going to the women's group tonight? "Now what was you just saying bout being nice? "I'll see, she giggled, "I'll have to see" and hung up the phone laughing causing Nada to laugh too.

Nada took her clothes from her garment bag and hung them in the closet. She carefully arranged her clothes in the armoire style dresser that along with the matching bed anchored the spacious room. "Wow! And I thought I lived well growing up" she said still looking around the beautiful room. After getting her things all arranged and speaking with her dad, she headed into the adjoining bathroom for a long relaxing bubble bath in the large Jacuzzi style tub. Billy, she figured was going about whatever he does when he's home and she felt very comfortable sitting in a tub of bubbles reading one of the magazines she found in the bath's magazine rack. After a while she was dressed and moving around the house looking for Billy. "Hello! She said passing the staff in different parts of the house as she went up stairs heading for Billy's study after getting directions. Nada looked from room to room looking at the décor chosen for each room. She saw the study door at the end of the wide hallway. Hearing the sound of soft jazz music playing she headed that direction stopping short to looked into Billy's bedroom housed on the second floor. His room was very masculine draped in rich shades of browns with silver accents throughout. "Hey! She turned a bit startled to see Billy standing in the door. "Hi, I was checking out your room, good taste! She acknowledged walking toward him in the door. "Thanks how is everything?" "Heavenly, Nada replied smiling, walking him back to the study. "Well someone's been busy, she noticed looking around at the oak wood desk top covered with files and papers. Always! That's why I'm glad you're here." What would you like to do?" he asked holding her hand. "Me! She teased well let's see, since I've never been to Maine" she paused. "This is tough relinquishing my independence to you," she said smiling "but I'm going to trust you with our entertainment this week. "Oh, so now what does that mean? He teased back. "You will be so dazzled this week, you may not want to return to Washington again! He said doing a jig around the floor. Right! She said pretending to be distracted by looking at a book on the massive floor to ceiling shelving unit along the wall. Billy stood behind her and put his arms around her. "Nada thanks for coming", he said, sincerely. "William I'm glad I came to, I really am, I admit, I was not sure when we were at the office. I was ready to get on a plane and leave," Nada confessed. "But I'm willing to see where this relationship goes," she added. "You're amazing and honest and I like that," he shared. They had moved over in the big leather chairs in the reading area of the room. "A girl could really get caught up with all this and settle for anything to have it" and I have to confess ten years or so it would have been me". "A very bad relationship and aging has matured me greatly," she said sharing her self with Billy. They sat talking and sharing each other's personal lives that they felt comfortable with sharing. Billy shared about Jillian his fiancée, he lost to September 11th, and of course Dana his son's mother. Nada shared about the man she thought she wanted named Colvin, with all his money. But lived to regret the day she met him at her father's restaurant. "Billy was moved by her honesty once again and felt so close to her at this moment. "Thank you for giving me a chance after that experience, now I know why you gave me such a hard time. "I understand, "thanks William". Billy got up to answer the buzz coming from the telephone "Thanks! He responded to the caller hanging up quickly. "Nada are you ready, our brunch is being served" reaching for her hand. The two friends went down to the dining room and dined on an elegantly served, and sensuously spicy, delicious brunch, Billy had requested before heading out to share a walk on the estates grounds and continue sharing and bonding with each other.

The night had just peeked through when Mollie pulled up a Dana's home Friday night. "Come in, do come in" she said inviting Mollie again into her home. "Hey do you have some dangly earrings I can wear with this outfit? Mollie asked removing her coat showing her newly purchased cowgirl outfit she was wearing. "That's nice, let's see" turning her around in the living room. Mollie followed Dana into her bedroom to get the earrings; trying on several pair before settling on a gorgeous diamond and pearl set, she just loved. "All right now once again before we head out let's go over the basic steps" Mollie suggested moving around in front of the mirror. "The basic steps because it will change from song to song". "Everyone as a different way of doing the same moves" you know that! "I know that! Mollie returned quickly.

"When we went over it several times at the office and then last week when you came by my place. I'm sure I have the basics, so all I have to do is put my personality in it." Dana and Mollie went into her family room where she had selected a tune to line dance by. "Okay, okay! Turn! Another turn! Oops wrong direction!" Okay! okay! Turn! Another turn, back step, front step, side to side, all right I think I've got it," Mollie said making a sassy move around the floor. "I've reasoned, it's the country version of the electric slide," laughing as she said it. This was a fun night out for the girls. Dana and Mollie had fun dancing the country styles to lively music. They squared danced and line dance late into the night. The dancing cowboy was there and so was Corky which Dana shared a few dances with throughout the night. They enjoyed the music of Garth who wooed all the ladies with his love ballets. The ladies left vowing to return the next night for more fun on the country scene.

Sonjee spent a pre-Thanksgiving holiday with her dad, sister, and brother's families before boarding her flight to Los Angeles to live with Doris Wright her birth mother. She knew she would probably never see or hear from Fonsworth her college friend again. And with the exception of the bad dreams every now and then she was content with that fact. Sonjee had to admit she was glad he had returned home, and would hopefully get some help doing his rehabilitation, with his drinking problem. "Wow, he actually wrote his mother about me! Well maybe he did care, she thought reclining her airline seat for the plane ride to L.A. She had driven down earlier in the month flying back to spend time with the family before returning to Los Angeles to live. Doris was anxiously waiting Sonjee's arrival. She had fresh flowers put into her bedroom, that was beautifully decorated in her favorite colors. Doris had been busy also, planning a big celebration for her nephew Michael's baseball team. The plans were to go to David Michael's finally playoff game, and then the huge planned celebration for all at Doris's home. "Sonjee took out a pen and a pad of paper. 'Let's see, there is David Michael, and Aunt Dana, Uncle Billy, Frannie, David Michael's girlfriend, will surely be there. Umm will there be other family members to meet she thought, writing down the names of the ones she had already met. "This is certainly going to be a big change for me coming from Gonzaga and going to U.C.L.A". "My advisor gave me her phone number if I need help with the transition". Her mind was moving from situation to situation. "Something to drink?" The stewardess asked pushing the small cart down the aisle of the plane. "Coke please," "Thanks! Sonjee replied taking the soft drink from the smiling stewardess, who then moved on to the next seat. "I must remember to call Candace and Bailey and give them my new phone number," she then thought making a note to herself. "I will be there soon, she sighed before her next thought. But soon her thoughts were off and running again. I'll be traveling back and forth quite a bit, mostly for dad. He seems to be handling being on his own really well. Although he did break down in tears at the dinner table on their family's early planned Thanksgiving. Bailey prayed for the meal, and family, while saying grace over the dinner table that Candace and Sonjee had cooked from learned recipes of his wife and their mother.

CHAPTER 28

Thanksgiving

It was Tuesday, and Billy was enjoying is houseguest, who had come unexpectedly to see him. He had not heard from Dana but expected a call any day now. "Hey you! Nada said greeting him with a kiss as she entered the family room where he sat reading his morning paper. "Thanks for the beautiful flowers in my room. "You noticed! He said holding her hand. "It was tough, but I finally saw them" she flirted back smiling. 'I'm having our breakfast served on the deck outback okay? "Sure, that's sounds wonderful. Nada replied. "I also thought we could go into town today, see some sights?" he suggested. "I'd loved that and thanks for the tour around the estates. My favorite places are the flower gardens". "Funny you would say that! My grandmother and I planted most of them. She loved flowers, and taught me the names of most of them before I reached sixth grade" he shared remembering his times spent with his grandmother. "So, I will know when I get flowers from you its heartfelt" Nada said. "I had never thought about it quite like that, but you're right, I have wowed a florist or two with my knowledge of the beautiful plants" he added heading outside for a lovely breakfast on the deck over looking a garden with various types of orchids, with Nada.

"Good morning" came a groggy voice over the phone. "Good morning, I guess, you sound terrible! Dana replied. "I know I was out late with Corky at the Corral. "Oh, you seem to like the place. "Hey you have to admit it's contagious". Frisco asked for you! "He did? Well I hoped you explained that I don't go out every night! "Honestly it didn't come to that, someone else came up and he was gone again". "I see, his loss", Dana responded. "Anyway, you have any plans for Thanksgiving? "Um I don't know, why? "I'm heading out to the ranch Corky says you're welcome". "He did! did he! Well what time are you going?" Dana asked. Around noon! I won't be out there long I have a date later" Mollie explained. "What, why are you going out there?" "Well one reason is because he asked, I find him to be very nice, down to earth". "I like sitting around with family on the holidays". "So, there's no cupids arrow in your heart?" "No not really, he's not my type, he talked about you most of the night" but since I haven't been asked by the other guys, I'll enjoy a family gathering at the ranch, Mollie shared. "Sounds a bit strange, how did he say Rusty was doing? "Who? "Hey doesn't matter, let me make some calls and I will let you know my plans". "Whatever? call me later anyway, to make sure I'm back safe! "I'll call you! Dana hung up the receiver and called her son. Finding out he and Frannie were having Thanksgiving dinner with her sister Doris, she thought about dialing Billy. "I don't want Billy's drama! I will go and be with David Michael, for the holiday" she decided. Knowing Billy, he's probably spending his day feeding the homeless or something I really don't want to be a part of, "she reasoned going out to catch a flight to Los Angeles to spend Thanksgiving with her sister and her son, leaving with a call of an explanation to her friend Mollie.

Nada had spoken with her dad who was headed out to Mt. Nebo with the Parkers to feed all those who will come by for a hot meal. "Billy is upstairs I think but I will tell him to call his mother" she said to her dad who had given her Mrs. Parker's message. Nada had enjoyed spending yesterday downtown finding a much-needed hair salon, and nail shop, while Billy took care of some business at his law firm. "Nada could smell the aroma of turkey and dressing and all the trimmings being prepared by the busy staff bustling around the huge kitchen. She had woken early but had not come out of her room, choosing to just relax reading a book. She also made phone calls to friends and of course her dad. She combed her hair and adjusted the jacket on her fuchsia colored Cashmere outfit she had chosen to wear today. "I wonder who else is coming to dinner today? she thought heading out to find Billy. "Hi! She said coming upon one of the cooks in the kitchen. "Hello Ms. Francois, it's good to see you again this morning, can I get you some coffee?" "Yes, thank you" she said reaching for the hot cup of coffee heading back to her room. "Oh, have you seen Billy, I mean Mr. Parker this morning? "Yes, he's out for his morning jog, got a late start this morning" he said. "He'll be back shortly, I'll let you know when he gets back". Thanks," she said heading in her room with her cup griped tightly as not to spill it. After a few hours things at the estate were underway. Billy and Nada welcomed their dinner guest. His brother Justin and a friend, Annie and her husband Keith. "Come in! Come in, whew, it's cold out there! They all admitted coming in with fur coats and warm hats and gloves. "Everyone this is Nada Francois, my dear friend and houseguest for the week. "Hello, Justin said, welcome to the family," giving her a hug. "This is my date Marissa Clinton". "Please to meet you, Nada said extending her hand and shaking all the guest hands. "Hi, I'm Annie, we met at the law firm and this is my husband Keith. "Sorry to have you waiting I didn't know you were a personal friend". She confessed. "Oh, no problem he wasn't expecting me anyway, I sort of surprised him" Nada replied. With all the coats hung in the guest closet. They gathered in the great room for conversation, drinks, appetizers, and games, before sitting down to a luxurious thanksgiving dinner, shared with lots of laughter, and fun, being made by everyone sitting at the elegantly decorated table.

Finley we're waiting for you! Doris spoke loudly into the intercom. "Coming my lady, he replied back with his voice coming over the intercom. Doris, Sonjee, David Michael, Frannie and Russell were all sitting around the long elegantly set dining room table waiting for Finley. The beautifully golden-brown turkey was now sitting on the center with all its trimmings. Cornbread dressing, yams, spiral ham, greens, cranberry sauce, and steaming hot dinner rolls! "FINLEY WE'RE GOING TO START WITHOUT YOU! "I coming madam, someone is at the door! He replied back into the intercom near the front entrance door. "Oh, my lady will be pleasantly surprised" he expressed giving the arrived guest a hug as she came through the door. FINLEY WHO IS HOLDING UP DINNER? She asked loudly over the intercom. Just as she turned back to the table Finley was standing in the door dressed in a three-piece suit. "Why Finley don't you look dapper," "Oh something new for the ladies! "Well Finley, I think you're going to woo the ladies, but right now please sit so we can eat! Well I have another guest to join us" reaching behind him bringing Dana from the hallway entrance. "DANA! "I'm so glad you are joining us! Doris said getting up to hug her sister. David Michael stood and hugged her too. "Great to see you Dana," standing and pulling out her chair. "Finley please do the honors of the grace" "Yes my lady," "God thank you for this bountiful meal you have place before us, thank you for each family member represented here. Bless each individual's incoming and outgoing, that they may share their abundance with someone else less fortunate. Thank you for those less fortunate you said, we will always have. Bless the hands that prepared this meal and bless this home in Jesus name we pray, Amen". With serving spoons flying in the air the meal started with lots of conversation, and laughter, and sharing of past, and present, experiences together as a family. "Pass the yams please!

David and Tetra went home to rest from a day of feeding the homeless and all those who came by Mt. Nebo for a great meal with all the trimmings. "God Bless this holiday season, was voiced by both during their time of prayer, and thanksgiving. The next day they spent a quiet dinner together, across a very elegantly set table. Later that evening Joey and his mother called, and came by with a gift to thank Tetra for helping them with a new start.

CHAPTER 29

A Night Out

Sonjee made a point to speak personally with her aunt Dana about an already scheduled plastic surgery appointment. Sonjee wanted her new look in time for the big celebration Doris was throwing for David Michael. She had also spoken with David Michael about being her roommate in the coming school year at U.C.L.A. Since he wanted to live off campus, it would benefit both of them, they reasoned. Things planned were coming into place nicely she thought seating in her room on the phone talking with Dr. Reeves her dad. "Gee! I can't believe this new life I'm living right now daddy! She expressed speaking daily to him. "Now Sonjee, you be careful, all that glitters isn't gold". He shared wisely. "What daddy? "Just keep your feet on the ground dear". 'OH! I know daddy, I promise. 'I'm leaving for the clinic now. "I'll call when I can from there." You have Godmother's cell phone number, right? "Yes Sonjee, I have it and I love you. "Love you too dad, bye". "Godmother, you ready? She asked looking at her watch and hurrying out the door in her sweats, and tennis shoes, casually dressed to go see a surgeon regarding plastic surgery on her nose. "Sonjee you're sure you want to make this change? "Yes, Godmother I'm sure. Soon they were in the car and headed to the clinic where she would have her nose made smaller and famine to match the rest of her body. "I want to change my hair to". What do you mean? Doris asked as they drove to the hospital where her surgery was to be performed. "I'm going to get rid of the dreads and perm my hair for a total change". 'What's with the big change? Well! I spoke with aunt Dana and she really loves her knew look". "I have a lot I want to leave behind and start new". OMG you listened to Dana! "At your age what could you possibly want to forget?" Doris asked the bubbling bright Sonjee. Sonjee, just smiled remembering what she went through only a few months ago. "Well, new place, new look! She replied heading into the medical building for surgery and a Hollywood nose job!

Dana had arrived home early Saturday after spending two beautiful days with her family in L.A. Of course, she purchased several new items from Doris's boutique and took Sonjee down Rodeo Drive. "Put my bags down here and thanks" paying and tipping the limo cab from the airport. She walked through her home noticing her message light was on. Pushing the button, she had a call from Mollie, but not one call from Billy. "Well! He must really be mad this time," she thought moving around getting all the things out of the way, and running her a long hot bubble bath. "Mollie, hey girl! "Dana good to hear from you, how was your Thanksgiving? "Wonderful, I had a great time! "What did you do? She asked. "Oh, besides shopping, I spent it with my son and my niece". "Thanks sounds relaxing anyway" So are you up for some fun? She asked excitedly. Where? Havana Nights! Where else? Tonight? "I'll have to see". "Oh, you're feeling that settle down with Billy tonight, aren't you? "Mollie you know me to well girl". "Maybe it's just me, but, how many messages did he leave on the phone this time?" "What do you mean? Dana asked. She was the psychiatrist but Mollie was always giving out the advice. "If I hadn't heard from my man in a week, and the last time we spoke we said it was over" Dana started to speak. No! wait, Mollie interrupted "and this has happened more than one time lately". "I would start looking somewhere else because I would bet you, he has! She stated in a matter of fact tone. "Billy's not going anywhere! Dana responded. "Okay, but if you need me, I'll be at Havana's" on the dance floor" Mollie concluded.

Good morning! Why, good morning! Billy replied seeing Nada standing by the front door. "Mind if I run with you this morning? "Billy was pleasantly surprised. "Which one of my staff told you I run in the morning? He asked. "Why are you going to punish them? She smiled. "No but that means they approve of you and that's good! I like you a lot too! He smiled pulling her close and kissing her gently. "So, you know I run about five miles around the property" he shared. "Let's go! And off they went for a brisk early morning jog together, sealing further their friendship bond.

Dana rang Billy's home phone twice, each time being told he wasn't in. She tried his cell phone before stepping out of her long bubble bath to get dressed and head out to the estate. "Ring, ring! Hello. "Why hello Dana", Corky! His twang came across the phone. "Howdy" she teased. "Hey, the old man is feeling pretty bad got a doc coming out to see him, thought you might" he suggested in an asking tone. "Well what seems to be the problem? He seemed fine last time we spoke," Dana added. "Well, probably my fault. I kinda told him you would be out for the holiday," went into a depression after you didn't show up. Started talking about how Donna jilted him again". "Oh, I'm sorry to here that, look I'll head that way now but I can't stay long," Dana explained. "Oh, I'm sure that'll do him good! See ya in a bit". Dana tried calling Billy again before heading out to the ranch to see her dear friend Rusty.

"So, you didn't tell me you enjoyed running? "A girl has got to have some secrets, right? Nada said coming back to the house from their fun five-mile run. "Come this way Billy suggested showing Nada another path to walk on. Soon they came to a beautiful wooden bench over looking a Koi pond. "My! This is gorgeous," she said looking around at the various flowers that had been planted in this setting. "Sit for a minute" Billy said, sitting on the bench and motioning for Nada to sit beside him. She sat and snuggled up beside him, and he put his arms around her. "Well have you enjoyed your visit so far? "Of course! I've enjoyed it all, every planned and unplanned moment," she confessed holding his hand. I especially liked our night of fellowshipping at church. I'm really glad you felt comfortable enough with me to go." Nada confided. "I'm sorry, that was a commitment I couldn't get out of". "Good I'm glad. I enjoyed you grandfather's friend, he's so very wise." "Yes, Reverend Jones he's blind. He served in World War II after that graduating from Seminary College. He's well studied and knows that bible so well, that you would never know he's not reading from sight, but memory," Billy shared. "He really encouraged me," Nada added sitting now holding Billy's hand playing with his fingers. They sat watching the beautifully colored fish swim around the man-made pond. And before leaving it shared a very meaningful conversation, and kiss, before heading back to the estate to spend the day getting better acquainted. There entire week was spent sight seeing Maine, and quiet lunches, out around town, or in one of the beautiful garden settings around the estate. Billy planned to take Nada out dancing at the Maine's exquisite Governor's Mansion Ballroom for their last evening together there.

Finley and Russell as well as David Michel, had come to join Doris, at the Cosmetic Clinic in Hollywood. "Finley, said Sonjee was headed to the hospital, so I hurried right over! He said running through the clinic doors. "No, Sonjee's fine this is cosmetic surgery to make her look more beautiful". "Finley! Michael expressed hitting him lightly on his arm. Finley shrugged his shoulders. As a matter of fact, you two can take me out to eat while we wait for Dr. Miles to call," intertwining her arms between Russell and Finley heading out of the clinic. David Michael headed back to the university. The team had to win only two more games to be state champions. "Tell cuz I'll call her later! He yelled back, heading back to his car

Dana made her way down the dusty narrow rode to the farm. Corky was standing out on the porch when she pulled up. Dana noticed another car parked out front also. "Hello, she said hurrying up to the porch. "Howdy, doc's in with him right now". "I just wanta' know if he's just depressed, I guess" he said opening the door to let Dana enter and he followed her in. After about twenty minutes the medical doctor came from the room. "Hello Dr. Bingham I'm Dana Williams, a friend, how's Rusty doing?" "Physically at his age he's fine" but he's severely depressed and that's dangerous" he shared after shaking Dana's hand. "Well can I speak with him? "You sure can, as a matter of fact I'd recommend it! He said going over to speak with Corky before shaking his head and leaving. Dana had pulled up a chair beside his huge bed with wagon wheel headboard and sat next to him. "Rusty it's Dana, what are you doing lying in bed?" He slowly turned his head toward her. "Dana, sweet young Dana, you still looking out for a old man like me". He responded. "Oh, you didn't think you would get rid of me that easy now did you? She teased causing a smile. She had sat by Rusty's bed about and hour and a half listening to his laughter and cowboy stories. Some even included his wife Donna. Before she realized the time, he had fallen asleep and she tipped toed out of his bedroom, finding Corky sitting in the leather reclining chair watching television in the great room. Seeing Dana come in he jumped up. 'Is everything all right? He asked. "He's resting now, when he's up to it we will go for a ride". "Thanks Dana" he said embracing her for her visit. Soon he stood watching her pull away from the ranch as she waved back.

Dana dialed Billy at home again. Getting no answer. She dialed his cell phone, getting only a recording on both. Deciding to leave a message, she drove out to the Corral for a few drinks to relax. Looking around it was the usual crowd gathered and ready to square dance. "Dana! Partner with me in this square dance will ya! Frisco asked standing by her table. Sure! She said getting up and dancing around the circle with other couples enjoying the night away. "JOIN HANDS! The m.c called out over the microphone. EVERYBODY GET'TA PARTNER! Well now circle the ring! Each of the couples were following the instructions being given to the beat of the music. Dana laughed, and had hours of fun, before quietly leaving, without being seen. Getting home around ten o clock, Dana still had not gotten a call back from Billy and she was starting to think what Mollie had said could be true. "RING! RING! "Hello, Dana said hurrying to answer. "Dana it's Frisco, I didn't know you had left I'd really like to get to know you better". "Frisco, I have an early morning, so I just slipped out". You guys have fun," bye! Disconnecting her line going to bed disappointed it wasn't Billy.

Several hours had past when Dr. Bingham called Doris to let her know everything went well. "When can we see her? The concerned Doris asked. Probably tomorrow she's doing fine but pretty sleepy from the antistatic." Thank you doctor Bingham I'll see you tomorrow. "Hello, Dr. Reeves? "This is Dr. Reeves. "Doris Wright. "I just spoke with Dr. Bingham and everything went well". I'll be seeing Sonjee tomorrow, she's resting now". "Good, so there were no complications! That's wonderful to hear" he replied. "My little girl as a mind of her own

Doris, and I know this was her idea to change her face, though I pray this is where it stops" he shared advise of concern about what this choice could lead to. "Yes, I hear what you're saying'. I pray the same thing". Some get caught up in the change of this, and then that, and there are even those who don't know when to stop." "You're right about that". "But I believe Sonjee will be happy and content after she makes this small change" Doris said. "I trust Doris, he paused "being out there in Hollywood can make one think things are better if we change it! But you're right. She has talked about this since she came back from Africa and begin attending college. So, I do agree Sonjee will be content with this surgery. Thank you for calling". Dr. Reeves paused, I'm looking forward to coming out soon" he added and please keep me informed". I will Jon, Doris responded. "And Doris please give her a kiss for me! He said with a smile in his voice. "I will, I most certainly will," she said hanging up her receiver understanding his concern and went into her room to pray. She would return Dana's call later.

Nada and Billy sat around the rest of the evening sharing stories, and playing board games, and having quiet time enjoying one another. He had noticed the messages on his phones but chose to ignore them, and deal with them, later, hopefully next week. He was enjoying his visitor. "Nada, I would love to take you out dancing tonight". "What? Are you kidding me! Where? "This lovely place in town" he shared. Our reservations are at 7:0 clock. "7'0 clock! She jumped up from where they were sitting in front of the brick fireplace. WILLIAM WHY DIDN'T YOU TELL ME EARLIER? I've got to fine something to wear! She expressed. "I knew you would say that, so I apologize, I went through your closet and you have something to wear that fits this occasion, don't worry". 7'0 CLOCK! She said again, heading out to shower and to get dressed for her evening. Billy played his messages from Dana as he prepared to get in his shower. "Hi Billy, I miss you! I'd like to see you, soon," please call me!" Billy shook his head; I have to tell her it's over again. I'm going to marry, Nada, I know it now. I know after this week, she's the one for me! He thought with a smile soaping his body down for an evening of fun with a woman he had truly fallen for.

My! My! My! Don't you look gorgeous Billy echoed seeing Nada standing in his sitting room entrance where he had chosen to wait after getting dressed in his Hugo Boss suit, looking very handsome. His over coat was draped over the arm of the antique armchair near the fireplace. 'That's the dress I thought you would wear! That color looks beautiful against your skin! He commented. "Thank you, I must say you look very handsome as well' Nada smiled. Nada had chosen to wear a gorgeous form fitting design by Klein she had purchased on one of her shopping time together with Madison. "Ready! No! I'd better get my coat its cold this evening" she acknowledged rubbing her arms heading back to her room. "Nada? "Yes, I'll only be a minute," she stated. "Look I have something for you" he said going into the guest closet near the door. "William what have you purchased now?" she couldn't imagine. She was already wearing the beautiful diamond earrings and necklace he had given her earlier last year. "I hope you like it! taking out a full-length mink fur coat, putting it over her shoulder". Oh, William this is absolutely gorgeous, a girl could really get use to this" she said putting her arms around him and passionately kissing him to say thanks. "I'm ready now, she said holding his hand walking out to the garage. "Let's take the Benz EX tonight" he suggested. "William what's that? That's the convertible Charger" for another time" He opened the passenger door of the sporty Benz with two seats and help Nada get in. Quickly getting under the driver's seat he pulled slowly down the cobbled road away from the estate. Driving around a few winding curves to the freeway and heading into town for a wonderful evening with Nada.

CHAPTER 30

Another Night Out

Sonjee had a very quiet night by herself in the clinic. She was sitting up in bed when Dr. Bingham came in. "Good morning, how are you feeling? He asked looking at her chart at the end of the bed. "Nurse said you were a little restless" is everything all right? He asked again seeing her vitals were fine and there was no high temperature. "Umm! Yes, She responded "Let's look at your nose" he said helping her to lay back and relax for the exam. "Well it looks great! He said pulling the bandages back across her nose and securing them. "He helped Sonjee sit back up in bed. "How long before I can remove the bandages" she asked smiling behind the large bandage across her face. "There is still a lot of swelling but that's expected right now". If things keep progressing like they are you should be out of the bandage by middle of next week". "Wow so about a week and half! She asked excited. "Now take it easy! I want you resting the rest of this week, and then we'll see" he said smiling, thankful her surgery had gone well. Sonjee being very active with her dancing, and in very good health, Dr. Bingham knew helped things go so well in the operating room. "See you later" he said leaving. Ring! Ring! Her telephone was ringing! Hello! Hi dad, I'm fine. "I know I sound funny" It's this big bandage on my nose" she smiled across the phone line as they continued in conversation "Okay daddy, I love you" bye". Sonjee sat around looking and reading some of the many magazines in her large private room filled with flowers that had been delivered from her dad, Doris, and cousin David Michael. "Here's your lunch! The nurse staff said coming in with a tray with a good nutritional meal to eat". She sat eating when in walked Doris. "Hi coming over giving her a big kiss and hug. 'How did you rest away from your own bed?" "Oh, all right I guess". 'Dr. Bingham said you were restless is everything alright? "Sonjee wanted to tell Doris about her restless nights. It had nothing to do with this surgery. Her nightmares started months ago. But since they were not every night Sonjee reasoned with herself, they would soon go away. "Dr. Bingham wouldn't let me see my nose without the bandages yet. He says it still has too much swelling" she said sounding muzzled behind the large bandage, secured across her face, as she talked. "Well other than your nose you look good and your spirit is high". "Yeah, I guess! David Michael made me laugh a lot" speaking with him a few minutes ago before you arrived. I told him he certainly couldn't go around talking about my nose job! She joked. "Doris, this is the one I chose," showing her the nose she had picked out from the portfolio. I chose one similar to Aunt Dana's, family resemblance you know! Sonjee smiled. "I'm certainly glad you and David or getting to know each other" Doris shared. Blood, right? "Yes Sonjee" she replied. She and Doris talked for a while about family and then discussed her surgery. "Well dear I have a meeting with my staff I'll come by later on my way home". "Thanks, Godmother for everything, embracing her as she leaned over the bed. "Oh, did you confirm my appointment for my hair? I'd like to go right over there from here next Friday". "Oh yes Sonjee, Doris replied, Lisa has you on her appointment book dreads off and all" she smiled and walked out heading to her all employee staff meeting.

Billy drove along the beautifully decorated streets on Maine's downtown. The city had been transformed with lights, garland and ribbon for the festive season to come. "This is gorgeous" Nada said riding along looking at the Christmas decorations hanging from the light poles of each street corner. Soon they were pulling up to the extravagantly decorated Mansion covered in hundreds of tiny little lights. The huge pedestals were wrapped around and around with sparkling strands of holly and garland filled with holly berries. The valets were busy parking the automobiles, as the invited guest arrived. Billy pulled up, stopped, got out, and went to the passenger side of the car, assisting his date, the beautiful Nada Francois from the car.

He handed the valet the keys, after helping Nada with her mink coat. "Thank you, she said putting her hand around his arm and walking in beside him. As they entered, they saw some couples standing out in the wide hall near the beautifully decorated Christmas tree, covered with ribbons, and bows, in glittering shimmer. Stopping by the coat check before entering the ballroom to mingle with friends, they secured their coats, and went in. "Billy! He heard someone say, slowly turning to see Annie and Keith coming toward them. "Well isn't this a surprise! Annie said. "It is! Billy acknowledge, wasn't I just with you earlier this week? He smiled. "You look great Annie! Nada said patting her gently on her small pudgy stomach starting to show. "Thanks, Nada it's good to see you again too! embracing each other. Is anyone else here from our firm? He asked Keith as they stood talking. "Haven't seen anyone" We only arrived a bit before you did," Keith replied. "Well Nada and I are going to find our table and get a drink you're welcome to join us". "Thanks man, but I'm here with my in-laws you two enjoy yourselves. "We will see ya around". Taking Nada's hand and leading her through the now crowded ballroom filled with beautiful evening dresses, dazzling gowns, tuxedos and lots of holiday spirit. Why hello Grant! He said coming upon another one of his attorneys from the Parker firm. "Hello, fancy meeting you here" he teased shaking hands. "This is my friend, Nada Francois". 'Please to meet you, this is my wife, Shelly Roberts" as she extended her hand to Nada and then Billy. "Well I'm glad you all accepted the Governor's invitation; it looks good for our firm" Billy admitted to Grant as they stood talking. "Yes, you're right but you know Shelly! Had I not come I'd be in the doghouse!" he laughed. "I saw Keith and Annie earlier before this place got so crowded" Billy shared continuing the conversation with one of the older attorney's who worked in the law office. "I know this is a great crowd for networking" though Shelly asked me not to!" he confessed. "She's probably right again," Billy said smiling "just relax and enjoy your evening" "Good seeing you Shelly" giving her a hug and a handshake to Grant they moved on. "CHAMPAGNE, CAVIAR? A waiter standing in front of them dressed in his fancy tails and silver tray perched on his arm asked smiling. "Sparkling cider please? Sure Madame!" handing them the requested glasses and small napkin with caviar from his tray. A nod of the head and he moved on. Billy and

Nada found their table after greeting and meeting many new and old friends. "The orchestra struck up the music. The methodical music flowed slowly across the room as couples began assembling on the floor to dance to it. "This is absolutely magical" Nada expressed dancing slowly in Billy's embrace to songs that expanded many decades of time. "Nada I'm going to miss you," he whispered as they moved as one to the music. "I'm going to miss you too" William Parker" smiling and then sharing a kiss on the dance floor, before going back to their table again, until the next dance, and awaited meal. "William Parker? He heard a voice call out. Billy turned to see Lon Anderson a very long-time associate of his dad. "Hello Mr. Anderson and Mrs. Anderson he expressed happy, and surprised, to run into him here. "Your dad told me you were making inroads around these parts, it's sure good to see you" Lon confided. "Thank you, sir, and it's good to see you as well" Billy replied standing smiling at a man he's known all of his life. "Oh, forgive me this is Nada Francois my date" he smiled. 'Please to meet you both" she shared extending her hand to the elegantly dressed and very distinguished looking older couple. The couples stood and talked a while then each headed in the direction of their table for a festive holiday evening of dancing and dinner with the state's governor. After and hour of romantic dancing and shared friendship the Governor shared a few words thanking each for coming and wishing everyone a great year to come. Keeping the topic light of politics, he shared words of encouragement to the attendees and sat down to enjoy a $5000.00 dollar a plate meal associated with this gala affair with the 200 guests in attendance. After dinner they socialized, danced and waltzed to more of Bach, Beethoven, and Chopin's romantic songs, along with an occasional chosen Armstrong's classical jazz tune, throughout the rest of the evening.

Things were going very well for Sonjee. Her surgery was healing and the day had come when she would get to see it. She was up early and hurried down to Dr. Bingham's office in the clinic. GOODMORNING DR BINGHAM! She said happily going and seating in his examining chair. "Well it's easy to see you're excited for today" he acknowledged. She sat and Dr. Bingham removed the small bandage from her nose. It had been changed now to the average size of a band-aid. "Oh, pretty, this is nice" he said looking at her new nose. "Okay! handing her a mirror. Sonjee took the mirror and looked and smiled from ear to ear. Wow! It's so tiny! She exclaimed. "Yes, I took the wide flat sides and closed up the nostrils a bit adding a length to what was there." He explained showing her the changes on her face. "It's amazing I look different but I really like it". Good, I like it to. It fits the rest of your body," he added. Thanks Dr. Bingham, leaving his office going back to her room for two more days of healing and recovery.

CHAPTER 31

Devil Woman

It was past midnight when Billy and Nada returned to the estate. "Umm" she said her head was on his shoulder fast asleep. He softly stroked her cheek waking her up. "We're home," he shared seeing her sit up and looking around. 'Gee that was fast! I'm sorry I went out on you, I guess I was tired," she acknowledged getting out of the car going into the garage door. "He put his arm around her and walked in. "William, I had a wonderful time". They shared a passionate kiss in his guest bedroom where Nada slept, before he left going to his room for a good night's sleep. "Wow, I want to be with her, but I'm going to wait because I want this to be right," he reasoned turning over putting the pillow over his head forcing sleep. "Was it to soon to think he'd want to sleep with me? Nada thought a bit disappointed he didn't. Sweet dreams of the first time of many nights together, she thought closing her eyes for a good night's sleep.

After spending breakfast together in his guest room Nada and Billy decided they would continue to build the relationship together. "You know when I said we're home last night, it sure sound good! He shared holding her hands lying across the bed. "You have made me feel like a queen Billy, I will never forget it! Both lay across the large bed getting better acquainted with one another through conversation. "I could stay here forever but my flight leaves in two hours so we'd better head out" she said letting him stroke her face as she talked. "Oh, do you have to go? He teased knowing she did. "If you want to teach my students, I'll gladly stay here" she teased back getting off the bed and putting her luggage on the rack to begin to pack it. Bittersweet ending to her visit, Billy left the room and she began packing her luggage. After goodbyes to the staff they were in the car and on their way to the airport passing Dana going up to the estate after no return call from Billy in a week and a half.

Dana hurried around the curves on the cobbled road heading up to the estate. Talking vigorously to Mollie on her cell phone she never saw Nada and Billy swiftly go by her in the other direction along the narrow stretch of highway. She pulled up to the estate noticing the car Billy usually drives was sitting in the driveway. She walked up and rang the doorbell. DONK! DONK! The dull thick sounding donk! rang out. She stood impatiently by the door waiting. DONK! She pushed the doorbell again. After a while a maid opened the door, and Dana walked in, not saying anything to her. The maid recognizing her slowly closed the door and made her way back to another part of the house. Dana looked around in the living room "Billy! She called out no answer. "Billy! She yelled a little louder walking around from the sitting room to another bedroom on the first floor. BILLY! She yelled louder going to the kitchen. Dante the head chef was preparing the weeks menu and tonight's dinner for Mr. Parker. BILLY! She called going into the kitchen. "Mr. Parker is not here! He said very frustrated and tired of her yelling. "I saw his car in the driveway, I know he's here somewhere! She shouted to his face. "Mr. Parker is not here! "Move!" she said pushing him aside and heading upstairs to his bedroom, still yelling his name! She hurried from room to room. The maid was changing the linens on his bed. She quickly moved out of the way and let Dana do whatever she needed before heading out the door. "I know you're here! What kind of game are you playing? She asked heading back down stairs running again into Dante who had grown weary of her yelling. "Mr. Parker is not here! He said to her again. "Then where did he go?" "I don't know he did not leave that information with me" he replied. "Then shut-up and get out of my way! Going down the hall to his grandfather's old study, Dana got a book, and then went into his grandmother's sewing room. She walked slowly by another guestroom. She stopped and sniffed smelling the scent of women's perfume. She slowly opened the door and walked into the bedroom. The bed was messy from the covers being thrown back. The maid had not gotten to it yet. She looked around at the fresh flowers and saw a note Nada had left for Billy. "Billy I really enjoyed our time together this week. I won't ever forget it, Nada". She ripped the note throwing it on the floor and walked out. She headed back toward the kitchen. Dante stood across the door so she wouldn't enter protecting something he had just put in the oven. She pushed him in his chest causing him to fall back. "WHERE DID BILLY SAY HE WAS GOING?" I KNOW, YOU KNOW! She yelled. "He didn't leave that information with me" he again replied now very angry at her persistent questions. She walked over and opened the oven door slamming it shut. MY SOUFFLE YOU STUPID! His strong Italian accent could be heard throughout the house and brought several other staff members running to the kitchen. He walked over to the oven where his soufflé was baking. He opened the oven to see the fallen baked good, shaking his head. Dana flipped her hair up with her fingers before heading out through the living room slamming the door with a book in her hand. "AH! I can't stand that woman!" He said going over to the oven to rescue his fallen soufflé.

Billy was back in his car after seeing Nada's plane take off into the wild blue yonder. Riding along down the highway his cell phone rang. "Hello, he answered. "Billy, what's happening?" "Hello Justin, what are you up to?" Hey just thought I'd come by tonight, get away for a bit and rest, you know!" he replied. "Oh, you need a place to hide out for a while, I understand," he teased with his brother. "Hey it's hard to turn off that Parker charm." "I know, but I've learned", Billy shared. "Oh, that beautiful lady you had over for Thanksgiving? She's the one I'm going to marry Justin! He said riding along smiling. "Let's talk later I'm being paged." "I'll be out around seven, see ya then we'll talk bro," he said disconnecting the line. "Ring! Ring! Hello! Oh, hi mom". It was wonderful". Nada and I had a wonderful week". No Dana, no drama! He said driving along speaking with his mother. No, I just saw her off, her flight left about twenty minutes ago". "Mom I think she's the one I'm going to marry". He explained. "Now don't hurry things are you speaking with your heart or another part of your anatomy! She asked. "No mom it didn't come to that". I want this one to be right mom". "Well

I'm glad, I like Nada, she's a class act, besides being a real nice young lady". "I know mom, I felt that too, he confessed. Anyway, the reason I called was to share I went over to see Mrs. Parsons". "Mrs. Parsons, he paused "how is she these days?" "She's good for her age" and very happy now Tyler is coming home for a real visit". "Oh, that's wonderful he spoke about that after Sidney's trial when he was there. "He travels around playing his saxophone I understand, Tetra added". When is he coming to Mt. Nebo mom? "He's on scheduled for next month the 22nd I believe, Tetra responded again. I'll put it on my schedule". "Hey are you and dad going to David Michael's game Saturday?' Yes, your dad scheduled our flights when you two got off the phone talking about it four weeks ago". "Should be fun," Billy replied. I've invited Nada". "Where does that leave Dana? Tetra questioned since her son was being so frank about his relationship. "Well mom I told you what happened the last time Dana and I were together" she left me in Kansas and ended the relationship." Mom it wasn't the first time but I would always go crawling back". But not this time, not this time" he stated driving along the cobbled path to his home. "Is Dana coming? "Don't know, probably". I'm hoping we will remain friends for our son's sake" though that's it." "All right son I'm praying things work out, and no drama ensues, understand? She stated. "I pray that to mom; I pray that too! Billy pulled into his driveway. Soon he saw Dante and the other staff standing outside to greet him. What's going on? He asked looking at each one standing near the garage door. "Mr. Parker" Dante said "We need to speak with you about that devil woman! As each followed behind, he and Billy entering the house.

CHAPTER 32

A Movie Star

Dana cried all the way back to her office. She was furious to say the least. She put the key in her locked office door, and went inside locking the door again behind her, since her department was closed on weekends. She threw her purse down by the chair in her office and angrily knocked over a vase of flowers on her desk. "UH! She said sitting the vase upright again, but to late to prevent all the water on the desktop and floor. "Darn it! She stammered around looking for some paper towels to wipe up the mess. "Oh no! She said sitting down in her executive chair crying like a baby. "I will find out who she is, if it's the last thing I do here on earth! NOBODY PLAYS WITH ME! Who does William Parker thinks he's dealing with? "If it had not been for an unfortunate circumstance, I would have had Jillian in a white jacket by now anyway! She said loudly yelling in her mirror on the wall. AND that wimp Annie was a piece of cake to get rid of! HA! HA! HA! She laughed. "Stop, Dana back to reality! She said using self-talk on herself in the mirror. You must be calm! You never know who could be watching". She paced her office floor. Then she looked at her credenza getting out a phone directory. "Let's see! Let's see I's she said turning swiftly through the pages. "I-N-V here it is investigator. Thumbing down the page Dana dialed and left a message for the agency to call her back. Then she wrote Nada's name in bold letters on a pad of paper and finished pouring the water from the vase all over it and let out a great big laugh. 'HA! Ha! Ha! Dana sat there about an hour before getting a call from Mollie. "Dana let's go to the Corral tonight! She suggested excitedly. "AHH! I don't know, Dana replied. "Are you still pouting about Billy?" He's moved on I told you! She added still sharing her opinion on Dana. "Mollie for once you're right". What? "Yes, I just left his place and someone had been there". "WHAT? What did you do? "Nothing yet I left" she explained. "I can't believe you left Billy there with a woman and nothing happened! Mollie expressed surprised. "No Mollie they weren't there but they had been there! All week from the note I read" Dana responded explaining details to her confidant and bosom buddy. "Who is she? Okay how long has this been going on". "Mollie, I don't have all those details yet! And I stress yet! But you can rest assured I will find out! Dana stated. "But you did mention the last time you left him in Kansas you were tired of playing his games" Mollie reminded her. "Mollie have I ever told you, you talk too much! Mollie laughed, well are you going to happy hour tonight? We can continue this conversation." "I do need a pick me up" I guess. I'll meet you there around six o clock," "Sounds good, Mollie laughed, wanting in on all the gossip. "See you there!

Sonjee stood looking at herself in the mirror. Her dreads were gone and her flat nose was now small thin and pretty she thought, touching it as if shaping it. "Sonjee! Doris called coming up to her bedroom. "Are you going with me? I'm going to have this celebration catered. All the players and their dates, that's a lot of folks for my small staff here" she said coming into Sonjee's room looking around. "I absolutely love your hair, it flows beautifully, and do you like it?" "Godmother I really like my new look. Though I must admit it takes getting use too". "I know it's me I'm looking at but it's kinda weird." Sonjee shared. "I'm meeting David Michael for lunch, you're welcome to join us." "Thanks that's very nice of you but I have lots to do for the big celebration" Doris explained. "Do you need me to come with you?" Sonjee asked. I really don't mind. David and I are just bonding" she smiled. "No, I enjoy planning big events, I just thought you were staying in again today" Doris replied. Have you seen Finley today? She asked Sonjee leaving her room. "At breakfast earlier, he mentioned having to go over to the church to meet Russell." "Oh, that's right we're starting that clothing drive for the holidays, I'll call him later" Doris hugged Sonjee and left out of the door leaving for the day.

When Nada pulled up to her front door in Washington it was around three o' clock in the afternoon. Ms. Manuel and Ms. Hazel her neighbor on her right was sitting out on the porch. King seeing the car pull into the driveway ran out wagging his tail stopping short of going out the yard. He looked back at Mrs. Manuel on the porch to proceed further. "Seeing it was Nada, she beckoned him on. "Go on! She yelled from the porch. He ran pushing the gate open running swiftly over to the car waiting for Nada to get out. "Hi boy' you're happy to see me! She said rubbing his head from the car's window as he waved his tail swiftly. "Good boy, good boy! She repeated as she got from the car. The big German shepherd was standing against her car door as she tried opening it to get out. "Move King! Ms. Manuel yelled again. "Get out the way!" He quickly sat back on his hind legs and waited for Nada to step from the car before approaching her again. "Hello ladies! Nada yelled waving her hand. "Hi Nada Jean! Glad you back and so is King! She yelled back getting up from her rocker. "Ms Manuel let me get these things from the car and I'll be over to tell you all about it okay! still speaking loudly from across the fenced yard. She knew Ms Manuel was on her way to that gate to stand and talk. "OKAY Nada Jean, I'll be right here! She yelled back. Nada took some packages into the house. King followed her to the door and sat until she came out again. Trip after trip he followed her to the car and back to the door. On her finally trip she stood with the door opened. "Come on in King we're finished with packages" allowing him in and closing the screen door. She had a present for Ms. Manuel and King but Ms. Hazel was visiting and she had not purchased anything for her. She looked through her purchases. "Oh, here's something! Taking a beautiful Dk designer scarf she had purchase for herself and putting it in a brightly colored gift bag for Ms. Hazel. "COME ON KING! calling to him from the door. He was sitting in her living room watching her go through her shopping bags. "Oh wait! She went back to the sofa and got a small brown bag. She opened it taking out a large bone and threw it to King. "WOOF! WOOF! King acknowledged his gift. He ran over to Nada and rubbed against her. "You're welcome boy, come on" she said heading toward the door. King's big body was barely escaping many of her delicate lamps and decorative picture frames she had displayed on her tables. He quickly grabbed the bone from the floor and headed out the door with Nada following with a gift for Ms. Manuel and Ms.

Hazel. "Hello again ladies opening the closed gate letting King run over to Ms. Manuel with his bone and dropped it in front of her. "What cha got King? She asked as he stood wagging his tail. "That's nice! She picked the bone up and looked at it. 'That's nice for your teeth, it's big too" she laughed giving it back to him. He took it and ran down the sidewalk chewing and pushing it around. "Thanks Nada Jean he likes that" she added. Ms. Manuel stood up and turned toward her door to go in. "Oh wait Ms. Manuel, I have something for you" Nada said. "Wait baby, I have to go and wash my hands from that wet dog bone". "I'll be right back," she acknowledged going into her home. Nada sit out talking with Ms. Hazel. "Have you and Ms. Manuel been friending a long time? Nada asked the sixty-nine-year-old Hazel. "Let's see I came here in 1957 with my husband Benny from Oklahoma". Virginia and I have been neighbors so long we sometimes think alike," she laughed. "Ms. Manuel has been here a long time, you both have" Nada conferred still making conversation as they waited. "Yes; now Virginia came in 1959 from South Carolina I believe" She bought her home before we did". Benny and I had to save for our down payment". Virginia loaned us most of it". Benny paid her back every cent before he died though" she confessed proudly. Soon Ms. Manuel came to the door. "Come here and give me a big hug and come on in and sit down". 'You to Hazel" she added holding the screen door wide open and giving Nada a hug as she came in. Nada brought the large box in and sat it on Ms. Manuel's lap. And here's something for you to Ms. Hazel. "Thanks, she acknowledged getting up to hug Nada too. Now what you done bought Nada Jean? looking at the beautiful wrapping on the package. "Open it Ms. Manuel! Nada said waiting to see her expression. Ms. Hazel had taken the designer scarf from the gift bag. Oh, my look Virginia! Isn't this absolutely gorgeous," she said getting up moving around waving the scarf. "Hold it still so I can see Hazel! For heavens sake! That is nice" looking at the box. AH UM! Now open yours Virginia! Hazel said anxiously waiting for to see her gift. "Knock! Knock! Yes, Garvey what you want? Ms. Manuel seeing him standing at her screen door) Hazel someone's at your house. He said moving away from the door and going back home. Hazel peeped out the door "Oh it's the pest man, let me see what he wants I'll be back later" hurrying for the door. "Thanks, Nada Jean for the beautiful scarf, I will have it on Sunday! She said stopping to hug her again on the way out.

"and Monday, Tuesday and Wednesday! Ms Manuel added with her nose turned up. "Now Ms. Manuel it's her choice". "Yeah, yeah I know, but I know I'm going to have to tell her to take it off" she stated bluntly. "Okay open your gift now so I can see whether you like yours" Nada lovingly suggested again. Ms. Manuel slowly opened the ends. "This paper is so pretty I hate to tear it," she confessed carefully removing it until it was opened. King came scratching at the door" Nada let him in. He lay near the door chewing on his large plastic bone still enjoying it. Ms Manuel lifted the box cover and slowly pulled up the thin paper covering her gift. "Oh, my goodness, it's my favorite color! She could see that. She lifted the suit jacket from the box reading the label "Jones of New York. "Oh, Nada Jean you bought me a red suit". "Do you know how long I've wanted a red suit?" she said carefully standing holding the jacket in her hands. "Oh, it's so pretty!" she said before falling back on her sofa putting her hand over her face. "Ms. Manuel are you alright? Nada quickly asked running over to her. "I'm fine, no one has ever given me anything like this before" she confessed wiping her face with her handkerchief she always kept in her dress pocket. "This is something I've wanted since I was a young woman". "Red wasn't worn by honorable women my mother would say" but I always wanted a red dress", she remembered still wiping her eyes. "Try it on Ms Manuel" Nada suggested helping her to her feet and carrying the box into the bedroom for her. Ms. Manuel followed her in the room, and closed the door after Nada walked out into her living room. She looked around in Ms. Manuel's quaint small home. "I wonder if there was ever a Mr. in her life? She thought. 'Umm funny no pictures anywhere" still looking at her beautiful decorations and her love for birds. After a bit the seventy-two-year-old Ms. Manuel came from her bedroom modeling her gorgeous red suit, matching white blouse with big tie front bow that was in the box also. She had dressed it up with her black paten leather pumps, purse, and a lace white hat. "My, don't you look quite the lady! Nada said smiling as Ms. Manuel walked into her living room also smiling. "What do you think? She asked Nada "You're going to be the envy of all your friends I'd say". 'You really think so! She asked again. Soon Hazel was back. "Virginia Manuel! You look like a movie star! She expressed causing and even bigger smile to form on Ms. Manuel's already glowing face.

CHAPTER 33

All that you know, good, do it!

Monday morning came quickly. Billy was sitting in his office thinking about his week with Nada. He and Justin his brother had spent last evening sharing dinner, watching the football game and catching up on each one lives. The Cowboys were tromping the New Orleans Saint's and he had stopped and took a moment to call and speak with Nada during half time. "So, she's a keeper? Justin asked seeing the demeanor of his brother after the phone call. "Yes Justin, she's going to be my wife! "Have you shared this with Dana? He asked. "Not yet we're having lunch tomorrow I hope." I left her a message I'm waiting for her to call me back" he responded. Billy remembered ending the night still waiting for Dana's call. "Ring! Ring! "Hello! William Parker answering the following morning from his office) Billy, Dana I'm returning your call," she stated. "Well you probably have an idea why I'm calling right?" he asked. "No, not really" she replied sitting having her morning coffee in her office. "I know you were at the estate yesterday Dana" he said. "So! She responded but said nothing else. "Dante! Remember Dante". "That stupid little man got in my way" what did he say? "Look Dana it's not about Dante but that will need to be addressed". I'd like to have lunch today to discuss our relationship" he informed. "Dana wasn't happy but agreed to get some needed info about the woman who had replaced her last week, anyway. "Olivetti's say 1:30 p.m. Billy asked. 'Sure! hanging up angry as she took her first client into her office for a private session.

David Michael hurried into the restaurant to meet Sonjee for lunch. They had decided on Cravers Restaurant near campus. "Sorry I'm late he said running in quickly and sitting down "Oh you're fine I just got here a little before you did" she replied. I had a meeting with the dance instructor. I have also gotten all of my courses and electives for next year. "Wow, you're nice looking! I like that he said regarding her new look." "Okay cuz, don't make me blush, you couldn't tell anyway but thanks", she smiled. "Practice was a bear today! Coach really wants to win this one! He said getting a straw removing the paper, putting it in his glass of coke. 'You know Godmother, is planning a big celebration for the team" since you all WON the championship and the campus I noticed is in an uproar! 'Yes, she told me. Coach Oldenburg has spoken with her too about it. Should be fun! "Thanks, they said after the waitress had brought the ordered entrées to the table. So, what do you think it's going to be like living together? "Umm fun I hope, David Michael replied. "I'm kinda dull". "Good, then we'll be fine" she added, me too! "HEY, HEY! Parker you didn't tell us where you were going in such a hurry! A group of his teammates had come across the street to have lunch too AND ALL FOUR WERE STANDING OVER HIS TABLE. "Hey guys, Sonjee". Sonjee, Jason, Eric, Paul, TJ". "Hi, hello, hey! They all said together. "Hi guys" she replied smiling. So, Parker when were you going to tell us? "Be quiet guy's I'm trying to enjoy my lunch. He teased back. LATER MAN! They said moving loudly to another table to harass the waitress before ordering. "Why didn't you tell them who I was? She asked. "Cause it's none of their business and besides I've got to watch out for you not throw you to the wolves" he said taking another bite of his meal and smiling at Sonjee. "Oh, I see you're going to protect me." "That's right, I know these guys! David Michael shared. 'Umm that's good you care cuz" thanks. They sat talking and getting to know each other better, finishing their meals before leaving going to see the condominium in Westwood that they would share for next U.C.L.A. colligate year.

Billy arrived early at Olivetti's and secured a table away from the line of traffic the restaurant has coming through. "Mr. Parker, can I get you something to drink" No thank you, I 'm waiting for Ms. Williams" he replied. The waiter moved away from the table heading back into the kitchen when he saw Dana arguing with one of the waitresses. Ms. Williams can I help? He asked coming toward her. "She claims she doesn't have my reservations! Dana stated to the headwaiter that was familiar with her. "Ms. Williams, Mr. Parker is right over here, come! He said escorting Dana to the table letting the frightened new employee wait on other customers. "What was the commotion about? Billy asked after hearing the apology from the waiter who had escorted her to the table. They moved my reservations" she responded sternly. "Oh, I'm sorry that was my fault. There was no need for two tables so I asked Ricardo to show you to the table". I apologize," he added helping her with her chair. "Dana I'm glad you came, how are you?" "Just wonderful now that I see you" she replied reaching over to kiss him on the lips. Billy didn't cause friction but gave Dana a cold none responsive kiss saying hello. Dana sat down feeling very open about their meeting. "Looking around for a waiter or waitress she was feeling positive about the call. 'Yes! A waiter said hurrying to their table after Dana got his attention. "Please bring me a bottle of champagne please? She asked kindly sending the nervous waiter hurrying off. "Dana, thank you for coming, I really need to ask you to please stop harassing my staff at the estate." "You're kidding right! She asked looking straight at Billy across the table. "No as a matter of fact they will not let you in unless I'm there". He explained. "I know you're kidding! She replied again. "No, that way it's not their word against yours it's easier that way," he concluded. "You know what? I can't believe you're doing this! I'm going to kill Dante when I get my hands on him! She said angrily sitting across the table, her face beet red from embarrassment. The waiter came back and quickly poured two glasses of the expensive champagne, taking their orders before leaving the table. Dana swallowed the first glass of wine quickly. "Dana, I hope we can a least remain friends for our son's sake" Billy started. "Remain friends! You're choosing your house staff over me! And you are saying remain friends!" She stated pouring another glass of wine taking a drink. "Slow down Dana," Billy said moving the bottle of wine to the other side of the table. Dana wasn't happy but she knew Billy was right about the wine. "So, what exactly did you invite me here to say?" she again asked trying to at this point keep cordial in this matter. "I just want to make sure you know it's over between us". He replied. "Over, is that what you want?" "Yes, now, that's what I want'. There was a time when I would have said no but I've moved on Dana". "When? When Billy did this happen? "IT'S BEEN COMING AND YOU'VE KNOWN IT" Billy stated. For over seven years we have been going back and forth with our relationship". You weren't ready for marriage you wanted to wait to be sure." I agreed over and over and when I began to press the issue you blow up and leave. There have been times when you leave for a week or two coming back after things have blown over in your mind. Kansas was the last straw Dana" I chose not to try anymore". He said holding his head up staring her in the face. "But Billy how can you finalize our relationship after a week with someone else?" Dana questioned. That's not true, and a bit unfair" he replied. "Oh, so this has been going on longer than a week!" she stated loudly. "Dana let's be civil please? He asked seeing the waiter coming back to bring their meal orders. Both handed the menu back to the waiter sending him away and continued their heated conversation. "Who is she, and when did you meet her? Dana's questions came quickly. "Dana I'm not going to discuss her with you" it's really none of your business". Dana took a deep breath. "Billy, what if I were to ask you to marry me now" she said smiling and wanting him to say yes. "No Dana, you're trying to patronize me by giving me what you think I want". "No Billy I really love you! "Will you marry me? She said holding his hand across the table. "No Dana, no, he repeated sending the angry Dana rushing out of the restaurant without a meal or a yes!

Hello Doris! Russell replied seeing her coming up to the thrift store. Wow! The clothing drive really looks successful," she acknowledged seeing all the bins out front beaming over with donations. "You're right our trucks just took away two loads of coats to various cleaners that donated their services to us to clean them. "Gee that's wonderful! She said again looking at each employee moving about getting things done. "Russ can we go up to your office, I just came from the caters who's preparing the team party and I'd like to show you something I think would be nice" Doris explained needing an opinion on something she had decided she'd have. "Sure, I'll meet you up there. Let me give Leo the instructions for the drivers and I'll be right up" he replied heading hurriedly toward the group of workers sorting through the large bins of donations. "Ring ring! "Yes, Doris answered heading into the door of the office. "Finley", I was looking for you earlier thought you were with Russell here at the store" she shared. "'No, my lady, I'm with Bethany at the boutique we're selecting a gift for the first lady" he responded. "Oh, that's nice, who is working today? Is it Sherry or Gisela? She asked regarding her clerks who run her boutique. "Sherry, I believe Finley acknowledged. "She's good just tell her who it's for and Finley the sky's the limit," Doris again explained disconnecting the line as Russell waked into the office. Russell walked in and put his arms around Doris and they shared a kiss. "No one knew they had become intimate and for now that's how Doris wanted it. "Russ look at this menu, do you think it's too much? You know how I tend to go overboard on things," she confessed handing him the paperwork from the caterer. "We're talking close to one hundred people at this affair! looking at the numbers and plans laid out on paper. 'Yes, there are the players and the girlfriends and any parent who chooses to come. "I'd like to know if you would come by tonight and help me with the invitations? She asked again holding his strong hands smiling. "I'd love to Doris" he responded with a kiss to her lips. "Let me get finished I have a staff meeting down town with some of the executives regarding the clothing drive and I'll see you around seven" he said holding her tight in his arms and sharing another passionate kiss before leaving. "Doris blushed and walked toward the big desk to use the phone. "Dr. Brewer, hello Doris Wright" "Doris, good to hear from you how are things? He asked. "Just fine doctor, I have been following your instructions to the letter and eating good foods, and exercising daily" Doris replied still in a very happy mood. "That's good to hear, her doctor said. "Well what can I do for you." "Doctor Brewer, I was wondering about having a relationship long term" you know how long can I depend on my body to behave right? She asked concerned about getting involved with someone. "Oh, I can hear it in your voice there's a special someone" Yes, Doctor Brewer there is" she smiled listening for his advice.

Justin opened the door to his bachelor condo. 'Rae! How did you get in here? He asked seeing her sitting on his sofa. "I'm sorry but I didn't know where else to go! She replied wiping her eyes that were red from crying. Justin sat down next to her and put his arm around her shoulder. You want to tell me how you got in here Rae?' he asked before finding out what brought her here. "You left a key for me remember we were engaged at one point" she reminded him. Umm I see" now remembering the key he had given her a few years ago now. "What happened? Why are you crying? Justin finally asked. He was exhausted from a long shift at the hospital and was coming home he thought to rest. He had been at the hospital sleeping for the past two nights and was in need of a good night's sleep in his own bed. "I really thought we would be married and have children," she stated. "It must be the holiday season! Why are you bringing this up now? He asked puzzled with his unexpected visitor. "I haven't seen you in two years! "Do you even still live in this building? Justin was full of questions". "No, Evan and I had a fight tonight! We moved to the suburbs a year ago" she confessed. 'So, what can I do? You're living with this man!" "He was messing around with a clerk as his office and I caught them together as they were leaving the parking lot," she admitted wiping her eyes as she spoke. "Well maybe it was an innocent ride home or just a chat Rae" "I wanted to believe that the first few times it happened! She confessed. "Rae I'm sorry," he acknowledged again with a hug. "Why Justin? What's wrong with me? She asked now whaling on his chest. "Rae, you're a sweet young lady, it's not you men or just dogs! I don't know" we don't know what we want! And further more we pass up the good ones! He shared searching for a comforting word to stop her crying. "Look! Just like you found Evan after me you can find someone who will love you and be true to you" he told her giving her a tissue to wipe her eyes of tears again. The front of his hospital greens was wet from her constant crying on his chest. "It's not going to be that easy Justin, I'm pregnant with your baby! She said. WHAT! He jumped up and stared at her sitting on the sofa. RAE, I HAVEN'T SEEN YOU IN TWO YEARS! WHAT ARE YOU TALKING ABOUT? This isn't funny". "Remember when you hurt me and I swore if I get hurt again, I would get you back someday" she shared full of hatred for all mankind Justin reasoned. "So, you're telling me you are going to put an innocent child in the middle of mess! why? Because unlike Evan you have the resources to care for it! She stated bitterly. "Rae listen" I know you're not thinking clearly and further more it only takes a paternity test to prove you're lying, why go through this just to hurt me". "Because you Parker's think you can do anything, and have anyone, at a cost! "I'm sorry if you don't want to own up to your responsibility! She stammered. "You're stupid Rae if you think you're going to drag me through the mud on this one" he said going to the door and opening it. "Get out! And good luck with Evan". Rae smiled getting up from the sofa. "I'll be in touch Dr. Parker". "RAE IF YOU KNOW WHAT'S GOOD, DO IT" HE SHARED with her now standing outside of his door. Hey leave my key please? "Sure, not a problem" tossing it to him as she walked away. Justin went back into his condo and sat on his plush sofa holding his head in disbelief.

Dana sped from the parking lot barely missing another automobile as she pulled onto the road. "Ring! Ring! Her cell phone was ringing. Reasoning it to be Billy she ignored the ring and kept driving heading to the ramp of the freeway to her office at the hospital. "Playing back her voicemail she listened for the message. "Dr. Williams, P-I Cavanaugh returning your call." I can be reached a 675-8976. "Oh no! Dana replied I wanted that call" pulling over to the side of the highway she dialed back the investigator's telephone number. "Hello Cavanaugh! He said cheerfully. "Detective this is Dr. Williams, I'm sorry I missed your call." Is it possible we could meet today say, in about two hours at my office, she asked in a business like tone? "Two hours! Pausing for a minute to go over his schedule Dana reasoned. "Okay I can do that, where's your office? Dana gave the detective all the details before heading back onto the freeway to her office. She had started formulating her plan in her head to win Billy back once again.

CHAPTER 34

Family affair

Dana hurried across the street to Billy's office. Her meeting with the detective was futile at this point. Not having a last name of the mystery woman or where she lived, she needed to do more investigating on her own, before she allowed him to become involved. Annie stood up to walk into another part of the office, Dana stopped and stared at her growing stomach that was making its presence known. "How may I help you? Annie asked. "Is Billy in? Dana asked quickly heading to his office without getting an answer. Annie turned and buzzed Billy's office to let him know someone was coming. "Yes, they must sign a writ" Dana heard him say speaking with someone on his speakerphone. Billy looked up to see her coming into the office now realizing his secretary's buzz. "A few more legal words flew around the room throughout Billy's conversation. "Hold for a moment" he said, I have a visitor. "I'll come to your office, continue the meeting I'll join you shortly" he advised grabbing a folder from his desk and I'll be right back," he said to Dana heading to another office to conduct the business at hand. Dana looked around the empty of Billy office space. He looked to be having a very busy day she thought. There were folders all over his desk. Moving them aside she decided to use his computer to email their son. She sat at the desk to log on but to her surprise he had it already opened. It appeared he had started an email and to none other than the mystery woman! Dana got up and peeped out of the office looking for Billy's return. Feeling the coast was clear she quickly sat back down and completed the email Billy had started using her own words. Nada,

I know you had a wonderful week with my man! "It's a shame it had to end. We are together now! Billy loves me and I him, you will never come between us! Dana Williams. Dana hit the send button and went back to her chair to read a magazine before Billy's return. "Dana what a surprise you're here! After leaving me to eat two entrée's the other day" he shared walking back after about fifteen minutes. And sorry about walking out we're in the middle of a big court case". 'Oh, I understand, I should have called" she said so innocently. "Okay ah, what can I do for you?" he asked looking around getting the documents arranged on his desk to be filed. "I apologize for the quick exit the other day" but I was upset, very upset!" Dana admitted. "Well, okay but as long as there is an understanding about the things, we discussed I forgive you" he said smiling keeping the mood jovial. Dana got up and closed Billy's office door. "Now Dana, what are you doing? He asked seeing her eyes began to flirt with him. "Come here William Parker," she asked turning Billy toward herself. Dana don't this can only end in pain" he responded not knowing what she was up to but wanted no part of it. "William Parker will you marry me?" she asked handing him a platinum band covered in diamonds. "Dana we've gone through this already" No! No Dana, pushing her hand along with the ring back to her. "WHY? You can't expect to leave me after seven years! Nobody's going to care for you like I do! She stated shoving the ring in his face again. "Dana I'm sorry. I can't! I just cannot marry you," going over and opening the door to allow her to leave peacefully. Dana's face was again red with anger. "You don't know what sorry is yet! She said under her breath turning to leave quickly out the door.

Billy hadn't heard from Nada all week even though he had left messages on her cell phone as well as at her home. He couldn't understand why she had not returned his calls. "Hello Parker's resident, Alfredo answered. 'Alfredo? Billy, how are you? "Oh, I'm wonderful" he said cheerful in his response. "Have my parents left for Los Angeles yet? He asked to the head chef. "Yes, they left this morning". 'Oh, I figured as much". So, have you spoken with Nada? Billy asked, his real reason for the call to his parent's home. "A few days ago, Alfredo replied. 'Why is something wrong?" he asked Billy. "I haven't been able to reach her and I need to speak with her". "She's coming later to bring my prescription

I'll have her call you". 'Thanks, I'll try her again but please have her call me" was his request. Alfredo got off the phone and dialed his daughter. "Hello dad, she said answering her cell phone from her desk at the university. "Nada, you did remember to pick up my prescription?" Yes, dad I shared that with you this morning did you forget?" "Wasn't sure just heading back to the bungalow. The Parkers have left for Los Angeles." "Oh? She said with a questionable pause. "Everyone's headed to watch David Michael's big championship game. "I know daddy, she said sadly. 'I thought you told me you were going" did I hear wrong? He asked still prying from his talk with Billy. "I CHANGED MY MIND". "Did you tell Billy you changed your mind?" "Billy! Daddy what are you talking about? Have you spoken with Billy? She asked happy he had called. "As a matter of fact, I have. He's been trying to get in touch with you". With me! She responded surprised. "Look Nada, I'm not sure what's going on with you" but Billy did ask me to let you know he was trying to get in touch with you". "Alright daddy, I'll be by later with your medicine" she said getting off the phone. That email from Dana was very misleading Nada thought. How did she get my email address anyway? Still saddened she went away wondering about the whole situation and to finish her day and head home.

Billy had changed his reservations after still not being able to reach Nada by Friday morning with still no explanation. He made his reservation at the Hilton in Los Angeles and headed to Washington first to see why Nada had not returned his calls. "Dad, hello, are you all there already? He asked calling his dad from the plane. 'Yes, son we're at the Sheraton here in L.A. Your mom and I are going to get breakfast." What time are you getting here?' "I'll be there in time for the game and ceremony dad, I got a late start". "Alright, mom sends her love". "Ditto dad, see you all at the stadium! he said putting his seat belt back on and prepared to land in Washington State. David Michael's team had won the state title. Everyone one was excited and was now headed to the stadium, to watch the team in action, for the final time this year. They had set up a rival with USC that had beaten them badly in basketball and a ceremony with awards being given was planned. David Michael had also shared the scouts would be out too! Billy secured a rental car and headed to Nada's home. It was Friday around four o clock pm and he knew the day at the university was ended. He had spoken again with her dad who shared she had just left his home going home. "Thanks Mr. Francois! I really need to find out what's going on". Billy pulled up in front of Nada's home. Her Lexus was parked in the driveway. He got out and walked up to her door. Ms. Manuel stood up looking and waved as Billy rang the doorbell. "Billy! What are you doing here? You're supposed to be headed to Los Angeles," she said still holding the door opened as he stood out on the porch. Soon up ran King growling and snarling! "King, down boy" It's all right rubbing his head and sending him home and letting Billy come in. "Nada I was a bit frightened, I'm sorry I called your dad but you didn't return my calls! He said pacing the floor. "And you have no idea why?" she asked in a matter of fact tone. No Nada, I DON'T! When I spoke with you Sunday night, we agreed you were coming with me to Los Angeles". "That was before you sent that email! She screamed. "Email? What email? I've sent lots of emails you didn't answer any of them," he stated. Their voices had gotten louder and King the German shepherd was now barking at her door. "King! Boy it's alright" (patting the big shepherd's head letting him come in. He laid across the entrance of her door listening again to their conversation. "You gave Dana my email address what were you thinking?" she said trying to make her point for not responding to his calls or emails. "What are you talking about? I would not even discuss you with Dana though she did ask" Billy replied. Well how did she get my email address?' she questioned. "I don't know Nada honestly I have no idea" he said holding her hand trying to comfort her concerns. "William, I want to believe you but I want you to be honest! Wait a moment let me get my laptop" heading to her bedroom and quickly coming back. Nada sat next to Billy and logged in online going to her saved email from Dana. 'Here read it for yourself" she said handing him the laptop. "What! I don't believe her! He said chuckling to himself. "Oh, you find something funny? Nada asked seeing he thought the email was humorous. "Dana was at my office Tuesday when I left to take a conference call in another office. "See, I was answering this email you had sent. I must have left it open and she emailed you" he responded shaking his head. "I'm sorry Nada, this was not my idea.' She found your note you left in my guest room also" he shared. 'What? Yes, when I was taking you to the airport Dana was rummaging in my home terrifying my staff." She wasn't happy. I band her from coming unless I'm there". What are you saying Billy? "I've shared with Dana that I am seeing someone else and she's not happy! As a matter of fact, she's asked me, oh never mind it's childish." Are you serious? Nada asked feeling better about the mistake. "Look Nada, it's not my intention to hurt Dana and it's obvious she's upset". But I have shared with her it's over" he said holding Nada's hand. 'I don't want you hurt by Dana, she can be very vicious." he concluded. "Come here William Parker," she said bringing him closer on the sofa. "I'm sorry I didn't trust you". I really didn't want to spoil our friendship we've build together". I think I'm falling for you" she smiled rubbing noses with him. "Nada, I think I'm falling for you too! And the two shared a passionate kiss on the sofa. The big shepherd raised his head and got up. Nada got up and opened the screen door letting King out. She closed her door, giving King permission to head back home. Before catching a flight out to Los Angeles, the next day, the couple spent a wonderful night together getting to know one another better.

Doris rushed around with last minute plans for the big celebration. Everything was in place as she walked from room to room inspecting each entrée the caterers had prepared. And the beautiful decorations that adorn each room and table setting were breathtaking. The elegantly decorated displays with flowers, ribbons and bows of festive holiday decorations covered many of the tables. There was caviar and hor'dourves of delicious cheeses, assorted meats for the hungry pallets of the baseball team players and their guest. Many tables had fried chicken, sliced roast beef, salads, macaroni and cheese requested by David Michael as a favorite. Doris was very pleased with the food and its arrangement around the spacious home. "Okay Finley are you heading to the stadium with Russ and I? she asked getting her purse and jacket to her sweat suit heading toward the door. "Yes, I'm coming he said leaving final instruction to the staff. Sonjee had left out earlier going to meet her dad Dr. Reeves at the airport who was coming in from a celebrity golf game in Palm Springs. She stood holding a sign reading Dr. Reeves. He had only saw her a few times right after her surgery. Her gorgeous new hairdo and the big bandage was now gone and she was excited for him to see the new lady she had become. She moved around as each one embarked from the plane. The passengers just kept coming and no Dr. Reeves. "Excuse me Miss? walking up to one of the stewardesses, are there any other passengers on this plane? "I don't think so, but wait I'll check. "Who are you looking for? She asked heading back unto the boarding deck. "My dad, Dr. Reeves, she replied concerned. "Alright just a minute, I haven't seen Jace yet". "JACE? Sonjee repeated not knowing the name. The stewardess walked further into the plane as Sonjee stood outside by the boarding gate waiting for some news. After a few moments out came the stewardess with Dr. Reeves and the pilot. "Daddy, I was worried! She said running up to him hugging his neck. "Oh Sonjee, let me look at you my! My! He said smiling and turning her around and around. "I send you off to school and you grew up on me" he said holding her close again. "Oh, forgive me, he said turning to the stewardess and pilot "this is my youngest daughter Sonjee". She's a student at UCLA" he shared. "We met" the stewardess said shaking her hand "I'm Ellen" and I'm Jace Ramsey" the pilot said extending his hand to her with a big smile. "Sorry for causing you concern" he said. "Hey it's not your fault son I was asking all the questions," but do keep my card we'll talk again" Dr Reeves responded. "Nice meeting you" each said with Jace the young pilot taking another long look at Sonjee as he and the stewardess walked away into the crowded airport.

The stadium was buzzing as David and Tetra made their way to their designated seats. "Hello! They said seeing Doris Wright as they entered the area. Hi! She returned glad you all could make it! She yelled. "Oh wouldn't have missed it for the world," David replied taking their seats on the bench in front of them. "David this is Russell Woods my executive director" Doris stated with a smile. "Please to meet you" David said extending his hand. "And this is my wife Tetra Parker". "Pleasure to finally meet you" he confessed standing to shake Tetra's hand also. "So, are we the first ones here? As far as I know," Doris eagerly chided. "Finley's gone to the snack bar" she laughed. "Finley! Tetra shared the laugh too. Soon up walked Justin, followed by Dana and a cowboy. "Hello everyone! Justin cheerfully greeted taking a seat near Tetra giving her a hug "Hi dad! How are things going? He asked to break the ice. "Just wonderful, glad you could get some time off for this". He replied. "Couldn't let my nephew down" besides we've got lots of interns to replace me" he teased. "Hello Dana! Justin remarked seeing her and her friend walking up to take their seats. "Well wonder's never cease! She stated looking at Justin. "So, what did David Michael promise you to get you out here? She asked bluntly. "Oh, now Dana, that's just not right" I have been here more times than you know" besides you're one to talk! Alright! Truce! David said coming between the two of them. "We're here to have fun". "Hello Tetra" Dana shared standing in front of the row in which they were to sit. "Why hello Dana, it's always a pleasure to see you where David Michael's concerned' Tetra stated with David nudging her leg. "Oh, I see this is jump on Dana day! She responded moving down away from the family. "Dana, please get back over here" you know that's the truth" Tetra said knowing Dana very well. "Hey, I apologize this is Corky, he came down to see David Michael too. "Please to meet you everyone said in unison. Dana moved back in her original seat. Tetra put her hand on her shoulder and smiled. Sonjee and Dr. Reeves were the next ones coming to take their seats. The stadium was filling quickly with excited baseball fans. The noise level was very high and filled with laughter. "Daddy I think you know everyone here' Sonjee said showing her dad to his seat next to her aunt Dana. "Why hello everyone it's good to see you," he replied standing waving around at those seated in the family. 'Dr Reeves, David shared getting up from the bench, this is my son Dr. Justin Parker." Oh, sorry Justin I didn't recognize you with the cap" Sonjee said smiling at him. 'Hey it's fine, pleasure to meet you Dr. Reeves extending his hand for a shake. The band came marching across the field and took seats in the stands. Finley had made is way back to his seat with an armload of goodies for everyone. David Michael! David! Sonjee yelled from the stands as he came to the field. He waved in her direction. Everyone else waved back with a smile. Dr. Reeves and David had struck up a conversation while Dana, Sonjee and Tetra were talking with Doris about her fall collection that had arrived at the boutique. Justin had made his way down on the field near the cheerleaders talking with David Michael and a couple of the other team members. "Uncle Justin" her name is Eden she's the head cheerleader". "Okay is she coming tonight?" I'm sure their all coming" David Michael replied. "Good just checking things out" he smiled walking back into the stands. 'Hey has anyone seen Billy? he asked. Everyone got quiet. The team had taken their position on the field. The announcer's voice rang out "PLEASE STAND FOR THE SINGING OF THE NATIONAL ATHEM! With the whole stadium standing as the Anthem was being song from down on the field in ran Billy and Nada through the crowds gathered for the game. "Excuse me! Sorry! Oops coming down the aisle to get to their seats. 'As soon as the home of the brave rang out" the cheering began. "Whew we made it! Billy said taking his seat. "PLAY BALL! The game moved along at an even pace. Cotton candy, popcorn, cold drinks were being sold throughout the large stadium as the game was being played. The band was playing and the crowds were cheering along with the cheerleaders to ignite their teams. "Tetra put her hand on Billy's shoulder. 'Glad you two could make it" she said smiling at his decision to bring Nada. Me too! He smiled back. "WHACK! The ball went flying into left field. All the men where on their feet! "Did you see that? "GREAT PLAY PARKER!" someone yelled loudly from the stands. David smiled his approval of his grandson's play as well. Each began to share their knowledge of the game of baseball. The game was getting tense. The score was two to three in the bottom of the fifth. "Who would have thought I'd be seating here watching my nephew play like a pro! Justin explained watching intensely at the field. Tetra and Doris headed to the girls' room. "Hey wait for me Sonjee said stepping across those on the bench next to her. The men had all gotten together to enjoy the plays of the game. The women were only there for David Michael and complained loudly when he was thrown out or when his fly ball was caught. They didn't notice the speed on the double play he made to end the sixth ending but the men certainly did and they were on their feet! "Sonjee wait I may as well go too, Billy's talking with your dad" Nada said moving down the steps to meet them. Dana got up bringing Corky with her feeling uneasy about the others heading in the same direction. "I'll get me a beer," Corky said looking back at the game Dana was pulling him from. "Not here you won't I'm headed to the lady's room silly! Dana explained as he turned and walked toward the snack bar. Doris and Tetra were enjoying conversation concerning the church, fund raisers, and her work with the local mission through her Thrift stores which she was actively involved in and doing well. Tetra explained how they were right in the middle of their Holiday toy giveaway for the church and donations were still pouring in. "The community really gets behind the children" she shared. 'Every year we are blessed to give every child that comes through those doors a very nice toy, lots of bicycles! She explained. "That's wonderful Doris added I know that's what the season is all about, giving". I agree Tetra said. "Nada, I love your makeup what is it?" Sonjee asked. "Oh, it's Mac, everyone uses it," she explained. "Not me, it's hard for us women of color to find a makeup that looks right". "You're right some are too oily, to dark, blotchy! name it, I know what you're saying but that's why I started using Mac and it's great". "I use Fashion Fae and it looks good for a while then it becomes very shiny and oily" "Right, that's what I used for years, but a friend of mind suggested Mac and sold me. "Look I'll let you try it when we get to the lady's room." "Sounds good! The ladies walked along talking and laughing together. Sonjee turned to see Dana walking alone. "Aunt Dana! Sonjee yelled back seeing her coming up on them. 'Why didn't you tell me you were coming we would have waited" she said slowing for her to catch up. "Thanks" Dana said and joined her and Nada. "Dana, there's no need for me to come that way, I'd rather be watching the game" Corky explained yelling, turning around to head back to watch the game. "Fine go ahead!" Dana chided and the ladies soon walked up to the waiting lines for the ladies' room. Doris and Tetra was in while the others moved closer to the entrance door. "Oh, I do remember meeting you at the Parker's home" Dana stated. "Yes, that's correct and I remember you" Nada returned. Sonjee was feeling from their tone this wasn't a good idea! "So, I do apologize, what was your name?" she asked inquisitively. "Nada, Nada Francois" Nada replied. "Oh, that's right you're the cook's daughter" it's all coming back to me now! So that's where Billy got you from," she laughed. "Excuse me! Nada stated, "My father happens to be a chef! And for your information owned a restaurant for years! She snapped back at her. "Hey! Hey what's going on here?" Sonjee asked standing between the two of them to diffuse the situation. A stall soon opened and Nada went in with Sonjee and Dana soon following as others became available. Nada was furious! "Billy warned me about her! She thought to herself washing her hands at the basin. "Look Nada I'm sorry Sonjee whispered toward Nada. "It's all right I can handle stupidity well! "Here's the Mac makeup try it, giving her everything she needed in her makeup purse. Everyone was moving in and out of the busy ladies' room. Dana had come out and said she'd wait for them outside, she needed to make a call. "Detective Cavanaugh please" was Dana's request? "The name is Nada Francois, yes F-R-A-N-C-I-O-S-, spelling it out for clarification. "Leave no stone unturned! I want to know the hour she got her first tooth!" She snarled to the investigator she had hired to find out about the woman who had taken her man!

With everyone back in the stands the wild fans cheer their team to victory. Billy and Nada sat very playful with one another as Dana watched fuming from her seat not far away. "Dana that was wonderful what you did for the Beulah Reeves foundation!" Tetra said to her a few seats away as the hoopla was just starting for the baseball team. "Thanks Tetra, that means a lot coming from you" Dana replied. "Well I know God is pleased and that's what counts dear," she said moving over to congratulate her grandson on a wonderful game. "Wow! You all came thanks guys!" he said getting hugs and high fives from his family. "UNCLE JUSTIN! Remember at the boys club I said I would do it!' "I'm so proud of you" Justin shared giving his nephew a shared hug. "Thanks Dr. Reeves and aaa". 'Oh, David this is Corky" Dana shared. "Corky, OH CORKY! No way! Wow! Good to see you, thanks for coming". How's the rodeo business? 'Hey it's great! He replied smiling at the young man he had taught to ride a horse. "Sonjee! Have you seen Frannie? He asked looking through the crowd of people. "No, but I spoke with her earlier she said she would call". Okay, she will but I hoped she would come, I miss her" he responded going over to his dad and Nada. "Hi guys did you see that play dad? He asked "Every one of them, son". Your granddad is over speaking with a guy he met in the stands. "Really, I told you there are lots of scouts out here". "Ray's good, isn't he?" he sure is son, the whole team is great." Billy responded. "Great game David Michael," Nada said gently extending a hug. 'Thanks, he returned with a smile. "David, I'll see you at home" his aunt Doris yelled leaving hurriedly to make sure things were in order for the big party. "Thanks Mr. Finley, and Mr. Woods for coming David Michael yelled as the three headed out through the crowds. It was a wonderful time for the whole family. David Michael got an honorable mention from the scout's present. "For a freshman you've got skills, we're going to keep our eyes on you," one told him shaking his hand. David Michael stood smiling alone with his Varsity teammate Ray whom all the scouts were interested in and speaking with.

"Bottley Crew"

Doris and Billy had arranged for three limousines to pick up the players and their dates for the evening. They wanted them to have fun and be safe. Doris had arrived home and was awaiting those who had stayed around until all the crowds had left the stadium. With everything in place Doris, and Russell sat waiting for the others to come. Finley was giving out orders to the staff on today for this grand event. David and Tetra along with Sonjee and Dr. Reeves made their appearances. "Come in, do go in, Finley replied standing at the door to greet them and take their coats. Everyone was gathering and the fun had begun. "Hi! Hello! Come in. Do come in! Doris and Finley were heard saying over and over again. "Aunt Doris this is magnificent! David Michael shared coming in with a group of his teammates. "Ray, welcome to my family's home, are you going to remember me when you make the big time? He asked teasing is buddy who was surely going to the pros. Ray's girlfriend Yola had come but no Frannie. The cheerleaders had made their way to the great room dancing to the music being played on the stereo. "David thanks for the compliment, I have a surprise for you," is Frannie coming? Doris asked. "Oh that's' right she left me a voice message, let me go up and call her" David Michael said leaving the crowd to go to another room. Dana and Corky soon showed up with Billy, Nada and Justin not far behind. "Wow, this has really grown from our first plans" Billy said turning to Doris. "Yes, you're right, but wait until you see the band I got! "Were you able to get the one we discussed?" "Yes! And I'm so excited Frannie's going to have a fit! The waiters were walking around with champagne and caviar for those over the age limit only. "There were lots of soft drinks and a dramatic punch bowl display for the young at heart. The place was buzzing. Doris stood looking at the crowd. The house had not been that active in some time she remembered. "This is nice," she thought before being interrupted in thought by Russell asking her to dance. "Please help yourselves there's plenty of everything! Billy voiced to the team players and their dates standing around asking questions. Some went to the huge buffet style table and piled their plates high. "To be expected" he told Nada as she looked on. "Babe let's dance Justin's wearing out the dance floor" Billy said pulling her toward the activity on the dance floor. Soon the music slowed somewhat and Tetra and David shared a dance. Dr. Reeves danced with Doris but Russell politely taped his shoulder. Everyone was enjoying themselves. Laughing, eating, dancing and socializing with everyone. "Ring, ring" hello Sonjee answered. "Hello Dr. Reeves? The male voice asked. No! This is his daughter; may I help you? She replied politely. "Yes, this is Jace the pilot, he responded. "Oh yes I remember" what can I help you with? Sonjee asked. "Your dad left his hat and scarf; I'd like to get it to him". "Oh, that is nice of you to call. Let me get my dad; I had his phone that's why I answered", just a moment" walking through the crowd to find him sitting in Doris's office talking with David. "Dad, here's your phone you have a call". "Oh, thanks dear". 'Hello Dr. Reeves" he said. "Jace Ramsey, Dr. Reeves your friendly pilot," he laughed. 'Oh yes son what can I do for you? He asked. "You left your hat and scarf on the plane sir; since I had your card and number, I thought I'd try and get them back to you" he shared. "Well now that's wonderful, my wife knitted that scarf I would sure hate to lose it, but where are you now son? Dr. Reeves asked. "I'm still here in Los Angeles sir, I won't fly out until noon tomorrow" Jace responded. "Hold for a moment son let me locate my daughter maybe we can drive back out to the airport and pick them up", still talking as he walked around looking for Sonjee. "Sir if you don't mind, I can bring your things to you" the very polite young pilot suggested. "Well now we're a ways out from the airport son" Mr. Reeves shared. "Sir honestly I don't fly out until noon tomorrow, I'm just going to my room and watch television". "Let me get the address, hold on son". "Doris? going over to ask her permission to have the young man come to her home. Doris spoke with him giving him directions to her home and retuned the phone back to Dr. Reeves. "See you soon" he said going to find Sonjee and let her know why he had called and to keep your eyes open for his arrival. The party was still buzzing with fun. The band was due in an hour; Doris told Billy, so everyone was still mingling with Dana getting her digs into Nada every chance she got. As Billy and Nada stood in the wide hallway cuddling Dana happened by. "So, Billy this is what you tried to replace me with? she chided, "Nada stood in front of her. "Nada don't bother, I know you're more woman than that" he replied putting his arm around her moving her back. Dana slapped Billy in the face! You'll be sorry! She stated walking off to another room. "Billy, we have got to confront this you know!" Nada explained. "And we will, but not tonight, and surely not now", rubbing his face to ease the pain from her viperous slap.

Jace entered the front entrance of the home pulling up to a huge iron gate. ON THE SIDE he saw a speaker with lots of buttons. "Wow, impressive! He thought but this is Beverly Hills. He pushed the button and announced his arrival. Soon the large gate was opening and a short way down the path was a guard's gate. "Getting cleared there he was at the front door of Doris Wrights magnificent home. Parking and walking up to the door, he was invited in." Come in" Finley said opening the door. "I'm here to speak with Dr. Reeves please, Jace Ramsey" he voiced extending his hand to Finley with a warm greeting. The scarf and hat he held in his other hand. "Dr. Reeves? He asked a bit puzzled. "Sonjee Reeves? Jace shared to clarify things seeing her past the hall as he stood at the door. "Oh Dr. Reeves, Sonjee's father right this way sir. walking him through the crowd of people in the home. The dance floor was still showing much activity and the dining areas were busy too. Dr. Reeves and David were playing a game of chess while Tetra sat and read some of the study books Doris kept in her library. "Hello! Dr. Reeves said seeing Finley and Jace coming into the library. "Hello sir, don't bother standing continue your game" he said handing him his hat and scarf. "Jace Ramsey this is Mr. and Mrs. David Parker. "Please to meet you sir," extending again a friendly hand. "My wife Tetra Parker' again turning his hand to say hello. "Dr. Reeves went on to explain who he was, and how he had met him, and of course his reason for being here. "Thank you, I would hate to have lost it. My wife knitted this from her sick bed" he said "it means a lot to me." After a while there was a loud shouting and cheering! Everyone gathered near the pool area to watch the band "Bottley Crew! Are you kidding it's really them could be heard throughout the as they left the room? "Where's David Michael? Everyone kept asking. With everyone looking for David Michael he was soon located in one of the guest rooms. "Hey David Michael the band is here" Dana said coming in smiling. "Okay, he replied. He and Sonjee were sitting on the bed talking. "Come on dear everyone's waiting for you" Dana explained escorting him up from the bed and out the door. Billy had now come up too. "Uncle Billy, Sonjee voiced seeing he was going out behind the crowd escorting David Michael out to see his favorite band play. "Yes, Sonjee what's happening? He asked playfully. "I thought you might want to know David's feeling a bit sad right now" Oh why what's happened? He asked concerned. "It's Frannie, seems she's fallen for her volley ball coach". "Say's the long distant relationship didn't work for her". Sonjee explained as they walked downstairs near the others. Nada had joined them now and the crowds were eagerly headed to enjoy the live music. "Thanks, dear, I'll speak with him later giving" Sonjee a hug and she went to find her dad. "Doris this is wonderful the kids seemed to be enjoying themselves David said, Tetra and I are going to turn in and we will see you tomorrow" he shared. Tetra stood speaking with Doris and each gave hugs around the room. Dr. Reeves was retiring for the night to and had sent for his overcoat. "David, may I ride in with you, these young children have more energy than I do" he smiled. Sure, where are you staying? David asked standing holding Tetra's hand preparing to leave. I'm at the Sheraton, is that out of your way? Dr. Reeves asked. "No, that's perfect we're there too" David explained, I would love to finish our conversation. "Sonjee had now made her appearance hugging her dad's waist. "Are you leaving dad? "Yes, Sonjee I'm turning in for the evening, will you see that Jace enjoys himself." "He's doing fine, I left him on the dance floor with Macie, he seems fine but I'll make sure to check on him from time to time" she stated giving her dad a goodnight hug. "I will see everyone at the dinner tomorrow! Billy yelled toward them as they walked out. Soon they were gone and the younger set was out by the pool dancing and grooving to the sounds of the band. David Michael had taken one to many champagne glasses from the tray as the waiter's walked by and he was feeling what he called goooooood! Finley being told soon put a stop to the champagne he was not supposed to be drinking anyway. David Michael and Billy sat talking about what was troubling him. Sonjee was keeping Jace with companionship introducing him around while Billy, Nada, and Dana were chaperoning the gathering of young college students. Doris and Russell had retired to the small sitting room upstairs and Finley was overseeing it all. Everyone had a safe good time including Dana we're told!

CHAPTER 36

Revisited

The year ended peacefully for the most part. Tetra's toy giveaway at the Mt. Nebo was a big success. David was growing mightily and was very active in another ministry work along with his wife. The drama department put on another great performance this year with the Christmas play. Tyler Parsons came home and brought the house down playing his "blessed saxophone" Mother Bean called it. She and her husband accompanied him on this trip to meet his family. She was an elderly woman devoted to God who was very instrumental in helping him get back on his feet. Doris's health stayed in check and she and Russell Woods where spending time together more and there was even talk of a wedding. David Michael had unfortunately taken the break up with Frannie a bit hard and despite Sonjee his cousin being there for support he had gone back to his old group of friends, not including his baseball teammates that were on hiatus until next season. Finley was actively trying to get David Michael and Sonjee involved with the young adult group at the church to fill what he called empty or lacking space in their lives. Sonjee thought it would be fun if she had time, she told him. She was very active again with her dance. She had been invited to dance in a festival in Washington D.C. She begged David Michael to come with her but he chose not to this trip. "Okay, but I won't stop asking. "I'm performing during summer break it's going to be fun' she shared with him. "How long does it last Sonjee? He asked after continually being asked by her. "It's a citywide event cuz, that last for six months at the Kennedy Center.

But I'm only doing it for summer break. "Promise me you will come before I leave there". She was selected to join an elect group of dancers from UCLA to attend this first ever event from a recommendation from her former teacher at Gonzaga. "Okay I promise," he said leaving his aunt's house once again to meet friends at the sports bar. Billy and Nada were growing closer together and spent New Years Eve in Time Square together. Things in life were moving on. Dana spent New Years at the Gala Affair the hospital puts on every year. A lot of her other time was spent at the office or at the Ranch with Rusty, who seemed to be improving. And of course, there was her good friend and coworker Mollie. Corky had started feeling possessive of Dana but she didn't notice his growing affection for her. She viewed him only as a friend. Most of the time at the ranch was spent talking with Rusty who was trying to relive the past with her. She and Corky would go out for rides on the horses occasionally. Mollie would also go, when she was there, wasn't her favorite thing to do! But! Dana wanted Billy and she was going to have him at any cost. "I'll let him have his fun but it will be over soon! She thought sitting in her office behind her desk waiting for that call. "Yes, this is Dr. Williams," she answered. "Happy New Year to you Detective" I hope you have some good news for me" she smiled. Before long she began listening to Nada's Life story. "This one's pretty easy he says, I feel somewhat bad about charging for this story" he shared. "Please tell me, she paused "and Cavanaugh don't spare any details! She stated harshly as he began sharing all the details he found out. Finding out about Nada's life growing up, her mother's death, and her family's lost during the floods in New Orleans, her old boyfriend she left behind, Dana's mind went to work to win back Billy Parker her love and kindergarten friend.

CHAPTER 37

The Last Straw

"Glen Reed please? Billy asked calling NASA space center. "This is Mr. Reed, he replied rolling up to his desk. "How's it going man? "Billy! Wow how long as it been six months I know!" he smiled across the telephone line. "To long, but how's the family? Billy asked taking a moment from his busy schedule to call his friend. "Everyone's fine and sends their love as always" he replied. "So how are you and Dana? He asked; has life settled down for you two? "Man no! He laughed. I'm dating someone else now". Seriously, whoa! I mean I hope it works, but, where is she? I know things ended rocky? Glen mocked. "Ended, I've been dating Nada for about three months and Dana hasn't gone away! She drops by my office unannounced to make life a living hell! 'I'M HOPING SOON IT WILL BE OVER! "It has been a quiet two weeks." He shared. "Quiet before the storm" Glen teased. "Anyway, when do I get a chance to meet this lady who has stolen your heart from Cruella? He laughed. "Yes, I'm beginning to believe that" he paused "Dana is evil" "Umm and what year did you make that discovery? Glen again asked having known her for years. "Yeah, but there were good times too I must admit" Billy added in her defense. "How's Cheryl? She's good, we would love to see you Bill" when do you plan a visit? "Oh, funny you would ask" Nada and I are coming that way on a Bahamas cruise next month and will stop in for a day or two". "Man, that will be nice! Glen exclaimed, just like the good old days". "That's for sure", how's the legs treating you? Billy had been evading the question but since he was going to visit it would surely come up.

"Man. I'm still in my wheelchair" he shared sadly. 'Can't run after the girls anymore" he teased keeping his spirit up. "Well, there's no need right you've got Cheryl now" he stated to his dear friend. "Yeah man you're right" look I look forward to seeing you man" we haven't talked in a while" he confessed with a heavy heart. Glen and Billy were bosom buddies growing up together sharing each other's families and lives. They talked often over the phone about once a month. But since the terrible accident that left Glen paralyzed from the waist down. These days they spoke more infrequent. But after speaking with Billy this time, it left Glen anticipating his dear friends' arrival. "I'll call soon" Billy shared getting off the line. "Umm Billy thought, his heart was heavy, he took a moment and whispered a prayer for his friend.

Nada was on her way to see her dad when Billy called. "Hello honey", my day was great! And yours? She asked with a smile in her voice. "Busy honey, very busy" I was in court most of the day," he admitted to her. "Oh, honey I'm sorry you have to work so hard" she voiced with sympathy for him. "Thanks sweetheart I really enjoy it but I am looking forward to our cruise". "Me too William" the girls are jealous they're always teasing me about being gone on vacation." "Well maybe soon you will go and not come back" he suggested speaking of keeping her in Maine. "Now that would be something," she replied liking what he said. "So, what's on your agenda for tonight? He asked. "Going by to see daddy for a while and Madison and I are going to dinner". "Madison huh? "Oh, Billy you know I only have eyes for you" she flirted. "Look sweetheart let me finish up here and I'll call you tonight say around 10:00 your time" he asked. "Sounds good honey I love you Billy". He sat for a moment reading some briefs Annie had given him. He had not taken his coat off and hung it behind the door as he usual does. The briefs he was holding had his attention. Billy was very interested in the documents his secretary had handed him walking in. After a few minutes he stood up to remove his sport jacket and in walked Dana unannounced again. He took a dept breath, Dana! surprise seeing you here" how are you? He asked being cordial anyway. "I'm great, haven't seen or spoken with you since last year, and you were not knocking my door down to see me! She stated coming over to hug him. "Happy New year" she voiced wanting more than Billy was willing to give. "Happy New Year" he said going back behind his desk looking again at the briefs. "Well, what brings you by Dana? he asked again, I'm quite busy". "I'm giving you another chance to come to your senses," she stated. "Look! Billy said standing up "this is not the time, nor the place for your foolishness Dana!" Things were getting a bit loud. Annie came over to the door. "Billy is everything all right? She asked "It's fine Annie", Dana is leaving". "WITCH! Dana yelled slamming the office door. "You mean to tell me you're going to let that, that, thing come between us! She stuttered her words. "Dana, look I'm not going to discuss my relationship with you! "Why? What does she have that I don't have? She asked coming behind the desk to hold or hug him. "Me, Dana, she has me!" "Look Dana, we've settled this more than once" when you left me in Kansas what? six months ago! You said it was over! Okay it's over, I agree". He replied ending the conversation sitting at his desk. "Billy, how can you just end what we had?" she asked now sitting on a chair she had pulled up to the desk. "Because what we had was going nowhere Dana! He was getting frustrated with her now. "But what can she give you? Exhausted from the conversation, he stated again, "Dana, I will not discuss my relationship with Nada with you! "How can you say her name to me? She screamed. "Look Dana I think you should leave now" he recommended getting up to open the closed office door. "LEAVE! LEAVE! she screamed. "You can not ask me to leave! She stated slamming the door shut again. By now the other attorneys and staff could hear what was going on. "Annie's husband walked over and knocked on the door opening it slightly. "Bill you, all right? "I'm fine, she is leaving" he said opening the door again standing near it. This time Dana picked up the heavy paperweight from his desk and threw it toward the door. Billy ducked and Keith pulled the door closed to keep the object in the room with her while he and Billy stood outside the door. "Bill you okay? He asked before opening the door to let Billy see inside of his office for damage. "Look I'm fine, she acknowledged before Billy opened the door further. "Everyone was standing around looking now at her fury. Annie had witnessed her meanness but nothing like the display she was putting on today. "Billy come in, please close the door, 'I apologize, I'm fine I'd like to talk with you privately" she asked meekly. "Billy looked at his staff's puzzled faces. "Okay Dana but make it quick please we have an office to run here." His patient with Dana had worn thin but he didn't know how thin until her next move. "Go back to your offices I'm fine," he said convincingly to Annie and the rest of the staff now gathered in front of his office door. Dana was sitting down now waiting for Billy's attention to turn again to her. "All right Dana you have my attention," he said waiting to hear what she had to say. "I'm sorry sweetheart I really didn't mean to cause a scene but you make me so angry! She said looking for sympathy from him. "Angry! I don't believe you, when I tried for years to be with you and care for you". "The last straw was when you left me in Kansas at the lodge! Remember the lodge Dana! He yelled louder than intended but she had made him angry. "Lower your voice, she stated knowing she had gotten into his head now. "Dana please leave, I have nothing else to say to you at this time" Billy stated again going over to the door. "If you would have just said yes to my proposal this would have all been over! She yelled from her seated position. "Dana leave," pointing with his hand toward the door. A slight turn of his head when his phone rang and Dana had her hands on him screaming and tugging at his shirt. "I hate you! She kept clawing and screaming! "DANA! He shouted GRABBING HER AROUND THE NECK AND SHOVING HER BACK ON THE CHAIR. His staff was again at the door. "Get her out of here! He stated, get her out of her now! Keith, Annie's husband assisted another attorney to escort Dana to the security guard waiting out by the elevator. "I don't want her within a hundred yards of this building" Billy affirmed returning to his office adjusting his clothes. "Which one of us is going to defend him? They asked each other going back to their offices shaking their heads.

CHAPTER 38

She did what?

Nada was having a cup of coffee with her dad when Tetra came home. "Why hello dear" she replied walking into her kitchen. "Hello Mrs. Parker" Nada said coming over sharing a hug. "So how long have you been here? Tetra asked, "for about an hour talking to daddy". "Well don't let me disturb you'. 'How was your day Alfredo? Tetra asked moving toward the stairs. "It was wonderful madam, thanks for asking". "Is there something I can get for you? he asked. "Not at this time you enjoy your visit with your daughter". Nada we will talk before you leave okay?" "Sounds great Mrs. Parker" Nada went sat back to the tall stool and finished her coffee and conversation with her dad. "Ring, ring! Her cell phone in her purse was ringing. "Hello honey! She said cheerfully, I'm still here at your parents' home I didn't expect a call from you" but its fine I love you too! She teased. Billy was quiet. "Honey are you alright?" she asked the silence was very misleading. "Dana! He stated. 'Dana, what about Dana? she asked excusing herself to another part of the house for a private conversation. "Dana just left; well, I had her escorted out! He shared again still angry from the incident earlier. "Honey what happened? Are you all right?" Nada, physically I'm fine" she just has a way of making me want to strangle her! "Oh, honey I hope you didn't get that upset". Sweetheart I did" I really did". He replied. I have got to settle this matter with Dana" I don't know what's she up to or capable of" he shared. "I would like you to stay at my parents for a while, just until this crazy woman settles down". "Look Billy I shared with you we would have to confront Dana!

Should I come there to be with you? "No Nada, I want you so far from Dana's wrath I cannot began to explain what she's capable of! "Billy, she is human just like us, she's wants us to let her scare us and I refuse too!" Nada chided. "Look Nada, I understand what you think you know but Dana, she's not human! 'What? Well, I'm joking of course but you didn't see the display she put on in my office". I'm going to let her settle down for a few days before I confront her again." I'll call you later. "Okay Billy but if I don't see you this weekend, I coming your way," she told him concerned for his safety and angry Dana was still causing problems. "Sweetheart think about what I said about staying at the house, I'm sure your dad would like having you for a few days". "I'll think about it, Billy". "Nada it's going to be fine, I love you" I love you too". Nada walked back into the hallway now seeing Tetra sitting in her great-room. "Mrs. Parker may I speak with you for a moment? she asked. "Oh, sure dear I was going to ask you if we could do something together besides sitting at the salon" she smiled patting for her to sit down. "That's sound wonderful Mrs. Parker". 'Dear you sound troubled is something wrong? She asked reaching for her hand to hold. "I just finished speaking with Billy; it seems Dana came by his office and upset him again" she shared concerned. "Oh my, Tetra exclaimed getting up from her sofa. "I just knew she was not going to let Billy have a life" she said frustrated at the thought. "Mrs. Parker is Billy safe with her hating him that much? She slapped him so hard at Doris' I was furious! "She did what! "Oh, Billy says he's fine." I'm going up to my room dear." Please stay as long as you like. I must go and do something upstairs." heading off to another room leaving Nada alone thinking.

Mr. Reeves had just retuned from the hospital visiting an old friend when Sonjee called him. "Hi daddy! sounding chipper as always "Hello darling how's the show going? he inquired. Daddy it's unbelievable! Standing O's every show. I even got a chance to see my dance instructor from Gonzaga." "Well, that's great what a coincidence! small world, he explained taking a sit to talk with his daughter. "No not surprised, I knew she would be there" "Candace is coming to the show this week". Oh, really now that's wonderful. Yes, and we're going to do some shopping while she's here "Doesn't surprise me a bit! You two always find time to shop," he laughed. They talked for a while catching up on things which was their daily routine. All the dancers had gathered in a hallway entrance to the stage for a quick meeting. Sonjee had just finished her conversation with her dad and stood waiting in the back with the others. "Excuse me someone said tapping her from behind on her shoulder. Her silky flowing shoulder length hair was bouncing and behaving from a newly touched up perm and her flawless skin was beautiful with the Mac facial makeup she had purchased and absolutely loved! Turning around she looked up into the face of Fonsworth Erickson her old friend from Gonzaga. "Yes, she said with her knees shaking from fear he would recognize her. She wasn't frightened of him she just wanted his story to end. The nightmares she was having for months had dissipated somewhat and she wanted nothing else to do with him even though she now understood why. "Does this girl dance with you? Handing her a picture of her with dreads and the nose she left behind. Sonjee was looking at the picture but Fonsworth was panning the crowd disappointed trying to find her. "No, disguising her voice "I'm sure no one has seen her here" she told him nervously looking at the photo not wanting him to make the correlation. A few of the other dancer's standing near her looked at the photograph and shook their heads negatively with a smile. Soon the instructor came out and motioned for the group to come to the stage. Sonjee handed him back the photograph, "Sorry!" she said running behind the others.

Billy was tired after his incident with Dana. He finished getting together some paperwork for court Tuesday morning, and spoke with his staff, and left with everyone else going home. 'Good night! They all shared going their separate ways. "Billy are you sure you're going to be all right? Annie asked walking out holding hands with her husband. I'll be fine. "I'm headed home to rest we'll be in court most of tomorrow, right" he said looking at Keith. "Yes, I'll meet you there Annie has an appointment in the morning also." 'Oh, do you need me to get Paulson or Magee to assist me? "Oh no I'll be there" Great! See you tomorrow" shaking his hand and a wave to Annie he was in the car heading down the highway. "RING, RING! Hello, Billy said answering. "Hey Parker, are you going to make the meeting tonight? It was one of his Christian brothers calling to remind him as he had asked anyone too from the last meeting. "Don, oh man I forgot all about it" Billy admitted. "I did to but Albert called me so I'm going to head over now otherwise I'd just go home and watch a game or worse work", he shared with a laugh. "You're right, look I'll see you there, thanks guy" "hey we all need reminders," later! Billy called and talked with Nada who was headed out to dinner with her friend Madison after which was going home to her own bed for a good night's rest. He on the other hand was glad he had gone to the meeting with his fellow brothers and went home for a good night's rest after calling saying goodnight to Nada around 10:00 0 clock in the evening.

David Michael was gathering his things from the dorm when a knock came to the door. "COME IN! He yelled still moving things around to find his stuff. The room was a disaster area most of the time. His roommate Kyle was a party animal and contributed to most of it. "Hey David! Oh Ray, I didn't know it was you, come in sorry for the mess, I'm moving out, he shared. 'Really you're not going to stay in the dorms next year? Ray asked. No, my cousin and I got a place a few blocks from campus". 'Really hey those or very nice and costly for a student." 'Yeah, but our parents or chipping in, you know how that goes right? 'Right! "Well look guy I came by to give you the good news and of course invite you to the celebration". David Michael stood waiting holding some clothes he was packing in a box listening for what his old locker buddy had to say. 'What man the suspense is killing me! "I signed with the Cardinals! "I'm headed to Saint Louis! WOW! GREAT! I knew you were the best! He exclaimed giving a high five to him. "Congrats dude! "Hey I want you to know I'm going to be watching you" keep yourself in the books and out of the bars I'll BE SEEING YOU IN THE PRO'S TOO RIGHT? Ray encouraged. He had taken David under his wing for the most part helping him to improve his game. "You're good man, I can't wait to see you there" he smiled leaving. "Oh tonight, what time? David asked after coming back down to earth from the good news. "Starts at 6 0 clock man, invites only though! He explained standing in the door. 'Got it, Thanks Ray" "I can do it, I can do it! David Michael said jumping around before settling again to continue to pack his belongings to move out.

Tetra sat next to David her husband in the pews listening to Pastor Edinburgh's message. They had just returned from the morning altar prayer remembering to pray for their son and his situation with Dana. Pastor Edinburgh had just returned from the Holy land and was sharing an experience with the congregation during his visit. "My he is full this morning" Tetra expressed watching the moving of the spirit throughout the church as he spoke. "I wouldn't trade walking on that Holy ground for anything else" he shared with tears streaming from his face. "I looked in the tomb where they laid him" IT'S EMPTY. The praises went up and swept over the entire audience present. The movement of the Holy Spirit took over and praises went up higher and rejoicing began. Some shouted, there was a clapping of hands, others shed tears of joy as God himself showed up in their service once again. "AMEN! David shouted.

CHAPTER 39

A Quiet Storm

The week was quiet. To quiet, Billy thought pulling into his driveway. "No Dana could it be over? Really over? He thought getting out of the car. David Michael had called earlier to say all his things had been moved into the new condo in Westwood and he was going to visit his buddy Tommy in Texas on his ranch for a week and would call him when he returned to L.A. Billy hurried in to call Nada. He would be working on a court case all weekend and didn't want her to worry or jump on a plane heading this way. He would be tied up in meetings all weekend anyway. "Ring! Ring! "You have reached the home of Nada please leave a message after the tone" the recording sounded so sweet. Billy smiled and dialed her cell phone. Ring! Hello daddy? She asked hurriedly. "No sweetheart it's me, what's going on you sound panicked? he asked. 'I'm on my way to your parent's home, your mom called me asking if I had saw daddy today? 'Why is everything all right? "Billy, I don't know.' She said he left a note stating he had something to pickup at the supermarket earlier this morning and hasn't returned since". This morning! What time are we talking about sweetheart? he probed. "Billy, I don't know exactly, look I'm pulling in the driveway now I'll call back when I know something" she shared still a bit shaken from the news. It was not like Alfredo to go off all day. Not to a super market without telling somebody. Tetra met her at the door giving her the note. 'Come in dear" she said hugging her. "I just came from the bungalow he's not there." I looked at the note for a clue or something' and I called David and shared with him" Tetra explained. "Thanks, Mrs. Parker for calling, look I'm going to go back to the bungalow to see if I can see something to tell me where he's gone". Looking again at the note, "this isn't daddy's handwriting, Nada said. Maybe the coat or clothes he's wearing will give us a clue or something. She moved quickly to the door with Tetra following close behind. Turning the key in the door they walked in. Everything was in place. Strange, nothing seems out of order Nada thought looking around. His morning's cup of coffee was still in the sink. After looking aimlessly around for something out of place she sat on the colorfully printed sofa and began to cry. She had been there an hour and still no call or contact from her dad. Tetra had returned to the house just in case he called or came back. His car was gone, where was he? She thought. "Ring, ring! Her cell phone in her purse was ringing. She sat up hurriedly and answered daddy? "No Nada 'its Billy, and you still have not heard from him? No! She cried trying to wipe tears flowing. She reached to get a tissue to blow her nose and next to the tissue box was something shining. Hers tears were distorting her vision so she quickly wiped her eyes and picked up a ring. It belonged to her dad; it was his wedding ring, which he never takes off. Some thing was wrong. "BILLY! she yelled into the phone. SOMETHING'S HAPPENED TO MY DAD! "Nada, Nada what are you saying, what do you see? He asked trying to connect across the lines. "I found daddy's ring! He never takes off his wedding ring! He's trying to tell me something, but what? "Look Nada I'm on my way! He stated. Nada looked up to see Tetra and David now standing in the bungalow door. "Billy, wait, your parents are here" she quickly stated before he disconnected the line. "Let me speak with my son" David asked reaching for Nada's cell phone. "Dad what's going on? "Look son, there's not much you can do here now! I have someone looking into this matter if there is one. "The police won't do anything until he's gone for a least twenty-hour hours". We may be jumping to conclusions" he shared. "I know dad but I would just like to be with Nada" Billy replied. "Well son I understand but your mother and I are here. I thought you shared with me you were in court now," trying to ease the hurriedness of the moment. "I am dad, but I can get Keith or Dan to cover for a day or two" Billy explained. "Well, it seems you'd at least wait to see if he's gone longer. His car isn't here!" "You're right dad, I understand, is she, all right? he asked. "She a strong lady Billy, she will be fine" Okay may, I speak back with her? he asked caringly. David handed her the cell phone and began looking around the bungalow for clues or something to give hint to Alfredo's disappearance.

Dana sat having lunch with her friend Molly in the hospital cafeteria. "Well, it won't be long now! She stated eating her lush green salad for lunch. "So, are you going to tell me what you've been up to? Molly asked sitting across the table from her. "No, but you'll find out soon enough". Well does it have anything to do with Billy? She again questioned. "Molly you ask to many questions, eat your lunch" she said smiling deviously.

Doris do you think the family is going to like the fact that we're getting married? Russell asked as they sat in their pastor's office waiting to speak with him regarding their wedding plans. "My family loves you, and of course I love you! She stated to ease his concerns regarding their future plans. "Ring! Ring! Hello Doris answered. "Hello God mother! How are you? Sonjee asked calling her cheerfully from Washington D.C. "I'm fine, funny you should call, Russell and I are here to speak with Pastor Grey about getting married". "Oh, so he finally asked Godmother? "Finally, she smiled. 'Well tell him I said congrats! "Sonjee says congratulations! Doris turned to Russell to share what her daughter had said. "Thanks" he smiled back to her. "Well, how's the show going? 'Oh, Godmother it is unbelievable! Candace was here last week and we had fun shopping after the show" Sonjee replied. "Good, Russell, Finley and I will be there soon". I have some important test to take this week but my doctor seems to think there's nothing to worry about" Doris responded. "That's great Godmother. I look forward to seeing you and I too hope the test are ok." "Thanks sweetheart. "Have you spoken with David Michael lately? Sonjee asked concern. "I haven't I know he's gotten all moved into the condo. Finley helped him take some of his clothes when he went over to see him" Doris said. "Oh, I see, I know Finley was trying to get him and I to participate with that young group of college students at your church" Sonjee replied. Yes, Sonjee that would be wonderful for both of you". "It surely couldn't hurt. David is taking the break up with Frannie pretty hard so I'm glad Finley is staying on him" Sonjee added. "Well Godmother if you can try and persuade him to come with you," she asked. I have been calling him and he promised he would before I left though, I haven't spoken with him lately, he's not answering his phone." "Sure, sweetie I'll see what I can do, remember Dana is his mother! He acts like her sometime I'm afraid," Doris said trying to explain away his behavior. "You take care I've got to go Pastor Grey is here." "Love you! They both said before disconnecting the line.

Sonjee had been around her hotel room most of the day. A group of her fellow dancers had stopped in Sonjee's room on their way to the Kennedy Center where the show was being performed. "Sonjee, please let me use your makeup? "Ahh! You like it, I told you! You'd like it." Lauren it's in that carrying case right there" she said pointing as she stood in the mirror putting her hair up for the performance tonight. "Ring, ring! Sonjee your cell phone is ringing" one of the six dancers replied. "Sonjee ran from the bathroom grabbing her phone from the vanity where she had lain it after speaking with her Godmother. "Hello, she said. "Hi! The male voice said. "Hello, who's calling? Sonjee asked not recognizing the voice. "Oh, I'm sorry I thought you saw your caller Id and was giving me a hard time" he replied. "Okay" she stated I didn't so whose ringing my phone? Its Jace, am I bothering you? "Oh, Jace I'm sorry I'm getting ready for a show? A show? He asked. "I'm dancing in the Shakespeare festival". "Oh, I was in L.A and I thought we could have dinner? he asked. "Great idea, I'd love too but, I'm in Washington D.C. at the Kennedy Center, Sonjee informed laughing at Jace as he laughed at himself. "Oh, I guess I blew that date uh? "Look thanks for calling I have to get dressed, I'll call you tomorrow and tell you about the show here" she said hurrying off the line. "Can't wait to hear from you," he said smiling as he disconnected the line.

Alfredo sat with his head down. He was sad, disappointed and quite upset because the guy still had not produced his daughter and two whole days had past, he noticed looking at the calendar of his watch. "Hey! Hey! He yelled from the dark little room where he sat tied with duck tape on his ankles and around his wrist. There was a time in his life when he could have gotten out of that tape without breaking a sweat! thinking to himself as he yelled. Soon in ran a big tall man.

"WHATS GOING ON? WHY ARE YOU YELLING! Look I need my medicine" you left my jacket in the other car!" WELL, I HAVE TO MAKE A PHONE CALL" STOP YELLING THOUGH". He admonished walking out of the room putting his cell phone to his head.

Nada sat in the bungalow still waiting to hear from her dad. Police now were aiding the family search for him. Billy had gotten his affairs in order with his law firm and came down to be by Nada's side. "Billy do you think we will find him soon?" she asked lying her head on his shoulder on the sofa. "I'm sure with everyone looking for him someone is bound to see or hear something." "You're right but I'm worried he's not taking his medicine". She voiced. "I'm sure he'll be fine". Billy was praying so it had been longer than he expected Alfredo to be missing. But he was keeping strong for Nada. "Ring! Ring! Her cell phone was ringing. "Hello, hello jumping quickly to answer it. "Hello Nada Jean? "Oh hi Mrs. Manuel" "Oh baby you still ain't found yo daddy?" "No, I haven't heard from him yet". "Well, I'm praying" she shared. "Thanks Mrs. Manuel that's sweet". Then there was silence. "Nada Jean, I don't won't to bother you but Hazel done got us loss! "Loss? "Yes, she said she know how to get to Nettie's house and we got forced on the freeway and I don't know where we's et now! You were going to Mrs. Blakins home? "Yes NETTIE! I SAID NETTIE DIDN'T I! "I'm sorry I know her as Mrs. Blakins". "Okay whatever we loss and I'm not letting her back under this wheel today! Now, now, Mrs. Manuel, please let me speak with Hazel." 'She went to Starbucks to get a cup of coffee to calm her nerves! I told her to bring me the whole pot! Mrs. Manuel stated. Trying to hold in her laugh Nada asked "Mrs. Manuel can you tell me where you are? the street and an address of a building? YES, I CAN hold for a minute while I get my glasses." Few minutes went by as she searched through her large handbag. "Okay, 79145 Expo Way". "My you two certainly have traveled a distance from home". "I know that's why I made her pull over and stop the car! "Let me speak with Hazel is she back yet? NO! BUT I AM NOT GETTING BACK IN THIS CAR WITH HAZEL ROSS DRIVING WITH NO DIRECTIONS! Mrs. Manuel was speaking very loudly into the phone. Billy had to laugh. "Listen Nada tell them to stay put we're on our way". Nada shared with Mrs. Manuel what Billy had suggested and disconnected the phone. "Billy you go I want to be here if daddy calls or comes back". "Nada you need to get out you've been in here for two days! Come on the fresh air will do you good besides Mrs. Hazel will welcome a warm smile," pulling her up from the sofa, putting on her jacket and out the door they went.

Alfredo hadn't heard from the man in the past hour so he yelled again. Hey! Hey! He went on for about fifteen minutes straight. After a while he heard a door slam! BAM! "Look I went all through that car and I didn't see a jacket! He stated looking now at Alfredo slumped over just about to fall over in the chair. He straightened him up and gave him some water. He could see the sweat beading on his face. "Hey! Hey! Tapping him on the face, you, all right? "I need my medicine," the weak sounding Alfredo said. "I looked all over for your coat I didn't see it! "It's in the trunk where you had me, remember! He yelled with all the strength he could muster. "Oh, that's right I didn't think to look there," he said rubbing his head. "Okay, I'm going to take you with me this time but don't try any funny stuff" helping Alfredo up loosening the ties on his legs and walking him like a duck out the door and in his car. "Nice ride you've got! the man acknowledged. "I guess thanks would be in order" Alfredo reluctantly replied sitting on the passenger side of his own car. "So, do you have my daughter or, are you wanting money or something? You seemed to be wasting both of our time! Alfredo expressed as they rode down the highway to the stranger's car parked in a lot. "Enough said! He responded and turned into the large parking lot and headed to the dusty car that had been parked there for days.

Hazel had gotten back with directions for getting them home but Mrs. Manuel was not budging. "Nada Jean said to stay right here and that's precisely what we're going to do! She stated to Hazel who was very capable of getting them back home if Virginia would just shut up and ride! "Look over there Hazel ain't that's Nada Jean daddy's car? "Hey! Hey! She was moving quickly across the lot toward the car yelling. "Hazel go put the hood up on the car, go! Go! I'm adding something to our story" she shared with her moving as fast as she could across the large lot. Virginia was slow but steady and she finally made her way to the car. She looked and saw Alfredo make a gesture shaking his head no! He motioned quietly with his mouth. Virginia squinted her eyes trying to understand what he was saying. The tall man soon came around from the other side of the car. "Oh, I thought you were a friend of mine," she said nervously. The big tall man stood with his arms folded looking very intimidating. Me and my friend is having some car trouble". "Where's your car? He asked in a gruff voice. "Over there! She pointed with Hazel standing by the opened hood. "Stay here, he told Alfredo and you come with me" pulling Virginia along behind him. "Look! If you don't want to carry me you might want to slow down a bit mister! "SORRY, I'm in a hurry, he said still moving to fast for Mrs. Manuel's comfort. After a bit they were at the car. "Keys, he said turning to Mrs. Manuel". "Keys! Hazel keys! I don't have them; you took them from the ignition! She exclaimed. They stood yelling back and forth at one another. "STOP! I can't help without the keys". Bye! "Oh wait, I think I have them" Virginia finally said and began digging into her large handbag. While he watched the two ladies going through their antics Alfredo was making his escape. The big man finally tiring of the ladies looked up and across the lot to see the door on Alfredo's car was opened and he had waddled away". He ran toward it looking around to where he may have hidden. Soon he saw a patrol car come in the lot and head toward the parked cars. He walked slowly away and took off running like lightening says Mrs. Manuel as she stood laughing. Minutes later Billy and Nada pulled into the lot. Mrs. Manuel and Hazel were both trying to talk at the same time. "Billy had stopped the car and he and Nada had gotten out. "Come on! Come on! Mrs. Manuel said pulling them by their arms toward the police car now in the lot. "What's happening? What's going on? Your dad is here somewhere! she confessed getting close enough now to the cars. "Hey that's daddy's car Nada yelled opening the door looking inside. Billy was now talking with the officer who had spotted the dusty car parked in the lot. One of the business owners had called to report it, and he was checking it out. Alfredo was nowhere to be found. "ALFREDO! ALFREDO! DADDY! DADDY! They walked from business to business in the strip mall. Hey! Hey! he here" and oriental man said running out pointing toward a building. Then hiding inside a drive thru car wash was Alfredo. He was soaked from head to toe and sneezing. "Oh daddy! I'm so glad to find you, are you all right? She asked getting a blanket Billy had retrieved from his car to wrap him in. "Let's get you to a doctor! She stated leading him to the car. "No get my medicine from that trunk and take me home! He said shivering from standing in that cold spray of water. The officer assisted with getting them into the dusty car's trunk. (And with a tow truck pulling it away Hazel and Mrs. Manuel followed Billy and Alfredo out of the lot with Nada now driving her dad's car heading home) "Colombo ain't got nothing on me! Virginia said to Hazel who was now driving home.

CHAPTER 40

Fancy meeting you here!

The Royal Shakespeare Company had just finished their amazing performance and Sonjee and the other dancers anxiously waited the cue to enter the stage. Sonjee had been given a solo part in their performance and was looking forward to showing her new dance instructor what she was capable of. Once on the stage she twirled flawlessly like a spinning top! Her jumps and leaps were perfect. She moved with the other's so effortlessly and the timing their instructor thought was impeccable. APPLAUSE! APPLAUSE! They out performed some of the pros that everyone had flocked there to see. The likeness of the Australian's Expressions Dance company ode to one of Shakespeare's most famous villains or the Classical Theater of Harlem's King Lear. Sonjee's dance group from U.C.L.A didn't miss out on a standing ovation from the enormous crowds that packed the Kennedy Center nightly for their performances.

Sonjee! Sonjee! She heard her name being called as they came out to greet the crowds who loved ballet. She looked up to see Jace Ramsey with an armload of roses. "Jace, wow! I most certainly didn't expect to see you here, tonight, anyway! She stated taking the armload of flowers from him he was handing her. "Great performance Sonjee" "Thanks but tell me how do you get around so quickly, I spoke with you what, less than twenty- four- hours- ago", she smiled speaking slowly regarding the time. "I'm a pilot remember! He joked. Anyway, I traded with a friend last evening when you called and told me about the show". "Silly me I didn't know you had it like that! She teased back. They shared a laugh together. "Look, a few of us girls are going out for dinner if you care to come along, you're most certainly welcome" she suggested not wanting him to come all this way to see her without being hospitable. She was taught manners! But truly Sonjee wasn't interested in a relationship now. Her love was ballet. Where are you staying? she asked. I'm at the D.C Guesthouse, a friend recommended it. "Good, we're all at the Willard. So, we will go to our rooms and change and meet you say in an hour at Logan's tavern for a great burger. "Sounds great! The smiling young pilot said. "Thanks again for coming and the beautiful flowers" reaching up to kiss him on the cheek before walking away. "Sonjee he's cute and flowers too! Ooh where did you meet him?

Hello! Didn't I tell you not to call me here! Dana admonished her caller sitting in her office. "What? You did what? That was stupid! "Don't call me. I'll be in touch later! She slammed the receiver back on the phone's cradle. "Well, that didn't work, all it did was send him running to her! she sat thinking to herself. She was angrier now and something must be done with Nada Francois. And she knew if she wanted something done right, she would have to over see it herself!

"Dinner is served" Tetra said coming into her great room to let them know her beautiful table was set and the dinner is getting cold. David, Billy, Nada and Alfredo all got up and headed to the beautifully arranged table. "Thank God for a good meal" Alfredo said pulling his chair out from the table to sit down. Billy and David assisted the ladies and everyone was sitting down to one of Tetra's great meals. David said grace, and with a smile the conversation and laughter now replaced days of uncertainty and grief. "So, David what about the car they towed away" Tetra asked. "Well, they went through it looking for clues. "The car was from the Louisiana area they're still looking into the matter". "I just thank God daddy's back home and in good health" Nada said reaching over and giving him a hug. "That was crazy how the guy just came up to the door early that morning." 'It was silly of me to drive away without saying anything to anyone else". "Won't happen again I promise" Alfredo explained now rethinking the matter. Everyone was enjoying the company and the great meal that had been prepared by Tetra for the evening. "Mrs. Parker thanks for this fine meal and time to re-coop" Alfredo confessed drinking a cup of coffee with the desert he was eating. "I'm glad thing's turned out well and you were not harmed." Tetra replied. "I sent Mrs. Manuel and Mrs. Hazel some huge boxes of See's candies to thank them" Nada shared. She's telling the neighbors how she's smarter than Dick Tracy! Everyone at the dinner table shared a laugh. Ring! Ring! They could hear the phone ringing from the great room entrance. After a while the Parkers housekeeper walked in with the receiver. "This call is for Mr. Francois" "Who is it Mae? David asked suspiciously after the ordeal the family had just gone through a few days ago. "Didn't ask, would you like me to?" "No! Dear that's fine David said reaching for the handset. "Hello! Alfredo? No this is David" Dana? He questioned recognizing her voice. "Yes, I wanted to speak with Alfredo is he in? she asked. "He sure is, hold on" he handed the phone to Alfredo and everyone looked as he spoke not knowing why she called. "Oh yes! I can get that to you" it's pretty simple but their going to love it". Okay, thanks for calling, bye. "What was that about? Nada asked knowing if Dana was in it, couldn't be good. "She asked for a recipe of mine she had eaten here before for a dinner party she's planning". "Something's up! Billy said getting up from the table. Something's up! "Now, now, let's not jump to conclusions" David responded. "I know Dana like a book, she probably just called to see if Alfredo was here, instead of lost somewhere" Billy informed. "No! You don't think she had anything to do with that do you? Alfredo asked looking at everyone sitting at the table.

Sonjee and the girls went back to their rooms and showered and changed before heading out to the Logan for a burger and maybe dancing. It was a spot where the young folk hung out. A kind of disco meets retro atmosphere filled with fun and laughter. "HELLO! Jace said greeting her trying to speak above the loud noise of the crowds enjoying one another. "HEY YOU! Let's sit here" She suggested pulling him over to an empty booth near the wall. Daphne, Kara, and the others were finding folk they knew and everyone was scattered throughout the spacious place. The colorful lights were bouncing off the ceiling and against the walls. "Wow this place is wild! Jace said looking around. 'Kinda, but you get use to it" Sonjee explained getting a waiter's attention and ordering some soft drinks for their table. Soon they were joined by Daphne and Nick a friend she had met since being in Washington D.C. "Hi I'm Nick, extending a shake. "I'm Jace please to meet you both" he said. "Are you from here man? Jace asked. "Yes, I do live here in our great state of D.C. he laughed. "You? No, I'm just here visiting Sonjee". "Oh, I see" he smiled. "You see what? Sonjee chided. "He's a friend of yours." "Umm-ah! She replied, "let's order". The guys had struck up a conversation and Sonjee and Daphne excused themselves from the table for a walk across the room after leaving the orders, in case the waiter came by before they returned. So, what do you find to do here in Washington? I mean it seems to be so straight laced and of course politics play a big role." "Right! Right, on both counts but this is gorgeous country. And somewhat of a tourist place", but for me I love it." Nightlife isn't bad. "How long are you going to be here?" Nick asked. "Oh, I'm flying out tomorrow, duty calls." "Okay, I've only known Sonjee for the four weeks she's been here but she has made it plain that she's not ready to settle down with anyone" he laughed. So, what do you do?" She's letting her guard down with you". Jace lifted his brow; do you have a problem with that? No man, understand I like Sonjee but she has sent many dudes skating since she's been here that's all I'm saying" holding his hands up. "Oh, I see, Jace recanted now understanding what Nick was asking. "I'm a commercial pilot for North Western". "That's great! So how long have you been flying? the excited Nick asked. "I started when I was about 16 or 17 years old. A friend of my father owned a small plane and he taught us to fly. I've always had a love for it." he explained. "So how long did it take you to get in your current position; you seem young for a pilot?". There were lots of hours put in even before I could get my student license to fly. Then there's ground instruction, where you learn about meteorology, navigation and flying regulations". "Mete –o what? Nick laughed. "Meteorology is the study of the weather". Then you must pass another exam before 40 hours of flying time". So, I'm twenty- four and you're right I had lots of doors closed in my face before someone final gave me a chance". Man, that's cool". So, what do you do? Jace asked after finishing his coke with the waiter approaching their table. "I make money! 'Funny guy, aren't you, we all make money doing something" right! Right and I make money". The girls were now heading back to the table and had heard part of Nick's story. "Is Nick sharing his make money story" Sonjee laughed. "Well apparently this story carries some weight," Jace acknowledged moving out to let Sonjee sit down. It does, he got me with that line too" she confessed. "Okay? Jace replied looking at Nick. "Man, I really do make money, he smiled I work for the Bureau of Engraving and Printing which makes our nation's paper money". "Ha! Ha! That's way cool man, so when I'm handling money, I will think of you". "Deal, and when I'm flying the friendly sky's I'll do the same" Nick acknowledged in return. Well, I see you two have been talking", Sonjee noticed from the over heard conversation. Here comes our order! they said in unison moving the soft drinks around on the table so that the waiter with his hands full of food could place down the juicy burgers they had ordered. They enjoyed the burgers and conversation. They danced to the latest hits played over the speakers in the upscale establishment. "Daphne came over to where Sonjee and Jace had sat still talking. "Sonjee I'm heading in now" she said. "Oh, is it time? She asked looking down at her watch. "Well for me it is Nick's waiting he's got and early shift," Daphne confessed. "I'd better head in too I'm not a morning person and my flight leaves early in the morning" Jace shared getting up to say nice meeting you to Sonjee's roommate. "Okay, that works for me Sonjee said let's head out too." Will you meet me for breakfast tomorrow? He asked now walking out with the two girls. "Maybe no promises" she smiled. "Nick it was nice meeting you and I hope to see you again". The two guys shook hands again after exchanging business cards with numbers. Jace walked slowly down the sidewalk with Sonjee heading back to the Willard Hotel. Well, were you serious about not meeting me for breakfast? "Jace honestly I'm not looking for a serious relationship right now" she stated to his persistence of meeting for breakfast. "I got that the first ten times you said it" I know you're my sole mate and I like my mentor A.C. am willing to wait for you to realize it". "Really? Well, someone forgot to share that with me! Sonjee laughed. "Good at least you're still laughing" Jace replied now standing in front of the Willard. We are here! Sonjee acknowledged looking at the entrance. Daphne had gone in already she and Nick traveled the four blocks by car. "Thanks again for coming to the show and of course the gorgeous roses" giving him a quick hug she was gone in and the door closed behind her. Jace walked off back to the D.C Guesthouse two short blocks from the Willard. He knew getting Sonjee to commit to dating him was going to be a challenge. He reasoned with himself he was up to the task. Nothing had come easy for him; he had worked hard to be accepted as a commercial pilot for a major airline. Graduating from a small college in Kansas he set out to make a career for himself in this big world. He knew to make it he'd have to work equally as hard. And also prove to Sonjee she really belonged to him, he smiled. Now how do I get her to realize it? "Hello", hello Jace so you're in now? Sonjee asked "Yes I am. I just wanted to say goodnight" and if I don't see you at breakfast continue to break a leg with the show" he shared. "Thanks, Jace, I had a great time goodnight".

CHAPTER 41

Mac and Cheese

Dana was sitting in her office writing evaluations on some of her patients when Billy walked in. She looked up slowly and smiled. "What a surprise, I never expected to see you in my office again? She teased getting up coming toward him seductively. He held his arm out to keep her at bay. "I'm surprised I'm here too." I just stopped in to tell you something, I think is important." I don't know if you had anything to do with Alfredo Francois' abduction, but I strongly suspect that you did! he stated. Before he could finish his statement, Dana interrupted him. "Now Billy what would I gain from hurting Mr. Francois? She asked turning to go back behind her desk. "Well just know, I'll be watching your every move, Dana, and if I find you did, I will prosecute you myself! he turned without saying another word and headed out the door only stopping when Dana yelled out to him. "Now that's love!

Sonjee tossed and turned most of the night. Daphne had woken her up twice during the night already because she was having that reoccurring nightmare again, she had share with her. Up early she looked at Daphne still sleeping with her head under the covers. Sonjee went into the bathroom and closed the door and began to pray. She prayed softly as not to disturb her sleeping roommate. Grabbing tissues from the Kleenex box she wiped her face repeatedly from the stream of tears running down her face as she spoke. After a while she got up and went back to her bed. Looking at the clock she had been up for an hour.

She laid back on her pillow and with a "thank you Lord" she was fast asleep.

Dana had just arrived back to her office after a long business lunch with one of her colleagues when her phone rang. It was Mollie calling to invite her out tonight. "What have you been up to lately stranger? She teased smiling. "Not much just working and trying to figure Billy out". "Dana, I know you are not still tripping over Billy! That man has moved on and you should do the same". 'Yeah, that's easy for you to say" I can't stand to lose at anything! 'Well, I believe that but when it comes to men you may have to! What do you mean? Dana asked seemingly puzzled at Mollie's answer. "You can't force anyone to be with you" they have to want to be with you, right? "Billy's just confused right now he doesn't know what he wants". "Umm ah, and that's what you choose to believe." Anyway, are you going tonight? Why not? I haven't been dancing in a while, it will be fun". I'll come by around 6pm we will ride together," Mollie suggested. "That's fine see you then. "I have a very busy day today, bye! She looked at her watch and put her briefcase and purse in her office after turning on the light. Sitting down she sat at her desk looking over her schedule for the week when two gentlemen walked into her waiting room. "What are you doing here? She asked after looking up going into the waiting room to confront them. "Hey you owe me! He yelled in a deep voice. "Get out, I'm going to call security! she yelled back. "I wouldn't do that if I were you! after all the car was in your name! he reminded her. Dana was angry, he was going to let everyone know she had something to do with Alfredo's disappearance. "Shut up and sit-down you idiot," she said bringing them into her office and closing the door. Obviously getting to work early hadn't paid off at all. "Look, it's not my fault you hired this imbecile and he left your car". Dana chided. "Spilled milk! Can't cry over that," he said now walking around in the office space checking it out. "All I want is my money and I'm headed home! he said boldly. "Money, I don't owe you anything for that hap hazard job! All you did was put them closer together! "Maybe I did, or maybe Nada just beat you at your own game! He laughed touching her under her chin. Get your hands off of me! SECURITY! she yelled. "Do you want me to open the door so you won't have to strain your voice?" he mocked.

"You called me and brought me here". "Oh, by the way here's a copy of our plans and conversation," he said pulling a small tape cartridge from his pocket and throwing it on the desk. Get out! Get out! She yelled. "Shhh someone might be listening". Look I'd like to leave by Friday, I really need to get back to New Orleans," he stated. Try and keep the money in small bills, fifty thousand of them", he laughed again still taunting opening the door leaving out. "You have my number unless you set up a different place, I will see you right here Friday!" Colvin Murphy stated walking out with his buddy close behind which after his mess up in Washington, said nothing as instructed before he went into Dana's office.

Jace was up early, his flight was leaving and he had to be on it. He ordered breakfast and sat drinking coffee while reading the Washington post newspaper. Every now and then he'd look at his watch and then look toward the door. "Refill on your coffee sir? The waitress asked as she went passed his table. "Sure, thanks" he replied going back quickly to his paper. After a while she was back with his breakfast. He had given up hope on seeing Sonjee before he left. He would call her after he got to the airport, he figures she was probably still asleep. "Can I get you anything else with your breakfast? "No thanks I'm fine" he said and began eating his meal. Just as he finished and pushed the plate to the end of the table Sonjee walked up. "Oh, I'm sorry I started without you, and I'm afraid I have finished," he said disappointed he hadn't waited. "Oh no, it's not your fault, did you enjoy your breakfast? she asked. "It would have been better if you were here" he smiled. "I thought long and hard about coming this morning, I really don't want you to get any ideas! she replied. "Sonjee look, thanks for coming to see me off". I'm not trying to rush you into anything, I will wait." he said smiling softly at her. "But Jace you don't understand, I may never feel the way you want me to". "True, but it's a chance I'm willing to take" he responded. "Refill on your coffee sir? The waitress asked coming up seeing Sonjee now had sat and joined him. "Another cup please flipping the waiting cup over and "refill for me" pushing his cup to the end of the table. "I don't want to make you late for your flight" Sonjee stated. "I have time! Looking again at his watch and folding the newspaper pushing it to the side. "Daddy says hi! I told him you came to the show." "How is Dr. Reeves doing? He asked interested. "He's remarkably wonderful he says," she answered sipping her coffee across the table with a smile. Please tell him I will call and we will watch that movie he suggested real soon". Movie? What movie? she asked sassy sounding. "Tuskegee Airmen" what else? He laughed. "Oh, I see that is one of his favorites of all times." The two sat talking until the airport limousine pulled into the parking lot of the hotel. Soon Sonjee was waving bye to Jace as he headed to the airport. Looking at her watch she hurried back to the Willard to get prepared for her performance a few hours from now she noticed walking now into the lobby. "Ms. Reeves! the clerk at the desk said seeing her come in. "Yes, she answered going quickly over to see why he beckoned her over. "Ms. Reeves that young gentleman has been waiting for you," he said pointing to a guy sitting in the corner reading a paper. She couldn't see his face and he was wearing a hat. Sonjee's heart jumped! It couldn't be Fonsworth again? She questioned. Had he followed here again? She had evaded him once, had he figured out who she was? she thought walking toward the silent stranger. "Hello" she said standing in front of him waiting for the big impact. When he looked, she smiled, "DAVID MICHAEL! You made it! she said reaching to hug him as he stood to return the embrace.

Dana sat in her den looking at some case studies when Mollie rang her doorbell. She walked to the door and opened it letting her in. "Hey you're not ready! She said walking in dressed for an evening out. "You're right I'm not going" "What? Why? Are you still sulking over Billy? Mollie asked. "Not really, I have other matters distracting me now". Dana, I don't believe you. You've got everything anyone could ask for or want and you are straight tripping." "I would give it all up to be sitting on a beach with Billy" she said going back into her den wiping her eyes that had start losing tears. "Oh Dana, I'm sorry to tease you, I didn't know you felt that bad! Mollie said coming over to sit beside her on the sofa. "Look let's you and I sat and watch, "Waiting to exhale" and be mad at every man we know okay! She suggested sitting next to her holding her arm around her letting her cry. "Ring, ring! Dana you get the phone and I will get the DVD from the cabinet" Mollie said getting up slightly helping Dana up also. Get the phone! It might be Billy! she said going into the cabinet near the television for the movie. Dana looked at her caller ID it was Billy's number. "Hello! She said with a smile. "Dana hello! You sound chipper this evening". "David Michael? She questioned. "Non other! Just in town thought I'd give you a call". "Oh, so you're at your dad's I see" she said sounding disappointed it was not Billy. "Yes, came in last night from Washington D.C. "I went and saw Sonjee's production at the Kennedy Center". "Wonderful dear" Dana replied. "You seem to be short on words, do you have company, am I bothering you?' he asked. "No, I'm getting some work done, just busy I guess." "Well anyway I am going to visit Mrs. Bea tomorrow while I'm here thought you might want to come along this time". She always asks about you" he admitted. Sure, why not, besides I'd love to spend some time with you" Dana confessed. "Good, then it's a date" see you tomorrow! He said hanging up the line. Dana decided to let Mollie out of her promise to keep her company and sent her off to enjoy her previous plans without her of course, telling her David Michael was coming by. Instead, she sat around studying what she could do to rid Billy of Nada François.

Sonjee hugged her friends she had met during her six weeks show performance run. Kara, Daphne had put their luggage in the lobby to be picked up and taken to the airport for the flight home. The show had concluded with a big cast party on the last night and Sonjee and the other girls were dragging around getting things ready to go home. "UCLA HERE WE COME! Kara yelled out heading to the lobby. Yeah! where's David Michael? Mindy asked. Kara had him pinned down the other night! She said laughing hitting Kara on her shoulder. "He's left for home baby, that's a sealed deal! Kara said strutting around in the lobby. Kara! Shy little Kara! Mindy teased. "Sonjee so will you still see that cute pilot that came to see the show? Mindy again asked making conversation as the airport limo pulled into the lot. Their dance instructor had now joined them with her plastic cup of coffee in her hand. "His name is Jace and I don't know we're simply acquaintances! 'Umm okay so why is he standing in the door right now! "WHAT? She turned to see Jace smiling. She shook her head and smiled back. "Where is Daphne? Their dance instructor said looking around the lobby as she sipped her latte. "Umm ohh, she left early to go to the salon before heading back to L.A. "Aha well one of you better call her now, we're leaving with or without her body in thirty minutes". Our limo is pulling up now" she said looking at the other six girls gathered in the lobby. Kara was busy dialing because she had gotten stuck with bringing her and Daphne's luggage to the lobby. "I hope you are close! Sandra is on a tear and we leave in twenty minutes" she expressed speaking on her cell phone. "I'm a block away, tell her I'm coming and hey did she buy the salon bit? "Just get here! Sandra stood looking at the door when Daphne walked in. "Wow that was close! Where's my luggage? "Over there! Kara said pointing to the pile of luggage the bellman was starting to take to the limo. "Daphne may I speak with you? Everyone got busy helping the bellman with the luggage. "You know you cut it close, I would have hated to leave you" "I know but I liked the way they did my hair at Premier Salon and wanted it nice to show my friends in L.A. "How's Nick? she smiled. "He's fine, he had to work". "Umm well I'm glad we didn't have to leave you" she replied walking away waving at the clerk behind the desk. "Ka-chi-fo she waved at the hotel staff before heading out to speak with the limo driver before the departure.

David Michael had arrived at the retirement home and sat in the lobby waiting for Dana. She didn't want him to pick her up in one of his dad cars, nor did she want to come on his property, so each came alone. He had already spoken with the nurse at the front desk and Mrs. Bea was getting prepared for their visit. He sat reading a magazine and paced a few times around the lobby before dialing Dana again. This time there was no answer. He decided to start the visit without her. He had visited Ms. Bea many times before over the years since she was put there and often Dana never showed up. Why should this one time be any different he thought pulling his chair up in front of Grandma Bea. Mrs. Beatrice Flowers had out lived two husbands. Her first lasted over fifty years and then to Deacon Willis that marriage lasted three years. "Hello Davie, my you've grown! She said reaching for his hand and accepting an embrace from him. "You still going to the boys club? "Not as often any more Grandma Bea I'm in college now". "I know I read all your letters" you know I'm so proud. I remember walking to that boys club" she smiled "boy you certainly liked that boys club there." The picture you sent me a while back of you and that bat "You're mighty handsome in that baseball uniform" she acknowledged patting his hand smiling "Thanks gram, he smiled remembering how she had cared for him. "Well, she sighed, I would have made you dinner but I haven't seen a kitchen since I've been in here" I remember how you loved macaroni and cheese! She laughed fondly. She was not capable of living on her own anymore and her daughter had put her in convalescent home. And at ninety-two her mind was as clear as a bell though she was wheelchair bound and needed total assistance for daily living. Oh! she sighed with her warming smile "I don't cook anymore and can't walk much anymore without a lot of help" "Well I understand Gram, but you seem happy" David Michael said. "Well good, I'm glad for you, good! I wouldn't want to spoil your visit" she said shaking her head. "Where's Dana? Is she working? that child is always working" she giggled. "She'll be here" he replied going out on a limb saying that. The nurse came in to check on Mrs. Bea and see how her visit was going. "Fine, you've met my grandson haven't you Michelle? "Oh yes I have. "Hello, she said turning to shake David Michael's hand. "He's quite handsome Mrs. Bea" she said turning her attention to her now. "That's right, headed to the pro's soon". Really congratulations! "Thanks. I hope to in a couple of years" he clarified back to the nurse. "You'll see! Mrs. Bea said now being assisted to the bathroom while David Michael waited in the hallway. While Michelle took Ms. Bea to relieve herself David decided to make another call. Let's see, he dialed. "Dana good, you're on your way" She's only asked about you one time already" I assured her you'd be here". "Oh, you did, how is she? Dana asked. "For her age GREAT! Look, do me a favor, make a stop and get some macaroni and cheese at one of your favorite takeout's please? He asked her. "What? It's for Grandma Bea, thanks.

CHAPTER 42

Not So Bad

Alfredo had prepared the week's menu for the family when the phone rang. "Hello! He answered. "Hello there how are things? David asked. "Pretty quiet around here with you two gone, are you enjoying yourselves? "We're having a wonderful time he replied. Mrs. Parker says hello and she can't way to get home to a good meal" he shared. Alfredo laughed pleased at what David had shared. "Has Nada been keeping you company? Yes, and I wish she would stop hovering over me! "Well after that scare a few weeks ago one cannot be too careful". "Yes, I know it's in the name of love" he smiled back. Well, the conference is going well". The speakers are awesome and the seminars are interesting and very helpful. I have some material to share with the men's group when we return". "Mr. Parker that's wonderful as matter of fact I'm heading out to the church around 6:0clock with Nada. She's picking me up and we're going to have dinner and then go to the meeting. She's meeting with the leadership group tonight also". Okay, give her our love, and you have our schedule, right? We're stopping in Norfolk Virginia to visit some old friends before our return home next Friday" "Yes, God Bless, he said hanging up the line.

Doris heard the doorbell rang as she sat in her study reading over some documents regarding her business matters. Finley! She called out. Finley! He didn't move as fast anymore and she understood that. He had busied himself with matters in the church and was always going or doing something. Understanding but now impatient she got up after a minute or two of calling him without and answer and made her way to the door. "That Finley! where on earth is he? She questioned going now quickly to the door to open it. "Oh, my Sonjee! You didn't tell me you were coming home today? Oh! she said seeing her weighed down with packages. "Here let me help" she replied reaching and getting some of the packages from her hands. FINLEY! FINLEY! I don't know why I keep him around lately he's never around" she shared with Sonjee. "Godmother Finley's getting my luggage, he picked me up from the airport when I called. I'm sorry I woke him up he looks tired". Where is he? She asked not seeing him at the door. She stepped out closer to see him pushing his luggage carrier to the door. "You certainly shopped I see! she smiled seeing Finley headed in the door. "Yes, you and I shopped and Candace my sister and I and of course the dancers, it was fun! David Michael even came to the show! She said heading up to her room. After putting the packages in her room Doris and Sonjee helped Finley get everything else including her luggage to her bedroom. Doris stayed upstairs catching up on the events in Washington and Sonjee's visitors and the outcome of the production. After a while she came down to see Finley sitting on the long bench in her entry hall holding his head. She smiled quietly to herself. "What Finley, twenty-four years now we've been together" He looked up at his lady as he affectionately called her. "Yes, my lady, I think you're right" Finley had just celebrated his sixty-second birthday and Doris had given him a bash with his friends from church and community groups he worked with. "Well guess what! "You and I are going to celebrate our years together too. "We're going to take a cruise to Jamaica! A whole month of relaxing and getting away from day-to-day activities! Russell and I are going to honeymoon while you do whatever you heart desires," she said looking at her aging butler. "So, you two have finalized your plans? He asked happy for her. Yes, we have February third on calendar at the church" now showing him her beautiful Calla Cut natural diamond ring she now wore. "Wonderful! I'd better get moving on it" he said getting energized again. Before he could finish his sentence, Doris interrupted him. "Everything is taken care of". "Oh! he said disappointed he had been left out of her wedding plans. "Well, I guess there is one thing, Finley looked up. "You must be fitted for the tuxedo I picked out for you to walk me down the aisle. 'Oh, my lady I would be honored! He said standing and giving Doris a hug and she was delighted to return the affection.

"Annie, are the papers for the Breneman file ready? Billy asked walking from his office. 'I'll bring then to you in a minute, you have a call on line one" she replied with a smile going back to her desk. "William Parker" he answered positioning himself behind the desk. "Hi hon." Nada, how delightful didn't expect a call from you this time of day." "Oh, is this a bad time? She asked. Oh no, I just wasn't expecting it. "How did the meeting go with the board?" "Well, for the most part. Vice Principal Ranglamente was not backing down from the committee trying to charge a higher fee per semester for electives, so it ran shorter than anticipated with a reschedule next week." Oh, sounds fun! But were you able to state your opinion on the matter? Of course, but they were taking a rough edge approach giving a select few opportunities to ask or address questions" So the vice took the floor" for the most part she's a force to be reckoned with" Nada responded. At least you didn't have to sit through hours before they decided to reschedule." That was a blessing, you are right about that." "I know this is changing the conversation but are you coming down this weekend? I mean you planned a few days to be here right? He asked again after rephrasing his question. "I do understand what you're asking dear" I do plan on coming though I am a bit worried about daddy." "Oh? "He's fine, I just worry to much he says. Just a minute, Billy said putting the line on hold to ask a question about a document Annie had just brought in. "Okay I'm back, look honey I've got some papers to get together before I head off to court. I love you and hope to see you this weekend". I would love to talk about maybe a June wedding! "Wedding, did I miss something during this conversation? Nada teased. "Look babe I have to go, but think about what I said, love ya! and hung up the line. Nada got off the phone smiling from ear to ear. It was a lot sooner than she expected but hey! The bible says be ye always ready! She smiled going to meet Madison in the teachers lounge. "Somebody's singing happily today must be time to go see Billy again! Madison said waiting at the table as Nada walked in. So, has he asked you to marry him yet? Carin butted in. "Not yet but soon! She said filling her cup with coffee to sit down. You seem very sure he's going to? Madison said teasing her best friend who knew her like a book. "You all will be the first to know when he pops the question" she smiled happily. "Well, what's going to be the answer? Carin jokingly asked. "DUH yes of course! Nada teased back. And they all laughed slapping high fives across the table.

Dana had made plans to meet Colvin Murphy and the goon as she referred to him at a small café downtown. She had decided to keep things to herself and pay him some money to be rid of this imbecile, she thought making her way down the street quickly. She walked up to the quaint little café with the red-checkered gingham curtains hanging in the windows. Looking around she could see a few patrons in ordering lunch to go. The place seemed clean enough to have a cup of coffee so she obliged the waiter by ordering a cup. She sat drinking her cup of coffee when Colvin walked in by himself. Seeing him walk in Dana laughed to herself at his outfit. "Where's the do-fuss? She asked looking up at the guy from her sit. "He's staying out of the way; may I sit down? Colvin asked nicely. "Sure, sit down let's just get this over with! Dana chided. "Look I'm really not a bad guy. We just got off on the wrong foot". "Umm, look I'm going to pay you ten thousand dollars and not a dollar more! She said taking money from her purse enclosed in an envelope. "Stop! he replied pushing the envelope back to her. "I don't want your money! I own my own seafood business in Louisiana," you know that, you're the one who found me! He said clarifying matters. "So, what does that have to do with anything? And what man does not want money? She stated with a question. "Me right now! I'm getting ready to head home, but I would like to at least take you to dinner to end this on an up note, he suggested trying to find the right words to please her. "This fiasco! Dana laughed. "I wouldn't give you the time of day! She stated before her phone rang to interrupt her abruptness. Colvin Murphy sat there smiling calmly as she walked across the small cafe to take her call in private. The waitress came with a beer from the back that he had ordered as she passed the table. Fifty thousand dollars, ten thousand dollars! would sure help my struggling business but why settle for ten when she's worth millions and she's very attractive too! I'm going to ride this wave, he thought to himself sitting waiting for her return. "The Black and White Ball is this weekend did you remember? her caller asked. "You must be there; we need your support.

The hospital is counting on certain businesses to contribute for our new children's wing we're building" Dr. Baisden stated again. "I'll see you there! He added and hung up the line. Dana stood thinking for a minute about the ball. She had gone every year since becoming a staff member of the hospital but with Billy. She knew he'd be there; he went every year to support what he referred to as a worthy cause. She hated it! Having to smile and be nice all night to contributors who have more money than they even know what to do with but love being asked in an open forum. She knew she'd have to put up with that Nada on his arm! She couldn't go alone but who could make her stand out against Nada. Certainly not Corky, besides he and Mollie had become and item now, and Rusty still wasn't up to it. Umm anyway" she said going back to the small table. "Look if you're going to forget I ever called you without having to pay you money then I'm saying goodbye! She stated extending her hand to shake his. To her surprise he extended his hand and shook her hand. "So, you're really going home? Yes, he replied "Without a word to Billy about this? "Yes, he again replied finishing his beer. "Thank you" maybe you're not so bad after all she smiled getting up from the table. "No, I'm not, thank you," he smiled back. "She walked to the door before turning back. "Look! dinner tonight, and please lose the loud colored suit, shoes and socks! she grimaced walking out the door "I'll call" closing the door behind her leaving Colvin smiling from his seat at the small table.

CHAPTER 43

"Yes, I will marry you"

Sonjee stood with her arms filled with items she had brought from her bedroom at Doris's while trying to ring the doorbell. After many failed attempts she put down her wares and put the key in the door opening it. "Oh Sonjee, I'm sorry I didn't hear you ringing David Michael said I was in the shower" now seeing she needed help bringing in things to their new apartment. "Hi, this quiet little voice turned also seeing Sonjee walk in. Kara, I see you found our new place" she smiled. "Sorry Sonjee" Kara said "David Michael invited me, hope it's alright? Kara said again looking at her. David got up to help Sonjee gather the things she was bringing in and took them to her room. "Thanks, cuz", Kara is fine with me" Sonjee replied going down the hall closing her door. David Michael and Kara settled back in watching a spy movie, his favorite kind she understood. "So, what's for dinner tonight? He asked her. "Should I cook you one of my Indian meals? She was from Indonesia and asked rubbing his shoulder as she sat next to him on the sofa. 'Sounds fun, would you? he asked after the movie finishes okay?" What about Sonjee, think she would mind? Sonjee! No, she's a cool cuz besides she going out with Jace tonight". "OH, I AM? She said coming from her room to hear what David Michael was saying. "Oh, he called and asked me to let you know" he'll be in around 7" o clock,' he replied walking in the kitchen showing Kara where they kept the onions, she needed to slice for her meal she was planning to prepare for him later. "Kara, when you get a minute, I'd like to show you something in my room" Sonjee yelled going back to put the finishing touches on her newly decorated bedroom of the apartment she shared with her cousin near the University campus.

Colvin Murphy walked quickly down the street and into the moving escalator that led to the Men's Emporium. He needed a new look for tonight to impress Dana Williams. She had called him to help her get rid of Nada Francois his old girlfriend who was now dating William Parker her old boyfriend. Failing to do so he thought up another plan to trap her into marrying him for her millions. His business had suffered a massive lost after the floods in New Orleans. Most of his clients were relocated after losing everything and the ones left struggled paying him for his goods on time using the excuse of trying to rebuild from the devastation. Nada's dad had threatened him to stay away from his daughter after their rocky relationship that left her broken hearted and sad. Needing money to keep his head above water he decided to help Dana with her scheme after she had contacted him through an investigator. But their scheme failed miserably. The clerk seeing him walk in cleared his throat. "May I help you? he smiled looking over the top of his glasses first at his feet then slowly moving up to the feather in his hat. "Yes, I'd like a business suit" Colvin replied. "Okay, I see, and what exactly are you looking for? He questions sizing up the bright PEACOCK BLUE colored suit he was wearing. "No, no, I'm looking for a total new look" he explained. "Good, the clerk sighed "right this way" walking him over to the designer suits near the wall. "Our clothes are very conservative you will find. Is that the kind of change you're looking for? He questioned again. "Yes, I want to walk out of here looking like I belong on Wall Street" Colvin stated removing his hat and jacket and sitting down. "Alright! The lively male clerk said removing a couple of suits from the selection he thought might do the trick. "After a few more attempts "Okay, I will need the total package, you know shirt, tie, and shoes" he said to the clerk going into the fitting room to try on still more suits. "Good! My name is Felix and let's do this, I know you like color but let's soften it for a sexier more appealing look" he said pulling some shirts off of the shelf putting then aside of the suit's jacket Colvin had taken into the fitting room. Here try these Kenneth Cole shoes they are the latest style came in last week" he suggested moving around quickly with his suggestions and choices like a bumblebee. Nice very nice! he replied what do you think? now looking at Colvin who stood in the full-length mirror. Felix removed the tape measure he had thrown across his shoulder and measured the trousers that needed a hem. "How long will that take; can I get these pants hemmed today? Colvin asked looking quite handsome in his new duds he thought. "A few hours you can come back and pick them up" he replied. "Okay now where around here can a brother get a haircut? Felix raised his shoulders "I don't know? Wait, you wait here! He hurried out of the store leaving Colvin standing at the counter with the salesclerk paying for his purchases. Soon he came back with an address of a barber. "Tell him Lenny sent you". He will make you look like your suit" he told Colvin smiling patting him in his chest. "See you in a couple of hours" Felix replied heading into his tailor with Colvin's trousers.

Look what I've done to my room! Like it? She asked Kara who was now standing in the middle of the floor looking around. "Wow! I really like what you've done. Your space is so much larger than our small apartment." "Thanks of course I got pointers from my mother's decorator". Sonjee admitted. Anyway, the reason I asked you in here is I like you with my cousin" Sonjee shared with Kara standing in her bedroom of her university apartment. But please don't rush things with David Michael he's coming off of a hurtful relationship with Frannie". "Yes, he told me Sonjee. You guys tell each other everything? Kara said. "No not really but we do look out for each other, because that's what families do! Right? "Right, we're just friends, Kara admitted. Other than here we've never been alone to speak of". "Well, I hope you two have what it takes to make it but I wouldn't rush things. "Knock, knock" they heard someone at the door. "What time is it? I hope it's not Jace! We have got to talk! Two times this month he's been by to visit asking through David Michael". COME IN! COME IN! they overheard David Michael say. Soon they heard giggling and laughter. Walking out they saw Sasha Brown, and Jada Bowman two girls David Michael had met at the campus bookstore that stopped by to pay him a visit carrying in two large pizza's and a smile.

"Babe look I only have three and a half weeks before the school years starts again at the university. My schedule will not be as flexible as it has been," Nada said speaking with Billy on their usual goodnight phone call. "Good, two weeks! We have two major trips I'd like you to take with me before that time" he said smiling across the line. "You're kidding right! No, I have a business meeting in Florida I must attend and I'd like to see an old friend there and would like you to accompany me? Okay that's one and what's the other? She asked thoughtfully to her man. "I would like you to accompany me to Kansas to visit Desmond". "So, you're sure you're ready for me to meet those important people in your life? 'Yes! Then there was silence from both parties. 'And when is this trip to start? Nada again asked. Well, you haven't said you were going yet" he teased. "William I will be glad to meet your friends" she confessed. "I will see you here Friday night and we will leave from here on Sunday after church" he shared. "Mother Buttons wants you to come and sing for us again" he confessed. "Share with Mother Buttons I'd love to attend the service again". "Oh, so that's it! he teased. "I love you too! Goodnight sweetheart"

Colvin walked in the store and went to the counter and asked for Felix who was not on the sales floor. The sales clerk failed to recognize him from his previous visit. "Just a moment sir" he replied paging Felix over the intercom. Colvin stood looking at some sweaters that were being displayed on a table when Felix walked up. "May I help you sir? He asked staring at him. "Yes, I'm here to pick up my pants" he smiled "Your trousers"? we have your trousers? "Felix man it's me! He admonished smiling. Felix stood back, "it is you! oh my I wouldn't believe it if I had not seen it with my own eyes! You look different! Lenny was right, come ahh! Ahh! You look great! You certainly look like a big executive now! he said leading Colvin to the fitting room. Colvin had the barber take all that hair from his head in a very today style cut. They trimmed his facial hair on his face allowing his goat tee to connect with is mustache in a tapered fashion. He looked every bit of the fortune five hundred men on the cover of "Men's magazine. After getting dressed from head-to-toe Colvin stepped out of the fitting room. "I DON'T BELIEVE YOU'RE THE SAME MAN WHO WALKED IN A FEW AHOURS AGO! Felix kept saying shaking his head from side to side. "Felix, show me again that Wall-Street walk, Colvin asked stepping around in front of the mirror. Like this, like this, he kept asking. "Yes, that's it I think you got it! Felix laughed standing watching Colvin practice his walk right out of the store. He was proud of what he had done to please his customer.

David and Tetra sat on their porch having their evening tea, when they were surprised by a visit from their son. "Son, when did you get in town? They asked extending their arms for a hug. "Haven't been in town long wanted to stop by to share some news with you both." "Oh? They both said looking up at him. "Let me pull up a seat, he said bringing another wicker chair near them. "Mom, dad, he said reaching into his coat pocket of his suit. "I going to ask Nada to marry me" handing his mother the engagement ring he planned to present to her. "Oh, my Tetra said starting to cry. David smiled and stood up with is son and gave him a big hug before they all hugged together. "I'm so happy for you son, she's a sweet girl" Tetra confessed wiping tears of joy from her eyes. "Have you told Alfredo? "Not yet he's coming with wine for a toast." I shared with him I was in town to close a deal and we're celebrating; he's bringing mom's favorite wine." "Here he is David said seeing him walk out on the porch with the ice bucket, and stemmed glasses on a tray. Putting the tray down on the table Billy pored the slightly sweet wine and handed it to his mom and dad. No one said anything. Alfredo just stood watching Billy. Then Billy handed him a glass of wine also. He took it not wanting to offend them but felt uneasy standing there. "Billy poured his glass and turned to Alfredo. "Mr. Francois I would like to ask you for your daughter's hand in marriage! He said nervously. "What? Really, oh my family! he broke down in tears from what Billy had asked flopping in one of the wicker chairs available from the surprise. He answered "Yes, yes I am honored and thank you for asking me. Her mother would approve of you too! She really would" he added. They stood and cried tears of joy and toasted what had just taken place before closing with a prayer. Billy left to go and meet Nada to now ask for her hand with her father's blessing.

Colvin had made reservations at a posh restaurant in midtown. He had come across it as he drove around sight seeing in Maine. Little did he know it was one of Dana's favorite places to dine. He had spoken with her after she called and made plans to meet her there. Getting there a little early he was shown to his requested table near the fireplace. "Thanks, he said sitting down. "Sir can I get you something to drink or would you like to wait for your guest? Yes, I'll order he said giving the waiter his requested drink of choice. He sat listening to the live band playing and enjoying the atmosphere of the magnificent dining place. "Mr. Murphy please? Dana asked coming into the establishment. "Oh Ms. Williams right this way", the waiter explained leading her to her date at the table. Dana dressed in a black designer dress followed him to the table. As she approached Colvin stood up to greet her. Turning to look at the waiter to correct his mistake for leading her to the wrong table of a man she did not recognize. "Hello Ms. Williams, she heard a familiar voice. She turned getting a closer look. Wow! It is you she said sitting down on her chair taking a drink of water from the glass sitting on the table. "The transformation is uncanny! You look, I'm lost for words" Dana said still trying to believe her eyes. "Well, I hope that means you approve? It does, have a sit" she said smiling at him from across the table. "And you did all this in a few hours! She said still finding it hard to believe he was the same guy she had saw early in the day. "What can I get for you to drink? He then asked changing the subject from his appearance though very pleased she approved.

Jace, so you don't mind that we're having dinner with my mom tonight? Sonjee asked as they drove down the L.A. highway. "I don't mind I'd like to get to know your family better" he confessed. "Well, it seems you and David Michael have a growing communication that includes me most of the time" Sonjee stated. "I'm so afraid you will say no! and I know you're the one for me". Jace admitted honestly turning up to the gate of Doris Wright's home in Beverly Hills. "Honestly Jace you lucked out this month my schedule is fairly light" but I promised Godmother I'd have dinner to discuss her wedding plans" she stated. "I shared with you that I haven't been told that you're the one, by anyone! WHAT? He asked laughing innocently. "That you're the man for me! She said sharing a laugh with him getting out of her car. "Dad said you were by earlier this week". Yes, I did a favor for a fellow pilot who needed a flight trade so I had a layover in Washington and I went by to finish our talk" Sure! I believe you" she said walking in shaking her head. GODMOTHER! I'm here she yelled going into the sitting room after hanging their coats in the entry. "Hello! Doris responded back. And this must be Jace" she smiled shaking his hand and hugging Sonjee after being introduced again. Come on in Russell and I are just going over some last-minute changes". "Sonjee, I have some dresses I ordered for my brides' maids I'd like you to look at" she said. "Godmother what happened to the other dresses you had chosen? "Oh, they are available but these are some that may allow them more flexibility to reuse" she shared sitting down now on the sofa with the catalog and fabric samples. "I have only four weeks before our wedding day of February 3rd and I'm still making changes" she said smiling showing Sonjee her plans made. After sitting discussing the wedding while the guys watched a basketball game Finley announced dinner. The men had now rejoined then in the dinning room "So Jace, how often does your flight plan change? Doris asked now with everyone sitting around the elegant set table. "We're allowed to bid for the shifts and seniority has its place of course. But I like the L.A. flight schedule because it allows me to see Sonjee! He exclaimed taking another bite of his steak and lobster dinner that had been prepared. "Oh, you sound sure she's the one" Doris laughed. "Oh, I am, I just have to wait until she finds out". Everyone enjoyed a laugh as they conversed through dinner about the upcoming wedding, careers, and his undying love for Sonjee. "He's a man who knows what he wants" Russell said now feeling more relaxed about his marriage proposal to Doris.

Dana and Colvin enjoyed a wonderful evening together. She was very impressed at all he had done to please her. Dinner was wonderful and they danced to the live music with pleasant conversation over dinner and her favorite bottle of doux wine. Maybe just maybe he might be the man she needed to make Billy jealous and come back to her, she thought laying her head on his chest as they danced. "Colvin how would you like to be my date for the Black and White ball this year? Without thought he replied "I'd love to Dana, when is the ball? He asked pleased she had asked him. This Saturday! "I'd love to be your date Dana" Colvin replied again smiling. When the evening was over

Colvin was urged to drive Dana's Porsche leaving the rental in the lot of the restaurant to pick up the next day.

Billy pulled up to Nada's home. Ms. Manuel was sitting outside on her porch talking on her home phone. "Hello Ms. Manuel! He acknowledged waving as he walked up the sidewalk to Nada's door. "Hi Billy! you in town! She yelled from her porch. "Shhh, I'm trying to surprise her, is she home?" He asked pointing to Nada's front door. "Yeah, Nada Jean came home about and hour ago, what's the surprise? She asked now standing next to the fence talking with Billy. He thought for a minute and walked over near her across the fence. "I'm sure she won't mind" he said pulling the small box from his coat pocket showing it to Ms. Manuel. OH MY! You goin to marry her! Give me a hug! Shhh she said to Billy after her outburst. "Go on in there! Go head! Ohh! Ahh, she laughed going back to her chair smiling as she dialed. As Billy walked up to the door it opened. "Sweetheart! (surprised to see him standing at her door) I thought I heard Ms Manuel," Nada acknowledged standing in the door. "You did she's on her porch". "Oh, hurry and come in before she gets off the porch" Nada said inviting him in. After sharing a passionate kiss saying hello "You didn't tell me you were coming" she said moving her papers to the side of the sofa for him to sit down. "As you can see, I'm getting ready for my school year. Since we have the trips coming up, I won't have time to get this done if I wait." "Not that I don't want to see you, she said, but why the surprise visit? Perfect lead in Billy thought pulling the ring from his pocket and kneeling on one knee. "Nada Francois will you marry me? He asked holding out a flawless five- carat solitaire engagement ring. "William Parker! she said with her mouth opened wide with surprise. "Of course, I will! allowing him to get up and share another intimate kiss accompanied by tears of joy as he placed the beautiful ring on her finger. Lovingly hugging and kissing on Billy Nada soon hears a knock at her door. Nada wrinkled her brow wondering who was at her door this time of day. Opening her door, she saw King the German shepherd standing wagging his tail along with Hazel and Ms. Manuel. She invited them in. They oowed! and ahhhed over her beautiful rock! With congratulations, hugs and smiles from her dear friends and neighbors she again stated, "yes William Parker I will marry you!

CHAPTER 44

Desperate Times

Sonjee sat on her flight headed for Washington State to spend a few days with her dad again before the school year began. She thought over her new life, and friends since moving to L.A. with her real mother. She had found out about her later in life from her parents who she felt had pains takingly raised her all those years. She loved them dearly and was glad many questions were answered and her life had finally made sense to her. "Hello! she answered her cell phone's ring. "Hi Candace, are you there already? Wow, I'm so excited did the twins come this trip? Good, I'd loved to see them." How about Uncle Bailey and aunt Myrtle? "They're off getting some r and r from the boys" ahh she laughed. Well, I should be down on the ground in an hour". "Are you picking me up or do I need to call dad? "What! Already he's got them on the course". "Okay sis I'm coming in on flight 586 West Air" around 2:30 pm. Sonjee reclined her seat and closed her eyes again to reminisce about the strong bond she had with her family. Their mom had passed away a few years ago and she thought often of her. She was so excited her sister and her brother's twins were there also this trip! She was going home again for a visit with the family she grew up with and the only man she ever knew to be her dad.

Nada was up early humming a tune as she prepared to leave for the morning. "RING! RING! Looking at her phone she answered. "Good morning sweetheart, how was the flight home last evening". "Oh, not bad at all, it was very quiet and I slept all the way" Billy shared with her. "Are you just getting up? she asked. "Me oh no I'm just coming back from my run" I wanted to be the first to congratulate you on your engagement" he teased. "Why thank you, I'm marrying the most wonderful man in the world" she replied twirling around in her small kitchen. "I love you! he said and I'll see you Friday! "Nothing could keep me away" she replied.

The stands were almost empty except for one lone body sitting watching the team practice. The season had not started yet but baseball practice was in full swing. "Hi David Michael" Kara yelled out across the field. She had come everyday to watch the team practice and of course to see David Michael who still had not committed to anyone since Frannie. Being a handsome hunk, he stayed in trouble with the ladies. Holding a trump card of just friends she showed up everyday to root him on. "Hello, he voiced "practice went a little long today glad you stayed, he said coming over to the bleachers where she sat. "See ya Billy! Some guys yelled. "Tonight, at your place, right? "Yes, that's fine the play offs are on we can watch on the big screen! Me too! Another yell. "Sure, why not! He yelled back. "Oh, so you have company tonight? She asked. A few of the team guys are coming by you're welcome too though Sonjee's out of town" he shared. "That's right she went to visit her dad". Yeah! So, I'm mister bachelor this weekend". "Umm maybe I'll stop in for a little while, but later is that all right? She asked as the two headed across the open field going home

Colvin passed by the front desk at the Maine Western Hotel where he had been staying since he arrived in Maine. "Are there any messages? he asked the clerk behind the counter. "Sure, mister Murphy lots of them" handing him a paper clip stack of messages. He wrinkled his brow seeing the first one on top. "Wow! An estimate statement had come in on a freezer. He needed to replace the one that no longer functioned. And the other messages were equally as grim. "I got to speed up this process somehow, he thought to himself going back to his $150.00 a night room still trying to impress Dana. "He looked at his bank statement. He had laid a lot of money down on his new look. Money he really didn't have. His cards were max-ed out and he was feeling desperate. "Yes, please send a dozen long stem red roses to

Mrs. Dana Williams immediately" Colvin said giving the address at the hospital. "This has got to work he thought laying back on the bed awaiting her call.

Sonjee was helping her sister set the table after they had returned from a family outing with her dad. "Dad you relax Candace and I will take care of things" she said suggesting he go in the living room until they finish setting the table. "You sure? Yes, dad I'm sure. He went into the living room almost being knocked down by the twins running in to ask a question. "Sorry granddad, both said trying to speak at the same time. "Aunt Sonjee! Momma said granddad is not your real dad! Is that true? They stood waiting for an answer. Sonjee looked at the kitchen door where her sister was putting the food into serving dishes while she placed the silverware on the beautiful silk tablecloth. "Is that why you're darker than aunt Candace and dad? The inquisitive eight-year-old asked. Sonjee was a bit surprise and a bit hurt they had asked but she knew now and wasn't bitter about the truth secret. "Yes, that's true but you know what? "What? "I was so loved by mom and dad Reeves that they took me home even when they didn't have to" she smiled. "Wow! You mean they asked for you and not another baby? "That's right, so you see how special I feel to be a part of this family" she added. "Well, we love you aunt Sonjee coming closer to her and embracing her at the waist before heading in to ask questions about Dr. Reeve's airplane collection that was very old and priceless.

"He's nice and very attractive" Dana shared walking back to her office from lunch with Molly. "So, he's going to be your date for the Ball." "Yes, I know he will make Billy jealous enough to give me a second look" she bragged walking along the hallway. "So where did you fine this one Dana? "Molly, somethings are not to be shared but I will say this, he has impeccable taste". Umm look I'll see you later" Molly replied turning to go down another hall to her section in the hospital. Dana walked into her office and saw the vase of roses sitting on her desk. "Rusty must be feeling better he's sending flowers again she thought walking over to get the card. "She smiled softly and sat at her desk and dialed the person who had sent her the flowers. "Thank you, those are gorgeous flowers" she said with a warm smile in her voice after he answered the call. "Oh, so you got the roses, I was just thanking you for a wonderful evening the other night' he replied. "So, you didn't forget about Friday, did you? Dana questioned. "No, but I really need to get some matters straight back home," seems you have to stay on top of everything going on". "You're not planning on abandoning me, are you? She flirted her voice. "Not entirely, but I need to get some monies changed around and other matter's that need my undivided attention" he shared. "There is only one day before the Ball I really don't want you to abandon me without a date! "A pretty lady like you will have no problems in finding someone to be by your side" Colvin voiced using his best lines. Dana had made her plans including him for Friday night and he was talking like he might be headed back home. "Colvin my treat will you have dinner with me tonight? She asked seductively. "Tonight? He paused looking at his last dollars scattered on his hotel table. "This has got to work! He thought to himself. 7pm I'll pick you up! Dana stated, hanging up the line. Colvin just smiled looking at the buzzing receiver he held in his hand.

Kara had thought it best to stay away from David Michael's invite and let the guys be guys. She knew Sonjee was due back Sunday around 5pm and thought that would be a good time to stop in. She walked up the stairs and knocked at the door. "Music was playing but no one opened the door. She turned slowly to leave when the door opened. This very big brut of a guy probably a football player she figured came to the door. "Come in! He said I'm just leaving. DM is in his room I guess" leaving the door opened and walked slowly down the stairs. Kara peeped into the apartment. "Oh my! What as happened in here? She thought looking around. Clothes were everywhere and furniture was moved around from its place. The once beautiful apartment that Sonjee had taken from a magazine was totally destroyed! There were cans, bottles and pizza boxes all over the place. She entered and closed the door but was surprised by a red head coming from the bathroom with her shoes in her hand. "Hi! She said stepping quickly over anything and heading out the door quickly returning after forgetting her purse and heading back out again. Kara stood shocked at the once immaculate space. Every part of the apartment looked as if a tornado had been there! She slowly walked into David Michael's room. She could see him lying across the bed. "She touched his foot. He didn't move so she panicked "DAVID! She yelled hitting him on the back. "AHH! He moaned turning over holding his head. "What happened in here? This place is a mess! She said seeing him now trying to sit up. "I know Sonjee's going to kill me! He moaned. "Things got out of hand, way out of hand," he moaned again trying to quiet the noise he heard in his head. "You really think things went to far! She stated hitting him again for good measure. "Ring, ring! Please answer it for me Kara, I owe you one" moving into the bathroom to throw up again. "Hello", hello Kara, Sonjee! 'Oh hi "I'm glad you're there I was worried David Michael would fall back into his old habits and we'd have to move out tomorrow" Sonjee teased not knowing the real situation. "Is he around? "He just stepped out to get something from his car" she lied. I'll have him call you". "Fine, but not really necessary he's in good hands though I will see you all this evening around five o clock". "Oh! Okay "See you then, Kara replied hanging up and flopping on a sofa covered with blankets. Then she jumped up quickly and ran to Sonjee's beautifully decorated bedroom. She opened the door and exhaled. Someone had been on her bed and ruffled the covers but her room was still in tact. "Thank God! Kara said going into the bathroom hearing David Michael throw up continually, leaving out after handing him a stomach seltzer she had found in his kitchen.

Nada's flight landed safely and she made her way to the waiting car Billy had sent for her. She was a bit tired because she had stayed out late with Carin, Madison, Marsha and some other girlfriends from the university staff informally celebrating her engagement. She already had spoken with Billy about the planned engagement gala in Maine and Washington and of course they would be invited. Right now, she and Billy were headed off to visit some of his old friends and wanted her along. Getting all of her luggage in the car she was off again to the estate. "Hi honey! I'm heading to the house now" she explained riding along in the back of the limo he had sent to meet her at the airport. "Great so everything went well with the car picking you up? Yes, but you didn't need to send a limo, I didn't bring that much luggage! She laughed. Nothing but the best for my wife! He said proudly. "Oh, William I love you! Sweetheart, please make yourself comfortable".

The staff is expecting you and I will be there around 5: 30 he shared knowing his case schedule wouldn't change much today. "Alright dear, I could certainly use a nap before this evening" Nada confessed to her fiancé. See you soon!

Dana drove up to the Maine Hotel picking up Colvin and heading to a cozy dinner along the river. It was a small restaurant out a ways, from the hustle and bustle of the city. She had taken a few close friends there and thought she'd impress Colvin enough not to stand her up for the big ball her boss was expecting her to show up for. Walking in and being shown to an intimate table in the corner he was smiling from ear to ear. "May I get you something to drink? The staunch waiter asked. One of your best bottles of chardonnay! Dana replied cheerfully. Right away Madame! He responded hurrying off to get it. 'So, you're in a great mood tonight" Colvin said removing his jacket before sitting down. "Yes, good friends, good food, and seeing the waiter coming back with two stemmed glasses and a bottle of very expensive demi sec wine she stated and great wine! What's there to be sad about?" Everything went just as she planned it. The entrees were to die for. The soft atmospheric music set the tone for the evening and Colvin's lines though heard before were music to a desperate woman's ears. She asked questions about his life and prying further about Nada his ex-girlfriend who now was dating her man. After dinner and getting little information that she viewed didn't amount to a hill of beans, Dana excused herself to go powder her nose as the waiter walked up with the check. "He placed the small folder on the table and walked away. Colvin picked it up and opened it slowly. Dana had eaten a rare kind of swordfish and he had a steak that would choke a horse it was humungous. He coughed when he saw the price of the bottle of wine they had gone through. The waiter stood afar off watching Colvin and smiling knowing his patron Dana very well. He closed the folder and pushed it over to Dana's side of the table. The waiter at this point was laughing with another waiter in the back. After a short while she was back. "Oh, I see he brought the tab," she said. "Oh, you're right I had not noticed Colvin replied quickly clearing his throat. "Are you ready? she asked putting her elegant lace throw shawl across her bare shoulders. "If you are beautiful lady," he replied getting up and reaching for her arm. She walked away leaving the bill at the table. If she's not going to say anything neither am I he thought following her out. As she passed the podium near the front she looked back and said "Raphael put it on my tab! and proceeded out the door with Colvin close behind sweating from her expensive taste. Very little was said on the way back to the Maine Hotel. Colvin was throwing small hints of money though Dana seemed to be ignoring them. "So that's all you can tell me about your old girlfriend? She finally asked. "Hey I told you she was a great lady with a mind of her own!" "She left me! He stated. "Oh, hush you fool! She teased him with a passionate kiss getting very close to him before letting him out of the car. 'See you tomorrow she voiced and do remember your tuxedo! were her words said as she pulled out of the lot heading home. When Colvin got back to his room, he discovered Dana had put and envelope in his jacket's pocket as she snuggled, he suspected. But he didn't mind it contained the fifty thousand dollars she had previously promised for kidnapping Nada's dad Alfredo.

Kara finally got David Michael settled into his room after clearing everything out of it that didn't belong and cleaned it up. She moved around quickly getting things in order while he sat in the messy living room moaning with a headache from too much partying. After cleaning his room to her satisfaction, she helped him into his bed with the promise of sleeping an hour to clear his head and he'd be good as new. "Just hold my hand," he asked as she sat near the bed wetting a cold towel placing it on his head to make him feel better. "Thank you, Kara, I owe you big for this one" he kept saying. After about twenty minutes he was sound asleep. She moved her hand gently from his grasp. Looking at the clock there was only a few hours before Sonjee would walk through that door and probably fall out she thought still looking at the mess in the once beautiful condo. "There's no way I can clean this spacious condominium before Sonjee gets home by myself" she reasoned. She grabbed a phone book from the shelf near the telephone. "Let's see what's the name of that service mom uses? I'm sure they have one in L.A. she thought thumbing through the pages. "Here it is she said dialing the number "Hello, I'd like to use your service for today". Yes today! I will need two possible three" okay two will be fine," she said after hearing the prices. "How soon can they get here? She asked giving them the address. She stood sharing all that needed to be accomplished giving all the details along with her credit card for payment. "How did I get myself in this mess! She thought out loud. She walked in again to check on David Michael and he was sleeping like a baby. I'd better get started she thought they will be here in an hour. Kara started in the kitchen and had the dishes done when they arrived. She gave the merry maids instructions and one started in the bathroom and the other in the living room while she finished up the kitchen. Without much conversation going on they buzzed around like three little bees. Within three hours the condo was back to its luxurious beauty. Kara quickly tipped the ladies for the much-needed help from monies she took from David's wallet. "Thank you! She said hurrying them out the door and falling on the now visible sofa. David Michael had still not made an appearance or woke up for that matter. Kara sat down with a good book. After reading a chapter or two the phone rang. "Hello, Hello Kara". Sonjee are you in L.A. yet she asked. "Yes, I called to let you know Jace is going to bring me home so I'll see you two in an hour or so". After hanging up Kara went into the kitchen and made a strong pot of coffee and poured a cup heading for David Michael's room.

CHAPTER 45

Out of the pit

Nada walked into a guest room filled with flowers. She smiled looking around the gorgeous bedroom. Millicent the maid helped her with the luggage the butler had brought in from the car. 'Thank you" Nada said as she left out smiling. "Glad you are here! Millicent added. Nada looked around she could hardly believe it. "I feel like a queen," she said spinning around the room looking at her fabulous diamond ring on her hand. Millicent had run her a hot bubble bath and she couldn't wait to relax before Billy came home. She put away her things in the drawers and hung her clothes in the closet before going to sit in the luxurious tub for a long relaxing bubble bath. "Umm let's see, how many brides' maids will I have? She thought still relaxing in her tub. "Wow a little girl from New Orleans! And now a queen in Maine! 'Wow if mom could only see me now! She thought out loud enjoying her quiet time to plan and imagine. After a while she got out and dressed comfortably for curling up in a big comfy chair near the bed reading a good book. She woke to Billy standing near her stroking her face as not to startle her. "Oh honey, I must have fallen asleep she said raising her head from the pillow someone had placed there. The room is gorgeous sweetheart you have out done yourself this time! She stated kneeling in the chair with her arms around his neck giving him a gently kiss to the lips. "Did you just walk in? She asked seeing he was still wearing his over coat. "Yes, I spent a good part of my day in Manhattan". "Manhattan! New York? She asked surprised. "Yes, I went to talk with a dear friend "Jillian's mom actually". I needed to close that chapter in my life and that's how I chose to do it! I hope you don't mind? He asked now sitting on the end of the bed with its elegant warm yellow duvet bedding. "Sweetheart thanks for sharing that", I'm glad you did" Nada shared "and of course I understand and I certainly don't mind". "Look I've got no plans for tonight other than snuggle up with you after dinner and talk about our wedding plans." "But tomorrow I get to show you off to the world! swinging her around in the air. "After a shared kissed Billy picked up his briefcase and overcoat, he laid on the side table after he came into the room. "I'm going to go up and get comfortable before dinner. Did Alfani or Millicent happen to mention if my tux was delivered? 'Not to me but I'll find out from them while you go up and get comfortable" she replied wanting to know what pleased her husband to be and began doing it. Billy headed upstairs and Nada went in search of Alfani or Millicent.

"Justin do you have your date for the ball? Dana asked passing the handsome doctor in the hall of the hospital. "As a matter of fact, I do she works in radiology. I'd better head that way and make sure of the time I'm picking her up! he voiced not stopping to hear why his brother Billy should still be with her. "Anything that moves these days, ah?" Dana teased as Justin kept going without stopping. "Hello, Mollie. "How's your love life? She asked now in her office calling her friend. "Corky and I are going up to the cabin this weekend" "oh sounds promising" Dana edged in. "He loves me and I have come to know him as reliable and that's more than I can say for anyone I've been with over the past few years or so" Mollie confessed. "So, you're not doing the ball thing? "Dana that's only for you big wigs he doesn't care if we laborers show up or not" she laughed "we would just clutter the place" "Well I'm hoping to walk out of there on William Parker's arm where I belong" Dana shared in a matter-of-fact tone. You have to come by and see my gown! She explained. "Hey I can do that I'll stop by on my way home from work" bye girl! Mollie voiced hanging up her line.

"Kara thank you for all your help today, David Michael shared after getting some alone time with her. Sonjee and Jace had gone out for dinner again the next day and he sat in the apartment later that evening with her. "You are welcome though I tipped them from your wallet I didn't have the change". "Don't worry about it I will give it all back every cent" he told her. "You will never know how much you saved me from much embarrassment and shame for letting things go to far with my old friends" "Okay I understand though you may want to change that behavior" she stated. "You're right, Sonjee has talked to me more than once and so has Finley" he's invited me to that young adult class at he and aunt Doris's church." "Yes, that is fun I've gone the last three times with Sonjee even this last week when she wasn't in town, I went by myself, she shared. So, it's interesting? He asked. "I'm a loner for the most part though I have found some friends who attend U.C and have similar interest." Our instructor really challenges us to bring the bible to our daily living." I have been helped a lot. Everyone there seems to enjoy it. Right now, there are about twenty of us regularly, last count, I think weekly though we're growing, Kara confessed. "I will definitely show up this week coming in. Mind if I ride in with you for accountability? David Michael asked now seeming interested in what Finley had been trying to get him to attend for a while. Sure! Look I'm getting ready to go. I'll see you hopefully tomorrow? She questioned leaving out of the door. "Oh Kara, I forgot to ask you, I received my Aunt Doris" invitation for her wedding. It's not until next month but will you come with me as my date?" Surprised but pleased she stepped back from the door. "David Michael are you feeling alright?" She asked teasing him for his question asked. "I'm fine thanks to you, and I would like you to be my date! He repeated to the somber drab and most of the time quiet young lady. "If you're sure of what you are asking, I'd love to accompany you" she smiled in her mousy little way leaving going home.

Justin walked in with his date looking dapper in his Valentino tuxedo and she chose to wear a white gown from the designer label Wechsler showing her trendy side. Looking around in the gala decorated room he saw Dana near the front with other's who had to give presentations for the prestigious affair. The Black and White Ball was an annual event and many of the hospital's top executives were in attendance. Dr. Baisden was making his rounds meeting and greeting everyone there and laughter filled the air. "Hello Dana, good to see you" he said coming over to speak and to ask her a question. "Dr. Baisden you look very handsome tonight" Dana expressed seeing him coming toward her. "This is my date Colvin Murphy she said allowing him to extend his hand to her boss. "Good evening sir, Colvin shared extending for a shake. "Are you affiliated with the hospital? He asked making conversation. "No sir I have a seafood business in New Orleans." Which now lead to another conversation about the disastrous floodwaters. Dana extremely gorgeous in her black designer Wang gown was quickly tiring of her boss and date discussing the events of Katrina. "Dr. Basiden we're moving this way I need to get some more info before my presentation" she shared grabbing Colvin's hand and pulling him away. Dana still had not seen Billy but she was looking. 'Hi! Hello! Hey! Could be heard throughout the glamorous old-world building where the ball was being held. Beautiful full-length gorgeous ball gowns were being worn by most of the attendees there. Local radio and television personalities were emceeing the annual event and as always, the turnout was great. "Something to drink? Colvin asked as they came upon the open bar in the corner of the room. "Champagne please" she replied reaching for the flute style stemware being poured by the bartender. "Hello, Dana said seeing Justin and his date Krista. "Dr. Williams" she said speaking to her colleague. "Krista, so you're moving up I see? 'Excuse me? She questioned looking at Dana. "Oh, it doesn't matter" Dana responded grabbing the arm of Colvin and walking away. "That lady is pure evil! Krista confided to Justin. "I wouldn't worry about it "Let's dance" he said pulling her gently to the floor. Dana and Colvin had returned to their table and sat talking quietly as each presenter took the podium to speak. "Excuse me Colvin I must go up front" "Do your thing babe! He shared as she moved to the podium for her presentation. Colvin sit listening to his women's (is how he thought of her) spoken words. She was so thoughtful to give him the money she had promised him for the botched job regarding the kidnapping of his ex-girlfriend's father. He had spent the earlier part of the morning in the bank getting his business affairs in order. "Hello, calling his foreman in New Orleans. "Thanks boss! I'm waiting for them to delivery that part for the freezer" he shared with Colvin. "Good and did you get the guys paid? I did boss and boy, were they happy! "Good I should be home Monday" he shared still speaking with his foreman of his small business. "Freda said the money you sent put us in the black for this month, something changed? "No, not really, just a windfall came through, glad everyone's happy for a minute anyway" Alright boss looking forward to seeing you soon." "Yeah bye! Dana was doing her thing at the podium as she made her presentation to the guest contributors for the event. "Excuse me mind if I sit here? A female voice asked as he sat waiting for Dana to return to the table. Colvin looked up to see a beautiful brunette wearing a white silk chiffon bloused number by Parkinson showing off her very shapely legs. "Sure, he said checking her out from head to toe. "I don't think anyone's sitting at that table he informed her. "Thanks, she said putting her purse down and heading to get a drink from the waiter across the room. "Colvin stood up as Dana came back after her presentation. "Great job, he said reaching to embrace her for a kiss. "Yeah! Yeah! Look I have to find Billy I'll be right back" she said moving away to find the man who she had come to see leaving Colvin sitting along at the table awaiting her return. "Hey are you alone? The brunette had returned with a stemmed glass in hand. "No actually I'm here with Dr. Williams" he replied. "Oh, so you're here with Dana" please to meet you, I'm one of her colleagues Dr. Helen Salinski, director of our neonatal center" she said extending her hand for a shake. "Oh, pardon my seat Colvin said getting up to shake the doctor's hand. "So where is Dana she asked gazing around through and over the crowd. Not waiting for an answer, she flirted "she's brave leaving such a handsome man all alone in this crowd of women don't you think? Smiling as she took her sit. Colvin sat talking with her as he waited for Dana. "Want to dance? She asked moving in her seat to the music. Colvin looked down at his watch, it had been twenty minutes and he was tired of waiting on Dana. "Why not? He said reaching out his hand to walk slowly to the dance floor with the flirtatious doctor. He drew her in and embraced her to a slow instrumental tune played by the live band present. The dance was over and still Dana had not come back to the table. The two sat conversing with Helen now sitting at the table with Colvin enjoying his company. After a while a catchy little tune was being played. "Oh, oblige me Colvin I like this tune! She said pulling his hand wanting to dance to the lively tune. "Whew! She swirled and danced around in front of Colvin. He was now involved in this dance and playfully flirted back moving around to the hip beat of the music. Helen swerved her hips with the asymmetrical-hem skirt flowing as she moved. They laughed and were having so much fun interfacing with each other's moves. Just as the dance ended, they stood together on the floor "hey you are quite a dancer" she shared smiling at him. "Well, you are not bad either Colvin replied with his arm around her waist when Dana walked up. "HELEN SALINSKI! who let you out of the pit? She asked seeing her with Colvin. "Now, now Dana don't lose you venom it's not becoming! She fired back. "You're right I forgot rattlers travel alone! Dana chided. "Dana come on let's get a drink Colvin said walking away with Dana to defuse the heated ensuing conversation taking place. Colvin looked back smiling leaving Dr. Slanski standing sipping from her champagne. Why Helen it's good to see you! Dr. Baisden said walking up from her left side. "Oh Major, yes you knew I'd be here" she replied cheerfully. "Where's the Mr.? He asked looking around for her husband. "Hermick was a bit under the weather this evening so I'm doing the solo joint tonight" she confessed. Hermick did all he could to keep up with the vivacious Helen. He was about forty years her senior and was viewed by most as her sugar daddy. "Well, it's certainly good to see your commitment to this event" Dr. Baisden confessed. "Hope Hermick feels better soon he added moving on to another group gathering in the room. "She's just a witch! Dana stated standing next to the bar waiting for Colvin to get the drink orders from the bartender. She looked across the floor and finally spotted Billy and Nada sitting at a table talking romantically to each other. Leaving Colvin to follow her she walked slowly toward the table. Her beautiful gown flowed as she moved toward them. "Hello William! She said standing over the table. "Nada! She said also coldly speaking to his date. "Hello Dana your presentation was great! You did a wonderful job," he said greeting her warmly. "You know Nada my fiancée, don't you? "Sure, she replied extending her hand to shake it. Standing seductively showing off her black Wang gown she began conversing with Billy ignoring Nada. "Dana I certainly believe you are committed to this event however I'm here with Nada and I really can't discuss this with you tonight" he shared with her putting his arm around Nada gently drawing her to him. Dana exhaled loudly put out by what he had said. Colvin finally discovered the direction she had made her way to and came to the table. Billy seeing him come up to the table stood up again. "Dana here you are! He said giving her the drink she had ordered. "Thank you, oh William this is my date. "Good! please to meet you, my name is William Parker" extending his hand to the mystery man Dana had brought to the Ball. "Colvin Murphy" he replied joining the shake. "Nada had been ignoring the conversation between Billy and Dana until she heard the name. She coughed! Is everything all right Nada? Dana asked sensing her uneasiness. Nada now stood to get a better look at this man who had a very familiar name. Billy put his arm around her and introduced her. "This is my fiancée "Nada Francois "Colvin said surprising Billy by finishing his sentence. "Excuse me" Billy said surprised now looking at Nada. "NO! This can't be true? Nada exclaimed taking a closer look at Dana's date. "Sweetheart how does this man know you? He asked holding her now trembling body. Dana stood smiling knowing she had caused a stir. Billy can we leave? I promise I will explain it all to you" Nada pleaded. She stood trembling in her gorgeous Pesce white gown wanting to run out of the event. "Sure, Billy replied "excuse me Dana I have to get my fiancée out of here she's not feeling well" sensing something is really wrong. Dana had missed what Billy said earlier about a fiancée but this time it rang clear. "Your fiancée? You gave her a ring? Come on Dana let's go! Colvin suggested reaching for her arm. He had moved away from Dana and stood to the side of her. Dana pulled her arm away from him and stood looking meanly at Billy. "WHAT'S THE SECRET TELL HIM? She yelled. There were on lookers now near to where they were standing "William let's go please? Nada pleaded. She was not about to satisfy Dana by causing a scene in a place with all of Maine's elite and radio and television hosts. Dana walked over and caught Nada by her arms standing in front of her shaking her to confess. "Get out of my face! Nada replied lightly pushing her back with her opened hand. "I knew you were behind what happened to my dad! "Billy this is Colvin Murphy the worm I told you about!" Nada confessed. Billy looked at him standing waiting for Dana's next command he reasoned. "I've got it now sweetheart, let's go" quickly walking toward the door with whispers now starting to fill the room. Billy stopped short of the door looking back into the crowded ballroom. Socializing and dancing was still going on. Only those in the immediate area even knew anything went on. Dana had embraced her date Colvin and was dancing to the music that just played through the whole thing.

CHAPTER 46

Are you sure?

"You look beautiful Kara! Sonjee said standing looking at her new makeover. Having cropped her long hair in a short cut tapered style she looked so sophisticated. She was showing off one of the outfits she had picked out during their shopping spree on Robinson blvd in Beverly Hills. "You think David Michael will like my new look? she asked. "I'm sure he will but what about you? Sonjee asked. Me? Kara replied pointing to herself. "Yes you! You have to like yourself, right? "Well, I really like it I hope he does! She said excitedly spinning around in the floor length mirror. "He will, because you look fabulous, she shared with the shy introverted Kara who loved to dance. Both are on the performing arts dance team at UCLA together and she is very good at it. "I'll take all of these" laying the outfits she had picked out on the counter. The clerk stood waiting for the girls to pay for their purchases. She smiled wide as she reached for the credit cards.

Nada stood waiting for the valet to bring the car up. Billy was getting their over coats from the checkpoint in the ballroom. "Hello dad! Hi sweetheart, how are you enjoying your visit with my son in law to be? He asked in a very good mood. "Daddy you won't believe who I saw tonight? She stated standing on her cell phone trembling with anger as she spoke. "Who dear? He asked still clueless of her real feelings as she spoke. "Clovin Murphy" WHO? Did you say Murphy? Are you all right where is Billy? Nada he's not bothering you, is he?" No dad I'm fine Billy and I are headed home". "Dana showed up with him to the yearly Black and White Ball event". "Let me speak to Billy! if he puts his hands on you! "Daddy! Daddy I'm fine I'll call you tomorrow I need to speak with Billy first okay? All right but call me or I will be on the next plane out! He shared concerned. "Dad I love you, I'm sure Billy will take care of me. I was checking to see if you were all right". "I'm fine having dinner with Ms. Phyllis, but I'll be home in two hours at the most and call me if you need me". "I'm happy for you dad, goodnight! She said seeing Billy coming to the car she was now sitting in after the valet had brought it to the door's entrance. "Sorry honey it took so long I got into a discussion with a client" are you all right? "I'm angry sweetheart, I can't say with certainty that she is behind all this mess though if I was a betting woman!" "Now, now calm down dear" he said holding her hand as he exited the lot to the street. "Please don't buy into Dana's foolishness" "I don't mean too" she said and broke down and began to cry" "I'm sorry Billy but I just don't know what to think of her most times" she admitted still wiping her eyes trying to stop tears. Billy comforted her thoughts and held her hand. "I was there, honey and I know Dana". I have had a detective following her every since the incident with your father but until tonight I didn't know the man's name". "What? She said sniffling and blowing her nose and wiping her eyes. So, you knew about Colvin and Dana? "Well like I said I didn't know what connection he was to this whole fiasco but yes I have had and eye on those two for a while". "William, I love you she said laying her head on his shoulder as he drove back to the estate. "I love you too Nada" he said feeling secure he had comforted her fears.

"Well honey! I thought rehearsal went well tonight Doris shared with Russell over desert. They had stopped off to have a treat at a restaurant call "Simply Desert" "The crust is very flaky I like it! I knew you would Doris explained that's why I suggested it". Honey did Paul or Bethany Ann call or write about our wedding? "No, Doris neither has replied. I really don't think they will" "Why? Why are you so positive neither wants to attend our wedding? "Because they were with their mother most of their life, and I'm sure she has turned them against all people having anything to do with me" he remarked. "Besides Doris, I'm sorry but I didn't tell them about you" he stated sadly. "What do you mean, you didn't tell them about me! Who did you tell them you were marrying? "You! He said again. "Okay, I'm calm help me to understand? She asked still somewhat puzzled. "Doris you have to understand you gave me my dignity back! You loved me knowing what I have and don't have! You trusted me with your life and I love you more and more everyday" I can't and won't let them come between us! He stated. "All right I understand she said remembering an earlier conversation" as the two finished their desert and got up to leave. "Well, I think I understand though to be honest I will have to pray about it". Me too sweetheart me too!

Sonjee, Kara and Daphne walked into the auditorium at Royce Hall for a called rehearsal. "Are you sure she said Royce Hall, this is our liberal arts building. "I know that! Sonjee chided but Kubunawa said Royce Hall six SHARP! Everyone was gathering and now looking at Kara's new look. "Wow! I like it" let me see turning her around. "Fierce! I really like it Kara! Other's were saying as all forty some dancers gathered looking around waiting for their instructor. GET IN ORDER PLEASE! Vanessa their instructor yelled walking into the room. She walked around and around looking to see who had come for the called practice. She said it showed dedication! Looking again over the assembly of dancers she asked, where is Kara? "Right here Ms. Kubunawa! Kara replied holding up her hand quickly. She walked over to her striking each step in her black leotards and stood looking at the new Kara. "Umm I like it! It's hot! Okay let's began with stretches! She shouted moving back to the front of the group of now chattering girls "thanks Ms. Kubunawa" Kara whispered with a smile.

Nada had taken a long relaxing bath and took time alone after they arrived back at the estates. Billy excused himself to make some phone calls he said and would return later. Nada was sitting in his guest bedroom after talking with her dad again to ease his concerns. Billy knocked on the door. "Come in she replied. She was feeling bad for spoiling their planned evening. "Sweetheart, how are you? He asked coming in all relaxed with a big smile. "Honey I'm so sorry, I should have handled myself better in that matter" I know you can take care of me" she confessed sitting up straight in the big chair as he snuggled in beside her. "Hey are you ready for our trip starting tomorrow morning? He asked ignoring what she was apologizing for. "I am, I just want to be with you! She admitted laying her head on his broad shoulder. "I can't wait either for you to meet Glen and his wife Cheryl and Desmond and his wife Mossy," he explained excitedly. "Honey do you think they will like me?" she asked. "I'm sure they will like you. I love you myself! He joked to get her to smile and then shared a kiss with her. "Ring, ring, hello, Hello dad! David Michael how are you this evening? I'm good had a scout come out and talk to me today" he shared about to burst with excitement. "He said he's going to be watching me this year! "Son that's great! So how is practice going? He asked getting up to pace as he spoke to his son. "Well dad, very well! And how is everything else we've been discussing" he asked with concern. "Dad I'm going to join this young adult group at aunt Doris's church" as a matter of fact I'm waiting for Kara to pick me up we are riding together; I need accountability you know". Son that's wonderful, look I'll probably sneak a peek in on practice in the very near future and you have a wonderful time with the group okay?" Sonjee loves it she's been going for a while she got Kara going and they both think it will occupy a lot of my idle evenings". "That's got to be good, call me and let me know how it goes tonight." tonight? "are you sure?" David Michael asked. "I'm sure I want to know. "And ah Kara, her name has been coming up a lot lately" She's just a friend dad not my type really but she's a really good friend" All right call me I'll be waiting to hear about the group" Any hour? Yes, son any hour," "Love ya, dad bye! later son.' "Sorry about that Billy shared turning his attention back to Nada "but he doesn't call often so when he does, I know he wants to talk." Nada just smiled she liked he had taken time for his son. Billy came and sat beside her again. "What are you writing? He asked. "Just scribbling something on paper," she replied. Looking he saw 'Nada Parker" written several different ways. "Has a great sound to it doesn't it? He asked her smiling. "It does!" she admitted looking at her beautiful ring on her finger. "I was sitting in my study going over some things that needed my attention, he said, "oh by the way I got Doris and Russell's invitation! They are getting married February 3rd. "That's great! Nada exclaimed "she shared with me it was her first marriage but Russell's second so she wanted it to be really nice since she only plans to do it once" Nada explained looking at the invitation Billy had handed her. "Well, I don't want to over shadow their nuptials though I was thinking June 20th for us. How does that sound for a wedding date? "JUNE 20TH! ARE YOU SURE THAT SOON? Oh, William Parker June 20th is just wonderful! I love you! She exclaimed hugging him tightly around his neck.

A surprise visit

"Sonjee have you spoken with Kara? David Michael asked as she came through the door. "I have, we just left dance rehearsal why? "We're riding together to the young adult meeting tonight at the church and she hasn't answered her cell phone all day! "Well, I'm sure she'll be here, just running a bit late" Sonjee replied heading to the shower. "Ring ring! Hello! Dave, hey man it's Brody! What are you up to tonight? he asked. "David Michael was hoping he would be gone before his old buddy called. "Brod, got plans tonight what are you up to? Thought we could hang out at your pad! I'll bring the brew! he said hoping to persuade him. "Man thanks, but not tonight headed out, take care" and hung up the phone. It had only been a month since Brody and some of his other old friends had came in and tore their beautiful condo up with a wild unplanned get together. Sonjee had showered and dressed when someone came knocking. "David get the door!" she shouted. he was now involved in watching a crime show on the television. Hearing Sonjee he jumped up and went to the door peeking out, he couldn't make out the person standing at the door through the small peephole. "Who's there! he yelled "KARA!" he looked again before opening the door. "Kara! I like it! Sonjee didn't tell me you had made this change". He hugged her and then turned her around. The outfit she was wearing he liked that too! "Are you two ready? Sonjee asked grabbing her jacket and heading out the door with both following.

Dana sat having her morning coffee and dialing Colvin's hotel room. Ring! Ring! Ring! Ring! He must be in the shower no one sleeps that sound! She thought dialing again on his cell phone. "You have reached Colvin Murphy leave a message after the tone" beep! Ahh! She exclaimed, now, where is he? She was starting to get agitated. She had been calling him most of the morning and no answer. "They were up quite late after the ball but anyone human should be moving at this hour she reasoned dialing again for the 7th or 8th time. "Ring, ring! "Maine Hotel lobby! the voice answered. "Yes, please ring Colvin Murphy's room for me please? She asked kindly. "Murphy? Murphy, he repeated again as if looking for something in a ledger. "Yes, Murphy room 4708! Dana stated frustrated with the desk clerk. "Oh him! Well Mr. Murphy isn't with us any longer" oh did he check out this morning? She asked. "No, he was already gone when I started my shift this morning at 6am" he replied. "Did he happen to say where he was going? Dana questioned again trying to get answers since she finally got someone to answer a phone. "Excuse me Ms. I'll be right back with you. I have another line ringing in". "Now where on earth has, he gone to? She thought waiting for the clerk to come back on the phone. "WELL? Dana asked as he picked up her line again. "He cleared his tab here last night I was told and left in a cab" don't know where he went, bye! Darn it! She said throwing her wireless handset against the wall. "Were men this foolish back then? She asked looking at the beautiful hand painted portrait of her mother she had hanging on her wall. She paced around her home most of the day getting only a recording from Colvin's mobile phone. By 6:30 pm she had had enough! She dressed in her white cowboy outfit from head to toe and was headed to the Corral but first she was going to call Billy. He may have something to do with Colvin's quick departure. "Ring! Ring! Ring! "Parker residence", came a greeting. "William Parker please?" "Mr. Parker is out" came the replied. "When is he expected in? "Mr. Parker will be gone for about two weeks" the voice again replied." "TWO WEEKS! Dana repeated hanging up the line abruptly. "I know that was that devil woman! Ha! ha! Dante said laughing with the other staff present.

Doris was humming around her home approving some last-minute advertising pamphlets for her boutique she had opened in the inner city. Russell had called to say the meeting he attended regarding her thrift stores went well. "Honey I'll see you at 7:30. I need to stop by the church and speak with Deacon Folgers about getting his group involved with the rest home in East Los Angeles" "Alright dear see you then. Hanging up she heard her intercom buzz. "Mrs. Wright there is some one here at the gate to see you" came the voice. "Trubul I'm not expecting anyone except Russ, who are they? She replied back. There was a pause while her attendant got the person's name. "Ms Wright it's a woman, and a small child around six or seven, he explained. "Says her name is Bethany Mcvey and her son Trendon" Doris stood for a moment going over the names in her mind. "Bethany, she thought. "Oh Bethany Ann! Russell's daughter! "Let them in Trubul thanks! Bethany drove the car through the large gate with Trendon watching it close slowly behind them. "Mommy where are we going? I'm coming to see a lady my dad knows," she explained to her small child. "Oh, she lives in a big house like grandma and grandpa Stacy." "Yes, she does" Bethany Ann remarked pulling up parking in the very spacious driveway. She got out and Trendon got out and met her at the door. He stood looking up at the very tall and very wide doors. Bethany rang the doorbell. After a while the door swung open slowly. "Hello! Finley said standing in the door. "Wow! He looks like the guy on Fresh Prince" Trendon thought. "Shhh, his mother said and took hold of his hand. "Good morning may I speak with Doris Wright? she asked very slowly looking at the smiling butler. "Come in My lady his expecting you," he replied. "Mommy he talks like him too, Trendon whispered as he walked in looking at the tremendously tall ceilings in the enormous size house. "Right this way" Finley said leading them to the great room where Doris had chosen to meet her. "Hello! extending her hand with a smile to greet them as they walked in. "Doris Wright, she said smiling at the very surprised young lady. Hello young man! Doris smiled. "AH! She gasped looking at Doris. "Doris smiled she knew she wasn't expecting to see a woman of her nationality standing in front of her. "I'm sorry, I'm so sorry" finally came out of Bethany Ann and she extended her hand to Doris. I wasn't expecting" she was almost in shock. "Please sit down, sit down" Doris suggested seeing she was surprised and close to fainting, she reasoned. "May I have a drink of water? She asked. Doris went to the intercom. Soon Finley came in with a tray with water and something for Trendon who had squeezed in between the handled of the chair and his mother. "Thank you she said taking the glass and drinking until it was all gone. "Mrs. Wright I'm sorry, but dad never said you were" she stopped. "Black" Doris said finishing her sentence. "We're from Utah! She stated. "So, is that a problem for you? Doris asked seeing she was clearly caught off base. "Ms. Wright can we talk alone" she asked not wanting to speak in front of her son. "Sure" Doris replied asking Finley to take Trendon to the game room. "I don't want my child to hear how I was raised by my mother. I grew up in Utah Ms. Wright and saw very little interactions between blacks and whites even today. I was in junior high when dad lost his great job and mom left him because she had lost everything and blamed dad for it all! I didn't see my dad again until two years ago." Mom is still very bitter and never allowed us to talk about dad and wouldn't answer any questions either. He often wrote us over the years and if mom didn't get the letters Paul and I would sneak and read them when she was out which as we got older was often because she traveled a lot with her new husband. We stayed with a sitter a lot when we were younger. AND by the time we were teens we were very self sufficient for the most part. "I understand dear, Russ and I have talked in great detail about you and your brother" Doris confessed. "I feel bad, here it is the year two thousand and I'm still explaining race! Bethany Ann admitted now pacing around the room. "You have been nothing but good to daddy he told us that" but yet when I saw you, I only saw your color! She shared with Doris. "I hope you know I love your father and he makes me happy. I hope I do the same for him". "We fell in love after spending time together and getting to know one another" I don't know if I've ever seen him as anything other than a man" Doris shared. "He told me what you did for him, giving him back his self esteem and his manhood" Bethany Ann explained. "Sometimes that's all it takes Bethany" allowing a person of any nationality to feel liked for himself. Not seeing him as a black man or white man but as a human being" Doris again shared. Ms. Wright do you have children? Bethany asked now sitting down in the great room drinking coffee. "I do, Doris replied smiling "I have a daughter she's a freshman in college. "Then as a parent you understand how it feels to raise a child? she questioned. Doris didn't respond not sure of where the young lady in her mid-thirties was going yet. "My attendant introduced you as Mcvey are you married? Doris asked now feeling comfortable with the conversation-taking place. "Yes, she said shyly but he doesn't know I'm here. We're both school teachers in Utah my brother is an architect but I was very close to my dad" she explained allowing Doris to understand that she probably went against her husband's wishes to come and he certainly didn't know she was here, she reasoned. "Oh, I do understand". "Would you like me to call your dad I'm sure he would rush right over to see you! She said getting up to call. "No please! She exclaimed, "I really don't have the time." touching Doris's hand over the phone receiver. "All right I won't. But understand I met your dad in a very down time in his life. I own boutiques, on Rodeo, and Robinson in Beverly Hills that's just a few of the things I busy myself with. Though the work I do in the inner-city missions and my church is what I'm passionate about." Doris shared. The young lady sat attentively as she spoke. "As a matter of fact, that's where I met your father at one of the missions!

"I interface with a lot of powerful people every day and they come in all colors and races. But I found the same race of people on the street and in the missions, the only difference is the pride of life and dignity and of course money" she admitted. "Doris handed her one of the pamphlets she had given out for the mission work she and Russell were still very involved in. "I didn't know! She said sadly reading over the mission statement. She got up from her chair and hugged Doris, and asked for her son she really had to go, she expressed. "May I keep this? She questioned speaking of the pamphlet Doris had given her. "Please! Doris replied. "Thank you for taking the time to speak with me. You have made him happy and I'm glad to have met you" she confessed and turned and hugged Doris again. "Is this Russell's only grandchild? She asked before Finley and the child arrived by the front entrance. "Yes, but he's never had a chance to meet him" she admitted sadly. "Are you sure I can't call; he will be so disappointed! Doris explained. "No Ms Wright I've stayed to long already now" reaching for her son's hand that wasn't filled with a balloon or popcorn. Goodbye again Ms. Wright. "Bye Finley! Trendon said sadly walking out the huge doors of Doris Wright's home. "Mr. Finley's nice too!

Dana had spent Sunday around her home. Everyone she had called was either out or she got voicemails. "I don't know when I've ever wanted Monday to come so badly! She expressed now dressing to go somewhere for the evening. She had spoken with her son who shared he was on his way to church with friends. She knew he had gotten that trait she called it from his dad. She was headed to the Corral for happy hour. "You have reached the voicemail of Colvin Murphy please leave a message" "beep" Imbecile! Where is he? She had tried calling most of the day, she thought driving down the highway heading for some fun. "That's right Mollie had called, ring, ring! "Molly, leave a message! Dang! No more calls she sped up and headed toward the Corral. After about a half hour she was pulling into the parking entrance that was waiting room only. "Who's here tonight? She asked herself slowly moving up the long line of automobiles waiting to park and be parked. "This is crazy! She thought dialing a friend of the popular nightspot. "Smokey here," "Smokey, Dana! Howdy! "Look, who is on stage tonight this parking lot looks like a zoo" she said now sitting in an overcrowded lot. "Ms. Tucker's singing tonight! he said speaking loudly above the crowd. "I could sure use some help getting in there! Dana requested of the club's owner. "Pull up by the door I'll send someone to rescue you darling! "Thanks Smokey, I owe ya! turning her Porsche carefully in another direction to the front entrance after getting the parking attendant to let her through. When Dana pulled up to the entrance a valet was waiting for her. "Dr. Williams? he asked reaching for her hand to help her from the car. "Yes, thank you, she replied getting out giving him her keys and making her way through the doors with Smokey waiting near the entrance. "Howdy pretty lady! Good to see ya out tonight! he voiced coming over to embrace her as she made her way through the crowded entrance of the club. "Wow! This place is buzzing tonight! She said returning his embrace. "Hey come on in I'm waiting here for a friend of my but you go on in and have yourself a good time ya here! Dana walked in and slowly went through the crowded club. "Howdy! Hey there! Dana! Excuse me, sorry she said speaking and making her way to the tall bar stool not occupied at this time near the bar. She ordered a drink of choice and sat looking at everyone chatting and dancing and mingling all around her. "Hello missy, can I interest you in a dance? This tall thin cowboy standing in front of her asked.

Dana's first instinct was to say no but she had watched him go around the room getting turned down so she obliged him. He caught her hand and the other on her waist and off he went. "Hee haw! He said as he went around and around the dance floor with Dana laughing and enjoying the fun. After a while it was over. He smiled, thank ya miss! He said now moving to some others who had turned him down. Dana was about to sit back on her stool when she heard her name. "Dana! Dana! It was her girl Mollie. "Mollie! She said seeing her come over to hug her. "I called you earlier to see if you would be here? "You did! "Corky and I just got back". Soon he walked up with two drinks he had gotten from the other side of the bar. 'Dana girl! Long time no see! he said hugging her with one arm. "How's Rusty? she asked, "Good! He was out riding Sugar the other day! "I HAVE GOT TO GET OUT TO THE RANCH AND SEE HIM! She said speaking over the crowd to be heard now that the lively band had began to play. "He stood behind Mollie. "Dana look! she said very excited. "Cork and I got married. We just got back from Vegas! What? Dana exclaimed. She held her hand looking at the beautiful Varna diamond sparkling on Mollie's finger. "Oh, Mollie I'm happy for you" and you to Corky" she said hugging the both of them. "You have got to come and see my pictures DANA! Mollie explained. Dana was happy but so sad it wasn't her wedding or her diamond. Doris her sister was getting married at the beginning of the month and she still hadn't won William Parker's heart and probably never will since he had given Nada François a ring! Corky and Mollie made their way to the floor for a big line dance that was taking place. "We'll be right back Dana" they yelled heading into the huge crowd of excited cowboys and cowgirls having fun on the wooded dance floor. Dana left without saying anything to anyone. She rode home still trying to get and answer from Colvin Murphy whose cell phone was still being answered by voicemail.

When Russell arrived, Doris greeted him as usually. "Honey I really need to speak with you before dinner" Oh Doris I want to share with you about this homeless couple who came to the store today! Thomas and Ellen, they" Doris interrupted "Russ I really want to hear, but honey! She said looking into his face. "What's wrong you sound so serious you're scaring me". "No, I 'm fine dear, sit down, have a sit please? She asked sitting beside him on the sofa. "Doris what's wrong? He asked now very concerned. "Bethany was here today," she said. "Bethany? My Bethany Ann he asked a bit confused. Yes, dear she asked me not to call you though I sure wanted to". "Oh, how is she? Is she okay? What did she say? He kept asking questions. She came to meet me and almost fainted when she saw me," "She didn't know Doris! "Yes, she told me, she loves you a lot! "Why do you say that?" He asked now pacing the room. She's married! "My Bethany Ann is married I didn't know; they never wrote me" did they get the letters I wrote? "Some" Doris replied. Russell sat now holding his head while Doris shared what his daughter had said "Russ she's a schoolteacher and Paul is an architect." They live in Utah. Bethany Ann lives with her husband who didn't know she was here". She told me she was very close to you when she was growing up". "Oh, I missed them so much! he said now resting on Doris shoulder. "Are they coming to the wedding? he asked. "I can't say Russ. She said Paul was a lot like his mother" helping him to understand why he never got in touch with him and probably wouldn't. "So, my baby was here". Yes, dear she said she was glad to have met me" he looked up, thank you God! And thank you sweetheart, I'm sorry I didn't tell her. Russ I understand better now". "I love you! I love you too Russell, taking his hand and leading him to the dining room. "And Russell hold on tight" she said "you have a sweet little grandson seven years old! "Really, what's he like? He questioned heading to the dining room table to enjoy a meal with his fiancée Doris Wright.

C H A P T E R 4 8

The wait continues

"David Michael I'm here" Kara said coming in the door. "Where's Sonj? She went over to the library with Crystal and Clark". They're working together in Wasman's class. "Clark? Wow he's usually a loner". "Nobody's alone when Sonjee's around you know that! true, true". "Ready! grabbing his cap heading for the door. Kara had come by to take him to practice. He was constantly being persuaded by Brent and the old gang to go out partying after practice and he had finally realized he couldn't win. Often, he'd come home wasted or there were times when he didn't show up at all. So, he asked Kara to accompany him. Driving up he could see they were waiting in the bleachers. The baseball team was standing near the dugout. David Michael got out the car and ran over and kissed Kara who was still sitting under the wheel. SHE SMILED. "Have a good practiced "she yelled as he took the field with the other players. She took their small tote cooler that carried Gatorade and water for her. "My book! She said "I must remember to get it from my backpack in the back seat of my cute little Jetta" she had just purchased. She walked up into the bleachers and sat down and began opening her book and started to read. Looking up she was interrupted by this big brut of a guy named Brent. He must be at least 275 lbs and stood about 6 ft tall. He was a lineman on the football team she knew that. "Babysitting again? he asked. Kara said nothing. David Michael and the team were way out in the field and looking around it was just she and his buddies sitting a bit further at the top of the large stadium. "I like your new look! He said rubbing her hair.

"Get your hands off of me! She yelled. "What? Your wimpy little rich boy won't hear ya! he mocked. She stood trying to bring attention to him bothering her. But the team was so far out in the field. She was only a dot from where they were. She started gathering her things up in her arm when he swatted the book from her arms. "STOP! She yelled again. "What are you going to do? Get the wimp! Call the wimp! I'll help you" putting his hand to his face making a mega horn from which to yell. Silently he pretended to yell David's name laughing. "I guess he can't hear me," he then said. Kara reached down to pick up her physics book when he pushed her and she dropped the tote to keep from falling. I'm not sure if Brent knew this small little 98-pound female and that was with clothes had this much fight in her. He leaned over to pick up her tote and she spun around with what wrestlers call a round house right up side of his head and the big guy went tumbling down the bleachers. She quickly picked up her tote and book and made her way to the field and sat down breathing quickly trying to catch her breath. The team didn't see a thing they were still busy at practice. Brent's friends came to his aid. "Get back! Get back I just slipped" he lied. Stupid witch!

Dana sat in her office writing in her journal when her phone rang. "Hello! Dana it's good to know you're all right! "I'm fine dear Mollie" "Well how was I to know! You didn't say anything when you left last night" Hey you guys were having so much fun I just slipped out "I had and early morning anyway. So, tell me about your wedding?" Oh girl! Mollie replied sharing her wedding story.

"William I must share with you I'm nervous about meeting your best friends" Nada explained as they sat in the airplane headed to Florida for a meeting first and then a visit to his childhood friend Glenn Reed. "Don't worry they will love you" you're bias! Umm that might be true" but I think they will still love ya, I do! He expressed tapping her gently with a magazine he was reading. Babe, mind if I change the subject for a minute? "WHATEVER YOU WANT FOR THE WEDDING IS FINE WITH ME! he said laughing, I'm talked out about it". "No sweetheart seriously this is not about our wedding" it's about the Ball." "The Ball? last weekend? Yes, you have selective memory? She asked.

"What happens if we run into Dana and Colvin again, they are in Maine you know!" I don't think we will have to worry about that". "You don't why? Umm hey they are just people, right? He asked. "True! But you're not telling me something" she reasoned. Quickly changing the subject, he asked "Nada should I get a band of gold or platinum one to compliment yours? He now asked holding out her hand looking at her five and a half carat sparkle. "Are you trying to change the subject on me? "Look sweetie I don't plan on going through life trying to avoid Dana and whomever she chooses to be with BUT if we see those two together again then we will deal with it okay! kissing her forehead as she turned to lay her head on his shoulder for the plane ride to see Glenn and Cheryl. Billy stared out the window. His investigator had shared some advice with Colvin concerning a kidnapping. If he wanted to stay out of jail he'd better stay away from Maine and Nada Francois.

Wow! Great practice! David Michael said walking over to Kara now sitting on the grassy field. Hey fun! She replied. Yeah! Did you notice coach put me in as pitcher? He said excited about that appointment. "I sure did what was that about? Oh, Stalen our regular pitcher hurt his arm and needed to rest it" what an opportunity to show coach what I'm capable of! He said spinning around joyfully. "Man, I going to call Ray tonight! He's going to go ballistic! he said I could do it! Wow! David couldn't contain the joy bottled inside of him at that moment. "Great arm Parker! Some teammates yelled heading off the field. 'WAY TO GO PARKER! That's show'em" others replied leaving to go home from what David Michael deemed the best practice ever. "Thanks guys! Kara got up brushing herself of the lose blades of grass on her clothing and headed to her car. "Kara what was going on in the bleachers earlier? He asked now calm from practice. "What do you mean? Kara asked avoiding his question. "I saw some guys talking with you and then you stood up and left were they bothering you or something? He asked. "Oh, you saw that? Well yeah, we were in a time out coach was showing Vaughn how to slide into home plate and I was looking at you sitting there alone until they came up." "It was just Brent and his gooneys." What did he say? "Nothing worth repeating' she said clicking the lock to unlock the doors. "How about pizza? Kara asked putting her backpack on the seat and the book she was reading back inside.

"Sounds great I'll call and order we can pick it up on our way home," he suggested. David Michael handed her the tote and put his dirty cleats in the trunk. "I'll drive he said catching the keys as she tossed them to him. "Those guys show up almost every practice wanting me to go out with them". "I told them I'm trying to do something different like become a pro-player". How did you meet them? Kara asked as they rode along home now in the car leaving the field. "They're on the football team and lived across the hall in the dorms. They kept our place a mess! That's why I moved out" he shared. Remy was Kyle my roommates' best friend and he invited them in most of the time". "I bet that was a mess," she echoed. "Yeah! Any way I'm glad to be rid of them, I totally forgot and let them come to our condo" YES YOU DID! And Kara, I promise I will never do it again" he stated pulling the car into the parking lot to pickup their large pan pizza. Arriving home and noticing Sonjee had still not arrived they waited before sitting down to eat. "David you shower I'll set up the pizza," Kara suggested going into the kitchen. "Thanks, he said and reached over and kissed her on her forehead moving to the room first and then the shower. She blushed and continued into the kitchen before acknowledging what he did. "She smiled softly as she took the plates and napkins back into the den and turned on the television. After fifteen or twenty minutes he emerged again "Thanks Kara you're great! She put two larges slices of pizza on his plate and handed it to him. "It's still warm," he voiced taking a bite. "I put it in the microwave when I heard you whistling in the room, I knew you'd be out soon. "Kara", he said eating and watching the show now playing on the set. "I got strawberry soda for you" she said handing him the ice-cold soft drink. "Kara, Fenton and Craig and I are up next Tuesday for the young adults meeting" I know are you ready? She asked smiling. He was taking a part in the group. "Sort of? It seems so different when you're at church" he confessed. "What do you mean David? I took public speaking in high school, so to speak in front of a group comes almost second nature butt! "No buts' you can do it! She said hesitantly touching his shoulder playfully. Soon both turned around as the door opened. "Hey guys! Hi Sonjee! Pizza great! she voiced coming over helping herself to a large piece. "How was the studying tonight? David asked relaxing back with his head behind his head. "Good really good! But I ran into Ms. Kubunawa" coming out of the library and we have an early practice tomorrow" she reminded me. "That's right I had forgot, I'd better get out of here I still have a chapter to read" Kara voiced getting up preparing to leave. "So how was practice? Sonjee asked. "Wonderful" he replied. After I walk Kara out, I'll tell you all about it". "Good, sounds good" Sonjee said walking into her room. "Good night Sonjee see you bright and early in the morning" she teased. "Don't remind me! No! Girl I'm kidding call me! Good night".

Doris had met with her coordinator for the final rehearsal dinner. "Marabelle did you get the flowers arranged on the main table? She asked moving around the beautiful now decorated Convention room in Century City Hotel. "This is only the rehearsal dinner what will you do for an encore? Marabelle asked looking around the elegantly decorated room. "I plan only to do this once! Doris smiled and might I say, "You have out done yourself again Marabelle! Doris complimented her over and over again for the beautiful work she and her staff had done, coming over and joining her embracing as they looked over the room. 'You have captured a distinctive atmosphere kind of a dreamy ambience I'd say" Doris replied. "Your color choice was so easy for me to match with your personality it was a pleasure doing it" Marabelle confessed. The towering bouquets and candles were placed at the room's entrance giving it style. The candelabras cast a gentle glow standing tall and filled with creamy white tapers adorning them. Other flutes and large vases were strategically placed around the room as needed for a very elegant effect. Marabelle had selected big-bloom flowers like lilies and hydrangeas, Doris's favorites she expressed. The head table was dressed with a low centerpiece so that all could see the couple of the evening. The pale lavender ribbon trimming the bottoms of the table skirts for a fancy finish as well as the silk ribbon on the back of each chair was to Doris priceless! "Oh, lets lay the gifts for the wedding party on the table, shall we? Doris jaunted playfully going to get them from another room. What fun they had getting everything ready for rehearsal dinner tonight for sixteen people including the bride and groom and let's not forget Finley!

Dad have you reserved your flight for Godmother's wedding in two weeks?? Sonjee asked speaking with Dr. Reeves on the phone. "I have Sonjee but I, oh never mind I'll talk with you a little later". "What daddy, I've got time, is something wrong? "No, no Sonjee nothings wrong." I was thinking of bringing a friend" he shared. Who dad, Uncle Wilbur? Oh no baby I would never ride on a plane with Wilbur, he snores to loud he explained laughing as he spoke. "Who your chess buddy Dr. Carter? No dear it's not important besides I've got two weeks by then I will have decided, okay? Okay daddy I'm headed out the door. "Oh, how's that young fellow of yours? Who Jace? She asked innocently. "Yes, Dr Reeves replied. "He's fine I guess; I haven't seen him in two weeks". Two weeks you're making that seem like an eternity? He shared teasing her because she claimed she didn't really care and he really doesn't matter. "No, I'm just saying" You're saying what, that you really miss him and would like to see him since it has been two weeks" he laughed. Oh daddy, please stop teasing me, I have to go". "AH um" he replied "we will talk soon. 'Love ya daddy! Hanging up now thinking only of Jace and what friendly skies was he flying right now.

Billy sat talking on his cell phone to Glenn when the flight attendant came over the loud speaker. "We will be landing soon, buckle your seat belts and put your seats in an upright position! Nada! We're here! He smiled securing his belt and making ready to de-plane. The landing was great and before long they were in sunny Florida heading to their luxurious oceanfront hotel room at the Regency Grand in Florida. "Honey the weather is humid" I need to shower and get into some very comfortable clothing" Nada said sitting down now on the bed of their gorgeous suite. "Welcome to Florida! Billy teased turning the air conditioner on. So, what's your agenda? She asked unpacking the suitcases putting things in their proper places. My meeting is tomorrow morning with Ellison" and then we will contact Glenn. I spoke with him earlier and shared when we would get in". "So today we can go to the beach? She asked anxiously smiling. "I'd love to honey" he replied going into the bathroom to shower and put on his summer attire. After about fifteen minutes Billy emerged again. Honey your phone rang while you were in the bathroom" oh really who was looking for me already?" he asked buttoning up his shirt. "David Michael! He wanted to share something with you" he sounds very excited about it. You might want to call him back" Nada said heading in the shower with her towel. "Thanks sweetie giving her a peck on the cheek as she passed. "I'll call and talk with him while you're in the shower", and then we can head out to the beautiful sandy beach. In less than an hour they were out sitting in the sun enjoying the warm climate of Florida near Cocoa Beach. "William this is wonderful thank you so much for inviting me." "You may want to get use to this it's my life that I want to share with you" he said laughing walking along the beach holding her hand. "Look sweetheart a volleyball game! Nada said walking along stopping to watch the players having fun. GAME! Someone yelled the volley went fast to one side then the other! Oh! yelled a tall guy lobbing the ball high in the air to the defending opponents' side. I got it! I got it! A lady replied jumping to spike the ball for the win! Hey! Hey! We won! We won! Re-match one yelled. "Okay let's switch sides! "Sorry guys we've got to go" a couple announced gathering their things saying their goodbyes. Hey you guys want to play? They asked Nada and Billy who had been watching the last ten minutes. SURE, THEY SAID LOOKING AT EACH OTHER WANTING TO GET IN THE FUN. They laughed and enjoyed several games of volley- ball. Conversations were light but each was learning a little about the other. Looking down the sandy shores there was fishing and water skiing and many were swimming in the warm Florida waters. What an enjoyable first evening they shared together. Billy said good night after a very romantic dinner he had ordered to be brought to their suite. He went into the other room of their large suite tossed and turned biting on a towel. (The thought of having Nada was a bit over bearing) He was determined to wait for his wedding night. Tonight, was proving to be challenging seeing Nada running around all day in her beautiful bikini with a long-skirted scarf tied at her hip line. Nada would never make it her idea but she wanted him to!

CHAPTER 49

What are you doing here?

Dana had given up on calling that slime ball jerk of a man! One more time SHE THOUGHT DIALING, "he should be at work by now" she reasoned sitting in her office dialing New Orleans. "Hello Murphy's seafood" Yes may I speak with Colvin Murphy please. There was a pause, and then "ah Colvin is out!" Dana recognized the voice. "Why I know you're covering for him! "I don't know you lady! The voice came back. "I know you and I know how to find you! She lashed out. THE PHONE WAS DISCONNECTED FROM HER HEARING ANYTHING. THE RECEPTIANT OF HER CALL HAD HUNG UP!

Billy was up very early and moving around quietly as not to disturb Nada still fast asleep. "My tie" This one will do the other one is in her closet," he remembered not wanting to disturb her or be late for his meeting with Ellison. "Honey?" she said quietly waking up hoping he was still there. "Oh, good morning dear!" he said coming over to her bed and sitting down. "Why didn't you wake me? She asked feeling bad he was up and she was still resting. "You look so cute when you're sleeping I just couldn't" he replied kissing her forehead. "My meeting should last most of the morning I figure until noon" he shared then we'll go to my buddy Glen's home okay?' "Sure, I can certainly fine something to do with myself until you return" she voiced. "Are you sure? He asked looking at his beautiful even when she wakes up in the morning fiancée. Coffee? Please and thank you for a lovely evening" sharing a morning embrace to start the day. Nada jumped out of bed and went into the bathroom while Billy got her coffee he had made and changed to his silk tie. "Don't leave yet honey! Nada yelled. "I'm coming right out" sounding like she had a mouthful of toothpaste. "I've got a few minutes" he replied back. Nada hurried from the bathroom now in her gorgeous silk robe trimmed in lace. She walked into his arms and gave him a passionate kiss to start the morning. "You make it hard on a brother to leave you know that? He smiled. "I'm just making sure you don't get lost in this city of beautiful women" she teased back." I ONLY HAVE EYES FOR YOU! tapping her behind, grabbing his briefcase, and leaving out the door to his waiting ride. See ya soon!

David I've made our reservations for Doris Wright's wedding" Tetra shared. "Doris Wright" he repeated remembering his first encounter with her at the Prizzy Palace. She had put together a skit to throw he and detective Masony off the trail of finding her sister Dorca who is now Dana. "She has certainly made a name for herself." That she has! I can't say how many times her name has come up when someone mentions doing good or a goodwill tour" David remarked putting his matching jacket to his suit on to leave for the office. I wish her the best and I continue to pray for her and her endeavor", "me too honey". "We have our own little Doris Wright, right her in Washington," Tetra shared. Who Tet? "Alexis Wimberley, little Joey's mom." "Oh yes, is she busy helping in the Center. "Yes, James said she has single handedly started helping other young ladies to find jobs and better themselves." He says she's usually there late working on the computer looking on the Internet and other job-related sites to help aid them in their searches. "Well, I would say that is a blessing and a great work to be called to". I agree sweetheart" kissing her husband as he left for the office. Oh David! She yelled rushing out behind him. "I almost forgot Billy and Nada have set the date for their wedding" she shared smiling from ear to ear. "Did he call? Yes, last evening you had gone to sleep." It's going to be in June" a beautiful June 20th wedding for our son" she confirmed closing the door as David left out now pleased and thanking GOD for answered prayer.

"If Colvin thinks I'm going to trip over him leaving he had better think again! Dana stated showing her client into her office for an hour session. "Ring, ring!" Dr. Williams. "Howdy pretty lady! Rusty my you're sounding great! How are you? I'd love to take you out riding on my new Philly." Well, it sounds like she's doing the trick" Dana replied. 'Well, I have a vet who comes by everyday to check on my horses and she's got them back to new! Sugar and I was on the trail yesterday and I declare! WE HAD A GREAT TIME! Rusty was so excited and very enthusiastic about what was taking place with his horses. They had seemed a bit sluggish he had explained to the veterinarian who was treating them. "Look Rusty I think that's wonderful and you seem to be doing great too! Dana affirmed. "I'll take you up on that offer soon" she confirmed then hanging up the line heading into her session. Dana needed for her own satisfaction to speak with Colvin Murphy. "He hadn't promised her anything neither had she him except the money for the botch kidnapping and she had made good on that so Dana figured that's all he wanted and he was gone. She had to fly to Los Angeles for her sister's rehearsal dinner before which she was going to pay a visit to New Orleans to see Colvin Murphy for closer. Rusty she will visit as soon as she returns. But for now, he will have to wait!

Nada had hurried out of her hotel room armed with an address and her navigational system in the rental car headed to the House of Ling a posh wedding boutique in Daytona. She had spent a good part of her day over breakfast speaking with her wedding planner she had hired through Tetra her mother-in law to be and her girlfriends in Washington regarding her wedding plans and date. "No Carin I have a wedding planner but thanks for offering your services," she finally said after her friend offered to decorate for her. She parked on the side of the red brick building and headed to the door. The huge windows that could be seen from the street had live models standing showing off their gorgeous gowns. Nada walked in. She saw rows and rows of white lace gowns. "Where does one start? She asked herself looking around. "May I help? A little old lady maybe 60 years old with snow-white hair and rhinestone trimmed glasses asked coming over with a tender smile. "I'm trying to get an idea of what I want for my special day" Nada explained, but where does one start? "Well let's see," she said "the dresses on this floor are mostly for second or third weddings, you know not as formal" she explained. "Oh, I see" Nada replied looking closer at some of the very pretty gowns by Vera Wang. "I would suggest you go up on the third floor, we have some elegant styles from the VII collection for the younger first-time brides there" she smiled. "Thank you ma'am" Nada looked for the stairs and headed up the moving escalator. It wasn't long before she was ooowing and ahhing over the styles and colors. One gown really caught her eye it was from "Mary's bridal collection" the train had to be a half- mile long embroidered with lace. It was to die for! "Oh no look at the time!" She exclaimed. She had lost track of time trying on and looking at all the beautiful gowns. Checking herself in the mirror after trying on a gorgeous gown by J Alexander she put back on her white linen pants and linen top for the hot Florida weather, her red halter top and leather sandals moving quickly stopping by the front counter to get a business card and a thank you to the nice clerk she got into their rental car to go and meet Billy. Arriving a bit late but forgiven they were on the highway to Glen's home, his childhood friend. "Did you remember to put the directions to Glen and Cheryl's in the navigational system? He asked as he entered the car. Oh no! I forgot I'm sorry sweetheart I had something else on my mind" Nada confessed. "I know the House of Ling right? "I'm sorry Billy but June will be here before you know it! "I know honey, don't worry about it, I'll call him" dialing on his cell phone. "Please leave a message" he had tried Glen's number several times with no answer only voicemail. Finally, he called and spoke with his secretary who shared he was in a conference and could not be disturbed. She would get the message to him as soon as it was over. "No, it's not an emergency" when he gets out is fine". Fearing they would have to go back to their hotel in Cocoa to get directions to get to Glen's new home in Daytona they decided to pull over to the side of the highway. While Nada was having fun looking at wedding gowns Billy was negotiating whether or not he would be going to trial on this very important case. "Ring, ring." "Parker and Associates" THE VOICE ANSWERED. Annie? Billy asked not recognizing the voice. "Annie's not in today" the voice replied. "A bit impatient while working on an important case he asked for Keith Poulton one of his attorneys of the firm. "Just a minute" the voice replied, putting him on hold. While waiting to be answered by someone at his firm he was still discussing their plans of action "Ellison, opening arguments should stress the points of this guys health" he suggested going over the strategy to use for the trial. After a minute or two someone was back on the line. "Parker and Associates" Yes this is William Parker' "Bill! Ramsey" he replied. "Ramsey what's going on there and where is Annie? He asked tired of being on the phone and still had not made is point with anyone. "Keith called he and Annie went to the hospital late last night! "Oh is it that time, how's he doing? He sounds like a first-time dad! We're taking bets on him passing out during the delivery! He laughed. "Okay so things are a little unsettling without Annie," he surmised. Yeah! That's and understatement. "We thought we'd have Annie until the end of this week but I guess it wasn't our call" he joked. "Ramsey, call the secretarial pool have Linda Freeman come she's as close to Annie as we are going to get for a while. "Ram; write this down, I need her to send me the Bitterman file. I'll be at this number until noon so as soon as possible" and keep me posted on Annie! "Will do boss". So how was your day dear? Nada asked now stopping again at a Starbucks to figure out their next move. Billy tried Glen's cell phone a few more times before remembering Cheryl worked at Daytona Junior High three or four blocks up the street. Back in the car he drove two blocks and turned right a block then a veer to the left and there set this gorgeous state of the art new junior high school where Cheryl worked. He had been there a few times with Glen over the years but not in recent ones. "Wow this looks like a college campus, they didn't have junior high schools that looked like this when I was going" Nada stated looking at the beautiful grounds that surrounded the school. It had small benches sitting under the trees in a park like setting. There was a small manmade pond with large geese walking slowly taking an occasional wade across it. Billy parked and he and Nada got out and walked to the main office to inquire about Cheryl. "Mrs. Reed is out to lunch she will be back in approximately ten minutes" she said looking at the clock. "Thank you, if you don't mind, we will wait out on the grounds" he shared. "That's fine Mr. Parker, shaking his hand as he left. They went out and sat on one of the benches near the pond. The water in the pond shot straight up in the air causing a beautiful cascading effect. This is a perfect reading spot Billy confessed. The water is awesome the way it sounds," he added. Looking in the distant under a tree was another couple enjoying the nice calm day as well. "It's great to be in love Nada said sharing a kiss with Billy. The young couple across the way seemed to be doing the same, enjoying and occasional kiss along with their conversation. Billy had taken off his coat and removed his tie before getting out of the car. "Nada, I have something in the car I got from a vendor today he remembered. He ran the distant to the parking lot and came back with a Frisbee. "You're kidding right? She said smiling. "Go out and catch it! He yelled. "Billy my hair will get messed up! She shared. "When I get to Glen's I'm heading to the pool after my hello" he confessed. "Oh yes and I almost forgot Annie had a little girl! "Billy how could you forget that? When? She asked amazed. "I called the office for some documents I needed and Ramsey told me. "Oh, Billy did we send flowers? And congratulations" he said "I called the florist and had them delivered. "I can't wait to see her! Nada exclaimed smiling. Looking he could see the couple had walked slowly arm and arm to the parking lot. They shared a passionate kiss before he got in the car and left. The lady was walking back up to the school when Nada over tossed the Frisbee causing it to fly over Billy's head and land in the hands of the woman coming toward them. "Hey great catch" he said walking toward her to apologize. As he got closer to her, he stopped cold in his track. It was Cheryl! Glenn's wife! And he saw her kissing and embracing another man! "What are you doing here? She asked shocked. You could buy her for a penny at that moment. "Doing here as in Florida or here at the school? He asked still in shock. Cheryl didn't care for his sarcasm at this moment. 'How long have you been here? She again asked "long enough Cheryl!" He stated. Soon up walked Nada and his cell phone rang it was Glenn. Billy backed up and headed to his car Nada followed.

CHAPTER 50

Coming together again

David Michael had waited as long as he could for Kara. "MAYBE SHE HAD SOMETHING ELSE TO DO! He thought getting in his car heading out the door going to practice. They were still using him as pitcher and he was so excited. He loved it! Practice was going well but he found himself staring up into the bleachers looking for Kara. She had been coming to practices regularly and she didn't seem to mind. With practice over he walked slowly back to his car after high fives and goodbyes from his teammates. Everyone was headed to their cars in the lot. When David Michael got closer to his car, he could see his tire was flat. "Oh, Parker need help with that tire? "No, I got it" thanks he said. He didn't know anything about the engine but he could certainly change a tire. He quickly put his things in the car while most of the guys pulled off. Park you sure? They asked as he quickly loosed the bolts and in no time was on the road again. Driving slowly out of the parking lot of the stadium up pulled Remy and the brut. "D.M want to go out? They yelled from the car with their heads sticking around the mirrors to the side. "Naw guys we just had a great practice and I am exhausted, going in relax and go to bed" he explained. "Oh, good then we will just follow you home! The brut suggested. No not tonight man I'm tired! David Michael weighed 145lbs with all his clothes on. Stood about 5'10" hoping for more height but satisfied. He had a baseball player's body. He was very tough and fit but tired. He pulled around the guys in the car that was sitting about four deep and headed down the street with them in tow. He stopped and pulled over a block from his condominium after he saw they were not going to go away. They taunted him all the way home pulling up beside him every few feet. Kara had left a message on his cell phone. She had a test in her physics class and her performing arts had another call meeting. Kubunawa was getting them ready to perform at the Hollywood Bowl. "Guy's look some other time, he replied now standing outside of his car. "All right D man we understand "Brent the brut replied getting out to call a truce and shake is hand. What happens next David Michael couldn't even see coming. One of the guys in the back seat had gotten out and took his keys from his ignition and the big guy picked him up and threw him in the back seat of their car and off they drove. "Yeah! Stop this! He kept saying while being pushed around by the guys in the back seat. Remy was under the wheel and afraid if he didn't follow Brent's orders, they would beat him up too. "Hey guys let's just let him out! Remy yelled. Shut-up and drive to the bar! We are going to have some fun tonight! David Michael couldn't believe this was happening. His cell phone was in his car though the blue-tooth headset was now in his pocket after he discovered he was still wearing it after that melee. Speeding down the highway they soon pulled into a sports bar. "Now rich guy if you want to get back to your car in one piece you will cooperate" Brent told him leading him into the loud club. The guys had secured his wallet from his pocket as he fought scrambling in the backseat of the car. Round for this table! Brent yelled holding up David Michael's credit card. 'Look guys I don't mind buying a round are two but give me my keys and my wallet! He stated standing up to make his point. Alright! Sit down and have one drink with us and we will take you to your car" Brent told him. Remy was up playing pool and drinking beer. He was now right at home and clueless to his buddies' plans. David Michael sat down and Brent again ordered drinks for the table. "I'll appease them and then get out of this place and go home," he thought to himself. Brent distracted David Michael and one of the other guys put something in the beer glass he had ordered. "Toast, Brent said lifting the glasses together before everyone began chugging them down. Remy let's go! Brent yelled. He dropped the pool cue and headed to the door. David Michael was glad to hear those words. Here's your keys D-man, oh and your wallet". The guy said patting him on the shoulder. "Thanks guys" he said getting up now a bit woozy. He knew he was tired but two beers had never made him feel like this. 'Look guys I'm fine I'm going to call Kara to come and get me" he said. "No need we've got you! They teased. They walked outside Remy noticed something was wrong with David Michael. "What did you guys do to him? Brent slapped him behind his head "Shut-up stupid, you're here too! Remy was scared. "Hey his dad is a lawyer guy! You better make sure he's okay," Remy added. A lawyer! Why didn't you say something before now? One of the guys asked. "Cause you guys told me to shut up every time I spoke" They begin arguing with one another. We were just going to scare him! When they finally turned their attention back to David Michael he was gone. "Where did he go? Where did he go? They kept asking. Get in the car he couldn't have gone that far. David Michael didn't have a cell phone. A bit woozy but determined to get home without the guys help. He walked hiding between buildings seeing them looking for him. "Man, I hope he's alright, Remy kept saying. Soon they spotted David stumbling by the church that was four or five city blocks from the sports bar they were just previously at. "There he is, there he is! Hey! They yelled as they saw him stumbling. "Were did he go? They said coming up on him where they thought they had seen him near the tall steps leading into the church. "Look if something happens to him his dad will surely find out it was us" Remy was afraid because he knew Parker the lawyer!

The guys got out running around looking in every dark corner for David Michael. David reached in his pocket and felt the small wrench he had put there when he changed his tire. He also put his blue-tooth headset back on his ear. He heard the guys coming to the back of the church where he had hidden from them. He slowly moved bumping the garbage can as a cat ran out. "Oh man it's just a cat" he's probably gone. Shut up and keep looking, I know he's back here. David Michael fell and got up with and idea. Praying was new to him but he was sure thinking "please help me! He made his way to the car parked on the curve while the guys continue to search out back. He used the wrench to lose the bolts on the tires before moving on, to slow them down. "There he goes! One guy was saying pointing toward him as he continued trying to get away from them. "Please help! He said he felt himself close to fainting. He hit the blue-tooth on his ear and it started ringing in his ear. He sat back in an ally a block from the church. "Hello, hello David is that you? It was Kara's voice or was he dreaming. By now he was weak. "Help! Help! Where are you DAVID WHERE ARE YOU! She could hardly hear him. "The church, the church" he said again before he passed out. Kara had been driving around after seeing his parked car near his home with his cell phone down on the floor. Hearing his voice she headed to the church in his car having an extra key. "What's at the church? She thought as she drove faster downtown where their church was located. She was trembling. Before long she pulled up in front of it. "Hey guys look there's D.M." s car. He may have called somebody! They all jump in Brent's car but not before Kara saw the group of them running to jump in it. She could still hear him moaning over the headset. David can you hear me? Where are you David? She got out looking up and down the block near the church. "GOD PLEASE HELP ME! He asked looking into the night's sky that had come since leaving the sports bar. As she walked down the block the moaning got louder. "Oh, David there you are, what happened? She asked helping him to his feet. Her tiny small frame being a dancer could lift quite a bit she thought putting him on her shoulder and helping his limp body to the car. "Kara it works! Prayer works! He mumbled now safe in her car going home. Kara nervously drove down the highway headed home. "Ring, ring, hello" she answered. Kara, Sonjee! Oh, hi Sonjee trying to sound cheery. "Have you seen David Michael? She asked. Your car is parked not far away about a block down from the condo but he's not home did he come home from practice? "He's with me Sonj" Oh good, I just had the worst feeling a little while ago and I tried calling him his phone's going to voicemail. "Yeah, you know David Michael she teased. "I'M JUST GLAD HE'S ALRIGHT I'LL TALK WITH YOU GUYS LATER" Okay" Kara said breathing a sigh of relief she didn't ask to speak with him. Kara decided to take David Michael to her place until he was able to walk on his own two feet any way. It wasn't late maybe 8:30 or 9:00 p.m. but during the week it's relatively quiet around town. Kara painstakingly helped David Michael into her small apartment. She was sure glad she was on ground level. He sat then fell over on the sofa. He moaned. She went in and made a hot stiff pot of coffee. She wet cold towels and put on his forehead. What ever he had drunk was working over time. But strangely enough there wasn't any alcohol smell on him she surmised as she tried making him comfortable. He moved his head from side to side as she pressed the cold towel on him. It seemed to make him feel better. After an hour he settled down from tossing and turning on the small sofa settling her fear of him falling off of it. Braving her strength again she helped him into her bed and let him sleep it off. She grabbed blankets from the closet for herself and went to sleep on her sofa listening for her houseguest.

Billy was angry as he opened Nada's door letting her get in. He started up the car and pulled out of the school parking lot. "Honey did you apologize to that lady? She asked clueless as to what just took place. Billy didn't say anything. Honey, what happened she kept asking? Nada please, I really don't feel like talking. "Honey was that Glenn on the phone? did he give you directions? Nada he's sending them through my phone okay! He stated. "Did something happen? We're going in the wrong direction". Nada we're going back to our hotel". So, we're not going to Glenn and Cheryl's?" Maybe later I'm not up to seeing him right now" he said, truly something was wrong. "Is something wrong with Glenn? She was really trying to help she reasoned as Billy drove speedily down the highway. "I shared with Glenn we would come by a little later, okay!" She had been with him long enough to know question session is over. She sat quietly all the way to the hotel in Cocoa. Is there something I can do? She asked getting out of the car seeing he was still distrait about something. They walked into their room. "William? She said before being stopped by him. "Nada the lady who caught the Frisbee was Cheryl and I'm having a real tough time having to see my best friend knowing what I saw" he explained so if you don't mind, I'm going to go for a walk by myself" walking out and closing the door behind him leaving Nada standing with her mouth wide opened only covered from sound by her hand. Nada had finally got the full picture of Billy's mood. "Oh God help me to be a good wife for him" she cried out falling to her knee's. She began pouring her heart out to God. Billy walked along the sandy beach until he was away from the few sunbathers still lying out in early evening sun. He walked and he walked far down the beach thinking of every time he had hurt Jillian his fiancée whom he had lost to nine eleven. He thought about Dana and how she continual hurt him with her actions. He wept quietly as he continued to walk and think silently to himself. After a while he sat down on a huge rock looking at the beautiful water with its endlessness. He remembered how he felt when he thought Jillian had betrayed him in New York so many years ago. Oh God! He cried out why does love hurt so! He remembered the nights he sat and listened at his mother's bedroom door when he was growing up. How she must have felt being alone with all that pain his father had caused her. Why God? He questioned. He was ready to commit to Nada and be a good husband for her, but what if! He thought trying to grip on to reality. Cheryl had made that promise before God to love and cherish Glen and today he couldn't believe what he had witnessed with his own eyes." Glenn had share how he wrestled with marrying her after he got injured but she convinced him she'd be there! Now what's next! forlorned, he sat in the white sands with his arms resting on his knees, head down between them and wept bitterly for deceit and betrayal.

Dana had made her plans for a cab to pick her up when she got off the plane in New Orleans. With a small carry on in hand she headed to the front entrance of the huge New Orleans International Airport in Kenner. As she walked toward the seating area at the front of the large airport she saw and elderly gentleman standing holding a sign. He looked and asked "Doc Williams? Instantly Dana looked around. "You ma'am I'm talking to you" he said still looking for the person whose name was written on his sign. "Yes, she answered still looking strangely at the aged man. "Well, you requested someone whose knows these parts so here I am! He stated. "My name is Smiley, luggage? He asked looking around behind her. "No, just this" holding out her small carry-on luggage case. She had no plans of being there any longer than two or three hours at most. "UGH UGH! He laughed "not staying long are ya? He said reaching for the lightweight tote and heading toward the door. "Where ya from? He asked in a gruff voice as they walked toward the cab outside. "Maine" Dana replied following behind the aged man leading her out the large glass doors. Dana noticed he walked with a slight limp as if one leg was longer or shorter than the other. Saying nothing else Dana continued to follow him. "What harm could he do? She thought following him to the cab. He stood with the door opened as she got in and sat in the back seat. He put her carrying case in the trunk walked around and secured his seatbelt and started out of the busy airport traffic. Where to ma'am? He asked as they made their way to the freeway. Dana looked in her purse for the card Colvin had given her and handed it to him. "Oh, you headed to Murphy's place?" he said looking back quickly over his small rimmed glasses. "Yes, do you know him? She asked sitting up straight in her designer original suit still a bit frightened. Ugh! Boy done good for himself, "who would have thought it! The most mischievous little child one ever wanted to see! He added shaking his head and laughing. "So, tell me about Colvin I mean Mr. Murphy? "Tell ya what? You's coming all this way to see somebody you don't know? He asked again looking back quickly to stare at Dana. The old gentleman's dark wrinkled fingers gripped tight to the wheel as he drove. Now sitting behind him she could see clearly that he did frequent a barbershop. His large ears with gray hair protruding from them and his large wide nose were a very dominant feature. His skin she thought looked like old worn leather. "Is this your cab? She asked looking around in it. It was spotless. "Yes, ma'am it is" he stated proudly. "You obviously have lived here a long time? Dana asked feeling more relaxed making conversation as they drove to the business district where Colvin's business was. "I've been here all my life, gon die here to I wrecken" he laughed. "Have they started rebuilding your city after the terrible flood waters sir? Asking about how Hurricane Katrina had devastated New Orleans. "Slowly, but God scattered us folks like he did in the time of Baal. He sent us all over this great country of his. "It was a shame what happened but some folk had become so satisfied with nothing and having nothing and doin nothing it was a blessing in disguise" he laughed. But clearly the pain of it all was shown in his voice as he spoke. "So, you seemed to have weathered the storms pretty well?" Dana was feeling comfortable now with the elderly cabbie and spoke freely. "You know it duden take much for me. I'm living close to the promised age." He confessed. "I's wake up in the moaning and thank God for another day. Have my cup of coffee and some breakfast if I choose to. Get in my cab, head out to make an honest living" he shared sincerely. As they got closer into the city Dana could see the devastation of the once beautiful town. The footage scenes on television could not compare to what she was looking at right now. Homes pushed to the side of the road. Furniture and old cars filled with mud and debris. "This is awful! She stated looking from the cab's spotless windows. Soon they were in the heart of the French Quarters "Jackson Square". The elderly man pulled the cab to the side of the street and parked it. "Murphy's Seafood is right over yonder" he said pointing in that direction. "Please don't leave me! I'll be right out" Dana acknowledged before stepping out of the cab. "Ugh don't worry ma'am, I'll be right here when you come out or right over there in that coffee shop" again pointing showing her the direction as he helped her out allowing her to secure her footing on the red brick sidewalk that lined the streets. She noticed his very bent fingers probably from arthritis as he held her hand. His plaid shirt and creased pants were neatly ironed and his winged tip shoes worn but spit shined. She looked back as she headed toward Murphy's. "You'll be fine! He yelled turning to go into the small coffee shop. Dana walked a block down the cobbled stone walkway before turning into the old warehouse style building next to the Pontalba Buildings. Entering she saw a man pushing a very large cart with boxes reading perishable. He was headed into the freezer she surmised looking at the large sign that read: cold storage. There was a buzzer there not much else she could see so she looked around as she pushed it. The cold cement floor was causing the building to feel like the Antarctica Dana thought waiting for some one to answer. After a short while a lady maybe in her late forties came out. Dana noticed her very small curls lined neatly on her head. "Kin I help you? She asked looking at the stylish Dana. The lady tugged at her checked black and white dress with large bow at the neckline smiling. "Yes, Dr. Williams here to see a Colvin Murphy" she replied. "Dr. Williams? Jus a minute I'll let him know you here" she said heading back from the direction she had come. "Colvin there's some doctor here to see you! She shared standing in the door with her hand on her hip. "Who? I know that woman didn't come here! He stated. Did you say I was here? Yeah! I don't' know what you was doin while you was gone! She sassily replied. "Louise remind me to fire you!" "Right, I'll send her in" beckoning for Dana to come to the back office holding the door until she entered and walked away. Dana reached and closed the door behind her. The small office was cluttered with papers that lined the back shelves and the small desk had paper clutter as well. And sitting behind it was Colvin in a fluorescent lime green suit and matching socks and alligator shoes she could see as he stood up to welcome her. Then a glance on the hat rack sitting in the corner was the matching lime green brim hanging on it. Dana said nothing but walked over and using her open hand she slapped him. Jumping up he yelled "WOMAN ARE YOU CRAZY? He gasped grabbing her hand to keep her from repeating the act again. "Dana if you hit me again, you'll be sorry! He said shoving her into the small chair in his office. She fell backward and was caught by it but her purse fell to the floor. "Did you think not answering my calls would keep me away? She chided. "Look I told you I had business to deal with! He fired back. "I see you've gone back to your old ways, those loud colored cheap suits! Dana was mad now. "My suits may be loud in color but they are not cheap! He confided. "Well, it's a shame they aren't! Seeing the yelling was getting neither one of them anywhere both settle down. "Why didn't you call when you decided you were leaving? It's the least you could have done! She admonished. "Look Dana I'm a man! You can't just talk to me any kind of way. "I worked to hard for what I got! He spoke. I kept the haircut! He confirmed rubbing across his head. "So why did you leave? She asked now almost in tears from anger but clearly hurt he had abandoned her. "I had business to take care of I told you!" up pacing the small office space now. "So, are you coming back to Maine? Dana asked wiping her eyes with a handkerchief she had taken from her purse. "Someday when the statue runs out," he mocked. "Statue, so Billy got to you, didn't he?" looking at Colvin now with disgust. "I didn't see no Billy woman! Colvin came toward her as if to kiss her. Dana said nothing else she got up and walked out of the small office and through the cold vacant feeling building without looking back. Once out side she walked to the waiting cabbie that stood talking with friends she reasoned. She looked back to see Colvin standing in the doorway as the old cab driver pulled off. Where to ma'am? He asked as he pulled away from Jackson Square. "The airport sir and thank you for a wonderful visit" Dana replied smiling relieved Billy cared.

With things back to normal Kara and David Michael walked into the cafeteria on the U.C.L.A. campus. Looking across the room David

Michael spotted Remy surrounded by a large group of people whom disbursed as he walked toward him. Remy looked at him as if he had seen a ghost or something. "David Michael man it's good to see you're alright! He confessed jumping up grabbing him into a hug. "Wow man we didn't know where you went, it's good to see you," he repeated over and over again. David Michael did not share his enthusiasm at this time they had wronged him and he wanted to know what they did. Kara sat down at the table and David Michael and the relieved Remy did too. So, tell me why did you guys throw me in that car yesterday? "Wasn't my idea man, Brent said he was getting back at you for what your girlfriend did" My girlfriend? looking over at Kara. "What are you talking about? "Brent said your girlfriend kicked him one day and you deserved what they were going to do" he acknowledged. But no one was supposed to get hurt. It was all supposed to be in fun he admitted. Brent decided to put that stuff in your beer. I don't even know where he got it from, one of the other guys I guess" he talked on nervously as he explained. When I saw they had gone too far with the prank I called a halt to my end but he took my car keys! "So where is Brent now? David Michael asked looking around for him to walk up anytime. "Oh, you haven't heard? Brent's in the hospital man! We sped away last night when we saw your girl in your car coming, we thought". Brent jumped under the wheel and clearly after drinking he shouldn't have. We fools followed him. "So, what happened? We hit a telephone pole on Wiltshire and 29th. Brent got pinned in the car. They had to amputate both legs! The other guy got a broken collarbone and Belly and I escaped with minor injuries he said showing off a bandage from a small cut he had sustained. "Man, you were right I really need to pick and choose more carefully when it comes to friends" Remy shared getting up and with see ya around" he was gone. Kara stood up to explain about the girlfriend thing. Surprisingly David Michael put his arm around her shoulder and as they walked out of the crowded eatery, "So you really kicked that big guy! He asked smiling.

As Billy and Nada followed the navigational directions in their automobile enjoying the great ocean views, they drove down the scenic highway. They spoke quietly of what they hoped the evening would turn out to be and soon within less than an hour they were at the front of Glenn's beautiful ocean view home in Daytona. "It's gorgeous! Nada said stepping out of the car looking at the large two-story home with the ocean being their backyard. "Wow! Billy gasped. Glen hadn't purchased his home on he and David Michael's last visit two years ago he remembered as he stood in front thinking over the years. "I love the windows this home has in it Billy," Nada shared as they walked to the door. He noticed the access ramp leading up from the massive driveway and wiped his hand across his eyes to prevent tears. "Take a deep breath honey," Nada said waiting for someone to come to the door. Within minutes one of the two beautiful wide doubled doors opened. There sat Glenn in his wheelchair. Billy looked and walked over and kneeled beside his chair and held on for a hug and cried. The moment right now was hard to script so I prayed through this one! Nada looked over to see Cheryl standing in the doorway with a look that pierced her heart. "She was so sorry about what had happened to her marriage and stood lost now for answers Nada felt as she walked over and hugged her introducing herself this time. "Man, it's been what two long years! How's David Michael? He's still throwing that ball? Glenn asked excited to see his old friend again. "Yes, he is! Billy replied not wanting to spoil this moment ever. "Man, you could always make me cry wiping his shared tears with Billy. "And this is the one uh" he laughed. Excuse my seat he joked. "Nada Francois" she said introducing and bending over to hug him. "A real pleasure to finally meet you, come in! Come in! Glenn acknowledged in a very gentle pleasant voice. "You've met my wife Cheryl", he said as she slowly walked into the large sitting room where they had gathered. "Can I get something for you to drink? She asked nervously not knowing anything of what had been discussed. "Yes, Cheryl please something for the Parkers and remember they don't drink liquor! He advised as she left the room. "Oh, listen to me I've already married you! So, when is the big day? Glenn asked looking from Billy to Nada. "June 20th Billy replied. "That soon, couldn't wait any longer ah buddy," he teased hitting him slightly on his leg. "Yeah man you're right" Billy confessed forcing a smile on his face. "You two are quiet for dating and getting married you know what I mean? He asked trying to be joyful at this moment. "Man, it's great seeing you and this home is fabulous, an elevator too! Billy could see from the large entrance to the hallway from where he sat. "They accommodated me well but then I don't have to tell you that I had the best lawyer money could buy" he laughed. "That you did" he shared back a tease of remembrance. After a while Cheryl was back with a tray of appetizers and sparkling cider or champagne in elegant crystal stemmed ware. They all sat around chatting and really enjoying the moment void of drama. "Man let me show you this room. Remember growing up" he said rolling his chair out of the room with Billy walking beside him laughing about early years leaving the ladies alone. Cheryl looked at Nada, she needed to talk. "Would you like to see our dream home? She asked almost in tears at this moment. Cheryl sat there waiting for the other shoe to drop she told Nada as the two started viewing the couple's spacious home. The first stop was in the guest suite downstairs. It was beautifully designed in rich colors of browns and gold. 'I love your color choice's Cheryl" Nada said touching the silk drapes and the soft duvet on the large bed. Thanks "I worked with a decorator", only the best for my wife he kept saying," repeating the words Glenn had spoke to her. Making it through that room they went to other beautiful rooms and a kitchen Nada wanted to take back with her to Washington. "The beautiful marble countertops and the spacious island in the center were fantastic! Nada thought sliding her hand across it. "So, are you two going to live in Washington or at that fabulous estate in Maine? "Billy handles the family business on the east coast so it's likely that's where we will be," she laughed slapping a high five. "I hear that! They had a wonderful time looking at the immunities that had been installed into the home to accommodate Glenn's handicap. They were tastefully hidden away so they did not take away from the beauty of the design. The swimming pool and spa with a patio for entertaining out back and the recreation room with all the exercise equipment for daily workouts, pool table, they even had a room for watching movies. This home was lacking nothing Nada reasoned as they made the rounds back to the great room still void of Glen and Billy. "Now where are those two? Nada asked smiling after getting to know Cheryl a little better. "Hey you will learn those two have gone through some stuff and you cannot separate what they have. One would think the two were married they are so committed to each other! Cheryl laughed but then realized what she just said. "I'm so sorry, she voiced. I love Glenn. The years together have been good for the most part. But of late he's been so frustrated with his rehabilitation. Life has been unbearable. "Do you think Billy is going to tell Glenn he saw me? She asked looking at Nada with fear in her eyes. "I don't know but if he does what are you going to do? I'm scared of my marriage ending! "One day he comes home and he's very positive about the outcome and another time he won't even let me in the same room with him. He pushes me away. "I know going to someone else is not the answer but I needed comforting too," she explained now crying on Nada's shoulder quickly composing herself. "I'm sorry I met you for the first time and I'm a mess excuse me" she said going into the bathroom to freshen herself.

Man, this is my seclusion. I come up here for hours at a time and just think. "Glenn have you forgot how to pray? Billy asked concern he had lost his way. "Pray after what happened to me? "Sometimes I think about it. I stopped talking to my mom and dad who is always asking me that same question," he confessed. "Man, I can't use my legs and my wife's seeing another man and you're talking about praying! Be real" rolling his chair to the window to view the Emerald coast with its white sandy beach and crystalline waters. "What did you say about Cheryl? Billy asked surprised he knew. "Man, I was hoping to get through this visit without you finding out". But you know me to well and I have to talk to somebody before I do something I'll live to regret! He said shaking his head. "Lately I have been impossible to live with I'll admit that and rehab has been slow, frustrating to almost no progress at all. I can't take Cheryl out dancing like we did when we were dating" I know she says it's okay but I see her face when we attend functions". I'd love to be able to go bowling with her and run along the beach with her, man you really don't understand if you're talking about praying. A lot of times lately I have refused to be in the same bedroom with her afraid I won't be able to perform there either" he confessed to his old dear friend. "But why do you say she's seeing someone else; I mean how do you know that? Did she tell you? No man would you tell me? He asked looking at Billy. "Bill for months now I've had a private eye following her" she stopped getting angry when I refused to sleep with her or cuddle by the fire like we use to do. And today when he brought the tape to me, I saw you and Nada at the school". "Glenn I'm sorry, I fought seeing you today but you know we're boys and I couldn't let anything separate our bond, he said embracing hurt. Billy shared his walk along the beach and his prayer to God for strength for him. "Bill you prayed for me? Always and I hope you're still praying for me. Your prays got me out of a lot of scraps I got myself into," he laughed shaking his hand. "Have you two tried counseling? No man, I haven't shared with her yet about what I know" I'm hurt and angry and honestly things may not go well," he admitted. "Glenn, did you and Cheryl read the books I gave you for your wedding? "No, things were going well when we first got together there was nothing to read about, we were always busy! Smiling through hurt rolling is wheelchair over to the floor to ceiling bookcase in his state-of-the-art home office he often worked out of for John f. Kennedy Space Center. He handed Billy the two books entitled: Outrageous Commitment seemly never opened only put in place neatly on the shelf. "A suggestion only" he said read these and get counseling and before any of that restart your prayer life! Reaching for his hand Billy prayed before going back down on the elevator to a meal prepared for a reunion of old friends coming together again.

CHAPTER 51

Five!

Dana left New Orleans headed to Los Angeles for her sister Doris's wedding and the rehearsal dinner. She had used her cell phone on the plane once the all clear was given to do so. Speaking with her office and Dr. Baisden the director over her department about an upcoming meeting in three weeks Dana stated "Dr. I will have those statistics all lined out for you on the overhead presentation I've prepared" she expressed. "Thank you Dana I look forward to seeing them, and have a wonderful vacation" he added disconnecting the line. Dana's rental car was ready when she deplaned at the airport. She stood waiting for her luggage when she heard a voice. Hello Dr. Williams! She turned to see a handsome man dressed in a pilot's uniform. "Excuse me, do I know you? She asked in her snooty Dana style. "Yes, I have met you a few times" he replied. "Well, hello, I'm always traveling somewhere so I'm sure I encounter a lot of people I don't really know" she said turning back as the luggage began to come down on the circling belt. Soon a stewardess walked up. "Jace are you bothering this lady? She knew he was single and friendly sort of guy always holding conversations with the passengers as he walked through the airport. "No not really? He answered. Dana hearing turned quickly to counter his claim. "Jace is it! Then she remembered the name. "Jace, Sonjee? Oh, I didn't know you were a pilot! She said surprised "good for you! "Why thank you miss Dana! He teased. I'm so glad you approved" he replied doing a tap-dancing shuffle motion with his feet. "No, I'm sorry you're right I prejudge you and please forgive me" extending her hand out to the young man. "So, are you coming to the wedding? Sonjee's invited me think I'll fit in? He asked smiling going back to is early joke. "The stewardess shook her head and walked away. "Jace I'll see you in the eatery in ten". Jace, we'd love to have you there. I'm Sonjee's aunt and Doris is my sister so you're more than welcome. And forgive me for not recognizing you with your uniform on" Dana admitted. "Hey, I understand we've only met a few times and that was in a large gathering so how could you remember? And there are lots of people and faces around here" he said as they stood in the crowded airport noise of busy folks going in all directions. Jace helped her secured her luggage from the belt and call a bellhop. "See ya round! Waving and faded into the crowd of busy travelers.

Billy and Nada went home from the Reeds knowing they were leaving Florida the following morning. He thought it best to leave and allow Glenn and Cheryl to work out their differences without hindrances from outsiders. He would hope and pray Glenn would share with Cheryl his concern before things got out of hand. He committed mightily standing in Glenn's study to do just that (pray for their situation). Later that evening He and Nada sat together a long time discussing about commitment. They talked about longevity in a marriage relationship and read quotes to each other from the book he carried in his briefcase "Outrageous Commitment" by R. Elmore. Nada surprised him she had her book too! Each found themselves laughing on parts they identified with and being very serious on another scenario's that concerned them. With yawns becoming imminent to both they prayed for Cheryl and Glenn's relationship, for David Michael, and many others were mentioned as the two petitioned to God with tears for strength and a better understanding of life. They turned in going still their separate ways. Billy wept alone for his dear friend.

Dana pulled up in front of the children's condo. She had been thinking of a lot of things since leaving New Orleans. Mostly Billy! He cared enough to run Colvin out of town! She sat thinking pleasant thoughts. Nada had not got him down the aisle yet so maybe there's still a chance? She reasoned getting out for a short visit with David Michael before heading to Doris's. Hello Aunt Doris! Sonjee greeted her coming in! Why, hello Sonjee how are you? "I'm wonderful auntie; my bridesmaid dress looks fabulous how about yours? She asked speaking of the dress rehearsal tonight before the dinner. "Its fine, you're jovial! Dana said walking in sitting putting her purse on the end table and kicking off her shoes putting her feet upon the large ottoman the kids used for extra sitting. Always! Sonjee replied can I get you something? No not yet but I did see that handsome older man of yours. She shared. "You did? Where? she asked coming over to sit next to her on the sofa. At the airport! Dana replied. "He's a pilot you know! Daddy likes him! She said excitedly. "What did you think Aunt Dana? Sonjee asked with wide eye anticipation for her answer. "Well, he's what four years older than you? "Yes, I know and that really concerned me when we first met, but he's different Aunt Dana". "OH! Dana expressed looking at Sonjee waiting to hear different. "Yea, he doesn't expect me to go to bed with him and you have to know that's different! She confessed. "Well how long have you known him Sonjee dear? I've met him what? twice? Dana asked knowing men was her business she confided. "We met right after mama died, so about two years I guess". And he's never! NO! And we have wonderful visits together and go places when he's in town and yes, we kiss but not to the point of wanting to throw each other in bed! She laughed sharing it with her aunt. "Umm are you sure he's not, No! on that count to Auntie. "There are men who are willing to wait to have a good woman." Sonjee shared in a confident sassy way. "You've convinced me, I think he's a very nice young man from what I've seen and heard so far" she acknowledged leaning over to hug her. "Oh, Aunt Dana, I must confess I was concerned about that gay thing until I spoke with uncle Billy" "BILLY" Dana wasn't as concerned about what Sonjee had to say but it did include Billy so she was all ears. Uncle Billy says's he and Nada have the same kind of relationship and he knows he's not! "Amen to that! Dana found herself saying slapping her niece a high five. OOOH auntie what are you doing thinking of Uncle Billy that way" Sonjee teased. "We share a son dear and we didn't buy him from a retail store! She laughed back. Soon David Michael and Kara were coming through the door. "We will finish our conversation later" Dana smiled. "I'd love too auntie" giving her a hug and turned her attention to Kara. "Kara come I'd like to show you this outfit I purchased at "Go Girls" today. "Hi Miss Williams" Kara said hugging her before going into Sonjee's room leaving David and Dana his mother to spend some time alone together.

I have spoken with Desmond and he and Mossy are expecting us. "Okay are you sure he's going to like me? Nada asked as they drove to Langley estates where the couple lived. My! Billy said noticing how the trees had grown so tall. They drove along admiring the beautiful tall rows of sunflowers slightly bending as the breeze blew. The path leading up to their home was shaded by gorgeous Cottonwood trees that once were not noticeable as you drove slowly along. "The house looks bigger! Billy said as he pulled into the open driveway. It still looked magnificent he thought. They had designed it themselves. And it had taken two years of waiting to move in he shared with Nada as they stood looking at it from the outside. After a few minutes or two from the time the doorbell rang Desmond and Mossy appeared together to greet them. "It's about time! Desmond laughed sharing hugs and kisses around the entrance greeting area of their home. "Welcome! Welcome come on in" we are so glad to see you, we've been waiting" showing Billy and Nada into their elegantly decorated living room. "Your home is gorgeous! Nada expressed looking around. I love what you've done to it! She said looking at Mossy. "Oh, thank you very much" believe it or not I did it all by myself" Mossy acknowledged back with a smile. Desmond and Mossy, Nada found very warm and down to earth. Their home was magnificent but their down-home hospitality made it so warm an inviting. She loved that feeling she thought sitting admiring her surroundings and love felt conversation. "So how was the flight in? Desmond asked. Mossy had returned from the kitchen getting something to drink. Everyone had requested coffee that she had accompanied with warm croissant or coffee cake. They sat around keeping conversation light and getting to know one another. And of course, the lady's talked about the wedding plans. After about forty-five minutes Nada noticed a tiny little head kept peeping around the door and then go away, she smiled and nudged Billy who was sitting next to here. "So where are the real lawyers around here? He teased. "Oh, believe me if they had their way, they would have met you at the car" Desmond smiled. We set a time limited on them so we could a least warn you before they appear" he again teased. "How many now Mossy? "Billy, we have five and you can have your chose of any one to lighten our load," she mocked. Soon another little head peeped out. "Come here! Mossy said to her little person who wanted in the room but wasn't going to until asked. Mossy explained how they had lots of business functions at their home and it is very important that the children know their place. "Come here Maya! Who was followed by Vlade! now that they had stepped out in plain view? The twelve-year-old came in. "Hello! He expressed very grown up like extending his hand. "Wow, it's been to long man this is the twin, how old are you? Billy asked bringing him over to sit beside him. "I'm twelve Uncle Billy! twelve? What grade are you in? Shaking his head to see how much the children had grown since his last visit. I'm in junior high now! He answered proudly. "I guess David Michael is starting his second year at U.C.L.A. so I guess" he said. Uncle David's in college? The twelve-year-old asked with a frowned-up wrinkle on his forehead. "He sure is! He didn't say anything else just sit back and smiled shaking his head. Maya had found her daddy's lap and was staring at both of us saying nothing. "So where is Maggie and the rest of you all? Desmond asked knowing they were soon coming. "Maggie's changing clothes again and Jordan's in his room listening to music and I don't know where Des is? Five! Man, you've been busy and Moss you have your hands full" Billy laughed. "I told you man I need someone to run this law firm" Desmond joked going over to the intercom and within minutes everyone was coming into the room. Hi! Hello, Hi Uncle Billy there was more hugs and kisses and laughing and embracing in this precious moment. "My! Jordan you are as tall as I am" Billy acknowledged. He smiled standing with is blue-tooth earpiece still on his ear from his iPhone cell in his pocket. You're what? Billy asked standing by him "Fifteen" he replied. Umh! Time flies". He said hugging the young man. Now who plays the piano? Nada asked looking at all of them stopping at Maggie, "Not me I'm going to live with Grandma Martha in California and become a movie star! She replied with a zany sense of humor she really believed it! "Okay, if you say so" Nada replied moving on. Being a singer, she had instantly noticed the pearl white baby grand piano walking into the room. "I do, Mostaliga replied. "I still had hopes of being a world re-known pianist but that was before number four came along," she laughed. "You, do you play? She asked turning to Nada. "Somewhat, I use to play back home for our church" Nada replied. Come on over here Moss said it's like riding a bike! Nada was very comfortable around Moss. She scooted beside her on the elegantly styled bench. All the children gathered around the large white grand piano to watch including Billy and Desmond. 'Okay let's start with chopsticks, remember that? Mossy asked. Nada tinkled the beginning of the song on the keys. Soon they were running up and down then with their fingers laughing and singing along. The children now had joined in the singing and laughing fun shared by Nada and Moss. After a while Nada asked who knows the "Ants go marching" I DO! I DO! Me too aunt Nada that's easy" the young Desmond junior voiced he was nine EVERY BIT THE AGE! And the cutest little girl one every wanted to see Nada thought named Maya she just turned five and she had been sat next to here on the bench. She watched Nada's hands very intently as she played. Okay here we go! Mossy had moved and Maya had nudged her way on the bench seat. Mossy stood clapping her hand and singing along with the others. The men sang for a while then left heading to another part of the house. Oh, my what a great start to their visit Nada thought getting up from her knees from praying heading to a good night's rest in the Owens guest bedroom. Billy was down the hall at his request in the newly added addition to the family's home enlarging it to seven bedrooms. And seeing the growing Owens family they needed every inch. She and Billy had without reservations accepted their invite to spend a week.

Dana enjoyed the time she spent with her son, Sonjee and her sister Doris in Los Angeles. The rehearsal dinner was wonderful and the food was a teaser to the entrée's to be served for the wedding day. Thank you for the gift Ms Wright" her clerks from the boutique expressed leaving the dinner. You are welcome dear and thanks for allowing your little one to be a part as well." Doris stood watching everyone leaving the elegant affair she had planned for her wedding party. The fresh gardenia place cards showing each guest where to sit was a fond memory. She thought it would be a great twist on tradition by preparing a sweet surprise. It was a beautiful small box embellished on top with white pearls continuing the theme and she had placed a chocolate with the flavor of her wedding cake inside! They absolutely loved it! The festive feast for tonight's rehearsal dinner were of course hors d' oeuvres, puff pastry pinwheels filled with diced olives, from age (French cheeses served on palette pleasers) one of Russell's favorites.

There were lots of finger foods. (Tender round of herb-and –wine-flavored pork tenderloin and flaky biscuits were also a crowd pleaser. Tart treats, tuck and roll, and prince wrapped asparagus and expensive wine. It was magnificent everyone thought as they gathered their very pricey gifts Doris had chosen for each of her wedding party attendee's bridesmaids and groomsmen. "Russell this is it dear, no turning back from this point" she teased. "Oh, honey I could never leave you" he said standing embracing her after everyone had left the dinner. "Sweetheart, have you heard from your daughter? She asked as they were preparing to leave now after all the goodbyes. "I haven't so I'm just going to keep praying and writing maybe someday I'll see my little girl again. "Honey I'm sure you will" she said getting into her car kissing Russell as he stood by her car door. See you tomorrow at the board meeting he replied back getting into his car and driving away.

The Owens home was in a buzz the next morning. Mostalgia was preparing breakfast as she did every morning when Nada walked in the kitchen. "Oh, I'm sorry did we wake you? She asked seeing her now standing in the door. "Are you kidding I can't even hear myself in that room it was a wonderful night's rest" she expressed smiling. "And I know there's a coffee pot around here, somewhere right? She asked "Right here Nada" the children want pancakes this morning so I'm kind of busy or I'd get it for you" she acknowledged back. Are you kidding, what can I do to help you? She asked getting a cup from the cupboard and pouring her coffee. "Are you sure it's your vacation!" Mossy replied. "Mossy I want to help" what do you need me to do? quickly swallowing her coffee down. JORDAN! MAGGIE! DES JR! Your breakfast is getting cold she yelled again to the children who still after the second call had not shown up to eat and the clock was ticking fast. "Nada if you could get four glasses from the cabinet and pour the orange juice it will be a big help" Mossy confessed busily getting the hot pancakes from the stove's griddle. Desmond made his appearance to the chaos! "Honey did you get Maya ready, Janie will be here soon" she asked still moving quickly around her kitchen. "Yes, dear she didn't even wake up when I washed her face this morning she must have played hard yesterday" he reasoned smiling. "Honey your breakfast is in the microwave and there is fresh coffee made. "Good morning, welcome to the Owens morning" Desmond said seeing Nada putting back the juice in the refrigerator after pouring the children's orange juice for their breakfast. William up yet?" he asked. "Not sure haven't seen him yet! Nada replied. "Thanks Uncle Billy" came a voice coming into the kitchen. "Good morning family! Billy announced coming over kissing Nada and reaching for a cup of coffee from Desmond with the other. "Dad, Uncle Billy was showing me a jumper it's pretty cool!" Jordan expressed sitting down to eat his prepared breakfast of pancakes, eggs and sausage. Soon in came Maggie and Valde and Des jr. and the room was buzzing conversation of the day. "Mom! Remember I have to stay after school! Yes, I remember Janie has your schedules". "Teacher's conference is scheduled too mom! Yes, dear I'm aware, that isn't until next week! MOM CAN YOU SIGN THIS? Vlade please remember to ask your dad about that then he'll sign it for you" she said now eat you don't want to be late! Janie was the sitter and she had been around through all of them. Mostalgia remembered they hired her when Jordan her oldest was two. So, she knew the routine. "Desmond had taken he and Billy's breakfast to the formal dining table and the children her busily chattering and eating getting their healthy nutrition for the day. "Here you are," she said handing Nada her breakfast. "Oh, you didn't have to" Nada confessed. "Hey I have to eat I need my strength" she laughed. "Thanks Moss". Just as the children were finishing up breakfast and Moss and Nada were making plans between answering the children's questions Janie came in. GOOD MORNING! GOODMORNING JANIE! Okay are we ready" she said after hellos. You all get your books and head to the car I'll get Maya and we are on our way" she smiled. "Have a good day! Mossy yelled after kissing each one on their way to the car. "Umm aunt Nada will you be here tonight? Maggie stopped to ask on her way getting into the car. "Yes, we will be here" oh good I want to show you some dresses for your wedding I think you'll like! She suggested. "Sounds great, have a good day! Running to the back door of the SUV waving as Janie pulled away. Mossy headed to the kitchen and Desmond and Billy headed to the Owens Law firm first and then golfing. The ladies were going downtown to a posh bridal store in downtown Kansas looking at gowns, and invitations for Billy and Nada's special day.

CHAPTER 52

Has it been that long?

Dana wasted no time getting back on a plane after the rehearsal party and headed back to Maine. "Umm so Billy has not consummated the relationship," she thought to herself reclined back in her first-class seat on the large 747. "I wonder if he's sure about that witch. Maybe there's room to slide in again? She thought dialing his home number, ring ring! Parker resident! The broken English of the voice told Dana it was Dante. "Oh, Dante, how are you? She asked so sweetly. "I'm okay how can I help you? He asked anxious to tell her no! "Is Billy in? "No! Mr. Parker is out! He said laughing quietly to himself. "Thank you, please tell him I called," she again said nicely. "Excuse me who is this? Dante asked because she was being so nice surely it couldn't be Devil woman! She started to say what she thought which wouldn't be nice so she just answered "Dr. Williams". Okay I tell him. It's her! falling down pretending to faint because she was so nice. The other staff laughed with him.

Des, man this is nice! You can see all over Kansas City from here" Billy acknowledged visiting the law firm he had built up since there college days. Wow did your granddad get a chance to see this? He'd be proud. "Oh yes, I brought him up when we first got in the place and he cried. He hugged me and if you don't think that put even more pressure on having to succeed in me it did! I can't even imagine how he must have felt. "Come here let me show you something in my office. They walked down at the end of the row of four offices. "Desmond pointed to and old desk. "I told him it would always be here, his spot in the office. "My, this is nice the role top desk, this is priceless" Billy stated looking through it. I know we had it restored from his old office and took it to our home for a while but it belongs in a lawyer's office and so this has been its home for the past two years. "What efficient manner does your firm use to get things to the court house in a timely fashion? He laughed. "You have that problem in Maine? All the time, you're there it's not! He joked. "You'd better prepare more than you need to get the job done! So right man". Why hello! Hello! Billy and Desmond returned the greeting. You know Henry Hampster? with Henry extending his hand for a shake. "Yes, my father says hello, it's a pleasure to finally meet my replacement" Billy teased Replacement? Henry questioned looking at Desmond. "William and I went to law school together and I shared with him we could work together". "Oh, I see, sorry about that! shrugging his shoulders. "No worry's he owns Parker and Associates in Maine". 'Well then it's a pleasure to meet you," he laughed extending a shake. "It was very nice of your dad to come down for my grandfather's funeral a few years ago now" he added. "Wild horses couldn't have kept him away he found him to be a friend" Billy patted Henry's arm and he left. Desmond spoke with is clerical staff and the two friends were on their way to the golf course. When the door opened on the elevator there stood Mostalgia and Nada. "Thought you two were going shopping? Billy asked hugging her around the waist before planting a kiss to the lips. "I needed to drop off some doc's tried to catch up with you two but your phone went to voicemail. "Desmond looked down at his cell phone attached to a side pouch "you're right! Turning it on giving her a kiss and the elevator closed. The girls got out entering the law firm "The color is gorgeous in here it doesn't look like your typical law office" Nada said noticing Mossy's touch throughout. And these pillars look so Greek! They bring so much detail to this space. Mossy this is a fabulous place to work! looking at the art on the walls and the floor to ceiling drapery. And boy what a space Nada thought heading to Mossy's office after being introduced to the staff as they walked in. "Henry here is the file on the Wesnick's divorce". Hey thanks! Are you out all week too? He asked moving papers around on his desk. "Yes, old friends visiting but you can always get us by phone, right? "Yes, just checking, I'm headed to the courthouse again". Okay leave Madelyn in charge of the staff and we will talk if needed. "Thanks Moss, and nice meeting you Mrs. Parker! Leaving speedily out the door with his documents needed for court. Nada smiled that name on her sounded pretty good!

The week was filled with so much laughter and fun but went by too fast. They visited fun places with the children and met a few of their friends. The girls shopped and the guys golfed but family time with all the children sharing each night was Billy and Nada's favorite. She like Billy had grown up an only child and loved seeing the interaction between the siblings. Jordan the oldest was a sport enthusiast; Vlade was the gentleman and businessman type. Billy said he reminded him of Desmond. Maggie was all girl and of course movie star. She helped pick out some styles of dresses she thought were perfect for the wedding day! Desmond junior was all of nine-year old boy. He played hard on his large wooden jungle gym outside in their backyard and stay in trouble for shooting his dart gun in the house at the others and the fat chubby cheeks of Maya were so kissable. She was the youngest and had stolen Nada's heart and she wasn't really ready to go but reality calls! Nada reasoned packing her suitcase for the final day. "You're up early," Mossy said to Nada coming into her kitchen at six in the morning to start breakfast. "Do you mind if I assist you this morning. I'm going to miss this! She told Mossy embracing her before getting started on a typical busy day in the Owens household.

Dana jumped in her new Porsche and headed out to the ranch. She had been back from L.A two days and still she hadn't got in touch with her old friend Rusty. Colvin, she had scratched off her list she wrote in her journal before leaving from her office that day. She rode along humming a tune from the radio as she made the familiar turn on the dusty road leading to the Higgins farm. I'm here she said to herself getting out of the car. She got out looking back at her beautiful red Porsche all dusty from the road coming in. "RUSTY! RUSTY! She yelled sounding so sweet. "There was no answer. "He's probably with those horses! She thought heading out to the distant stables. After about fifteen minutes she was walking into the stables. She saw Sugar one of his prized possession horses tied loosely to the outside post so she decided to surprise him. She tipped toed up to the barn door's room where he usually prepares himself to ride. Slowly Dana made her way to surprise her old friend who recently found new life since his horses were feeling better. She started in the door ready to say, "BOO! But he couldn't see her. Rusty was passionately kissing a woman. Dana swallowed and backed away from the door. Just outside the stables she cleared her throat and yelled "RUSTY! He came running out. "Hey Dana gal, how are you? I'm fine, she said sadly. "What's wrong ya come to see my new Philly? He asked. Dana wanted to say she had seen too much already when the lady walked out. Her long golden blonde curly hair hung to her shoulders. She had on tight jeans and her cowboy boots though worn were cute on her tiny small feet. The woman Dana thought could be close to Rusty's age but with women it's hard to tell. "Russ? Oh, Bliss this is Dana Williams" Rusty expressed standing between both of them right now. Please to meet you" Bliss replied extending her hand. "Dr. Williams" Dana responded a bit teed by what she saw. "Dr. Joliet I'm Rusty veterinarian". And a very good one too! Rusty added smiling. "UMM! I bet." Dana turned up her nose and walked toward the house. "You want to see my philly don't you? He said yelling back at her. Dana was mad now! Someone was trying to move in on Rusty. SHE HAD PAMPERED HIM OUT OF THAT DEPRESSION DONNA LEFT HIM IN and now some other woman had moved in on her while she was gone. Granted she had no intention of coming back but no one knew that! "Yes, I'll see her! She stammered coming back to the stables. "She's right over here Rusty said. And thanks to Bliss she's as healthy as can be". She's pretty Dana said patting and rubbing her shinning coat" I'd like to take her out for a ride! Dana suggested. "I wouldn't recommend it!" Bliss stated and whispered something in Rusty's ear. "Maybe tomorrow pretty lady we just got back with her and she's young. I wouldn't want anything to happen to her, vet's orders" Rusty replied. Dana was fuming and Bliss was smiling turning away so that Rusty couldn't see it. "Look Rusty can I speak with you? Sure, go right ahead. In private! Dana stated. "Russ, I have to go anyway later though okay? "Sure, sure, Bliss" SHE WALKED OFF WITH DANA QUIETLY MOCKING THE WAY SHE SAID "RUSS." Dana helped Rusty get the horses put away in the stables and went to the house. "So how long as Bliss been working with the horses Rusty? Dana inquired as they sat drinking some expensive wine Rusty had in his cabinet. "Bliss has been here three months, and she's done a fantastic job with Sugar and other horses" Rusty replied. Is that all to it? Rusty got up walking around to evade the questions Dana was now firing at him. "Dana darling it's been a long time since you came to the ranch. What have you been doing? He asked pouring another stemmed glass of wine. "Oh, you know I was always thinking about you Rusty! She confessed coming over rubbing up next to him touching his eyebrows rubbing across them as well. "So, I see you're doing a lot better now than you were six or seven months ago! She smiled remembering their spent time together. "You're right it's been that long I thought you had forgot about me." "Rusty please, she said coming over holding his face and giving him a kiss. And he didn't fight to stop her. The two sat talking becoming acquainted with each other again over the wine and appetizers his housekeeper had prepared. Rusty telephone! His housekeeper BARKED IN HER GRUFF VOICE. "Mavis, who's calling I'm busy please take a message" he replied. "It's about Sugar! "Oh, hold on excuse me," he said getting up going to the phone. "Dana, sorry for the interruption I need to get Sugar ready for the rodeo in a few months. "That was my buddy Hitchcock we're going out for a drink, you're welcome" he told her preparing to leave to go and meet his friend. "No not tonight but I would like to see you this week if you're up to it! She flirted rubbing his face and gently kissed his lips as he walked her out to her car. Dana was satisfied she had gotten rid of Bliss for today anyway. She didn't have the time to spend with Rusty tonight but his name had gone back on her list. And she'd work on finding out some information on Bliss Joliet. "Hey pretty lady if you want to see me just call let me know when okay? He said. Dana got into her Porsche and drove away smiling. Rusty watched as her lights faded off down the road leading to the highway before he headed back into his house. Mavis you on your way out! He asked seeing she was preparing to leave after the phone call. "Yep! I'll see ya tomorrow, say noon! "Thanks Mavis that will be fine, stew tomorrow for supper he requested. "I'm here for ya, and nobody is gonna hurt you anymore!" she said in her very gruff smoker's protective sounding voice. She was sixty-five and would have retired but why, she worked for the best boss there was. Mavis was very manly in appearance and gestures but got along with all the cowhands and ranchers on the large 150 acres ranch. She's been with Rusty a lot of years and stuck by him through his Donna years and even the depression Donna had caused him after his undying devotion to her. Bliss had helped bring him back to his old self, she was closer to his age, and Mavis never like Dana anyway she was too young, BOSSY, PUSHY and just using him moving in on a married man! "Anyway, see ya! She said going out the door heading to her two-ton Chevy truck she drove off. A half hour after Mavis said her goodbye Bliss showed up again. Rusty met her at the door giving her a passionate kiss inviting her into his home for the night.

That was wonderful I'm going to miss all that chaos in the morning" Nada shared laying her head on Billy's chest on the plane heading back to Maine. "You know you're right! I never thought I'd want any more children after David Michael". "Oh! Nada asked "Well that's when I thought I would marry Dana" he confessed. "And now that you're marrying me! She asked looking into his eyes "Well God says bless the man whose quiver is full! He laughed. "Two! Nada said holding up her fingers, "just two! Speaking of babies let's go by and see Annie and Keith's new arrival before I head back to Washington tomorrow". "Are you leaving me tomorrow? Billy asked pretending to make a sad face. I want June 20th here so that I won't have to leave your side ever again" kissing Nada's lips. "I love you too Billy Parker, gently returning his affection. "Oh, by the way Nada, Ms. Manuel called early this morning while you were in the shower" he said. "I assured her you'd be home this week". Good I have been keeping her and daddy a breast on my trip, how's she doing? "She's fine she was catching me up on the latest news from her newspaper" he smiled. "Good, reading written information is a lot better for her than that neighborhood gossip she listens to". "Yes! giving Nada a kiss of agreement. "Honey I can't wait to wake up with you! Nada confessed. He reached over and hugged her even tighter confirming he agreed in this matter as well.

CHAPTER 53

Let's make magic

Everyone had started gathering at the beautiful Los Angeles Praise Center church downtown where Doris and Russell were having their marriage vows performed. It was the church where both were active members so the pews were filled with family and friends of all nationalities. Marabelle had performed her magic again with the decorations for the church and the reception that would be held at Doris's gorgeous home in Beverly Hills. The decorations were fabulous! There were huge silver candelabras strategically placed all around the sanctuary. The center of attention was a magnificent pillar candle encircled by a wreath of full bloom white roses and tiny white buds for an elegantly sweet effect. White chocolate swans filled with almonds tied decoratively in thin tulle were given out as favors to the guests when entering. The snow-white accents with silver sparkles brought a shimmering glow to the nuptials of the happy couple and their many guests who had come to witness it. After most of the guest were seated and settled into a seat the Pastor came out and stood in front of the pews. He nodded and the groom and his best man walked out to the sweet mellow music and stood in the front of the church to the right of him. Russell was dressed in a Perry Ellis tailed styled black tuxedo with his best man in a short-tapered style Ellis tuxedo also black. The music playing softly was "Minnie Ripperton" loving you, Russell's song to Doris. After a verse or two of the song another couple made their way down the wide aisle slowly. Sonje her daughter looking beautiful in her white satin form-fitting bridesmaids' gown with lavender trim band across the bust line and three tiny stringed pearled earrings hanging from her ears. Her escort David Michael looked equally as handsome in his Ellis tux being the first of the four beautiful couples dressed identically to walk out arm in arm. After each couple made their way to the front out came Dana her sister in a very sophisticated white silk bodice fitted gown with rich lavender silk skirt bottom extending to the floor. A thin lavender ribbon tied in a bow accented her waist. The photographer moved around to get great shots of the couple's big day. With Dana now in place standing elegantly with her precious bouquet of miniature mums to coordinate with the others in her wedding party Sophie made her grand appearance! She was Gisela's seven-year-old daughter and there were three other little darlings dressed just like her coming in as well. Gisela worked at Doris boutique on Rodeo and was very pleased when Doris asked her and her daughter to share her day. Sophie's precious gown was light lavender with small white pearls gathered all over the full shirt with thin shoulder straps. Her hair was pulled up in a grown-up style showing off her tiny pearl stud earrings. They looked as cute as each walked down dropping white Rose petals along the aisle making a soft elegant path for the bride. From the stage came a soloist that rang out again as Russell nervously awaited his bride. Looking around a few late guests where still coming in. Soon a loud cord struck from the piano! The ushers slowly open the two big wooden doors to reveal the most beautiful bride every known Russell thought standing anticipating her standing beside him. "Here comes the bride all dress in white" Doris had chosen for herself a tapered waist white bear shoulder satin gown with delicate white embroidery inlays leading down into a very full shirt attached to a train designed by A. Angelo. It like Sonjee's was trimmed across the bust-line with lavender. Her headpiece was a simply band of small satin roses with tulle lace to cover her face that hung to her waist in the back. She chose delicate matching pearl earrings and necklace finished her look. "Look at that bouquet" some could be heard whispering. It had every imaginable white and lavender flower of the season. "Lilies, roses, mum, accented with lots of white ribbon, bows and greenery to bring it all together. Finley was almost invisible though quite dapper in a black Ellis tails tuxedo as he escorted his lady down the aisle proudly with all the middle age women vying for his attention with a wave. "Mommy look there's Mr. Finley! Doris heard someone say as she made her way to the front to meet her groom. She turned slightly to see Bethany Ann and Trendon sitting near the middle of the church. She smiled and held back tears as she approached. "Who gives this woman to be wed? The pastor inquired. "I do! Finley stated and sat in his designated sit up front. Doris caught Russell's hand she couldn't wait to tell him about his daughter and grandson. The minister prayed over the couple. The photographers were working over time capturing timeless moments that could not be repeated. "Is there anyone her who thinks these two should not be united speak now or forever hold your peace" again the Pastor, stated pausing long enough for an answer. The packed church was silent. REPEAT AFTER ME! The vows were laid out so beautiful with an explanation of what the rings meant. (A never-ending circle.) The couple lite each candle together and then blew them all out except one. This was a representation of coming together as one is how the officiating Pastor explained it. When Doris handed the bouquet to Dana for the exchanging of rings Dana actually cried real tears. David Michael handed her a handkerchief from his inside pocket. Repeat please, WITH THIS RING! It seemed so long Russell thought as he stood waiting for the words then exhaling again the moment was here, "I now pronounce you man and wife, you may kiss your bride! Nada looked at Billy, their day was soon approaching and she became very emotional when the words Doris recited to Russell in the traditional vow rang out. It was a beautiful ceremony as the couple turned to the audience. "Los Angeles Praise Center it is an honor to introduce to you Mr. and Mrs. Russell Wood. They kissed again smiling at one another. Then Doris leaned over and whispered to Russell as the wedding party followed them out. "Bethany Ann and Trendon are here" she smiled. "Are you sure "I didn't think it was possible to be happier today sweetheart! embracing his new bride and new life.

Everyone was moving around and smiling introducing one another to each other. The children were running around now because being quiet now was over. The limousines parked outside WITH CHAFFURES on the busy street in Los Angeles were waiting for the wedding party who was greeting their guest and families. All were taking photographs with lots of hugs and kisses shared before heading to Doris's home for a grand reception. "Hi Finley! He looked around to see Trendon and his mother coming to greet the bride and groom. "Sonjee? Doris whispered as she stood next to her dad Dr. Reeves in the greeting line "please see that that lady and her son get in one of the limo's please? Sure, mother I'll ask" she said moving out of the line to greet her. Bethany walked up to her father and tears came flowing down from both their eyes Doris as well. Most looking on couldn't understand the burst of emotions coming forth right now as Russell and Bethany stood holding on to each other while the beautiful bride looked on. Tetra looking stunning in her La Belle brown sequined bodice and chiffon layers ankle length gown she had chosen to wear as she held David's hand praying, I was told. With cake cutting and a toast at the church for those not attending the very formal reception an hour later all the limousines with lots of tin cans tied behind them were carrying the wedding party and the loud cheering guest moving down the street in L.A.'s busy traffic headed to Beverly Hills.

Arriving at the gorgeous Beverley Hills home Marabelle had draped the thick rod-iron gates with large white bows and assorted flowers entwined in the gates with their initials R & D. "Very nice touch Nada thought looking at what Doris's wedding coordinator had designed. The long line of limousines slowly came through the wide gates and pulled up to the front entrance. Everywhere one would choose to look you would find a festive embellishment of the day. The reception was being held out doors and the weather was absolutely perfect Doris thought getting out of the car with Russell's assistance with the long train. Her home was striking her guest said moving slowly through it heading to the festive affair to take place out back. The garden like setting of Doris's five-acre estate was magnificent. The lush lawns and the elegant gardens gave her guest such a romantic feeling" Nada shared. She voiced to Doris that Marabelle had captured with many of her design ideas a perfect day! The double doors on the back of the house were opened for those who wanted to be inside relaxing from the fanfare. Everyone looked up as they went into the great hall leading out to where Marabelle had once again performed her magic. She had set the cake in a tented pavilion. It was the prefect-gathering place to see this work of art her baker had decorated for display. A lovely white tablecloth covered a round table with tulle draped all around it. The beautiful five-tier cake looked delectable. The white smooth icing was decorated mimicking embroidered lace on each luscious layer. Again, the elegantly frosted monogram Marabelle, R&D initials were on the tallest tier and very tastefully done, Tetra thought as she and David stood admiring it from where they were standing. The base of this large cake set in the center of the table with assorted lavender flowers circling its' silver base. Absolutely lovely cake! The junior bridesmaids all wore sashes' the same color lavender that was repeated throughout the settings and they were running all over the large estate. "Hey what's your name? Trendon asked wanting to get into the fun "Sophie! she answered standing with two other's giggling. "And what's yours? Sophie replied. "Trendon! He said looking at her for the next question. "Well do you want to play with us" Sure what cha playing? He asked "Hide and seek its' fun". Okay! and off they went. The main seating area was filled with reception tables set with delicacies and a bountiful banquet of flowers. The very tall flutes Marabelle used that stood high in the air had a very dramatic affect. Tulle hung throughout the trees softened the visual effect of the gardens setting. "Stand still please? The photographer asked taking a picture of Doris and Russell standing near a lush patch of grass with their initials monogrammed in rose petals front and center. The Banquet tables were cover in lavender colored fabric with a sheer embroidered overlay mimicking the cake and Doris's beautiful gown. The table setting also boasted very wide strips of satin ribbon so elegant and fitting of the forty–two-year-old bride's chic style. There were flowers everywhere dahlias on the chair backs, clustered of hydrangeas in clear-glass containers running down the table's center. The gorgeous hydrangea-and-rose arrangement at the head table added a quiet elegance to the whole setting. "I'd like to thank you all for coming" Doris voiced now preparing to partake of the delicious entrée's prepared by the caterers. There were deliciously beautiful banquet tables strategically placed all around the lawn to satisfy every palette. Russell had now rejoined Doris and both made their way to the main table with the adults from the wedding party. The children were still playing in the game room inside when they were not running around the grounds. Russell and Bethany were in the sitting room when they first arrived. Doris thought that to be a good idea since she would be leaving soon and wanted him to spend some time with his daughter alone. "Thank you" Bethany said approaching Doris at the head table. "Oh, I'm so glad you came I'm sorry I'm unable to spend more time with you and Trendon" Doris replied. "Doris, I understand, thank you for everything giving her a warm embrace. "We're leaving soon after the meal if I can round up Trendon he's having a blast! Bethany smiled. "I'm glad dear you decided to come" hugging her again and she turned and walked off to find a table of which to eat. "Hi! Bethany, right? "Yes" she said looking at the lady who was in charge of seating. "Right this way, leading her over to where most of the family was sitting. "Bethany and Trendon" she said pointing to the delicate monogrammed place card with their names on it. "Thank you" she smiled sitting down introducing herself around the table. The three-tier place setting of white china trimmed in gold with the monogrammed menu lying across was signature Doris! A delightful china cup and saucer boasted a monogrammed favor also mimicked throughout the wedding. The monogrammed table marker and stemware were elegantly displayed and in very good taste for the evening directing each one to the designated tables. "Dana, I see you came alone? Gisela asked as they came back from the banquet table sitting again to eat. "I did! I have been visiting out of state and I came right here without going back home to Maine" Dana shared. "Oh, I see, so you're going to be catching the bouquet with the rest of us uh! She laughed. "You're right on that! Dana responded. Gisela was expecting a harsh answer from Dana, but she was much softer. Hello everyone! Kara expressed walking over to the table to see David Michael who had ridden in the limo from the church. "Excuse me ladies! Hi Kar, did you get lost or something" he asked her moving away to talk to her away from the crowd. Finley was so proud! Smoked Salmon Pate, tapenade-filled palmiers and marinated feta cheese and olives were a popular favorite. Sour-cream-topped mini quinces, and lavender shortbread bites as well as tarragon chicken salad and so much more. Sparkling wines and champagne and cider were also available at the tables chilled to perfection. Pork tenderloins with fruit chutney and crab cocktails were also served to the many guest who had gather at this gala reception. After everyone had eaten to their delight including rounding up the children from their play Doris and Russell shared the first dance.

Bethany his daughter had excused herself and said her goodbyes to Doris and Russell wishing them well shortly after finishing her meal. Everyone watched the couple laughing and enjoying their first dance together before joining them in the fun. The tossing of the bouquet brought all the single ladies together especially those ladies with eyes on Finley! "Doris smiled. Russell's guarder toss landed in a tree! "Great toss Russ, I'd aim higher next time! Guys yelled teasing him without mercy. All had a very good time. They laughed they danced to a live band that kept everything moving right along. Conversations where shared friendships were made and yes Dana said she had a wonderful time. She just knew there was still a chance with Billy. Nada was so impressed with all the wedding coordinator had accomplished to show Doris's true taste and style. And when all was said and done each guest were given monogrammed petal cones as the happy couple prepared to depart. These were filled with rose petals used to toss at the bride and groom as they left in their vintage Bentley. Waving goodbye to the two hundred plus guest still tossing petals Doris and Russell left for a luxurious honeymoon cruise for a month starting with the Riviera Maya and on to the beautiful cities of the Caribbean with Finley too!

CHAPTER 54

More laughs are in order

Nada arrived back home early afternoon from her wonderful time with Billy in Maine. As she pulled into her driveway King the German shepherd dog leaped from the porch where Ms. Manuel was sitting and ran jumping up by the car window of Nada's Lexus. "King hi boy! Are you happy to see me? She asked pushing her way out from his big body on the door. She stood rubbing his head and waved at Ms Manuel. "Hello Ms. Manuel, how are you? 'I'm fine Nada Jean how you doing? "Wonderful Ms. Manuel" "Where is that handsome man of yose? She laughed. "He's in Maine Ms. Manuel" "Yall still getting married right? "Yes Ms. Manuel" "Well I missed you glad you home" she said. She had walked over from her rocker on her porch. "I'm going to go and take a nap before the meeting tonight" now standing by the fence near Nada. "I'm going in to rest as well Ms. Manuel I have a lot of planning to do for my wedding" Nada explained reaching across the fence to hug her elderly friend. "Come on boy! She said calling him back to the porch as she returned to her rocking chair. "Ms. Manuel, I found a gorgeous dress for you to wear to the wedding". "Dress for me! She yelled from her porch. "You can't ride in a limousine and not be properly dressed," she teased. "Oh, Nada Jean you goin let me ride in a limousine? "Yes, ma'am you and Hazel" Nada replied. "Ha! ha! Ha! Ms. Manuel laughed "ain't nobody goin say nothing to me now! "I'll talk with you later about it." "All right Nada Jean I goin call Hazel! Dialing the phone as Nada went into her home with King close behind. Nada's day had started early when she headed to the university from the airport. She knew she was only scheduled for a half day so the two classes she was giving lectures in were nearly full. She sat in her living room remembering her student who had visited her between classes wanting a handout to study for an upcoming exam. "Ms. Francois I missed your class! He confessed standing with his buddy laughing outside the door. "I see and why did you miss the lecture? UH! uh I don't know I forgot this was an important one" Phil confided. "Well first of all! All the lectures are important and if you expect to graduate from this university you had better show up for every one of them! Got it! "I promise Ms. Francois" we will not have this conversation again." "Ok" he nodded. "Good, since this is your first year, I'm going to cut you some slack on this one but you still will need to read the chapter associated with this handout." And I expect a B or better. "Okay Ms. Francois, I promise, I promise". He expressed now just wanting the handout so he could exhale a sigh of relief for missing the meaningful lecture. Handing him the printout Nada stated "Phil I'm writing your name on my list of students and I'm going to keep it there until you graduate." "Okay thanks Ms. Francois" taking the printout and leaving relieved. Nada turned on her television and curled up in the corner of her big chenille fabric chair with one of her favor throws. Making a list for her wedding needs she fell asleep with her four-legged friend lying in his favorite spot near the door.

Dana had returned from Los Angeles and called her friend Rusty. She had invited him to the wedding in Los Angeles and he had refused but said he'd love to see her when she returned. After a day at the office, she had gone out to the Corral for happy hour and then she headed to the ranch. She parked and got out knocking on the door. Come on in pretty lady how was your trip? "Good I had fun" she said wish you could have been there! He said nothing just hugged her. The sun had not gone down it was dusk and the weather was cool. "Rusty let's go out for a ride! Dana asked still feeling good from the drinks she had from the Corral. 'Are you sure? Yes, I am giving him a soft kiss on his lips. They headed out to the stables and after saddling the horses they were on their way. "Wow! She does have get up and go! Dana noticed riding up on Cocoa Rusty's other stallion after catching up to them. "Yep! Bliss is a great vet! Rusty shared. Speaking of Bliss is she married? Dana asked going right to what interested her. "No, I don't think so why ya asking? He asked. "Well, you two seem to get along very well" Dana expressed. "Well, when Sugar got ill, we spent a lot of time together with her. She stuck in there and made my mare well again." Rusty said rubbing Sugar's mane down to his back. "That's it! Dana said riding slowly by his side. "Well, we've remained friends. I've hired her to take care of all my animals". Besides I met her through Mavis they have known each other for a while I understand". Umm! Really? Mavis ah? Dana expressed. After a while they stopped riding and tied the two horses to a tree and dismounted and went sat on a bench under an oak. Rusty sat down chewing on his straw hanging from between his teeth. Dana sat next to him flirting with her every movement. It had been a while since Colvin left and she was feeling what she deemed lonely. "Rusty do you think Donna will come back someday? holding his hand entwining their fingers as they spoke. I doubt it seriously, though I will never allow a woman to hurt me like that again! He stated firmly. "Oh, Rusty you know I would never hurt you! He didn't say anything he just reached and pulled her face to his and kissed her gently. She fell into his charm and then his embrace. Not allowing this moment to pass Dana took her blanket from the saddle laying it on the grass now with the dusk turning into darkness she and Rusty renewed their relationship they once had.

"Good morning Mrs. Parker" Nada said calling to speak with her regarding wedding plans. She had sat up late that night before filling in her wedding planner guidebook and she and Tetra were going to look for a location to have the reception.

Item	Average cost
Average cost	
Bridal consultant	$12,500
Marriage/license	$40.
Bride's Gown	$28,00.00
Medical test	$40.
Bride's accessories	$1,125

Officiates fee	$500.
Bride's hair and makeup	$270.00
Photography	$2,000.00
Bride's headpiece	$1,150
Reception	$17,00
Bridesmaids' gifts	$1,200
Reception music	$3,000.00
Bridesmaids' luncheon	$1175
Rehearsal dinner	$2,500.00
Ceremony	$1200
Videography	$850.00
Ceremony music	$175.00
Wedding rings	$18,000
Flowers	$1,750
Cake	$1,200
Groom's accessories	$1,140
Transportation	$600.00
Groom's attire	$1,100
Favors	$1,100.00
Groomsmen's gifts	$1,200
Wedding suite	$2,500.00
Honeymoon	$5,000
Invitations and stationery	$1,350
Total cost	$93. 465.00

"Mom, Billy and I have allotted $20, thousand dollars for our reception I hope we can find someplace big enough" she questioned speaking with Tetra. Twenty thousand! Tetra exclaimed repeating what her daughter-in-law to be said. "Wow things have changed. David and I had a very high-profile wedding and we only paid 30 thousand for everything she laughed referencing her wedding years ago. "I know that's true sharing a laugh. So, are you still going with me after work, say around 3:30 pm? I have two places lined up my consultant recommended. "I'd love to dear it should be fun", Tetra replied. "Oh, and if you don't mind, we can stop and look at some dresses I've picked out for Ms. Manuel and Ms. Ross" Nada added. Sure, I'll put on some comfortable shoes and I'm all yours." "Thanks Mrs. Parker" "Mom is fine dear".

"Nada so who's in the wedding party besides me? Carin Wilson asked coming into the teacher's lounge where Nada had come to get a much-needed cup of coffee and relax from a busy morning. June was right around the corner and she had been very busy making phone calls, looking for dresses and working very close with the wedding consultant for her big day. "Well good morning to you Carin" Nada replied a least speak before you start asking questions! She suggested teasing her younger friend. "So, it's me and Madison and his cute brother, right? "Carin you're a mess! Yes, Justin will surely be there." "He's a doctor right? Do you think I'm his type? Nada just shook her head smiling. "Madison and I are going to look at bridesmaid dresses Wednesday and another opinion we don't need but you're welcome to come." Nada joked. "Ring, ring, her cell phone was ringing and there was only five minutes left in her break. She looked and her caller ID said it was Billy. "Hi honey" Sweetheart, how are you? He asked. "Honestly tired but your mother is going with me I have an appointment to see two places for the reception the consultant recommended. "Good, but look I don't want you to be so exhausted you can't enjoy your day" I know honey but we have only four months to put everything together" she explained. "And are you letting the consultant do her part? That's what we're paying her for you know! "I know honey I just want everything perfect" I'm sure if you are involving mom you two will put me in the poor house! He laughed. "Now honey" she replied. "Well anyway, sweetheart I have all my groomsmen lined up David Michael, Justin my brother, I'm leaving a place for Glenn, and of course Desmond's whole family said yes! He laughed. "Oh, good thank you sweetheart" so all I have to do is see if Madison will be standing with her husband or one of the other guys." She's my maid of honor so she'll have to be escorted by David Michael your best man! Right? And of course, Mossy will be one of my bridesmaids". She was still talking as she waved to Carin still sitting at the table and headed back to her classroom. "Babe I'll be back at the class soon so we'll talk later. "Thanks, oh and sweetie I have finalized the honeymoon! He said. You have! She asked excited. Where? "It's a surprise, talk with you later! disconnecting the line.

Sonjee was moving around the apartment quickly getting ready. She had just come from the theater arts building on campus where her class was being held. She stopped to chat with a fellow classmate causing her to run late getting home. She took a quick shower and got dressed. Looking at her watch she let out a sigh of relief. She put her book bag by the door with her purse waiting for David Michael and Kara. She didn't want to be late for bible study tonight at the church. Hi! Hello Sonj! They said coming in just as she took a sit on the sofa to wait for them. "So, who read the lesson besides me? You know I did! Kara said. "Don't look at me I read my lesson as well, ask me anything! Go ahead. Hey I believe you but you'd better hurry and shower unless you're going in cleats! David headed for the bedroom and the girls sat talking when the phone rang. "Hello! Hi Sonjee, Jace! "Yes, I saw the name on the caller ID" she replied. "Okay well I'm happy to hear your voice," he teased trying to get a smile across the wave line. So, what happened to you? "Oh, the wedding I knew you were avoiding my calls. I was trying to explain but I only got your voicemail or mailbox full". Umm this otta be good! She responded excusing herself to her room. "No really, I shared with you I had taken those days off but a pilot friend of mine had an emergency and I owed him one" he expressed waiting for a response. Sonjee said nothing. "Then I still could have at least made the wedding but the plane I was piloting was grounded due to bad weather on the east coast. I know you saw it on the news! He hoped anyway. "Okay so what do you want now? She asked. "I'd like to see you, I'm here for the night I fly out early tomorrow morning." "Well, its good hearing from you and have a safe flight" she said in her sassy Sonjee way. "Sonjee I'm sorry please have dinner with me? He pleaded. "Look Jace tonight is not good, I'm on my way out to the church". "Oh, that's right I forgot babe". "Sonjee! The name is Sonjee! She stated. "Sonjee well will you call me when you get back? He asked knowing he was not going to persuade her to meet him tonight. Maybe! "I love you Sonjee! She hung up the line. David Michael and Kara were waiting when she came out of her bedroom "Why are you two looking at me I'm still going where I was going before the call" she shared gathering her bag and purse near the door. "How's my main man doing? David Michael inquired. "He's fine, you're driving let's go! Sonjee replied leaving from the condo. Arriving at the church seeing other young adults as well David Michael, Kara and Sonjee entered the west side of the very large sanctuary. Hello! Good evening! How is everyone? Each greeted another in their own way. Some hugged other's shook hands glad to be a part of the gathering. "HELLO! Their instructor voiced coming over to greet old students and be introduced to other's coming for the first time. "We are growing! Praise God! He voiced. "We will be meeting in room 406 down the hall this way". Everyone headed out behind him. After they arrived and got seated David Michael went back to get Kara's book bag, she had left on the pews up front where they stood around making conversation until the other's came. He walked down the hall and out in the front of the spacious sanctuary "Oh there it is" he said to himself reaching down between the benches to get it. When he rose up, he saw a man in uniform standing in the door. "Hello! The stranger yelled from the door. "Hi! Michael responded walking toward him. As he got closer, he could see it was Jace in full dress pilot's uniform. "Hi guy! greeting him with a manly embrace. Does Sonjee know you're coming? No! I wanted to make sure I could, I spoke with her from the plane earlier" he shared. Where is everybody? He asked looking around at the empty seats. "This way man, our class of young adults meets in room 406 walking with Jace down the hall. Jace had taken off his hat when he walked into the sanctuary. He smiled walking into the class of 20 plus students. "Hello everyone, look who I found! David Michael teased looking at his cousin Sonjee. Sonjee looked up "what are you doing here? She asked surprised. "Now sister Sonjee you should be saying welcome! The instructor said smiling. "Have a seat young man we were just about to pray". He found a seat next to Sonjee and bowed his head like everyone else in the room. The instructor prayed with anyone joining if they chose too. After an introduction of new members or guests the class study began. Jace Ramsey and a few others stood and introduced themselves. The class moved along well with everyone including Jace answering and asking questions. After and hour and a half of intense study and fun the class was over. Kara led the group in closing prayer. David Michael, Kara, Sonjee and yes

Jace all went out to TGI Fridays for more laughs and some good food! THANK GOD!

Nada stayed on pace with her wedding plans. Two weeks had passed before she and Tetra found the perfect place. They had fell in love with and old historic brick mansion in Washington State to host her and Billy's reception. The wedding nuptials will be rendered at Mt. Nebo and Dr. Cornelius Hathaway would be officiating. Sweetheart that's wonderful! So that's all finalized right! Good! So, who is making the trip here for the wedding announcement party? He asked speaking with his fiancée from Maine. "Madison and her husband, Carin and of course my dad and mom and dad Parker" she replied. "All right, just making sure" The staff will be very busy this weekend' he added Desmond's bringing his family out and David Michael is coming with a friend." Glenn apologizes he can't make the party but he looks forward to the wedding". "Umm that's too bad we will continue to pray for them, Nada said. "Yes, he and I pray every morning". He called me today before I could call him. That could be a good sign" Billy confided. "Yes, dear you're right. Sweetheart I will see you Friday my plane lands in Maine Thursday night at 9pm Maine time". All right dear I love you! "Oh Nada, I almost forgot the article came out today in the society page of the Maine Bugle News regarding our wedding announcement". 'It did! Oh, sweetheart you are the best! She said very excited. "Did you keep a copy? She asked still very excited. "Let's see one, two, three, four, should I continue? He laughed. See you Thursday sweetheart". Good day hurrying back to her class at the university.

Justin hurried to the nurse's station to answer an overhead page. Hello Dr. Parker! He replied greeting the caller. "JUSTIN! She replied. "Oh Kat, I should have known, how are you? "I'm fine, I was just reading," She started to say when he cut her off. "The Maine Bugle, let's see the society page" he laughed. "Oh Justin, I was wondering who you were taking or if you had a date? She asked slowly. "Kat, you know I always have a date, that's what bachelors do! He again admitted to his mother. "Well, I was wondering? She asked. "No Kat! You didn't give me a chance to ask my question" she replied. "Kat how old am I? He asked. You're my son I know how old you are? What kind of question is that?

She inquired. The kind that says no I'm not going to take you to the estate! He stated again. "Okay, who's on the guest list? She then asked. "I am! I'll talk with you later! and disconnected the line.

Dana had been keeping time with Rusty in between Bliss's visits and neither lady was the wiser. Rusty was determined that no woman would steal his heart again and hurt him the way Donna his wife did! Work, work, work, is where Dana found herself most days when she wasn't out at the ranch or having lunch with her cowboy as she referred to him. Molly and Corky had bought a home closer to town and besides at the hospital she saw very little of her close friend. Mollie lunch? She asked passing her in the hallway. "No Dana some other time I'm really busy today" she stated and kept going. Mollie couldn't tell Dana Corky didn't want her hanging with her anymore. She was a married woman now! So, she avoided Dana a lot even at work. Dana walked out into the open Bistro of the hospital where Rusty was waiting to have their weekly lunch date. "Hello pretty lady! extending his open arms to her giving her a hug before sitting down. They sat eating their ordered sandwiches when a couple of doctors came by. Why hello Dr. Williams extending his hand. Dr. Bagalari! Dana said surprised. "What are you doing on this side of the world? She asked grinning from ear to ear! He smiled "this is a colleague Dr. Rugger" please to meet you as well extending a handshake. Dana had met him in Paris at a convention and was very pleased to see him. She stood talking and forgot about Rusty sitting there. "Maybe we can go out for drinks later? He asked looking at her then Rusty. "Hey you think your father will mind? Bagalari asked in his best English "my father?" "Oh, I'm sorry he is just a friend" "Rusty Higgins' Rusty said standing to extend a hand to the good doctors. "Look I'll let you finish your lunch and I'll come by your office later". He smiled walking away. "Nice meeting you." The rest of her lunch was futile. Dana's mind had wonder off to the marvelous time she had in Paris. And hopefully she would reminisce about it a little later. Did you see the society page of the Bugle? Rusty asked. No, I haven't had time to read it. What's so important you would ask if I've read it? She asked thinking mostly about her friend she just discovered was in the states. "Well, I read that your friend William Parker is having an engagement party tonight." "Are you saying that because you heard I may meet Dr.Bagalari later? "No, I'm saying it because it's true" handing her a copy of the Bugle sitting on the table left from someone earlier. Dana read it for herself and threw it in the trash as she left going back to her office. When Rusty called Dana later that evening she was unavailable and he got only voicemail. He hung up and called Bliss who charmed him with a delightful dinner for two at her home where he spent the evening.

The thirty-six-year-old Dr. Justin Parker showed up in a stylish tuxedo by Oscar De but alone. "No date tonight" Billy asked inviting him in the door of the estate. "Are you kidding all the ladies that are going to be here from your list now that you're no longer eligible" and besides that group of young ladies Hope, Truth, and Love who sings with the band I'll be all right! He laughed embracing his older brother and moving on to greet other's. Later Billy! I'm sure I won't be lonely. "Man, you're crazy! And I know because I use to be the same way" he confessed laughing. The estate was decorated with beautiful flowers and lots of candles setting the mood of elegance. "Sidney! Good to see you" You to man, it's been a while" this is Jamie Gregory my date for the evening" Please to meet you" Billy said. After extending his hand to the couple he made his way through the invited guest. He and Nada stood in front of their guest and thank them all for coming to their engagement party. "We will be sharing our vows in Washington State where she now lives on June 20th. The whole room of invited guests applauded. And all to the happy couple of the evening shared hugs and kisses. Annie and Keith were there, David Michael and Kara had come along with Sonjee and Jace. "Hi dad, he greeted "son welcome introducing himself and welcoming Kara, Sonjee and Jace into his home. "Uncle Billy this is Jace Ramsey my date" Sonjee replied. "Nice to meet you, are you a student at U.C.L.A. as well? He asked. "No sir I'm a pilot for Northwestern sir" Jace replied. "Well, it is certainly a pleasure meeting you, though I must admit times are changing. I can't remember when we had our own private pilot to travel with! He teased smiling with the young group". "You all enjoy yourselves! He said moving on now looking for Nada who had excused herself to show Madison and Carin her best friends around the estate's beautiful home. Her dad had come earlier with the Parkers and had been shown the beautiful estate grounds the day before. The weather was absolutely perfect and the guests were roaming around everywhere in and outside. The orchestra music was playing softly as everyone took on conversations with one another. Then David Michael caught up to him again "Dad I haven't spoken with mom lately, have you? He asked now standing alone with his dad. "Not since Doris her sister's wedding, what? Well over a month ago I guess why? I just have not been able to reach her, I've left messages but she doesn't return calls! He confided. "Did you go by her house? I did come in from the airport but of course she wasn't there" home still looks lived in though" he smiled. "I would try again but we're flying out tonight got a big game tomorrow! "That's right I've been watching I will be down for that rival game against the number two seed in May for your division". Great dad! Should be a doozy! slapping a high five. "David Michael you seem happy? embracing him around the shoulder. "I am dad I've found another group to run with". "Oh! Billy said sounding like a concerned father. "My Tuesday night bible study group! Very good, it's working son" and look I'll see what I can do about getting in touch with your mother" just not tonight I'm looking for my fiancée right now! Billy smiled relieved moving on. Tetra and David were enjoying themselves over in one of the sitting rooms talking with Desmond and his wife Mossy. "So, who would believe you two would have five children now? Tetra loving said to Mossy smiling. "Yes ma'am, and I have called it quits with bottles and diapers" she replied laughing sharing the moment. The live band had sat up out by the pool and everything was buzzing joyfully around the 20,000 square feet of living space in the estate's home. The original plan layout of the large home was 16,000 square feet build by his grandfather in the early sixties but when Billy renovated the home after his grandparents passed, he added an additional 4,000 square feet for a theater and game room. "Hello Parker! A group of his attorney buddies yelled standing grouped at the opened bar. "Glad you could come, he responded extending a warm shake to them all. The waiters had caviar and sparkling expensive champagne for the eager palettes delight balanced carefully on his tray as he moved from room to room. The banquet tables were elegant and deliciously decorated in white, yellow and silver elements to match the chosen wedding colors. Billy walked back into the sitting room "Oh I am very proud of my son" he heard his mother say. "Mom are you telling them all about my stories in this house? He asked embracing her standing next to her side. "No! She teased your dad's doing that! Ha, ha! Everyone was having fun including the ladies who were checking out the home's master suite. "Oh Nada, you are a queen in here! Carin boosted looking at the bedroom's furnishings and bedding. "Is this where you and Billy sleep when you come for a visit? Madison asked sliding her hand across the very soft stylist and elegant duvet cover. "No! This is where Billy sleeps" Nada replied. "You mean? Really? NEVER? Carin asked coming out from the adjoining gorgeous bath. "GIRL PLEASE, my hips would still be swiveling around in that bed! making a motioning gesture. "Oh, believe me there have been times when I wanted to throw caution to the wind! But we chose to wait! She confessed enjoying girl talk with her best friends. "Uh isn't there something in the bible about asking for forgiveness? Carin asked, "I would have done it and asked forgiveness every time! She said laughing as she fell into the big comfortable chair in the sitting area. Carin you are a fool! but I love ya! "Nada I am happy for you" Madison voiced and proud too" me too! Carin acknowledged with all three giving a group hug before heading back down the wide spiraling staircase to join the engagement festivities in full swing. "Can I borrow that room tonight if I find a man up in here? Carin asked pointing to one of the other elegantly decorated bedrooms she had visited.

CHAPTER 55

Can it get worse?

Dr. Williams please," calling Dana that following Monday at her office. Dana Williams", she responded answering the phone. "Hello it's Billy, "Yes, I recognize your voice why are you calling? She asked sharply. "David Michael said he had been trying to speak with you but you were not answering your phone". "So, you're hired to see that I do! She stated sharply again. 'Dana take the chip off of your shoulder, I'm making sure things with you are well since you're not returning calls." 'Is David Michael still here in Maine? 'I can speak with him myself she chided. "No, his flight left last evening he did come by but you weren't home". "Okay I'll call him," she conceded. "Please do, he wants to share with you I'm sure". "Share what? Probably about how well he's doing with his group." "Or that, you've turned him into a Holy Roller! And now all of his talk is when am I going to convert or pray or any of that churchy stuff you all do! "Dana please, he's happy and doing a lot better since joining that group of young people". Okay so what you're doing is all right and what I'm doing is totally wrong! She huffed. "Dana I'm not going to argue with you, please call him," Billy suggested getting ready to hang up the line. "So, when were you going to tell me about the engagement party you had? She asked angered by the whole relationship. "Dana you knew at the Black and White ball I had asked Nada to marry me" he confided. So, an engagement party was imminent," he replied. "So, you're really going to marry her? a cook's daughter!" 'Yes, Dana I am" he replied. "Then this is goodbye and good riddance! Dana stated disconnecting the line with a SLAM!

Hi Dana" Mollie voiced coming into her office at the hospital. Hey you! Where have you been? "Got married and got lost uh? Dana asked teasing her friend. "No, just stopped by to see how you were doing" Mollie confessed. "I'm fine why are you asking so concerned?" "Oh no reason" Mollie replied looking down. "Look Mollie I know you better than that, so what gives? Dana asked coming over putting her arm around her shoulder. "Uh, just the buzz around the office about Billy" she said quietly. "Oh that! Yes, I spoke with him earlier he's going to marry that tramp from the sticks! It probably won't last long she has no class when it comes to men. I know that for a fact! Dana chided moving around to her desk. "OUCH! Mollie responded. "So, whatever you were doing with her old boyfriend backfired? Mollie just had to ask. "Look Mollie I'll give him six months before he throws her out and comes running back to me! "Well Dana girl you go! making a sassy wave with her neck and hand. "So, I heard you were seeing Rusty again? "Yes, Rusty's my cowboy but there's this pest of a vet who I'd like to get rid of! She confided. "Oh, Bliss she's nice and knows her horses! Mollie said. "Oh, so you know Bliss? looking at Mollie now sitting in her big chair near her desk. "Well, I see her from time to time when Corky and I go to the ranch". So, do you think she's Rusty's type? Dana questioned her friend. "I can't say, I know before you came back, they were seeing a lot of each other". "You were with that other guy though, what's his name? "Oh, shut up Mollie about that! She admonished getting up from her desk. "So, she thinks she's going to have Rusty now that he's back feeling better". "Dana, I didn't say that, I don't know what relationship that have other than working with the horses together". "Right, you didn't say, but I have already caught then kissing once when I came back months ago though I'm sure that's over! She said looking directly at Mollie. "Dana, I wish you well with Rusty, he's a nice guy and I'll leave it at that" Mollie replied. 'Oh, did you see Dr. Bagalari? He was here last week! Dana's mind was now on Rusty, and Mollie knowing her well knew it! "Look, Corky and I have been discussing when we will start a family" Mollie said changing the subject of Rusty. "Dana was looking away her mind seemed to have moved in another direction. "Look Mollie it's good seeing you I have a client to get ready for" going back to her desk sitting in her executive chair taking out a folder and began to write. She didn't even look up when Mollie walked out saying "see ya later!

Nada walked into the administrative office of the University of Washington where she is an instructor on staff. "Hello Ms. Francois" the secretary greeted seeing her come in. "Queen Nada! Carin yelled from the back office hearing her speaking to the secretary. Carin was showing off her pictures from the trip to Maine. "Oh, hi Carin, have you stopped talking yet! She teased smiling. "No! I brought in my pictures today" you did! Did you get some good ones to share? Nada asked. "Yes, they are all back there looking at my limo ride from the airport and the beautiful flower gardens, every single bedroom in your fabulous house! I told them you were the bomb! I got proof now! She said still very excited. Nada had paid for her trip since she and Madison were in her wedding. She wanted to do something special for them and it was! She treated them like royalty. It was a trip Carin probably will never forget. "After a while Mrs. Strasser was back with the document Nada had come in to get. "Thank you she said reaching across the counter. "Oh, I hear congratulations are in order," she asked. "Yes Mrs. Strasser, June of this year" Nada replied smiling. "Oh, right around the corner". "Yes, ma'am it is" she said realizing it was the end of April. "So, are you getting married in Maine on those beautiful grounds? "No, that would have been idea, however since his family and I are here we're getting married here in Washington at Mt. Nebo Community and our reception will be held in the Old Mary Hill Castle in Mary Hill over looking the scenic Columbia River Gorge." "That's wonderful $$$$$$$" she said looking over the top of her rimmed eyeglasses smiling. "I TOLD YA! Carin said waving bye to Nada going back to her desk that was in the adjoining office. "Thanks again for the file Nada responded to Mrs. Stasser walking out knowing her guest list probably just got a bit longer.

"David, dinner's ready! Tetra said going into her dinning room to sit at her table. "How was your day? She asked as he came in to sit down. "Oh, honey it was fine". Not much going on differently at the office." But I did volunteer to teach for our Wednesday night study he confided putting the serving spoon down from the seasoned potatoes he had just served on his plate. "Darling that's wonderful it's been a while since I heard you teach". So, you're going to be there supporting me? He asked. "And I will be praying for your guidance and strength through each lesson". Thanks, honey I love you he confessed. I you darling" sharing a kiss to agree. "Well soon our son will be a married man," Tetra said spooning up some apple crumble in her dessert dish. "Yes, honey, and I think he's found a Godly mate in Nada". They seem to compliment each other". I agree, we have been having so much fun together with her wedding plans I feel like I've known her a lifetime". "Good, family relationships are important in any family". "David do you think they'll have children? She asked. "I hope so, David Michael came to us late but I still enjoyed the years we were blessed with him as a young child and even now! Me too David I hope they do!

"Rusty come on there is going to be a big crowd tonight at the Corral! She voiced coming in the front door of the ranch. "Oh, Dana are you sure this is what you want to do tonight I will be just as content going to your place" he said. "Here's your hat you and I are going to go out dancing I know you miss that" she said handing him his cowboy hat and showing him to the door. "Mavis I am going out! be home later! He yelled to his housekeeper. "Should I hold dinner for you? Mavis yelled back from the opened style kitchen. "It won't be necessary! Dana replied now standing with the door opened to leave. Dana I'm not speaking with you I was talking to Rusty" Mavis responded teed at Dana's response. "Well Rusty won't need you tonight dear you are welcome to leave". Mavis had now stood in the wide door opening with her hand on her hips. "I take orders from Rusty and not from some," 'Now, now ladies, name-calling ain't necessary". "Mavis thanks, please keep my food in the conventional oven as always I'll see ya later" he said and gave Dana a slight tap on the shoulder and both walked out of the door together. "If I'm going to be around Rusty, you're going to have to get rid of Mavis! and I have an appointment with a vet in town tomorrow for the horses" she shared as they drove in to the Corral. "Now Dana, Mavis has been with me through some tough times she's not going to take kindly to you coming in and taking over her kitchen" he smiled. 'And Bliss well she's irreplaceable with my Sugar! Thanks, but no thanks honey buns for your help! He told her getting out of the car at the popular country nightspot. "We'll see! She replied walking in on her cowboy's arm.

"Ms. Manuel, Nada said walking up on her porch to ring the bell. RUFF! RUFF! King could be heard barking from the other side. Soon she was at the door peeping through the keyhole before opening it. "Morning Nada Jean, what you doing up so early? She asked standing in her flannel nightgown and slippers. "I'm sorry to wake you but I need to know if you and Ms. Hazel will be available for a fitting today on your gowns for the wedding? "Fitting, Nada I tell you I have learned a lot from you and you make me seem so special" she told her standing at the door. "Have you had your coffee yet? No ma'am, I just needed to catch you before I left this morning for work". "Baby come on in". I've been up and the coffee is still hot" she shared inviting her into her quaint little home.

"Dad thanks for coming down to the game it was great seeing you. Hey I wouldn't have missed it for the world son. "Granddad and I had a blast throwing with your teammates." Ha! Ha! Ha! They enjoyed it too! David Michael acknowledged laughing. "Kara and I are having dinner tonight with Aunt Doris and Russell we're going to see the slides of the honeymoon cruise. "Great son that should be fun! Then there was a long silent pause in conversation "Dad I don't mean to bother you, I know it's very close to your wedding day but do you think you could do me a big favor? "Well son if it's in my power" he replied. "Dana promised me she would be down for the game and the game before that but as you know she wasn't here". Son I'm sorry she's taking you through this" I'll see what I can do but I'm not on her A list right now either". He said sadly. "Dad I do understand that you can't make anyone do anything they chose not to do". I have tried hard to talk with mom but she's becomes very combative and usually just hangs up on me. "Maybe I should just let her alone" he concluded sadly. 'Well son she's your mother so I'll see what I can do" no promises but I will pray for her and you do the same. "I will dad and thanks! Love ya son.

Billy walked into the hospital to pay Dana a visit a few days after his son had called concerned that he could not reach her. Unable to reach her by phone either he decided to go to her office. Walking in he could see her door was closed to her inner office so he got a magazine from the rack and sat down to read. He looked at his watch the time seemed to be moving slowly but he was there now so he waited. He would talk with Dana because more or less his son had asked him to. Billy saw how happy he had become with his new friends and he just wanted to help Dana understand his change of heart. After about forty minutes her door opened. A short little man with curly blonde hair stood in the door shaking her hand. Billy looked back down at the magazine ignoring whatever instructions she was imparting to the gentleman and with "thank you Dr. Williams" he was gone. Dana went back into her inner office and sat at her desk. Billy put the magazine down and walked in. "Hello Dana! He said to a very surprised look on her face. "What the hell are you doing here? She asked without returning his greeting. "I tried calling you, are you busy? He asked seeing her shift through paperwork. "That's a stupid question, I'm at work, aren't I? She stated back to him. "I do apologize for interrupting you but". "BUT WHAT? She repeated getting up from her desk angry he had disturbed her. "Are you having a bad day? "I wasn't until you showed up! She responded. "Anyway Dana, David Michael says he hasn't been able to reach you" but before he could finish the sentence Dana replied. So! She returned standing with an I'm grown and can do what ever I please look on her face. "Dana are you trying to hurt David Michael to spite me? He asked moving from her reach in the smaller office space. "Hadn't thought about that but thanks for the idea William" she was being evil and sarcastic he thought looking directly at her stern demeanor. "Look he's happy he's not drinking and he's enjoying life doing what he likes. The least you could do is support him! "And stop telling him you're coming to his games when you don't intend to do so! Billy was miffed now regarding their son. She said nothing but walked toward him looking evil and swung her fist at him. He moved to keep her from hitting him. She just smiled. "You know maybe that's the best thing you could do is to stay away and let him live is life!" Billy added turning to walk out of the office. A vase of flowers flew by his head and hit the door's frame shattering it into pieces. He ducked but still apiece found his cheek and cut it. "DANA WILLAMS! He yelled going toward her. "Get out before I kill you! She yelled going back behind her desk and pulled her small pistol from her desk drawer smiling. Billy walked out and stopped in the hall to wipe the blood on his handkerchief before leaving. "Lord have mercy! is how he started his prayer.

David Michael had taken Sonjee to the airport. She was going to Oregon to visit her dad on their three-day weekend and looked with anticipation for the trip. "Thanks guy I'll see you and Kara in three days behave yourselves! She said teasing him with a hug. "Have a great time cuz, I'll miss you! he said. "I will miss you two! And off she went through the crowded airport with her rolling luggage. David was back in the car and headed home when his phone rang. Dad, hi dad! "Hello son", he said sounding a bit down. "Dad what's wrong you sound different" is what he finally came out with. "Well son I just tried to speak with her mom earlier and I think I made things worse" he confessed. "Dad what happened? Son I think your mom just needs some time alone she seems stressed," he concluded for her actions toward him. "Was she mad? "Son she was furious that I was even there! "Dad I'm sorry maybe I'll have a better chance with her, she's probably angry because you're marrying Nada". Oh, I'm sure that's involve to, though she seems to have reached a boiling point and I think she needs to go for a long vacation and just relax." "Dad you're probably right so I'll let things calm a bit and maybe try calling her later in the week." Sounds good son and David please pray for your mother". "I will dad, I will" David Michael replied turning into the parking lot of Kara's apartment.

Daddy! Daddy! Sonjee yelled walking into his home. "Hello dear" this sweet-sounding voice came from the kitchen. "Oh, I'm sorry she said looking around is this Dr. Reeves condo? "Yes, dear come on in," she said going back into the kitchen. "Put your things down dear, your dad should be back soon" she smiled. Sonjee didn't know what to make of this lady, definitely retirement age though very bubbly in character. The lady kept referring to her as dear so she decided to introduce herself. "I'm Sonjee Reeves, his daughter and you are? extending her hand toward her. "I'm Ernestine Melroy, please to meet you". This tiny framed, white hair full of life persona of a woman was now standing extending her hand back to her. "Jon has shown me many pictures of you children, he's so proud." She replied pouring a glass of tea with ice from the crystal pitcher. "Can I get you something? She asked. Sonjee was in her father's home and this lady was acting as though she lived there! "Come on in and sit in the living room dear I'm knitting and we can talk there," she suggested. Sonjee had no intentions of talking to this strange lady about anything but sat down looking around at things. "How was the flight? She asked very involved in what she was knitting and looked up quickly then put her head back down. "It was good" Sonjee stated. "You're not very talkative, are you? She asked smiling at her. "Look Mrs. Melroy how long did you say my dad would be gone? He and his friend Dr. Carter went golfing early so I'm sure they should be headed back real soon." She said looking at her watch. 'Dear is there something you'd like to watch on television? She asked again. She was doing her part in making her comfortable but this was her daddy's house and WHY WAS SHE HERE? Sonjee thought rolling her luggage into the room where she usually sleeps when she comes for her visit. "The curtains and bedding had changed. Looking around she saw other feminine touches throughout the spacious and charming three- bedroom condominium. "Excuse me, is it all right if I just leave my luggage right here? She asked now standing back in the living room feeling like a total stranger in her dad's home. "Sure, just hang your things in the closet dear," she said getting up to assist. "No that's alright Mrs. Melroy." "Just call me Ernestine" going back to her comfy chair. And just in a nick of time Dr. Reeves was coming through the door. "Ernestine I'm home! He yelled closing the door behind him. "Boy! Boy! Carter is a critic on the course! He laughed coming into the living room. "Sonjee! You're here! Come here what has it been four five months since you were here! I know I saw you at Doris wedding 2 months ago but you're home now! He said coming over to hug her. Her body was limp and lifeless as he embraced her and he kissed her forehead as he always did. "So how long have you been here? He asked smiling at her. Long enough! she said in a low voice sadly. Dr. Reeves looked at his daughter he knew exactly what was bothering her. Sonjee said nothing she just flopped down on the sofa and started to cry. "Ernestine please give me some time with my daughter please? He asked lightly squeezing her hand gently as she made her way out the back patio door of their home now. He sat next to her on the sofa and put his arm around her and let her continue to cry. He held her tightly and cried with her.

Billy rode along the highway home. He wanted to call Nada and share with her his concerns regarding Dana but really it was his matter, he reasoned. He needed to think, so he turned left instead of right and headed to his home church in Maine. It was the one he had now become an active member of and had renewed his love for Christ as he once had as a younger man growing up. He walked in turned off his cell phone and sat in the back pews and just listened to one of the choirs practicing their glorious music with the accompaniment of the harp. Nada had just finished speaking with her wedding consultant about the music for her wedding when she heard a knock on her door. It was not quite dark and she could see a woman standing on her porch. As she approached, she asked "who's there? Before she pushed open the screen door to see Dana standing holding out her hand. "Truss, she replied smiling. "Shocked but willing Nada walked forward returning the handshake RELUCTTANTLY inviting Dana into her home. "Cute! she smirked looking around before sitting in a Queen Anne style velvet chair. "Can I get something for you? Nada asked hospitably before sitting on her sofa to hear what Dana had to say. "No thank you, she responded sweetly sitting her purse beside the chair. "Well, I guess you and William are going to get married" she exclaimed still looking at her very small but stylish home. "Yes, Dana we are, we're in love" Nada said smiling. Love! does anyone really know what that is? Dana asked sarcastically. "Yes, I know what love is. It's a very strong bond between two people," she explained SHARPLY. "William and I were in love before you came along" Dana stated. Nada was starting to feel uneasy about her visitor and walked to her opened door and stood there looking for her next move. The sun had now gone down and dusk was all that one could see. "Dana what is this visit about? Nada questioned now standing by the door. "I wanted you to know personally that I will never stop loving Billy! and you can believe he will be back in my bed in a few months! Besides you don't even know what you're buying! Word is you've never slept with him! "Dana please leave" holding the screen door open for her. "Why you can't take being a woman gal? She said with her evil look on her face. "Dana if you don't get out, I'll" and with that announcement all hell broke loose! Dana had leaped over to the door and slapped Nada with the back of her hand. Nada was a country girl and though city bred she certainly was not going to stand for a licking. She balled up her fists and began swinging furiously on Dana who seemed to be being hit by cotton-balls that made her even angrier. "GET OUT OF MY HOUSE YOU WITCH! Nada yelled. "TRY AND MAKE ME! WHEN I FINISH WITH YOUR FACE NO-ONE WILL WANT YOU! She kept saying. "Nada somehow turned and kicked her causing her to fall across the coffee table. She jumped up and grabbed Nada's neck and began choking her. Nada tried screaming but the more she tried the tighter Dana's grip grew on her. She flailed her arms panting for air before falling to her knees. Dana wasn't giving up. She jumped on top of her and began clawing her face. Nada finally managed a scream turning her face from side to side to keep her face from being disfigured with scratches. Her wedding day was only a month away but right now she was fighting for her life she thought kicking and screaming on the floor. Dana had gone in for another grip to finish her off when RUFF! RUFF! Grrrr, this mean German shepherd with vicious long teeth was breathing on Dana's neck. He had torn his way through the screen on the screen door and was now ripping at Dana's arms and legs! He tore at her arm tearing her blouse biting her causing her to turn Nada's neck a loose. Dana jumped up and ran toward the door. King held her inside with his mean vicious stare as he growled. Nada laid on her side coughing trying to catch her breath. By now Ms. Manuel had made here way to the porch and sees Nada on the floor. "WHAT IN HEAVEN'S NAME IS GOING ON HERE? SHE ASKED LOOKING AT KING AND THEN DANA. "Who are you? She asked standing with her cane on the porch. "Mrs. Manuel call 911! Please call 911! Nada said still trying to breathe properly holding her neck. King looked at Nada struggling to get up from the beating and went to aid her in getting up from the floor. When he turned Dana grabbed her purse and hit the door running. Mrs. Manuel held out her cane as she was nearing the gate and she stumbled falling into the fence headfirst. Her stockings were torn her hair was a mess and looks of red scratches were covering her pale skin. King the dog stood by her now barking "Grrr! Ms. Manuel was just making her way into her house to call when Dana seeing the dog was more concerned with Nada still lying on the floor broke away again making it to her car parked on the curve and sped away into the dark of night.

Sonjee met her dad at the restaurant of the hotel where she decided to stay for her visit. She didn't want to talk about the lady staying with her dad and showed up with one of her old friends from Gonzaga University. "Hi daddy she greeted walking up to the table to sit down and have a planned breakfast with him. That was the decision they made yesterday when she left his home shocked and upset with her dad regarding his companion that lived with him. Okay she had her own room but she was still in the same house! She sat down with the forced hug to her dad and picked up the menu to order. "Sweetheart how was your evening? He asked drinking his hot cup of coffee. "All right" she replied saying very little giving all her attention to the menu in her hand. "Sonjee, Candace will be in tonight." "Candace! Really oh I can't wait to see her! She said smiling from the news of her sister's visit. "Are you coming to the house after we finish eating breakfast dear? He asked after everyone had ordered their meals. "No daddy Angie and I are going shopping I'll see you tomorrow when Candace gets here". Sonjee was avoiding him at every turn and he knew it. Sadden by her actions though he understood how she felt. He wanted to explain she's just a friend and someone to talk to when he gets lonely. No one would every replace Beulah in his heart he had tried to explain to her. Angie said very little as they sat eating the delicious breakfast that had been served. "Dr. Reeves, why don't you talk Sonjee into coming back home?" She finally asked to break the massive silence. "I can't! I told you there's nothing here for me" Sonjee stated taking her last bite of eggs. Dr. Reeves was saddened by his young daughter's words. He had no intention of hurting her. He had thought of telling her about Ernestine before Doris's wedding but he held off for later. He reasoned things would be different later on somehow. He continued with light conversation between the two young ladies trying to put on a front but he felt bad. "Daddy what time is Candace coming today? Sonjee asked finishing her orange juice and looking at her watch. Her flight is coming in pretty late dear; would you like to stay in the extra guestroom at the house and wait for her? He smiled looking at her for a yes answer. "No dad, thanks, Angie and I are going shopping and then a movie. So, we will probably be out late too but could you call me when she gets in if it's not too late" she asked. "I can do that dear" he replied disappointed with her answer. "Okay daddy we're going to go, thanks for breakfast, I'll talk with you later" she shared getting up from the table. "Bye! Mr. Reeves remember what I asked" Angie reminded him as she left going to her car from the restaurant clueless of the matter at hand, she walked hurriedly out the hotel door. Sonjee took a moment and hugged her daddy before walking behind her friend Angie out the restaurant leaving Mr. Reeves sitting at the table sadden.

Dana had returned the rental car she had got from the airport and boarded a taxi to another rental car agency and was headed out of town. She was a step ahead of the authorities that now wanted to question her regarding the incident at Nada's home. "Hi dad what's happening with you? David Michael asked cheerful answering his dad's call on his cell phone. "I'm fine, have you spoken with your mother? "No dad, I told you I have been trying for days why? "She showed up at Nada's home and caused trouble! He explained. "WHAT! She did what? What happened dad? Is Nada all right? He asked with Kara asking him questions in the background. They were together studying for Tuesday night group meeting over the long weekend. Sonjee was visiting her dad and had called to say she was staying a bit longer than planned. "Son, Nada's alive, bruised and beaten pretty badly" he shared sadly. "I haven't spoken with her at all. I wonder what happened to set her off! She does have a tendency to hold a grudge but she seemed to be getting better" "David Michael voiced. "I know son, I blame myself, I think when I paid her a visit regarding your concern it brought back the vile hatred, she as built up inside." "Dad I'm sorry it was my fault I should have listened to you when you said to let her be!" "Well son, she's your mother you had every right to be concerned. But really no ones to blame but Dana" I have tried to love her through all this but she's gone to far now! He stated. "Dad I'm still going to pray for her" David Michael contended believing in what he had read in his studies. "Son, as much as I hate to agree right now, you're right!" I'm going to pray for her too. Son if she does call please let me know" Dad I will! God Bless you son. God Bless you dad".

Nada had just arrived home after spending a few days in the hospital. She was sitting up in bed when Alberto brought her in a tray. She covered her face that had been drenched with tears for hours it seemed. Billy was down in the study speaking with the authorities that needed more information on Dr. Dana Williams. "Sweetheart" He said putting the tray down on the bedside tray table. "Oh, daddy I was so happy! She said now falling upon his shoulder and hugging him tightly as she cried. He held on tight to her to, thanking God she was still alive. Mrs. Manuel called him after she called 911 and he rode in the ambulance when they took her bruise and beaten body to the hospital. After two days she was released but now living under the Parkers roof for healing, recovery and protection. "Sweetheart, I've prepared one of your favorite soups, I need you to eat something okay" he said wiping the tears from his eyes as he looked upon her face of scratches and bruises. Large red finger prints where around her neck from being choked almost to death and she was hurting all over from being banged around in her small place. After a while she composed herself and sat up trying to eat something as Alfredo looked on. Daddy how could this happed? Why would God allow this to happen to me! She burst out in tears again. She pushed the tray from in front of her and turned her back and covered her head. Alfredo removed the tray from the bedside table and stood holding it by her bedside. He prayed fervently to God to help her understand and that He was still with her even in this!

A few days had past when Dana walked into attorney Patterson's office in Los Angeles. "Hello Dr. Williams please come in" he replied extending his handshake inviting her into his law office. "Thank you, Dillard," it's good to see you again. Did you get all the paperwork I requested? "Yes! Yes, I did," he said moving back behind the large desk to spread out the documents. He was her attorney who had taken care of all the legal documents with her sister Doris and knew exactly what Dana wanted in this matter. "Now I see you want to give and equal portion of the estate to your sister and your son, right? along with this letter" He asked moving quickly knowing how Dana liked business handled. "That's right Dillard securing the papers and signing them and giving them back to him. "This portion of your estate goes to the Beulah Reeves foundation. "And this portion goes to your niece Sonjee

Reeves" looking up at her to confirm what he was asking. "Yes, she so much wants to be like me, I'll give her a start! Dana smiled signing the document and handing it back to him also. Now let me repeat, this. It is to be kept for a year after your passing or in a sudden case of any accident leading to death," then this will be distributed immediately when things are settled is that correct? "You've got it Dillard! She smiled again becoming restless from being there over and hour at this point. She had resolved all the matters over the phone but she had to come in to sign the legal documents. "Just about finished" the attorney replied moving quickly securing the signatures and getting all the legal documents together in one file folder. 'Now I was able to purchase that taxi company in New Orleans for a reasonable price since we had the cash money, he smiled showing all his teeth. Hearing correctly, it was to be put in a Mr. Smiley's name, right? "Yes, that's correct Dillard, and you have sent his papers out to him already?" she asked. "The papers making him the legal owner of that business went out this morning," Dillard confirmed. "Good! And you have an attorney who will follow up in explaining all this to him right? "Yes Dana, just as you have asked. "Very good! She said getting up shaking his hand and "you have a great day! Smiling walking out of the office and getting in the car and off she went. So far evading the authorities was still a success for now.

CHAPTER 56

What you don't know

Sonjee had cried and prayed most of the night regarding her dad's new friend. She had not gotten a call from her dad about her sister so she stayed in her hotel room alone. She had spoken briefly with Jace and made plans to see him when she returned to Los Angeles but for now, she waited to talk with her older sister. "Hi this is Bailey! Did I wake you? Her older brother asked calling her from his home in Arizona. "No! I was just reading, she replied. "Dad says you're having a pretty tough time right now" he stated concerned. "Kind of," she said. He could hear her sniffling slightly as she spoke. "Hey, we know no one will ever replace mom, right? "Right" she replied sadly. "So, what do you think mom would want us to do for dad? He asked to get her thinking. "To love him", was her answer. "That's true but we already love him, right? Yes, she quietly answered again. "We have our lives and our families and we can't be with him everyday". "I know what you're saying Bailey, but he moved her in mom's home! Sonjee belted out. "Sonjee that's not mom's home she's never even saw the place". But her things are there! "You're right some of her things are there but what was she always teaching us about things? "That they're replaceable," Sonjee shared smiling. Bailey still doesn't know what he said that convinced the change but he heard it in her voice something had taken place. "Thanks, Bailey, for the call" she said. "Hey I needed it to! When are you coming for a visit? He asked. Soon brother, real soon!

Dana drove into the parking lot of David Michael and Sonjee's condominium. She wanted to speak with her son in person before Billy totally turn him against her. She took the one rolling luggage case out of the cars trunk and walked to the door. She rang the door-bell and waited nervously looking around. After a few minutes she rang the doorbell again still not getting an answer from the inside. He took her keys from her purse and opened the door and went in. "HELLO! HELLO! Is anyone home? She yelled loudly. Satisfied no one was there she settled in? First taking a long hot shower to relieve her aching body and remove all the heavy makeup she had used to cover the bruises and scratches she had sustained in the big melee! She most certainly could not have gone to her attorney's office like that! She rubbed herself very carefully with Neosporin and coco butter to help repair her scarred skin. "These will work," taking a pair of sweats from her luggage, putting them on and sat down to relax and wait for David Michael or Sonjee. She looked over and saw the blinking light indicating a message was waiting. Fearing it may be Billy calling to warn the children about her she decided to listen to it. "David! Sonjee "How are you and Kara doing? Hey I decided to stay some extra days with daddy, I'll see you all Tuesday" bye. That was the left message. "Oh, good Sonjee's visiting her dad, Dana thought I'll be alone to talk with my son", thinking about what she'd say. She looked in his room. There were notes on his mirror and bedside. She also noticed them in his bathroom. Psalms 34:17 the righteous cry and the Lord heareth and delivereth them out of their trouble". "Scriptures I want to remember is what was typed on each one. Dana walked through reading them. Another read: "Pride goes before destruction and a haughty spirit before a fall". "Why am I reading these? she asked going to sit down in the living room to get away from the words that seem to be speaking to her. She looked at her watch and waited for David Michael to come home. Dozing off she began to have a bad dream and woke up startled. "Oh, my I can't believe I almost killed someone again! She said now up pacing the floor. Why did Billy make me angry! He should have just stayed away! She cried out loudly. Okay, Dana just be quiet don't say that again! self-talking to herself. You gave them Edith on that one" it's over and done with". "I HATE YOU WILLIAM PARKER! She yelled, "I'm sorry I don't mean that, I love you but you make me crazy! She confessed crying again. "Oh, help me somebody help me! She screamed. She had fallen to the floor and balled up in the corner to get away from it all" she told herself. Lying there for and hour crying and confessing her wrongs Dana heard a "CLICK! David Michael turned the key coming in. He heard whimpering when he walked in and held up the bat, he was carrying to strike the intruder. AWE! He yelled pulling back his bat to strike. "No David it's me," she said from her crouched position in the corner. "Dana! Dana is that really you? He asked not seeing her face. He reached slowly and turned on the light switch. Oh, my goodness your face! "Yes, please don't call your dad! She pleaded over and over again. "David closed the door and put down the bat and went over to help Dana to her feet. She had drenched her sweatshirt with tears and her eyes were swollen from continuous crying he guessed. "Come on Dana get up and sit here," he said helping her to the sofa. "Promise me you won't call your dad until we talk" she continued to ask. He wanted to help her by calling Billy as he had asked him to but she was his mother and she wanted time to talk to him as well, so he figure what harm. "I'll call dad after we talk, he thought to himself. He got her a box of Kleenex and made her favorite rosette tea. "Thank you, son," she said reaching for the hot cup of tea on its saucer. "Billy made me do it you know! Why are you saying that Dana? He asked puzzled by her accusation. Because he came to my office admonishing me for being a bad mom, for not supporting you! He's going off marrying someone else when he knows I love him! She reasoned. "Dana how many times did you tell me you'd never marry dad! "I said not now! "Now he's chosen someone else! She cried out. "I'm sorry Dana things didn't work out for you and dad. "I still love both of you," he reminded her with a big hug. "But you can't go around hurting people". "I know, but she has everything, she's got Billy! She yelled again. Her son put his arm around her. He felt so sorrow for her pain right now. In this moment he began praying within his newness in Christ. He prayed silently and waited for an answer letting her cry some more.

KNOCK! KNOCK! Sonjee heard someone at the door of her hotel room. She walked slowly and peeped out. "Hi Candace" she said rubbing her eyes trying to sound excited but was woken only by the knocking. "Hey! Sleepy head how's my little bumblebee?" She asked embracing her with opened arms. "I'm fine, come in" Sonjee replied heading to the bathroom to brush her teeth and freshen up. "Dad didn't call me what time did you get in? she asked as she stood washing her face. "It was quite late he was sleep when I got there". Ernestine was up getting some warm milk she says she was having a tough time sleeping". She wasn't ready to go back to bed so we sat up talking. She explained to me that she and dad met at the recreation center. The Center had a retirement expert come in and speak to them. "Jon understood investing better than I and he was kind enough to help me with some of my questions," she told me. We talked a bit and found other interest we had in common" Ernestine shared while she sat drinking her warm milk. "He's such a good friend I don't know what I would do if I lost him" she confessed sadly. She and I sat and talked. I guess it was close to eleven o' clock". "Oh, I see" Sonjee replied coming over now to hug her sister and kiss her cheek smiling. "Are things better now? Candace asked. "Dad was concern you would never visit him again". "Better, Sonjee chided. Bailey called last night". "BAILEY! Our brother Bailey called. No, no, no, wait you mean our brother who barely finds time to see us on special occasions called" she laughed getting up from sitting on the bed. "Well, I know something good has to come from this! She stated. Candace sat in the chair crossed her legs and asked. "What words of wisdom did he share to make you feel better? Cause I could have saved airfare" she joked smiling as she said it. "Now sis, you know I love seeing you on any occasion, but I didn't know daddy had called either of you" "Anyway Bailey just reminded me of mother's teachings". "Mother's teaching? Candace questioned searching her mind. "Yes, anything and everything but mostly the fact that things are replaceable and people aren't." "Umm okay" she said still waiting. "I was tripping because daddy had moved her into mother's home and using mother's things! And Bailey simply said that mother never saw where dad lived. "Remember she was always telling us that what you don't know can't hurt or affect you" and that you can always get new things". Sonjee explained. "Oh, I see where you're going with this". "You're right you know" but Bailey was listening to her! Mr. know it all intellectual! Maybe there is hope" Candace sighed. "I'd rather have daddy happy than to not have him at all," Sonjee reasoned. It was selfish to think I could have him all to myself all the time" Sonjee finally confessed. "I do understand, and Ernestine is quite a lady, a retired principal she told me". "Really, I got that when I spoke with her coming in the other day. She listens well". Sonjee added thinking about her first meeting with Ernestine. So, she and daddy enjoy conversation with each other. She even caddies for him! he shared. Candace laughed. "I FEEL BAD! I probably caused her to lose sleep over this" Sonjee added. "Well, she and dad were preparing breakfast when I left and I shared I'd be back are you coming? "I wouldn't miss it! She said give me a moment to shower and change I'll be quick". ALL RIGHT! "I need to call my office" Candace responded. After a short while they were at the door of their father's home. Ernestine was now in the kitchen pouring flour into a bowl. "Hello we're back! Candace yelled coming in. "Good, how are my favorite girls today?" Dr. Reeves asked extending a fatherly embrace to both. "Just fine daddy" they said in unison. What are you making Ernestine? Candace asked walking in to meet her leaving Sonjee alone with her daddy. "Your dad showed me these great cookbooks your mother had" I hope you don't mind me using them. I'm trying to bake him some homemade biscuits" she smiled looking at Candace. "Oh no we don't mind as a matter of fact I'll help you" is that all right? Thanks, dear I wanted to ask you to" she responded sweetly. "Daddy I'm sorrow I was selfish about your love for mother and me" Sonjee said sitting next to him in his favorite chair. "Sweetheart you know no one will every replace your mother or you! He smiled and embraced her feeling she understood. "Oh, I know Sonjee smiled back. She wasn't a thing! "You're right! He smiled confirming what Sonjee said. "Hey, did I hear one of you say something about eggs? She yelled to the kitchen. "Nobody prepares eggs over easy better than me! She teased going in to join Ernestine and Candace who were having lots of fun cooking a homemade breakfast for the four of them.

David Michael finally got Dana composed again. "Look Dana this problem is easily resolved. No one died right? He said looking into her eyes. "Dana may I pray for you? He asked carefully. He realized prayer could change situations soften hearts, change mean folks, and brutal folks. And Dana needed all that to face what had taken place. "Will it help after what I have done? She asked. "Yes, have you ever tried praying? "Your dad tried teaching me long ago but I didn't believe just talking to someone I can never see would help me" she confessed. "Oh, but believe me you're wrong" he said getting excited about the Word. Dana sat quietly and listened. "First know He's always listening. David Michael shared his testimony of the guys who tried to harm him. "Did he answer? Dana asked. "I'm here talking to you aren't I" he replied smiling. "Will he accept me after what I have done? "Dana, Jesus does not condemn us for wrong doings". In a book called Romans he says: There is no condemnation for those who are in Christ Jesus, who walk not after the flesh but after the spirit. Romans 8:4 he smiled. He got up now pacing in front of her, "Dana but you must confess and admit you're wrong then He can help you" he said. "Is that all I have to do? THE BIBLE SAYS: You must confess with your mouth and believe in your heart" Dana interrupted as he spoke. "Believe what David? He turned and held her hands, "that Jesus Christ died and was raised from the dead". You shall be saved! "You're saying this voice that I hear saying good things is God". 'He does speak to us through a soft sweet voice." David was surprising himself with his learned knowledge to questions. He was new in Christ and already he was witnessing. That's what their lesson study was about for Tuesday's meeting, he smiled. "David help me, I want to change" I want to hear his voice, that leads me to do the right things and not hurt people". I want to be saved," she said starting to cry. "Dana I can't change you, only God can do that" he shared lovingly. But only if you are willing." Is that what Billy was asking of me? 'What? to be saved? "I suppose so Dana he must really care! David smiled. Then using the book of Romans, he had her repeat after him the road map to being saved and lead his mother Dana to Christ. "I love you Dana! I love you to son, "Goodnight! When David Michael woke the next morning, Dana was gone!

CHAPTER 57

A new mind set

Dad, I'm sorry I didn't call you Dana was here last night," he said calling early the next morning. "What! she was in L.A! He asked very surprised. "Where is she now? Don't know she left sometime during the night. We went to bed after I lead her to Christ and" "Wait! Wait, whoa! You did what? Billy couldn't believe his ears. All those years he had tried and one swoop it was done. "Dad, when I came home last night Dana was here'. She had been here sometime I guess looking at her face. Her eyes were swollen from crying and her shirt was drenched from tears. I FOUND HER CURLED UP IN A CORNER CRYING. She begged me not to call you and I listened and let her talk. We talked about a lot of things but I did share that she would have to admit what's she done and get help". "I'm listening son". She cried and admitted guilt she said for a lot of things and then she asked to be saved. "Thank God! Billy said loudly. 'So, you're not mad at me for not calling you? "Son, you were able to do something I had tried doing for years". "You got her to repeat the road map to Christ! I'm so proud of you, God smiles on you," he said rejoicing. "But dad I don't know where she's gone or if she's saved" He confessed. "You're right, only God knows, though you can rest in the fact that the bible says God's word will not return void but it will accomplish. "I love you dad! I love you to son!

After two and a half weeks or so the authorities were still looking for Dana she still had not surfaced. Her office reported her off for vacation and no one saw her around her home. Things for the most part were getting back too normal. The report on the local news had somewhat faded from memory and most who didn't know her anyway had forgotten all about it. "Nada are you feeling better now? Carin asked seeing her back at the university. "Physically better, but sadden it came to having to be watched all the time." "So where is she now? 'I don't know and don't care as long as she doesn't come around me, she's fine wherever she is". "So, did you press charges?" "Yes, I did, she hurt me pretty badly, but I've chosen to forgive her". You what? "That's what Christians do; they forgive". "Well, pray for me cause if I were you and I saw her it's over! She stated making a movement of shooting a pistol at her. "We leave all judgment to the Lord and believe me she'd rather I shoot her than the wrath of God'" Nada smiled. "Glad you back! Thanks, see ya later. Leaving headed to her class across campus. Billy hello! How's your day going?" Not bad I have to get to the courthouse right now, what time are you leaving today". 'I'm working till noon. I'm meeting with Nicky to go over some last-minute details for our reception" she replied. "I don't want you worrying. I have hired body guards for the wedding also to give you some peace of mind". "Thanks honey, that certainly helps. "It's so eerie I almost feel any minute she'll show up". "Sweetheart you have nothing to worry about I have so much security around you right now I'm surprise you don't see them." Billy shared. Really! Really? Look honey I've got to go I'll call later" love ya bye! Nada looked around. She got several waves from the janitor to the gardener and students, she just smiled and began instructing her class of students.

Dana hi! Hello son" she said answering his call. "It's good to hear you. Are you alright? He asked. "I'm fine I just needed to get away for a while and think but I'm fine. "Good, where are you? He asked "BUZZZ". The line disconnected. David Michael held Kara's hand and prayed.

Billy hurried into the courtroom. His case was on the docket for the morning's session and he sat down and listened to the bailiff as he stated. 'ALL RISE THE HONORABLE RAY WINSTON PRESIDING". He waited patiently his cell phone at his side was buzzing over and over again. He looked down and saw the caller ID read Dana Williams.

With court in session, he whispered to the attorney on the case with him to take over he had to take and emergency call and hurried out to the hallway. "Hello! Hello! He said hoping he had not missed her. "Hi Billy" she said sadly. "Dana are you alright?" He asked hearing her sad voice. "Billy I'm okay" I just called to say I'm sorry" and please forgive me for hurting your friend" how is she? She asked. "I do forgive you but you must turn yourself in and pay for what you've done" he informed her. "I know I am going to do that" that's why I called I going to need an attorney right? "Probably" He stated seeing where she was going with this. "Thanks William". "Oh Dana, David shared with me about what happened at his condominium, you accepting Jesus I mean. "Billy I only wish I had listened to you long ago" it's the best thing that has ever happened to me" she confessed very tranquil sounding. "William, take care". You to Dana, he said sadly knowing as soon as she shows her face, they are going to lock her up. He turned and went back to the courtroom. Dana walked out from behind the wall where she stood speaking to him. She wanted to see him again. In her own twisted way, she loved him!

Tetra, David and Nada sat down eating dinner when the phone rang. Hello Nada Francois, please? The voiced asked. Stating to Alfredo he was the baker calling her. Due to the wedding no questions were asked. "Hello! Nada said pleasantly greeting her caller. "Hello Nada, Dana replied. "Please don't hang up, I'm so sorry I caused you pain". "Why are you calling me? Nada screamed throwing the phone across the room. David and Tetra jumped from their seats and rushed to her side. She was very upset and crying. Daddy, why didn't you screen the call more carefully?" She stated. I did he said he was your baker" Alfredo replied feeling bad about the call. "Look I'm sorry everyone but I'm still feeling a bit uneasy about her still being around". 'We understand dear they said going back to their seats. Nada went to her room she didn't have an appetite for anything at all! When Billy called later that night, he was given the third degree to even speak to his dad and then Nada after a long explanation shared.

Having used all three weeks of her vacation time Dana had to come from hiding in order to turn herself in. She knew the authorities were looking for her and they were probably waiting for her at her home or office. She was going to turn herself in but first she wanted to explain to Rusty what has happened to her and share her plans. According to Billy she knew she'd have to serve time for what she did to Nada and then she could get on with the new life she had accepted in Christ. With that thought in mind she went out to the ranch. It was a nice day and Bliss was swimming in the pool having fun when Dana drove up. Dana sat out in front of the house writing in her journal. Assuming everything had faded regarding the earlier incident she walked into the back yard smiling. "Howdy Bliss! She said loudly. "DANA! WHERE HAVE YOU BEEN? She asked shocked getting out of the water wrapping a towel around her waist. "Oh, just needed some quiet time you understand" she said making her way to the side of the pool where she was. Bliss's eyes were as big as saucers and she looked as if she had seen a ghost. "So where is Rusty and Mavis? Dana asked securing a chair to sit down. "Bliss's first thought was to run inside. She had heard about the beating of Nada Francois on the local news little less than three weeks ago and now Dana was there. Not being one of her favorite people Bliss kept her distant and kept looking toward the house where Mavis had gone in to check on the dinner she was preparing. "Mavis is here" she said nervously, I'm not here alone! She added looking again at the kitchen door. "And the old cowboy, where is he? "Rusty left with Hitchcock to look at some horses this morning" Bliss replied. "Dana looked at her watch moving around anxiously in the chair. "Look Bliss I know I haven't been the best person in the world. As a matter of fact, down right mean sometimes" she confessed. "But just know this day I'm sorry for any pain or sadness I've caused". Bliss looked at Dana strangely "is everything alright? She asked getting up from her seat. "Things couldn't be better" Dana replied standing up going over by the pool looking into the crystal water. "It's not going to be easy to convince anyone I have changed but I have and I know it! She voiced. I just came by to see my cowboy and let him no I'll be going away for a while' she said sadly. They stood talking and still keeping her guard up. Bliss had gotten comfortable with her. Suddenly the towel Bliss had around her waist begun to fall off. Dana jumped to grab it to keep it from hitting the water. Bliss grabbed at it at the same time and they bumped heads laughing. That's not what Mavis saw when she came out of the kitchen's door. SHE HAD JUST BEEN TALKING WITH BLISS EARLIER ABOUT HOW DANA HAD WALKED INTO NADA FRANCOIS'S HOME AND BEAT HER WITHIN INCHES OF HER LIFE! SHE SAW BLISS HOLDING HER HEAD AND DANA'S HANDS IN THE AIR. "STOP! She yelled and ran back in the house getting her pistol from the kitchen drawer and fired two shots hitting Dana causing her to fall down. "No! No! Don't Bliss yelled. But it was too late. Dana hit the cement on poolside very hard knocking her out. "WHAT DID YOU DO? Bliss asked looking up at Mavis now standing over Dana. "Is she dead? Mavis asked in her gruff voice. "I don't know she's bleeding pretty badly let's call 911 Bliss suggested kneeling down beside her to take her pulse. She could see she was bleeding and the pulse was faint. "Are you kidding, I'm not going to be caught with a felon?" Mavis chided. "WE CAN'T JUST LET HER DIE! Bliss yelled crying. "SHUT UP! And Mavis slapped Bliss with her opened hand across her face. "Now help me get her to her car, and you get in my truck and follow!" Mavis barked giving out orders. "She could still be alive we need to get her help! Bliss continued to say. Mavis took the pistol and waved it at Bliss. It wasn't easy but they got her in the passenger side of her Porsche and Mavis took off with Bliss frightened to death following her closely in the big truck. They drove until they came to one of the jagged cliffs of the Atlantic Ocean. "What are you doing? Bliss asked getting out. She was still in her bathing suit and scarred stiff. Dana had made whimpering sounds moving her head from side to side. "What are you going to do she kept asking? I'M GOING TO LEAVE HER HERE AND LET HER DRIVE HERSELF HOME' sarcastically pushing Bliss away from the car. HOW? SHE'S HURT AND BLEEDING Bliss reminded Mavis. "Bliss, get in the truck and shut up before I shoot you! She admonished the frightened veterinarian. Mavis was mad and Bliss knew to do what she says or else! Dana was just about to wake up focusing her eyes when Mavis hit her hard in the face with a fist and she went out again. SHE QUICKLY SAT Dana's small frame behind the wheel of her car. "NO! NO! Bliss yelled knowing what Mavis was about to do. Mavis shot up in the air! SHUT UP BLISS! She walked over to the truck pointing the gun at Bliss. "You know what I will do don't you! she said. Bliss just shook her head yes acknowledging her. "I want you to go two miles up the road and wait for me!" she gruffed meanly. Bliss was crying and very frighten at what was about to happen. Mavis had so much on her thar was hanging over her medical practice Bliss felt she had to co-operate she thought getting under the wheel again and pulling off.

Good! Mavis sighed feeling now she could finish what she reasoned in her mind would end this nuisance in Rusty's life! She walked back to the car to start the ignition and send it over the edge with Dana in it. Mavis leaned in to start the ignition with Dana weak from the loss of blood. Dana grabbed her around her neck delirious and confused in her state of mind. Mavis was beating and moving Dana's weak body around like a ragged doll but she held on falling out of the car. They began tussling on the dirt of the ground. "LET ME GO $$#$%%$@$%% Mavis ruffed getting angrier by the minute. She flung Dana over by a rock and looked around walking a little way down the road for something to finish her off. When she looked up Dana was gone but she was leaving a blood trail to follow from all the bleeding she was doing. Mavis followed her easily and Dana was growing weaker. She moved a short distant down a thin ledge near the shore and found an inlet. She continued walking and stumbling and many times in her condition lost her footing along the thin ledge. The jagged cliffs down below were steep and death was imminent to anyone who went over. "Dana! I'm coming Mavis mocked moving carefully behind her. The rushing river was down under her when Mavis heard "AHHHHHHH! A LOUD SCREAM AND THEN A THUD! LOOKING DOWN SHE SAW SOMETHING HIT THE COLD CHILLED WATER OF THE ATLANTIC. Mavis backed up slowly and carefully along the ledge until she had safe footing. She smiled and took the pistol from her pocket and tossed it down in the rivers rushing waters and made her way back to the car, started the ignition, put it in gear, and sent it falling over the cliff as she walked down the street without looking back. When she made it to the point where Bliss was, they drove back to the farm. Bliss was silent and Mavis was barking out the plot she had planned. Bliss was shivering from fear but she was also still wearing the small swimsuit she had on earlier. "Look when Rusty gets here you let me talk! You hear! Mavis exclaimed. Bliss said nothing but drove on into the big gates on the ranch. Two hours after they had arrived and still standing on the porch Mavis got a big surprise! Police swarmed them. This way, this way! Bliss yelled pointing toward the swimming pool in the back of the ranch and showing the authorities the blood trail left by the victim Dana Williams. "SHUT UP YOU FOOL! Mavis yelled. "Let's hurry, I'll show you where the car with Dana in it is, hurry! "I have done some mean things in my life Bliss admitted but nothing as guiltless as murder" she shared riding now in the police vehicle. The search around the area turned up blood samples that proved through DNA to be that of Dr. Dana Williams. One of her shoes were found down by the water's edge. Reasoning suggest she lost her footing and went plunging down from the narrow ledge into the fast-rushing waters where blood samples were also found on the rocks below. They dragged the area for miles in the dangerous fierce ice chilled waters along the Atlantic coast for weeks. "With Mavis going to jail in cuffs for a long time Bliss confessed turning state evidence to her part of this bizarre murder. The Porsche was pulled from the rushing Atlantic river but Dana's body was not found.

When Billy got the news days later, he rushed to be by his son's side. He was crushed from the news. He prayed mightily for his son as well. He never wanted anything bad to happen to Dana. And such a horrible brutal way to die he thought reading his morning newspaper. He realized he was the only family she had besides her sister Doris in Los Angeles whom he planned to see also. "Oh Dana! He cried out sensing her loss with a pain deeper than he could ever imagine he had for her. 'GOD PLEASE HELP ME TO UNDERSTAND YOUR PLAN" Billy asked praying piteously after he found out about his long-time friend. "WHY Lord? He questioned she had just started to live! He held his head down in disbelief of the news he had received about his son's mother. Now sitting on a plane headed to Los Angeles to give him the gruesome news he cried. "Hello sweetheart" answering his cell-phone from the plane "I LOVE YOU" Nada shared feeling his sadness. "I love you too Nada' I'm just trying to find the words to say for comfort right now". "Honey, I'm sorry, I know I said some mean things about her but I never wanted her to die" Nada confessed. "I know dear, but it's over now" she could hear him sniff as though crying silently. "Billy do you need me to come and meet you? She asked caringly. "Thanks, but no, I want some time with my son, okay" he stated. "I understand, call me when you get settled in" Nada asked knowing he just needed some alone time to grieve for Dana. Their wedding day was only four weeks away and Dana Williams had managed to steal Billy's heart once again. But now she was relieved it was her LAST TIME!

CHAPTER 58

Oh, happy days

Everyone in the Parker family was trying to forget about sadness shared from a few weeks ago at Dana's very elaborate funeral gathering held in Maine by the rivers edge where she was last seen. Besides her sister Doris and her son David Michael and niece Sonjee, Dana had no other family to speak of. The Parker family, Rusty, Mollie and Corky and of course Dr. Justin Parker was also in attendance. Mollie cried through the entire services especially when Rusty got up to share his feelings and broke down in tears before finishing. Putting all that behind him Billy now had to focus on the family wedding and moving on with their lives. Because of their son David Michael, he placed a headstone for Dana in the Parkers family plot with his grandparents. He and David Michael lead everyone to the place where authorities say she most likely went over the cliff. Sadden grievously by seeing all the blood that was lost as she tried to run away from Mavis brought on more tears from the attendees just thinking of the terrible way she had died. They all tossed beautiful pink roses into the rushing water. They were Dana's favorite flower! Billy gave no thought to the placed headstone in his family's plot. It's where he always thought she would be anyway! closing another chapter in his life. He sat thinking after he boarded the plane to Washington for his wedding day!

"Ms. Manuel, the limo will be at our homes around 5:30 for me, you and Ms. Ross, for the rehearsal dinner okay" Nada said calling to remind her neighbor and dear friends. They really didn't need to be there but Ms Manuel had asked if she could come also Nada obliged after all she had saved her life! She wanted everyone happy. Madison and Carin were riding in the limo with her also and Billy was coming with his family. The rehearsal dinner was being held at the very posh Governor's Mansion behind the capital. David and Tetra reserved the Mansion for them and had planned the evening's gala affair. Billy sat at his parent's home anxiously waiting for his son and Kara to get there. This was going to be a long weekend ending in his marriage to Nada Francois. He wanted nothing to dampen the affair for her. Truly they had gone through a lot already. "Mom what time was David Michael's flight? He asked again pacing for the eleventh time Tetra reminded him. "Look son he said he'll be here it's only 1:30pm. You've traveled enough you know how the airport is sometimes, right? giving him a loving hug to settle his nerves. Tetra left and went upstairs. Soon David his father was standing in the door. "Can I interest you in a game of chest? He smiled, "mom, right? "Yes" he nodded. Things were moving along great. Everyone was calling to let Tetra know they were in town and had directions to the Mansion. With nerves settled and everyone in place they all headed out for a fun filled evening. Elegant was the evening's festivities Tetra had planned. One of the first limousines that pulled up belonged to Hazel and Ms. Manuel. Dressed in their designer gowns and large hats they were carefully escorted out directly in front of the Mansion. "My! My! Look at this place Hazel said touching the large pillar in front of the entrance. "I've been here practically all my life and have never seen this beautiful place" she confessed to Ms. Manuel. "Ha! Ha! Ms. Manuel laughed "now Hazel you know this place hasn't been here that long. It was only built in the turn of the century" she teased. "But I will say this, Cinderella better watch out for Virginia! laughing walking slowly into the elegantly designed Mansion. "The limousines were all parked outside of the gorgeous Mansion in Olympia that stands on a wooded hill. Nada's sixteen wedding party guest plus escorts and friends were in for a treat of their lives. Lieutenant Green was invited along with his wife Madison who was Nada's matron of honor. He had just arrived. Ms. Manuel and Hazel noticed the fabulous expensive tulle was strung and draped with beautiful white Rhododendrons, roses, and lilies, all around the large space. A live band was present and the delicious looking endless banquet tables were strategically placed around the room and were a heavenly feast for the eyes to behold. Silk tablecloths rippled flawlessly around each one of the round table settings. And silver place settings with Egyptian crystal stemware brought a shimmer and sparkle to the décor. They walked in and found their names on the place cards, smiling and took their seats. Mossy had dressed her girls in beautiful white-laced dresses which Maggie had picked out for them. Where's Uncle Billy? Vlade asked his dad Desmond sitting waiting for the couple's entrance. They will be here soon" Mossy replied trying to keep Maya settled in her seat. Carin was in heaven she still couldn't believe she could be invited to something like this. "Wow! She thought looking around at the magnificent room. Sparkling lights from candles and waiters with champagne and caviar! "I have died and gone to heaven" she teased with one of the other bridesmaids she sat next to. "I know what you mean this is fabulous! Charming favors and dazzling centerpieces flanked each table that caused a smile. There were finger foods THAT WAS SURE TO PLEASE! She thought looking around in amazement. The cake Tetra shared was called Ivory Splendor. It had four tiers covered in pleats of Ivory chocolate. It boasted ivory lilies and ribbons all in ivory chocolate and very tailored. "That's so Nada, Mossy replied standing looking at the cake after getting a brief break from the children. The guests were now up mingling and introducing themselves. Maggie noticed the children had their own beverage, dinner and cookie favors buffet decorated elegantly too as suggested by the wedding consultant Tetra had hired for this event. Jordan the oldest son of Desmond Owens was over talking with the band members. Desmond and Maya the youngest were over helping themselves along with the other guest to the delightful banquet buffet. It was adorned with two flutes towering over each end filled with a bouquet of assorted flowers. Sliced thin Pork Tenderloin prepared on a large tray with Fruit Chutney at the center. A bright and festive side dish made with tomatoes of all sizes, chunks of mozzarella cheese, crabmeat cocktail one of the groom's favorites and jumbo shrimp appetizers were also presented. There were desert buffet tables and breads and chesses elegantly displayed for the waiting pallets. "The theme Tetra shared was "Royal Romance" and from the baby roses at each table in small silver bud vases to the elegant dinner menu to be served displayed on their settings. It was magnificent! When the couple made their grand entrance, Billy looked handsome in his Valentino black tux and Nada in an exquisite sheath style hand beaded and scalloped laced gown with pearls and sequins. Both said hello and welcomed their guest to this fabulous evening to the start of their lives TOGETHER.

CHAPTER 59

A wedding fit for a queen

Sonjee had call Doris to inform her she was headed to the airport. "Jace and I are flying out tonight we're meeting Kara and David Michael". "That's fine, thanks for calling. Russ and I are coming tomorrow for the wedding". "Should be lots of fun for them" Sonjee voiced. "Yes, bitter sweet but I know how hard he tried to make it work with Dana." "Well mother I think we should just let that be over and move on. I don't think anyone loved auntie more than me but she's gone now and its Nada's day. We don't want to spoil it". "You're right dear God knows Billy deserves some happiness." Have a good flight, love to Jace," she said hanging up the line. "Russell we're flying out tomorrow morning to Washington" tapping him on his foot as she passed him in the room. "Tell me tomorrow I'm still on that fabulous cruise" he replied relaxing in their master suite's cozy chair. Their month-long honeymoon was great! They went on a cruise for relaxing and getting to know each other even better. Meeting people and laughing and dancing and enjoying the get away from business and meetings and resolving issues WAS OVER WAY TO FAST. "Finley are you attending Billy's wedding? She asked using the intercom to ask her butler. "I am since I've thrown my hat in the ring for a good woman, weddings are a great place to meet single women" he laughed answering. "Finley please I saw you maybe twice the hold time on the cruise you should be engaged by now! She teased responding to his statement. "They were fun but to old! He laughed.

Tetra hummed around the kitchen it was like old times she said getting a tray to take up to David. "He was upstairs in the library at the end of the hall with his son and grandson talking. "David Michael, I brought you juice you're not drinking coffee yet are you" she smiled asking. "Gram everyone in college drinks coffee it goes with cramming but thanks I like orange juice also". So, what do you guys have planned today? Dad and granddad are taking me to the golf course" "So their going to teach you the ropes of the business I guess," she said. "Something like that" Billy shared hugging his mother. "Dad I'm glad you all accepted Dana into the family. I know you and mom never got married but you still put her in with great granddad and great grandma and that sure helped me through a tough time" David Michael confessed. "Son I always saw her in the family" Billy replied embracing his son. "Dear your dad told me you guided your mother through the plan of salvation" I did grandma! He was so excited. He shared excitedly the whole story as they sat around drinking coffee and eating muffins and croissant. He was healing through it all and Tetra shared tears for the young girl she once knew whom through her grandson had come to accept Christ. Halleluiah what a wonderful day!

The house was buzzing now around the breakfast table. "Pass the butter please, okay but send the bacon this way" more pancakes anyone? could be heard time and time again as each joined the large formal dinning table at the Parkers home. "David Michael could you answer a question for me" Kara yelled from the stairs. "Sure! He replied excusing himself to go and assist her. All the men were up earlier and Desmond and his sons had arrived to play pool and help Billy to relax they say. So, Alfredo was preparing a huge southern breakfast for the family. "Biscuits are up! Alfredo yelled. "Now that's what I'm talking about" Billy said coming over to get the serving dish and put them on the table. Bacon and sausages are over here! David Michael said now sitting next to Kara who was being so quiet and shy around mostly the men. "Goes with pancakes you know! He told her smiling. "Anyone want grits? Me! Tetra voiced smiling. Everyone was laughing and having so much fun. Jace and Sonjee had now joined the family coming in from the airport. "Grandma Tet, are we going to meet Nada and Mossy for our nail appointments after breakfast" Sonjee asked. "Yes, dear as soon as we finish here "are you eating grits to?" she asked seeing her picking up the serving bowl Alfredo had placed again on the table. "Yes, I don't get them very often, mother used to cook them all the time. They are my favorite salty breakfast" she replied covering them in butter. Jace was having biscuits and fitting right in with everyone else who had come for the wedding's festivities. Soon there was a doorbell ringing. Tetra hurried from the table to answer it. "Hello, come in, Tetra said embracing her guest. "We're all around the table come in and join us" she shared walking him to the dinning area. HELLO EVERYONE! "Justin! Are you by yourself? Billy asked coming over to welcome and introduce him. "Yes! He smiled it's a wedding! thinking of the single women. Billy was pleased as he looked across the noisy room of family and friends who had come to share in his wedding nuptials. The only thing that could have made him happier would have been to see Glenn Reed his childhood friend come through the door.

"Hi honey!" Nada said, calling Billy's cell phone. Hi sweetheart, "What are you guys doing? Just having fun laughing and cheating in pool" he teased looking at the guys in his family's game room talking loud and having fun. "Okay has mom left yet to meet me? Yes, she, Sonjee, Mossy and Kara left about twenty minutes ago" he replied. Your turn Bill! Someone yelled. "Coming gotta go babe" love ya. Nada, Carin and Madison were still sitting having breakfast at the hotel. All the guys were at his parent's home. The girls were going out for a day of pampering themselves with manicures and pedicures and of course shopping! Their assignment was to keep Nada busy and away from Billy the entire day. With jeans and tennis or a very comfortable pair of sandals Tetra would say they soon met the others. Where to first guys? Let's get to the nail salon first then we can shop for sandals! Mossy voiced. "Yeah! That works for me! Me too! Others chimed in. They headed to the car when Nada's cell phone rang! "Hello! Mossy said she was in charge of screening all calls that was Billy's. "Hold on, it's not him". Are you sure? Tetra asked smiling. "I'm sure," Mossy replied smiling giving her the phone. "Hello this is Nada." Nada hi! "Melanie? You sound horrible! She exclaimed. "I know, I shared with you I felt bad at the rehearsal dinner but I'm not going to make it in the wedding! She explained sounding like a frog was in her throat. Oh, no!

I'm so sorry is there something you can take? I don't know, she replied coughing constantly through the conversation. I ache all over and I'm feverish" I wanted to call you in hopes you can get a replacement for me". "Oh Mel" I don't want you to feel bad I understand" I really do" Nada said. "Nada what's wrong? Mossy asked with the other's now listening and wondering about this sad conversation. "Melanie's sick" "Melanie's what? She's not going to be able to stand in my wedding? She was starting to cry. I knew something would go wrong" Nada shared. "Look we have enough of us that are not in the wedding here". "What size dress does Melanie wear? Melanie what's your dress size? Nada asked with her still on the phone. 'Size 7 she replied. "Not a problem I'm a size 6" Sonjee responded "and Kara is a 4 I'm sure one of us could stand in her place okay" hugging Nada to comfort her fears. "Melanie we'll be by later for the dress and you get some rest all right" bye! Hanging up sadden by the news of her sick bridesmaid. The girls comforted her fears then went on to have a great day after visiting the ailing Melanie. They also went to the university where Nada worked, Nada's favorite eatery, and shopping all the boutiques possible. Tetra finally waved bye to the young ladies and went home to her husband. All the ladies spent the night in a spacious hotel suite laughing and having girl talk. The guys went out to a sports bar and left Tetra, David and the young Owens children at their home enjoying themselves.

Mt. Nebo was decorated with beautiful white bouquets of an assortment of flowers and satin ribbons, bows, candles and candelabras. Guests were arriving and the church was buzzing with each one arriving for the wedding of the century! The Reeds were standing near the front and saw Tetra come in. She wore an elegant off white beaded gown that was absolutely stunning Phyllis thought as she got closer. "Are you sure you're not the bride? Phyllis teased coming toward her for an embrace. She had been in the room near the pastor's study with Nada and the bridesmaids trying to keep calm and timelessness. "Hello Phyllis", Oh no! When you see this gown, she picked up in Florida while they were down visiting Glenn you will hardly remember what I have on" Tetra replied smiling. Tetra paused. Speaking of Glenn is he coming? She saw the look on their faces and extended a hug to both of them. The Reeds both had become gray from age and Phyllis's silver was beautifully curled in loose ringlets. "When did you all come in? She asked smiling changing the subject as she spoke. "We got in last night early" why didn't you call? Oh, Tetra you had so many people at your home I didn't want to bother." "Well, you're right the house felt like old times again but you're always welcome to join there is plenty of room". "You must come and spend some time with us before you go home alright? "So, where's David? Phyllis asked. "Here he comes' she said waiting as he came up the hall. "My! My! this is certainly and elegant affair! David was sporting white tails like his son Billy and grandson David Michael. "Might I say the same for you two" David responded smiling and embracing old friends. This old thing! Phyllis teased smiling glad to see the Parkers again too. She wore a charming black taffeta form-fitting gown covered with a nylon sheer jacket. Flattering! Tetra expressed. Phyllis noticed the huge bows and small bouquets attached to every other pew. "Nada's a real girl" in every sense" Tetra said sharing her taste in the decorations everyone was admiring. "Excuse me these are reserved," she said turning to a couple coming to sit on the lower floor. Billy wanted everyone who wanted to be there here. So, three hundred invitations were given to guest who would be sitting on the main floor everyone else was welcome but balcony seats only. There was Ms. Ann, and Ms. Christine, and James Captain and his family were all taking their seats on the main floor. The Reeds took their seats and Tetra and David were helping everyone find their seats along with the ushers. Coming in were many of Nada's friends from the university and of course David, Tetra and Billy's friends from the law firms in Washington, and Maine. After and hour or so Mt. Nebo was filled to capacity with those who knew Billy and his family or those who just wanted to see this magnificent wedding being preformed. Mrs. Hathaway was sitting near the front in a beautiful summer hat and was soon joined by Miss Manuel and Hazel. "Hello first lady Hathaway" they said taking their seats. "Hello, my you ladies are sure looking lovely today" she replied. "Thank you" Hazel replied. You're lovely to! "I'd hate to sit behind her today! "Shhh! Virginia" Hazel said nudging her on the arm. Looking up you could see the balcony was filling quickly as Alfredo dressed in his Perry Ellis tuxedo headed up the stairs to speak with his daughter. "Knock! Knock! He said tapping on the door. Oh it's Mr. Francois" Mossy said peeping out. "May I come in for a minute? He asked politely waiting patiently for an answer. "Oh, hi daddy!" she voiced coming over to him. Mossy gathered Sonjee, her girls and the other bridesmaids asking them to step out and give them a moment together. You look so beautiful sweetheart. I only wish your mother could see you" wiping a tear. "Now daddy don't do that," you will have me crying and I will smudge my make-up". "Sorry dear, I know you have made a good choice. Billy loves you and will take good care of and provide for you" he shared holding her hand gently. "Your mother would be proud," he said reaching and embracing her gently. "Daddy I love him; he is a good friend and we have fun together! Her eyes were sparkling as she spoke to her daddy about her soon to be husband. "My little Nada Lillian Francois" touching her face gently in his palms. After about five minutes Mossy was peeping through the door. 'We've got to finishing getting her dressed" she said opening the door wider. "Come on in! Alfredo said moving toward the door blowing a kiss as he left to all the ladies. Mossy and Sonjee were fussing with Nada's train on her gown. "It has to be a half mile long" Carin reasoned finishing up her makeup. "15 MINUTES! An usher yelled in to tell them. Down the hall we heard "Thank you Pastor Hathaway" Billy voiced leaving his office in a white Jean Yves tuxedo with tails, heading down to the sanctuary to greet his guest. "Billy man I thought for a minute Pastor wasn't going to let you out" Desmond laughed teasing him. "Man, you have the ring, right? Desmond patted his chest and then reached in and pulled out the tycoon cut diamond ring. "It was sparkling even in the dark from its flawlessness! Both walked out to see the other groomsmen standing around talking in their white Claiborne tuxedo's and winter mist yellow vest. Hey guys! "Bill you nervous? Justin asked putting his hand on his shoulder. "Not yet probably after I see Nada, you all kept us apart for two whole days! "Everyone laughed. "Billy! Finley voiced in his British voice, he was sporting a plaid gray, light wool Boss Hugo suit with alligator shoes. "Ouch! "Don't hurt them Finley! The guys teased. Everyone was laughing and meeting each other. "Hi William' he turned to see Winnie. "The guys cleared out and walked away. "You look as handsome as ever. So, this is it for you" she said holding his hand. "Someone has finally captured the only man I longed for so many years ago' she teased remembering the yester-years. "Thank you for coming Winnie" he smiled embracing his dear friend. They stood and talked for a few minutes ending in a friendly embrace. Billy smiled as she moved away wearing a mauve tapered bodice dress made of silk and lace. The skirt was tastefully flared swaying around her gorgeous set of legs. "Congress will never be the same! He expressed turning away to join the others. Doris wearing a gorgeous Purcell gown and Russell a black Cole's tux had taken their seats. Billy made a point to go over and welcome them. After a while a hush came over the room when Dr. Hathaway walked to the middle of the aisle in the huge sanctuary. He gave a nod and the background music was silenced and the piano was heard being played softly. Out from behind the stage came a voice so sweet and so "Chelsea! Billy gasped. He didn't know she was coming. His mom and Nada had put together the program themselves. He sat in the front awaiting his cue to stand but right now he was caught up in the moment. "She came! He thought as he listened to her sweet melancholy voice delighting the guest. The song was mesmerizing, as the notes seemed to touch the heartstrings of listeners. She finished her solo and curtseyed and bowed before moving slowly away from the front waving a friendly gesture at the man of the hour! Billy took out his handkerchief and wiped his eyes to disgust his crying. Soon Dr. Hathaway was back up again. With a nod Billy took his place up front next to him smiling nervously. The piano player changed the song being played and out walked David Michael his best man and son to stand by his side. Billy looked out to see Sidney Owens and Brittany and her husband as well as Annie and Keith. He looked up in the balcony of people. Focusing he saw an image, no it couldn't be besides it's coming from the balcony. Billy dismissed what he thought just to be his imagination. Spitting image! Miss Ann whispered making reference to Billy and his son. The presentation of groomsmen and maids moved along nicely. There fabulous winter mist yellow dresses were a bridesmaids' delight. The little girls were darling in lots of lace and white tights and patented shoes. And Maya stole the moment when she came down the aisle handing out petals to the guest as she walked by. With all sixteen of her wedding party attendees in place there was silence. Now everyone's eyes were on the back of the room. Everyone waited in anticipation FOR THE PIANO'S MUSIC! The double doors opened wide and in them appeared the most beautiful woman anyone has ever seen is what

Billy saw. Then he heard the bride's song being played by non other than Tyler Parsons, the now famous world re-known gospel trumpet player. Billy could hardly contain what he felt at this moment. His friends had all come together to share in the most blessed day of his life. As Nada walked closer and closer to him her fabulous hand beaded gown brought whispers all around the room. Being escorted by her dad Billy tried hard to hold the tears. "Who gives this woman? rang out from Dr. Hathaway. "I do! Alfredo Francois said proudly stepping back to his seat and allowing her to finish her journey to the front. Her huge bouquet an assortment of white flowers draped down the front with green foliage leaves accented its arrangement. Dr. Hathaway officiated the nuptials in a light grand fashion. The couple lit their candles and then blew them out leaving one to represent their oneness. "THE RINGS PLEASE" Desmond handed the ring to David Michael and he handed it to his dad Billy. Mossy in turned handed the ring to Madison who in turn gave it to Nada. "Repeat after me! Dr. Hathaway said. With this ring" and the couple laughed and repeated the vows in seriousness and became one flesh. NOW BY THE POWER INVESTED IN ME "I now pronounce you man and wife! You may kiss your bride!" CLAPS AND APPLAUSE COULD BE HEARD ALL OVER THE ROOM AS THE COUPLE EMBRACED AND SHARED A VERY LONG KISS!

CHAPTER 60

To beautiful endings

Nada Francois-Parker most certainly had to feel like a queen. Not only was she wearing something old (the beautiful handset diamond necklace and earrings Billy had given her two years or so ago) something new (the gorgeous hand beaded Italian silk and laced $28,000. wedding gown) something borrowed (a diamond hair broach from her matron of honor Madison) something blue (a blue sapphire diamond tennis bracelet from her in-laws Tetra and David Parker) Everyone wanted to meet them and give them a smile, hug or handshake. The gift table her wedding coordinator had set up was running over with presents many had bought for the blissful couple. "My aunt Nada it's going to take a long time for you to go through all of those! Maggie voiced walking looking at the silver and white bows and ribbons used to wrap all the gifts of those who brought them to the church instead of being delivered from the stores where they had registered. Nada exhaled a sigh and then formed another smile. Both were very accommodating as the long lines of guest went by them. "Thank you! Thank you very much. "Hi Uncle Billy" this young lady said standing in the long line of greeters. "Congratulations! "Hello! He said not really hearing her greeting. She stood looking for a reaction from him. "You've forgotten me, haven't you? She asked. "He had he thought to himself searching his mind. "This slender young lady with braids hanging to her shoulders was waiting for him to recognize her and he was clueless. "Your wife his beautiful" she said shaking Nada's hand. "Why thank you dear." Hoping she would move on and give him time to remember her. "MIGHT I SAY

YOU'RE AN AWFUL PRETTY YOUNG LADY TOO" Nada voiced what's your name? "I'm Suraka." SURA! SURA JENKINS! Brittany and Meldon's little daughter" Billy now said looking at her smiling. "Well, I've grown up Uncle Billy! That you have," he said hugging her. "How old are you now? I'm nineteen remember two years behind David Michael! That's right". He looked around for his son who was standing down at the end of the line. "David Michael look who's here, these two were a handful together". He shared with his wife remembering their childhoods. Sura! Did dad remember you? David Michael asked coming over after Billy got his attention. "Umm not really but his wife helped him out" she teased. "I WON'T FORGET AGAIN! He yelled to her going off talking with his son. The line went slowly at times but the couple stood patiently greeting every guest who came in it. Then Billy looked in the line and saw the face he had imagined earlier. "You made it! He exclaimed shaking his hand. "I wouldn't have missed it for the world" Glenn replied. "Hello Glenn" Nada voiced bending over to embrace him too. "Did you just get here? She asked smiling glad he had come. "No, I was in the balcony, beautiful wedding man," he said. "You are going to the reception, right?" Billy asked hoping to talk with him there. "Hey a promise is a promise! And I told you I'd be here and yes, I 'ill see you both there". Giving Billy another heartfelt handshake and allowing the line to move on. Billy wiped his face to keep from crying. He looked as Glenn rolled his wheelchair away and stopped to speak with Winnie Hathaway another dear friend. The newlyweds greeted many friends, especially the ones who were not attending the formal reception being held at the Mary Hill Castle.

After the photographers had finished all the candid and posed shots in the church, they wanted of the happy couple Billy and Nada Parker walked out the front door. Waiting directly in front were two white horses and a carriage to wisp them away. While the photographers took photos of Nada in her carriage Billy looked over and saw Tyler standing in front of the Center. Walking over he said "Thanks man I was not expecting this! Billy said shaking his hand again. "Billy I was just admiring this magnificent tribute to my father thank you! Tyler shared. "Oh, it was a joint effort for all who knew and loved him" Billy replied. "Oh, he is being modest he single handedly orchestrated the endeavor" Pastor Hathaway said walking up placing his hand on their shoulders. They all looked at each other and smiled. "See ya at the castle" and walked away. The five limousines carrying the wedding party attendees and the family members and dear friends including Virginia and Hazel her neighbors left heading to the reception to be there to greet them. After more photographs and more last minute well wishes guest blew bubbles around them waving goodbye as they departed. The royal couple left for the castle in a horse drawn carriage allowing some quiet time alone before attending a very gala wedding reception of 300 family members and close friends. "I love you Mrs. Parker! "I love you too Mr. Parker! Embracing and sharing a kiss

The elaborate Mansion was a perfect place for a prince and princess to celebrate their togetherness. Built in 1926 by multimillionaire Samuel Hill many were told as they walked in looking around the ageless gray stone structure. Tetra and David entered being some of the first family to arrive to keep things moving smoothly. "David come here this is what I fell in love with she shared walking in across the spacious room to a beautiful rockwork patio with a gazebo and a panoramic view of Columbia River Gorge. "Wow this is absolutely surreal," he agreed standing there embracing his wife in his arms. Entering the beautiful mansion Nada's wedding consultant and her designers captured an explosion of flowers. By using very tall flutes closely linked along the walls as you enter the elegant room where the reception was being held. Giant candelabras with beautiful candlesticks were causing a sparkle and shimmering glow setting a magical mood of atmosphere. "And I thought the reception dinner was beautiful" Ms. Manuel expressed looking around. "This has that beat by a landslide! She shared walking in touching lightly all the sparkle in the space. The place settings sat on placemats made of lace and even the stemmed glasses boasted a lace pattern. The gold trimmed china dishes were magnificently arranged on the circular tables. The tables had been draped with white satin tablecloths accentuating the gold lace pattern on the fork as well as other eating gold ware used for this occasion displayed in napkin panache. The banquet tables covered in white satin strategically placed in areas to allow mingling and conversations to be held and enjoyed. There were also small bouquets of white hydrangeas on the backs of the chairs. Clusters of hydrangeas in clear crystal vases ran down the center on some of the banquet tables. White small roses and hydrangeas arrangement flanked the head table where the bride and groom were to sit. The guests were coming in and the room had now become a buzz regarding the happy couple's arrival. The bridesmaids and groomsmen were already getting into the fun of things as the live band struck up a favorite tune. Finley! Doris chided being pulled to the dance floor for a cha cha. Soon they were joined on the dance floor by Desmond and Mostalgia his wife, Sidney Owens Desmond's older brother and many other guests who were ready to celebrate the newlyweds. "Come on Madison relax let's have some fun! Her husband Charlie said moving around to the beat on the dance floor. "I will, another trip to the bar and I'll be underway" She replied smiling starting to get her groove going. Even the stiff shirt older attorneys were having fun! Everyone was in relaxed mode sipping champagne and sparkling cider beverages of choice. The open bar served only champagne drinks and a ride home was available for anyone who needed it! "They are here! They are here! And attendant came in yelling. Everyone got ready to yell congratulations to the couple as they entered. Nada had taken off the diamond- studded train that hung from her gorgeous gown allowing one to see even more of the elegant hand beading in its pattern which allowed free movement for dancing. The photographers certainly had their job cut out for them. They were busily moving about snapping photographs of the couple's friends and guest as requested by the couple. The waiters smiled balancing their silver trays of caviar and bubbly! making their way through the lively guests present. "The dance floor ceiling was trimmed in hundreds of tiny gleaming lights! Shh! Shh! each were saying across the large room. "Ready! 1-2-3 CONGRATULATIONS! Everyone roared. "Oh, Billy look this is magnificent! Nada said seeing it all dressed up for the first time. He turned and kissed her again gently. After the roaring stopped the couple spoke. "We would like to thank each of you from the bottom of our hearts for the love, support, and kindness each of you have shown to us today and many of you throughout my entire life" Billy stood sharing. "And to my dearest and closet friends thank you for calming me and helping in my decision making and really just being there for me" Nada expressed "WE LOVE EACH OF YOU! "Let's celebrate! And the band started playing. Billy and Nada went to the floor alone. After the first dance a short time later while Justin tapped Billy's shoulder handing Nada a $20 dollar bill and smiled at Billy as he relinquished the floor. Soon a line had formed to dance with Billy's gorgeous bride. Billy asked his mother to dance and others were also on the floor. The money dance was bringing lots of fun and laughter as each man tried to give a larger denomination of money than the previous one that was tapped on the shoulder to move on. After a while Billy made his way back to his bride when David his dad tapped his shoulder. "Hello! Honey are you having fun?" She asked slow dancing with her husband. Before he could answer he felt a tap in his back. Billy looked back and then down it was Vlade with his bill in hand for a dance. "Billy politely moved over and allowed the dancing to continue. Just as the music was about to stop Vlade yelled! Uncle Billy she's all yours! Everyone who heard laughed in the moment. Finley asked Ms. Manuel who was ten plus years his senior to dance and she was feeling pretty good and obliged leaving her cane at the table. "Justin had his eye on one of the brides-maids most of the evening and had found his way back to the floor several times. Laughter, tears joy and triumph were emulating from this gathering. As dinner approached everyone easily found his or her place setting and with grace from Pastor Hathaway the exquisite meal was served. Billy looked around the reception room. He noticed laughing and lots of smiling from his very close friend Glenn who was not going to ruin this day for his buddy despite his own misfortunes. (Cheryl was no longer in the picture) Son" Tetra said sitting next to him at the head table. "I'm certainly glad you decided to let God lead" she smiled embracing him quickly around his shoulder. "Mom you don't know the half of what I've gone through but God has given me Nada and I'm thankful mom". "Okay hush before you have us both sobbing" she voiced teasing him to smile again. "Well dad I know now I'll get all that learned advice about marriage, right?" "You're kidding right? I'd learned so much from talking with you and watching you I have improved my own marriage" he joked continuing to eat the marinated feta and olive salad with his meal. "Its official you are my lovely daughter –in-law and I can't wait for the three words! she teased now speaking with Nada. "Three words mother Parker? Yes! She said very coy. "IT'S A BOY! Aye! Wait you can't push me out that soon! David Michel said joining the conversation of laughter shared. "Okay you're right! "It's a girl! Now that's better," he replied to laughter. The conversations at each table were priceless I'm sure, Nada thought. Because Miss Manuel had her table in stitches of laughter but then again it was Miss Manuel! "Mom you have to see the ice sculptor of and elephant on the patio! Maggie expressed tugging at her arm to come and see "This way it is absolutely to die for! She giggled along with all the other young girls following her too. "See mom I told you! The punch is coming from his trunk" she said excitedly "Think I can get one for my birthday party? She asked Mossy. "We'll see dear, we will see". After dinner some guest said their goodbyes and left. Chelsea Parsons-Major shared another song for the couple. Her husband was an elected official on the white house staff. He was staying safely in the background he said "vowing to his wife not to talk politics today". Her brother Tyler Parsons now a famous well known gospel trumpet player did a duet with his sister that brought back memories from gentler times a Mt. Nebo. Dr. Hathaway, pastor of Mt. Nebo a well-known television icon all over the world shared light-hearted stories of the earlier years. Billy stood there with is wife Nada. To him he had come full circle and his life had just begun. Sonjee Reeves did a solo dance tribute to the blissful couple. It was a favorite from the show performed in Washington D.C. Her friend Jace Ramsey looked on lovingly as she stretched her body to its limits gracefully. With faces smeared with cake, and Nada's stocking guarder over shot and hanging from a crystal chandelier to Hazel and Virginia vying for the bouquet this celebration was fun for all. "Toast after toast and a very heartfelt one from his dad to end the night, and dance after dance Carin will remember this wedding fondly as they all made their way to the limousine to be carried to their perspective destinations safely. Russell and Doris shared the floor with Billy and Nada in a final bridal waltz of newlyweds. Annie and Keith joined in and soon many others. Alfani and Millicent had come and took all the younger children back to the Parkers home. Leaving the grown ups to enjoy a fun filled evening. And that it was! With the night slowly coming to its end Billy left Nada standing near the door and went back inside to get Justin who apparently had wondered off in the gardens and lost track of time and needed a reminder. "Hello! Charlie said standing next to Nada. She jumped "Oh! "Sorry didn't mean to startled you" "Oh that's all right I'm sure glad you could come Lieutenant Green" she said smiling at the tall soldier now sporting a handsome black tuxedo for the occasion. "Hey its June bug remember? he smiled. "We haven't done so bad for two little kids from the bottom" he voiced. "You're right! Nada smiled tip toeing embracing his tall statue. Madison was off taking photographs with Carin and the other bride's maid and walked up to meet her husband standing near the door. "Now what are you two talking about? Madison asked coming up to join them. "You really want to know? Charlie asked. "I'll tell you' he said holding her around the waist and escorting her to their Maserati." Congrats again! Both yelled back to her. Billy left instructions for the staff regarding the Castle and headed Justin to a limousine to get him safely to his hotel suite. He and Nada were headed to their luxury suite for the evening and had a flight out tomorrow to begin the honeymoon to Paris, Rome and Italy for a month before returning to their estate home in Maine. "William be gentle" she voiced now in the luxurious bed. "I love you Mr. Parker" ummm! "I LOVE YOUUUUU TOOOO! Mrs. Parker.

CHAPTER 61

Dejavu

Doris was sitting in her office at her posh boutique on Rodeo when her mailman brought in the letter. "Hello ladies! He said as he did everyday passing by on his daily mail route. "Hello Stan" the clerks replied with him handing off the boutiques mail. Gisela put it in Doris's mail slot in her office and went back to the floor waiting on her customers. Hey honey busy day? Russell asked stopping in during the lunch hour. "Oh no not really I was just thinking about Billy's wedding and Dana" she replied. "The wedding" That was a year ago, what brought that thought up?" He asked sitting next to his wife on her French style love seat that sat in her office space. "I always thought she would change and marry Billy" she confessed. "Oh Doris, remember we committed that to Jesus, right?

"I know honey, I was reading my bible and I understand from David Michael that she accepted Jesus before she left his condo that night" she said she had changed when she called me from there and I was trying to understand why now would Jesus take her away?" she confided. "His ways are not our ways" Russell reminded her now holding her in his arms as they spoke. Because truly there was no acceptably explanation to satisfy the thoughts Doris was feeling. She laid her head on his chest and wiped tears that had started to fall. "Sweetheart you haven't opened the mail today have you? Did that inventory slip for the thrift store come in? he asked changing the subject to business to diffuse the sadness. "I don't know? let me see" she said getting up wiping her eyes going to her mail. "I'm sorry honey I didn't mean to concern you with my thoughts" she shared kissing him gently on the lips. "No worries! I do understand dear-heart" he added. "I'm headed to the Westinghouse meeting at 2:00pm downtown are you sure you don't want to come? He asked still holding her hand to comfort her. "I'm sure you can handle that one alone besides the proposal you wrote for his company was really unbeatable and he knows it" she shared sitting down now at her desk totally focused again on her business day. "Here it is! handing Russell the large envelope. We will look it over and discuss it later tonight okay." "Sounds like my cue to leave" Russell leaned over and kissed her before heading out the door. I'll see you tonight" Doris waved without looking up she was still going through her pile of received mail when she came upon an envelope addressed from Dana. "AH! SHE GASPED almost in disbelief. Looking closer she saw it was sent from her attorney's office and she opened it and settled in to read it. Dear Sis, if you're reading this I'm probably locked away in my cell. I know what I have done to Nada was wrong! I have asked for forgiveness in that matter. I have also asked forgiveness for my parents the Demato's. I most certainly didn't know Richard was my real father when I helped Edith kill them. I didn't pull the trigger but I could have called somebody! Edith was mentally ill I know now but as a child many things I did not understand with her. I'm feeling just as guilty as she. "I have come to accept Jesus in my life I have left on this earth. David Michael showed me in the bible where he forgives all sin so, I'm praying and believing he will forgive me! Sis I know this is something you didn't know and I never wanted you to but I'm coming clean of everything! "I'm hoping first you will forgive me and try to understand what I went through in that house. Secondly, I hope you will come and visit me as you are really the only true family, I have besides my son David Michael. "I hear from Sonjee you are a terrific mother; I knew you would be. Take care of my son and please write me every now and then. "I'll soon come out of hiding and turn myself in to start my sentence. And know that I finally understand what Billy was trying to share with me so long ago. Love Dana. Doris burst out in tears when she finished reading the letter. "Oh my God! She exclaimed falling to her knees. There was so much she didn't know about her younger sister and now this! She had read both pages of the letter but there was a third page that read. This is my final entry in my journal before turning myself in to face the wrong I did to Nada. I'm going to trust the rest of what happens to my life to God. Doris noticed the date was the same day she fell victim to the chilly waters of the Atlantic.

If I had known and accepted the power from above
The reach of his forgiveness and the dept of his Love
I'd not have failed to see what my future
with God in my life held for me
Dana Demato-Williams

Doris stayed on her knees in her office for a very long time praying and trying to understand why?

Nada and Billy walked from their finished nursery into their family room. She waddled over and sat in her comfortable chair. "Long day? He asked helping her to position the ottoman at her feet. "Can I get you something sweetheart he asked now sitting near her on the sofa. "I'd like my ice cream and plums! Dante said he found the kind I liked at the market today" she replied. They had been married now for a year and a half and were now anxiously waiting for the stork in two months. "I'll be right back," he said walking out. RING! RING! I GOT IT! Nada yelled! Hello Parker resident she greeted. "Hello dear! Mother Parker, how are you? Oh, I'm fine I'm calling to see how you're doing? Tetra stated. "Good, ready for this to be over but I'm good! She explained. "Is Billy home? She asked I tried calling him several times today at the office" "Yes, mother Parker he's home now but he is in court all week" and most evening he's in seminary, she shared with her mother-in law. "Oh, I see, well, just have him call me when he gets a chance! She asked. "Sure, mother I'll have him call" it's not an emergency but I do need to speak with him about a legal matter". "Hold on I'll get him now! "NO! don't you dare, you should be resting". "I am we just sat in the family room" Billy was finishing up a message he's giving to the men's group Sunday. Oh, yes, they finished the nursery today" it's so cute mother Parker! "I SURE CAN'T WAIT FOR YOU TO SEE IT". "So, you and Dad Parker are still attending the conference in New York in a month and stopping for a visit, here right? She asked wanting to see them. "Yes we are and I'm hoping we time it just right and be there when you deliver." "Oh that would be wonderful, Billy will probably faint! They both laughed. "So, everything is good! It is mother Parker. So, how's the relationship with David Michael? Oh, David and his father have gotten closer since Dana's death" I don't hide the fact that she's an intricate part of their lives. So, he feels comfortable in talking about memories or times when something reminds him of her. We have a great relationship" as a matter of fact he and Kara are coming this weekend". I don't travel long distances even by plane right now. Most of my travels are to the university and home". "Umm I see, "So how long are you going to work dear? "Next week is my last week until after the baby comes". Then I'll decide if and when I'm going back" she shared. She had gotten a position on the university of Maine staff science department as an instructor. The staff in Washington hated to see her leave and some missed her very much! "Billy and I are letting David Michael and Kara help name our baby' so it should be lots of fun this weekend". Are they out for their break? Tetra questioned regarding their visit. No! Mother Parker their down for the long Labor Day weekend". "I'll see you soon and give my love to Dad Parker and dad too, is he in? No dear he's out with Priscilla". Nada laughed I see. Well tell him I'll call later this week" Love ya dear! Tetra shared lovingly. I LOVE YOU TO MOM, bye" Billy had come in before the conversation was over. "I'll call her" dad has told her what I'm going to tell her but she will accept it from me simply because she's mom". Well did you finish your first sermon? Yes, Billy smiled. I've decided through prayer to use Matthew 16:26. I'm familiar with that passage.

Knock! Knock! Oh! Finally hearing the knocking on the door "come in" David Michael said getting up to open the door. Thanks, are you almost ready? Kara asked. I am sending this text to Sura she says hi by the way". "Cool, tell her I said hi! He replied not raising his head at all. Kara moved around the condo busily waiting for David Michael to move so that they will get seats in the theater to watch the live play being performed at the university. Where's Sonjee? She left twenty minutes ago. I guess! He replied feeling disturb. "Well, are you going? She asked again picking up a post card he had received from his dad and Nada on one of their many getaways. "Wow this looks beautiful have you talked to them since they have been home FROM Hawaii? David! David Michael! she yelled hitting him to get his attention. "What on earth are you reading that is so interesting? She asked. "A bible" he replied. "Okay I hear that! we read all the time what book and verse? Come on share it! She teased. "No this is a child's bible and it's old so I have to be careful I don't lose pages". I think it belonged to Dana it had her name in it." "Well not really it had Dorca's name which was her name before she changed it! Really! May I see it! Kara asked reaching for it carefully. "How did you get it? "It came by express mail today and I just happened to be home to sign for it." "Where did it come from? "Let's see! David Michael said looking at the brown envelope that it was wrapped in. "Doesn't have a return address on it. Boy I can't wait until I visit Dad this weekend!

"Boy will he be surprised! Putting the bible safely on a shelf and walking out the door to enjoy a live play featuring his peers.

The end